THE HIDING PLACE

THE HIDING PLACE

KAREN HARPER

THORNDIKE
CHIVERS

This Large Print edition is published by Thorndike Publishing, Waterville, Maine, USA and by BBC Audio Books Ltd, Bath, England.
Thorndike Press, a part of Gale, Cengage Learning.
Copyright © 2008 by Karen Harper.
The moral right of the author has been asserted.

The text of this Large Print edition is unabridged.
Other aspects of the book may vary from the original edition.
Set in 16 pt. Plantin.
Printed on permanent paper.

LIBRARY OF CONGRESS CATALOGING-IN-PUBLICATION DATA

Harper, Karen (Karen S.)
    The hiding place / by Karen Harper.
      p. cm. — (Thorndike Press large print core)
    ISBN-13: 978-1-4104-1271-3 (hardcover : alk. paper)
    ISBN-10: 1-4104-1271-7 (hardcover : alk. paper)
    1. Women detectives—Fiction. 2. Single mothers—Fiction.
    3. Large type books. I. Title.
    PS3558.A624792H53 2009
    813'.54—dc22   2008041879

BRITISH LIBRARY CATALOGUING-IN-PUBLICATION DATA AVAILABLE

Published in 2009 in the U.S. by arrangement with Harlequin Books S.A.
Published in 2009 in the U.K. by arrangement with Harlequin Enterprises II B.V.

U.K. Hardcover: 978 1 408 43246 4 (Chivers Large Print)
U.K. Softcover: 978 1 408 43247 1 (Camden Large Print)

Printed in the United States of America
1 2 3 4 5 6 7 12 11 10 09 08

Thanks to the Jason Kurtz family for a
great time in Confier, especially to
Heather for all the support and advice.

As ever to Don, for being a
great travel companion to
parts known and unknown.

PROLOGUE

Near Black Hawk, Colorado
May 20, 2004

She was terrified she'd be too late. Tara Kinsale-Lohan took the next tight turn on the slick road faster than she should have. She'd been driving Colorado mountain roads for years, but never at this speed.

The big sedan fishtailed, but she steered it back onto the narrow, two-lane road, running with spring rain. Thank God, there was little traffic in this weather. She longed for her old four-wheel-drive truck, but her husband, Laird Lohan, liked only luxury cars. The road became a twisting, one-lane gravel path. When the next widely spaced driveway came into view, she hit the brakes again. Gripping the steering wheel in both sweating palms, she squinted to read the numbers on the mailboxes through the mountain mist. Her windshield wipers slapped gray rain aside, *whap-whap* . . .

whap-whap. She was getting closer. She prayed she'd get there in time.

How could a bright woman like Alexis have been so stupid to try to snatch her child back? Rats like her ex-husband, Clay, a moral coward, could be vicious when cornered. And how, Tara berated herself, could she herself have been so careless to let her dear friend sneak into her office and take her skip trace report on Clay? One of Tara's cardinal rules when she started her one-woman private investigating firm, Finders Keepers, was that the locate information went first to a lawyer or law enforcement, not to an emotional woman who might mess everything up, trying to take her child back on her own.

She'd simply trusted Alex too much, but they'd been close ever since they'd roomed together in college. Tara was an only child, and Alex was the closest she'd ever had to a sister. Like sisters, they sometimes argued, but when an outsider threatened them, they'd always come to each other's rescue. When Tara's parents had died while she was at the university, Alex's widowed mother had taken her in for holiday visits. With no family of her own, Laird's close-knit clan had looked so appealing to Tara — until she got to know them.

But Clay was the enemy now. Even for Alex, Tara did not like taking risks. She did almost all her work from her office on the phone or online. She never did her own surveillance or ventured out to serve a summons or subpoena where things could go bad. She had promised Laird she would not do any fieldwork, though she'd recently gone Dumpster diving — perfectly legal, though he'd had an absolute fit, just as he did each time he saw that she was not going to be remade into his picture of the perfect Lohan wife.

Their agreement, actually part of a prenup, was that she could still help women get their children back, if she agreed to hand Finders Keepers over to someone else when she and Laird had their own children. Laird was obsessed with having an heir for his share of the Lohan family fortune. The thing was, shortly after their honeymoon, their marriage had become so rocky that she had told him she was staying on birth control pills until they smoothed out their differences.

She'd seen numerous times that, if a marriage wasn't on solid ground, having kids only made things worse for the adults — and damaged the kids, too. Lately, to her amazement, it seemed that Laird had accepted that. The last few months, he'd become amazingly understanding, though she was pretty sure he still thought children could bind any marital rift.

Tara hit the brakes and felt the big car skid. At this altitude, way above mile-high Denver, she was actually driving through clouds. She began to creep, squinting through the windshield, straining to keep control of the car and her fears. The road narrowed even more. As if protecting their lofty realm, tall lodgepole pines and blue spruce loomed like mythical giants as they closed in around her.

At least, Tara thought, trying to buck herself up, she was getting close, but why did it have to be a place like this one? When Clay Whetstone, Alex's ex-husband, had snatched their four-year-old daughter, Claire, six months ago, Tara had agreed to trace him. Both she and Alex assumed he'd head out of state, which was why it had taken her this long for the locate. Clay loved to gamble, so Tara had spent precious hours online checking Las Vegas and Reno area U-Haul records, change-of-address Web sites, and expensive state-sponsored databases.

But Clay had outfoxed them. He'd been living — probably gambling, too — less than forty miles away in the casino-studded town of Black Hawk. She had finally located him through a hunting license he took out, since that required an address and a Social Security number. Clay and Alex had shared custody, but he'd only had Claire every other weekend. When Alex went into the hospital for an operation, he'd taken off with some house furniture and their child. Tara was worried, not only for Alex's safety, but that she might cause Clay to panic and run with Claire again before he could be arrested.

Yes, there it was, 4147 Elk Run! Tara had cross-checked the address through purchasing the subscription lists for two of Clay's favorite magazines, *Western Big Gamer* and *Poker Player U.S.A.* Now Clay was the hunted and, she prayed, his hiding game was over.

To doubly confirm Clay's location, Tara had used an online telephone directory, then phoned Clay's neighbor to the north, pretending to be a previous owner in the area. She'd asked if the Brown family still lived at the 4147 address, claiming their phone number had evidently changed. Pretexting, it was called; P.I.s used the chat-someone-up practice all the time to get information.

"Oh, no, the Browns don't live there," the woman had told her. "Carl Weatherby and his cute little daughter, Claire, live there now. Moved in 'bout Thanksgiving, though they kinda keep to themselves. He keeps funny hours, goes to play poker in Black Hawk sometimes. Steve — that's my husband — saw him there once. I mean, Steve don't go there much, 'cause we're churchgoing and all, but Carl does, comes and goes, you know . . ."

Unfortunately, everything the woman told her about "Carl Weatherby" and his daughter, Claire, was also detailed in the report that Alex had evidently pilfered from Tara's active file on her desk.

The road here was so narrow and steep that she couldn't park on the berm, nor was she going to take that crooked, single-lane driveway to Clay's residence. She couldn't even see the house from here. Could Alex already be here and have driven in? Surely she wouldn't approach like a storm trooper, however desperately she wanted her daughter back. After all, Clay was an avid, skilled hunter, so that could mean guns on the premises.

Tara had planned to phone the Central City P.D. today, so they could take Claire into protective custody and arrest Clay. But with Alex possibly on the scene, she was afraid to get them here in case it turned into a hostage situation. Little Claire was like a niece to Tara and she wanted to protect the child, as well as Alex, at all costs. If she could only find a place to park on this narrow road, she'd sneak onto the property to look for Alex's car. Then she'd escort Alex — hopefully with Claire — out of here and call the cops.

Just past the property, Tara pulled as far over as she could, parking tight to a line of precariously tipped pines. After she hit her warning taillights on and killed the engine, she got out and opened her umbrella. The rain drummed hard against it. The mud and grass were slick where she started up, veering off the twisting driveway so the trees would hide her. The shifting air, unfortunately, had cleared some of the mist away; it would have made perfect camouflage. The wind seemed to howl as if in protest or warning, and her footsteps crunched incredibly loudly.

She almost went down to her knees in the slippery pine needles. Hanging branches shuddered more cold water onto her. The wind changed again, whipping the rain sideways. She closed her useless umbrella and left it on the ground. At least these thick boughs provided some cover from which to view the house.

From behind a shroud of shivering, new-budding aspens and spiky blue spruce, a small A-frame of dark-brown-stained boards emerged, with an attached one-car garage. This place was a far cry from the beautiful home Alex had up for sale in Evergreen. Knowing Clay, he had big plans for recouping his losses and moving onward and upward in the world soon. Maybe he just needed time to buy himself a new legal identity as Carl Weatherby, then find a job. As he'd often said when pushing his opinion about anything onto others, "You can bet on it!"

No, Alex's car was not parked outside. Surely it wasn't in the small garage. Could she have been wrong to assume Alex had come here with her information? Had she come and gone, maybe with Claire? If so, Tara knew she'd better get out of here.

She went farther up toward the back of the house. The line of trembling, drooping trees threw cold water on her each time their branches moved. Rocks and thick forest fringe clung tight to the back lot line, but she didn't want to go higher and get cut off from a quick exit to her car. Her sopped hair stuck to her face and neck and dripped cold water down her back.

Oh, no! Alex's car *was* here, driven around in back, parked on the grass next to a sodden sandbox that must be Claire's. Her stomach lurched. Could Clay and Alex have reconciled? In her wildest dreams, she never thought that was a possibility. Or had something else happened?

Bending low, she rushed toward the back deck. It was elevated, with a narrow set of wooden stairs going up. On them, her footsteps sounded too loud despite the eaves and gutters spouting noisy rivulets of rain. Above, two house windows stared at her like blank eyes, running with tears. If she could just glance in . . .

No lights shone from inside, even on such a dark day. Surely Claire would be home from school by now. But where could Alex have gone?

Her heart thudded so loudly it almost drowned out the rain. Tara huddled against the wooden back door on the deck, then leaned slowly inward to peek in the closest window.

Alex! Alex, sitting in — no, tied to — a kitchen chair! Slumped over. Dead? *Oh, dear God in heaven, help her — help me!* She didn't see blood, but it was so dark in there. . . .

15

Tara's first instinct was to scream her friend's name, to break a window and climb in to help, but her gut told her that Alex could be bait. Where was Claire? Worse, where was Clay? This was a crime scene.

She thudded down the stairs, fumbling for her cell phone in her pocket as her car keys jingled. *Hide back in the trees,* she told herself. The number of the Central City police was on her instant dial. *Call them. Hide, wait, watch until they come.*

She hit their number, tried to whisper for help, then just shouted, "Nine-one-one! Forty-one forty-seven Elk Lane, above Black Hawk — a woman's been hurt —"

Her panicked cry was prophetic. She slipped and went down in slick mud and pine needles, twisting her ankle.

In the screaming wind, she heard fast footsteps behind her. A man's booted foot slammed on her wrist. Her phone skidded away.

A moment's stunning pain screamed deep into her brain. Blackness fell on her. Was this death? She wanted to live. Hide! She had to hide.

In that dark, secret place, some scents and sounds still clung to her: sharp, stabbing smells; muted music; her heart pounding in her ears and someone crying, crying, crying.

1

September 6, 2007

"I'm really kind of nervous today," Tara told her new doctor's nurse as the spiky-haired blonde prepared to take her blood pressure. "Because of my coma and rehab, I haven't been to a personal physician in years, only specialists and physical therapists. I figured I'd better get back on track with pap smears and all. Here I am, thirty years old, and I feel like a teenager facing her first time again — for a cervical exam, I mean."

The nurse, whose name tag said only Pamela, nodded and smiled. She was young but seemed kind and efficient. "I've got to tell you," Pamela said as she inflated the blood-pressure band around Tara's arm, "I've never known anyone in a coma that long — a whole year?"

"Eleven months, and then a lot of physical therapy to get my body working again, especially my left leg. I went from a walker to a cane. I'm finally back to normal, though I guess I'll never be the same person again."

"I read that article in the paper about you, and about your friend being lost. I'm really sorry."

Tara blinked back tears and said, "Thanks."

She lay back on the examining table while Pamela prepared to draw blood. B.C. — Before Coma — she used to hate needles and shots, but they were familiar ground now, as were doctors, medicines, pain. But all that was nothing next to the agony of these last long months since she'd been out of the coma. She could recall no events from the day Clay had struck her with the butt of the gun with which he'd shot Alex, but other people had pieced everything together for her. Alex was dead, and Clay Whetstone was serving a life sentence for murdering his ex-wife, though his lawyers had claimed it was in self-defense. Seven-year-old Claire was in effect an orphan, but Tara had moved in with her at Alex's family's home when the girl's maternal grandmother had died. So much loss and grief . . .

At least Claire's needs and love had kept Tara sane while she mourned not only Alex's death, but the death of her own marriage. No wonder this stranger and others pitied her. It was public knowledge that during her long coma, her husband had divorced her and left the area to start a new Lohan Investments office in the Seattle area. She had not seen or talked to him since. Tara had tried to tell herself it was all for the best. She'd been crazy to marry Laird, however wealthy, handsome and charismatic he was — Prince Charming in the well-toned flesh. Laird Lohan had, as the old saying went, swept her off her feet.

Why had he wanted her, when he could have had almost anyone? Since he hadn't stuck with her when times got tough, she had only one answer: he'd been hooked by her looks, lust at first sight for her red-gold hair, green eyes in a heart-shaped face, and her slender, graceful frame. Probably he'd been initially drawn to her independent nature, too, though. Until that fateful day she'd gone after Alex, she'd taken few risks.

At first, she had thought Laird was a gift from heaven. His apparent adoration had gone straight to her heart. He'd declared that she was his ideal woman, but he'd obviously only meant superficially. Some men joked about being a legs man or a breast man; Laird had been a face man. "Just wait until you see what our kids look like!" he'd boasted to his parents and his brother.

"We got your medical records from Dr. DeMar." Pamela interrupted Tara's agonizing. She pressed a cotton ball to the puncture on Tara's inner arm where she'd drawn the blood into a plastic vial. Tara was surprised that part was all over.

"Yes, Dr. Jennifer DeMar, my old doctor. I mean, my *former* doctor — she's not much older than I am. She got her chance to be part of a bigger clinic near L.A. None of her patients were happy to have to switch doctors, though I'm sure Dr. Holbrook is good and your office is not far from where I live."

"He's *very* good. He's not even taking new patients, but he wanted to — to help you. Bet your Dr. DeMar misses our lifestyle here — clean air, the mountains," Pamela rushed on. "Ick, L.A., with all those cars and smog. Now, if you'll remove your clothes and put this lovely little gown on, tied in the front." She forced a laugh. "I know everyone hates these things. I'll be right back, and Dr. Holbrook will be right in."

With a sigh, Tara followed orders and lay back on the examining table, staring up at the white ceiling with its recessed lights. That was what she remembered seeing first

22

when she came out of her coma: instead of darkness, she saw blankness, then cautious, curious faces staring down at her as they performed their cognitive and physical tests on her. But no Laird, no Dr. Jen, who had been a friend as well as her physician. Yet Alex's mother, Linda MacMahon, had been there for her, visiting almost daily, even bringing Claire now and then. Laird's mother, Veronica, had come to see her, too, holding her hand, filling her room with bright sunflowers and saying, "So, so sorry about how things have worked out between you and Laird. Maybe it's for the best he's moved away. . . ."

Tara sensed her former mother-in-law's visits were secret, not at the behest of the rest of the Lohans, who never showed up or even called. Still, it was through the beneficence of their family clinic that she'd been so well taken care of all those blank months.

Tara sniffed and tried to stop her tears, but they ran down her cheeks into her ears. She swiped the tracks of water away. Her new doctor didn't need to see her crying. She'd been doing so well lately, working hard to resurrect Finders Keepers and growing closer to Claire. Tara was pretty much back on her feet when Alex's widowed mother had suddenly died of a stroke. Tara was certain it was partly from grief over her only daughter's death. She'd been given temporary custody of Claire by Claire's new legal guardian, Nick MacMahon. Claire's uncle Nick was working in the Middle East helping the troops train tracker dogs. Tara and Claire's makeshift family included his pet dog, Beamer, a beautiful, smart golden Lab.

The good news and the bad news was that Nick was coming home soon. Claire was so excited, but she didn't fully realize he would probably take her and Beamer away. And then Tara would be alone again, with only her job helping strangers find their children to focus on.

Nick MacMahon, still in fatigues and field boots, dropped his heavy rucksack in the front yard of his boyhood home on Shadow Mountain Road. He inhaled deeply, grateful not to breathe in hot desert dust. The air, crisp and clean, bit down into his lungs. Thank God, he was home where he didn't have to watch his back, where the sun felt warm instead of scorching. Nothing like being nine thousand feet up in the fresh air of the Colorado sky, above the little valley town of Conifer.

His family home, surrounded by rocky

outcrops with thick pine and aspen forests, stood where Shadow Mountain and Black Mountain hunched shoulder to shoulder in the foothills of the Rockies. His family had always described their location as about twenty miles and forty minutes southwest of Denver on the edge of the Arapahoe National Forest.

He lifted a hand in farewell to his buddy. With a *honk! honk!* their rented truck roared away; Jim was eager to get back to his fiancée near Vail by dark.

Nick heard Beamer start barking, either at the sound of a stranger's vehicle or because he just plain scented his best friend and partner. Nick couldn't tell if the dog was in the house or around in back. Leaving his gear where it was, he jogged up the gravel driveway. Though he was in good physical shape, he felt the altitude and slowed to a walk. He'd have to get used to "high living" again, as his dad had jokingly called it.

Nick's carpenter father, who had died eight years ago, had designed and built the cedar house and its elevated wraparound railed deck with his own hands almost twenty years ago. Yeah, his dad had known how to build a house, and a strong family, too. Nick could remember helping him clear the lot of heavy stones. The place had large panoramic windows and side wings, which made it seem poised for flight. The interior boasted two-toned hickory flooring, well-insulated paneled walls and custom-made cabinetry.

Three bedrooms and two baths were upstairs; the middle floor had a kitchen and a two-story great room. Downstairs, the large garage was one way, and down a few more stairs was a huge area which had once been his dad's carpentry workshop. Now it was a rec room that could double as a guest suite. He and Alexis had been their only children, but the senior MacMahons had planned space for lots of grandchildren visiting. At least to their only one, Claire, it was home for now. Nick figured he'd never sell it. Maybe he'd lease it to Tara Kinsale, if he decided to take the job in the East.

"Beamer! Beamer boy, your partner's home!" he shouted, but the dog was not in the fenced-in run out back. The run was required by law, whether to keep the dogs safe from marauding bears or smaller wildlife safe from dogs, Nick wasn't sure. Beamer was not a hunter; he retrieved escaped or lost people. He was one of the best dogs Nick had ever trained. Put a working collar on him, give him someone's scent and he was off to the races. What a team they'd been. At eight years, Beamer was getting pretty old to work long days now, but he'd always have a home as Nick's pet.

No other sounds came from the house but frenzied barking. Nick was glad to be here before Claire got off her school bus from West Jefferson Elementary. They'd passed the school below and he'd been tempted to have Jim let him out there, to find Claire's classroom and hug her and tell her everything would be all right now that he was home.

The kid had been fighting battles of her own. She'd lost her mother — thanks to her bastard father — and her grandmother. He wanted to assure her that she would not lose her uncle Nick. It was his duty to take care of Claire. He had a great job offer to train more dogs at Fort Bragg in North Carolina, though his dream had always been to start a school near Denver for tracker dogs and their human partners. Wherever they ended up, Claire would have to learn to love it. Though he'd never been married or had a child of his own, he had no doubt he could somehow learn to be both parents to her.

"Beamer!" he shouted again as he walked back around to the front of the house. Puffing from the altitude, he went up on the elevated deck. The Lab jumped on his hind legs, trying to paw his way through the picture window. Considering this manic display, he was sure no one but Beamer was home. Nick's reluctance to leave his beloved pet was one reason he almost turned down the military consulting job with Delta Force in the desolate, dangerous province of Nuristan, Afghanistan, but duty called.

Nick cursed the fact he didn't have a house key. Maybe there was one still hidden where his mother had always left it. It was so bittersweet to come home but not find her here for the first time in his life.

He strode behind the house and heard Beamer follow him to the back door. He had hoped Tara, his sister's best friend and Claire's temporary guardian, would be home. He should have called her from the Denver airport, but at the last minute he and Jim had flown standby from Dulles in D.C., and then he thought it would be fun to surprise them.

Nick had met the beautiful, redheaded Tara here at the house a couple of years ago. He couldn't quite recall when, but he could recall her. It was before he'd signed the contract with the army to train dogs to sniff out the cave-clinging Taliban, including Bin Laden, who had a reward of a cool fifty million dollars on his head. They'd located a lot of the enemy but not the man himself, a small regret compared to his tragic failure while he was there.

Trying to deep-six that memory, Nick glimpsed a photo of Tara and Claire together, all dressed up for some event. The picture was on the coffee table, in great danger of being swept off by Beamer's tail. The photo reminded him of Tara's lavish wedding to big money. She still looked like how he'd picture an old-fashioned Irish lass though, not someone on the society pages of the paper. She was a natural, windblown-looking beauty with red hair to her shoulders. He only really knew her through a couple of phone calls and their sporadic e-mails, all dealing with Claire. He'd been stationed so far out in the boonies with the Delta boys that he hadn't even known Clay had murdered Alexis until she'd been buried for over a week. Anyway, if he'd been here, he probably would have tracked Clay down and then strangled his former brother-in-law with his bare hands.

This homecoming was also tough because Nick had been incommunicado with a Delta chalk squad when the stroke killed his mother. Tara and some distant relatives had taken care of the arrangements, as well as of little Claire. He owed Tara Kinsale big-time.

He checked for the house key under the flower crock where his parents had always kept it. Negative. With walls still between them, he and Beamer raced for the front of the house again. He'd just bivouac on the front deck, waiting for Claire and Tara to show. But if he didn't calm Beamer down, the high-ceilinged great room was going to look like a bomb blew up in it. He shuddered at that image — that memory.

"Good dog," he shouted through the window. Time to see if Beamer still knew who the senior partner was, the alpha pack dog, after their time apart. If Beamer obeyed him, he'd take that as a sign that Claire would happily do whatever he decided was best. After all, how hard could it be to take care of a young girl when he'd trained dogs and given orders to the Delta boys, no less.

"Sit," Nick commanded solemnly. "Beamer, sit. Beamer, quiet."

Tears blurred Nick's vision of the big, wide-eyed, panting dog as he immediately sat silent with his tail thumping the floor like a pendulum.

Tara wished she'd been able to find a female doctor who was taking new patients. She really did miss Jen. They had met at a social event years ago and had been friends before they'd been patient and physician. But Jen could never understand why Tara didn't gladly toe Laird's line. Jen hadn't brought it up, but Tara suspected she probably blamed Tara for their divorce, despite the fact that Laird had left her. Though Tara was grateful to be out of a bad marriage, it did hurt that Laird had deserted her in her hour of need. It was so strange to be married to him, and then, when she awoke from the coma — which felt like the very next day to her, though it was almost an entire year — to be divorced and not to have any contact with him. A blessing, in one way, but a curse to her psyche, too, one that counseling had not quite erased.

"A dream catch," Jen had called Laird with a sigh the first time she'd laid eyes on him. "Wish I'd been the one doing some social work with patients at the Lohan Mountain Manor Clinic. You sure were lucky, running into the eligible fair-haired son there."

Jen and Tara had talked via cell phone several times while Tara was rebuilding her life, but she knew Jen was busy starting over, too. Lately, they spoke less and less. It seemed, at least on Jen's part, they had little in common now.

31

Dr. Gordon Holbrook, Tara's new G.P., came into the examining room and said cheerily, "Good afternoon, Tara." He was fifty-something, with gray etching his temples and prominent crow's-feet and worry lines on his pleasant face. He sat down to chat about how she'd been feeling since waking from the coma and to go over the extensive medical records he'd received from Jen and from the Lohan Clinic, where she'd spent the last nine and a half months of her coma, then two months of rehab and counseling.

In short, Dr. Holbrook seemed to have a good bedside — or examination tableside — manner. He was thoughtful enough to call Pamela back into the room when he began the cervical exam and pap test, so Tara would feel more at ease.

Tara was still tense, but responded to his small talk about how the property values were skyrocketing in the area. He had friends who lived on Shadow Mountain Road, but not as high up as her. She didn't know them. She explained that she'd only lived in the area since her foster child's grandmother had died, because she didn't want to uproot Claire again. Their nearest neighbors lived about a football field away.

When he was done, Dr. Holbrook slid the

stirrups back under the table, covered her legs with a light blanket and had her sit up. He told Pamela she could step out. He had stopped the light talk; in fact, he stopped talking at all as he went to her folder. He scanned it again, frowning. With all Tara had been through after the coma, she could tell when bad news was coming. She gripped her hands tightly together.

"What is it, Doctor? Is something wrong?"

"No, simply an incomplete record here — by far. There is nothing I see here about your pregnancy or your delivery of a baby. Was the child lost or perhaps adopted?"

Her insides cartwheeled, then she actually snorted a little laugh of surprise. His question didn't give her a lot of faith in him now. "That's because I've never had a baby."

"I do understand," he said, "that you might have private reasons for not wanting to admit to a pregnancy or having borne a child. But I'm not here to judge you in any way."

"Doctor, I have not had a child. Besides, I was on birth control pills the entire two years I was married. What gives you the idea I was even pregnant?"

"Several key indicators," he said. Sitting, still frowning, he leaned slightly toward her. Her pulse picked up and her stomach cramped. "Tara, you have all the signs of having had a pregnancy and a vaginal delivery."

"Oh, you mean the stretch marks on the sides of my stomach. Those are from lying comatose so long, I think, even though they moved and massaged me and —"

"I didn't even notice those. There are telltale indicators of a pregnancy that must have gone at least nearly full-term."

"What? Doctor, there is no way. I said I was on birth control pills and —"

"There have been instances of pregnancies while someone is on the Pill. One missed pill, or even counterfeit ones coming in from China that have found their way into reputable drugstores or other suppliers."

"It's still impossible. You've read my record. That's all there is!"

"Tara, your vagina is relaxed, not tight."

"I was unconscious for almost a year! Every part of me was relaxed!" She kept shaking her head. This was ridiculous — impossible. She didn't know whether to laugh or cry. She even felt insulted. But when he'd said the words *vaginal delivery,* for some reason, she'd felt the earth shake.

"Also," he went on, "your cervix is open about one centimeter, and it doesn't have the tip-of-a-nose-with-dimple appearance of a woman who has never been pregnant and delivered. But the first thing that I noted was external body signs, beyond the stretch marks you mention. From your naval to the pubis, there is a slight dark line called the *linea negra,* which pregnant women present. On women who have not had a child, it would be much lighter — a *linea alba,* or white line. And I'm sure you'll note that the areolas around your nipples are darker than they used to be."

Her heart thudding, she stared gapmouthed at him. This man didn't know what was normal for her — not before today, at least. Yet she was riveted, trying to take in each word.

"Tara, whatever you share with me will stay privileged from everyone, unless you choose to release the information. Since so much of your private life has been made public lately, I can understand your reluctance to trust me. But as we embark on our professional relationship, this is something very important you should consider sharing with your physician."

Tara actually couldn't talk. She sputtered, half-furious, half-stunned. She blinked back tears. He — he had to be wrong. Even if by some fluke she'd gotten pregnant while on birth control pills, there was no way she'd had a pregnancy or a baby, not in a full-blown coma! She was getting out of here right now. She'd pick up Claire, go home and hide out with her and Beamer, where things were normal, safe and sane.

2

"Uncle Nick!" Claire exploded, and pointed out the truck window. "It's Uncle Nick! He's here!"

The child screeched in excitement as Tara pulled the truck into the driveway. She watched as Nick, grinning and waving a bit sheepishly at the raucous greeting, hurried down the steps of the front deck to greet them.

Nicolas MacMahon was taller than Tara remembered from their one meeting. He was big shouldered and bronze skinned; his close-cropped blond hair and white beard stubble glistened in the September sun. He was the only man she'd ever seen who did not seem to shrink in this vast mountain setting. Though still in pale-colored combat fatigues, he didn't blend in with the background but seemed the center of the scene.

Claire was out of the car like a shot to hurl herself into his outstretched arms. He lifted and swung her around while she squealed in delight. After losing his sister and his mother while he'd been away, Tara thought, this must be the moment he knew he was home.

Holding Claire in one arm as if she were a toddler, he met Tara partway around her truck. His ice-blue eyes glinted from under straight, pale brows and his teeth shone white in his tanned face as he smiled. Despite her height of five feet eight inches, he stood more than half a head taller. The late-day sun threw shadows in the clefts of his cheeks and a wayward dimple to the left of his mouth. His prominent nose was a bit crooked but it suited his look, a blend of ruddy and just plain rugged. He didn't really resemble either his sister or his mother; from photos Tara had seen, he had clearly inherited his father's form and face.

He finally put Claire down. A moment of awkward silence stretched out between him and Tara, as if they'd been caught by a slo-mo camera. Something loud but unspoken arced between them before he threw his free arm around her shoulders and hugged her hard against his rock-hard side, then let her go.

"Welcome home, Nick," she said, shoving her hair from her face in the sudden breeze as she took a step back and looked up into his happy face. "Welcome home!"

She meant it and was happy for him and her precious little Claire. Family at last, for both of them. But another loss loomed for her, unless she could convince him to at least stay in the area. The house was his, Claire was his, even Tara's best wishes were his, but in a way he was her enemy.

Ashamed of that thought — or blushing from the closeness of the man himself — Tara turned away. She hurried to the house and unlocked the door while Claire chattered to Nick about her two best friends at school, about how she and "Aunt Tara" were going to go to the Denver Zoo and to a concert at Red Rocks and would he go, too. Thank heavens the seven-year-old had no hang-ups about her uncle, whom she hadn't seen for over two years except for e-mailed photos and one face-to-face online interview. The child was so happy she flaunted the gap-toothed grin she'd been shy about ever since she'd begun to lose her baby teeth. Her brown eyes danced in her narrow, freckled face while, in her excitement, she stood on first one sneakered foot and then the other.

Tara stood frozen for a moment, gazing at them, her mind racing. She had to try to

39

convince Nick not to take Claire away — at least, not far away. In that split second of mingled frustration and fear, she sensed what her clients must feel in that moment they realized their husbands or exes or boyfriends had taken their beloved kids and disappeared.

With a sniff, she turned away to open the front door. Instead of his usual single bark and gentle greeting, Beamer tore past her in a blur of movement and strength. Nick saw him coming and put Claire behind him while the golden Lab nearly leaped into his arms. Another moment to remember, Tara told herself, then realized she felt left out — almost jealous. Today of all days, when she'd needed her closeness to Claire and some peace and quiet to deal with her own problems, this!

Nick hugged Beamer and knelt to bury his face in the dog's hair. The three of them looked like a matched set, all golden haired, perhaps with golden futures. Tara leaned in the doorway with tears in her eyes, then realized she was resting both hands protectively on her belly.

What Dr. Holbrook had told her today hit hard again. He was mistaken, of course. If the birth of her own child were a fact, the only possibility was that it had occurred while she was comatose. But that was impossible. Insane. Yet, just to ease her mind, she was going to use her online skills to check it out, phone Jen in L.A., too, and perhaps even get a second opinion beyond Jen's. But even comatose women didn't have babies they never knew about, especially not while they were on birth control, for heaven's sake. The man was wrong, and she'd told him so.

Now, she just had to prove it to herself.

However strange things seemed without his mother here, the old house seemed to welcome Nick. He'd held the door for Tara, and his words — *After you* — echoed in his head. Yeah, he could really see himself going after a woman like this. Yet she seemed more than wary, as if she had an invisible fence around her that she — or he — dare not cross. Hell, he couldn't blame her, since she probably figured he could take Claire away from her. Maybe she was scarred from her sudden divorce, too, even if that was a while ago.

After his excited niece dragged him from room to room, as if he'd never seen the place he'd grown up in, he sat at the kitchen table with a Coors beer, taco chips and Claire while Tara fixed a salad and spaghetti.

41

He filled them in on his flights home, then told them how he'd left the ten dogs he'd helped train with their new partners in the mountains of Afghanistan and how they wanted him to train even more here in the States. Beamer, tight to his leg under the table, seemed to listen to each word, too.

"Aunt Tara showed me where you were on the map and I can spell Afghanistan, too," Claire piped up. "And I think that's where afghans like that one on the sofa Grandma knitted first came from. Beamer missed you. Aunt Tara, too. We all did, 'specially after Mommy went to heaven and Daddy went to prison."

That incredible last sentence, delivered in the child's light voice, reminded Nick of some sappy Western music lyrics. Hard to believe it was all true and had happened to his family. Tears filled his eyes. Crying in his beer already. Man, he must be exhausted as well as jet-lagged. Everything was getting to him today. His eyes met Tara's green gaze again over the steam from the boiling pasta. What was this woman really like? Was she that lovely inside, too? She had tried to save Alex at the risk of her own life and had taken such good care of Claire. In the coma Clay's attack had caused, she'd lost almost a year of her life and had lost her husband, the life she'd known. He knew she ran a P.I. firm that searched for lost kids. She must have a heart of gold.

He could tell she forced a smile before she looked away from him. She was tall but shapely. Any moron who'd been living with men and looking only at the occasional woman swathed in black burkas for the past two years would appreciate that. Her grace and femininity made him weak in the knees, yet she seemed to have an edge to her. Her sunny looks often crashed to frowns or near tears. Damn, they had a lot to say to each other. He could only hope she'd understand his dilemma about taking Claire and leaving.

Tara intended to let Nick read Claire her bedtime story and tuck her in tonight, but both Claire and Nick had insisted she come into the child's bedroom, too. Ironically, Claire had chosen *Alexander and the Terrible, Horrible, No Good, Very Bad Day* — she liked any book title with a resemblance to her mother's name in it. Nick shot Tara a what's-with-this-book look, since the child seemed so happy. He'd soon learn, Tara thought, that Claire had lots of problems that came out in lots of ways. As Nick read the familiar book to his niece, Tara's mind drifted. She could have written *Tara's Hor-rendous, Impossible, Ridiculous, Gut-wrenching Day.* She felt both emotionally exhausted and keyed up; for once, the glass of red wine she and Nick had drunk with dinner was not making her sleepy. She was as revved up as if she'd downed a whole pot of coffee and she was dying to get online to search *comatose woman + childbirth* and to phone Jen. But she needed to talk to Nick in private first.

After they tucked Claire in bed, they sat out on the deck overlooking the darkening mountains. For the first time in the thirteen months since she'd moved in with Claire, Tara felt like a guest. It was an amazingly peaceful scene and yet she felt so uptight.

"You're probably very tired," she said, feeling she should give him a way out of further conversation if he wanted to be alone — with man's best friend, that is. Beamer trailed him everywhere and now lay two feet from the rungs of Nick's rocker.

"I'm kind of jazzed, tell you the truth."

They shared small talk, things about Claire's daily schedule. He with another beer, she with herbal tea, they rocked and watched the setting sun stain the western sky bloodred. To the northeast, down the mountain and over the darkening silhouettes

44

of spiky pines and leaf-rattling aspens, they could see the distant lights of Denver coming on in twinkling pinpoints. Behind them, up the mountain, the thick, black tree line loomed.

"Lots of memories here," he said softly, then cleared his throat. "I guess it's pretty tough to have lost some memories, when you were . . . hurt."

"Besides losing Alex, I lost my husband. That was just as well though. No woman wants someone who isn't in for the hard times as well as the good. We had a lot of differences." She switched to a news-reporter-style voice: "Independent, self-supporting, middle-class woman weds big money and becomes property of the lord of the manor, along with the loyal-only-unto-themselves Lohan family." She dropped the elevated tone and went on. "Laird Lohan gave me a shock when he left me — and left town — but also saved me some heartache. I'm slowly getting my real self back, becoming just working girl Tara Kinsale again. And Claire's been such a big part of my life and recovery."

"Alex had a tough marriage, too. Things were bad with Clay, obviously, even before he took Claire from her." He shook his head. "I guess I was in my own little

45

freewheeling-bachelor and dog-training world during most of that. Thank God, the cops found Clay, and he's locked up for life."

"Yes, but you should know that his family, especially his younger brother Rick, really took Clay's conviction personally, as if it was Alex's, or even my fault. She wasn't around to blame, so Rick berated me. Told me off in person and later sent me a threatening letter, which I saved."

He frowned and shifted in his chair so hard it creaked. "Yeah, that sounds like Rick. Not the sharpest knife in the drawer, but he's more of a blowhard than someone with the guts to do something. He doesn't have a family and never quite made a go of things professionally — keeps changing jobs, even careers. He hasn't bothered you since his initial eruption, has he?"

"Haven't seen hide nor hair of him."

"Beamer would growl if he came around here."

"You'll have to have a chat with Beamer," she said, glad to change the subject. "He doesn't growl, but he barks anytime a fox or elk or bear is around."

"He just needs a bit of reeducation on manners. So . . ." He drew the word out as if he hesitated to embark on whatever he

46

was going to say. "I take it that happy, smiling Claire still has her dark moments — that book she chose tonight, stuff like that."

"Yes. I think hearing about another kid's difficult day comforts her. It teaches her she's not the only one with problems and losses, although few suffer what she'd been through. The two of us are open about her losses, and she knows about mine —"

Her voice caught. But did she have a loss Claire didn't know about — one that she herself didn't know about? No, she could not have had a child of her own, a baby who would now be — let's see, probably around two and a half years old. If, by the wildest stretch of imagination, that were true, where was the proof? Where was the child?

"Go on," Nick prompted, making her realize she'd stopped in the middle of a sentence. It took her a moment to get back on her mental track.

"Claire and I have leaned on each other," she said. "But don't be startled if you hear her shrieking in the middle of the night."

"Bad dreams?"

She nodded. "Very." She didn't tell him that ever since her recovery from the coma — or perhaps even during the coma — she also had been stalked by the monsters of warped, horrendous nightmares. She'd

47

received counseling for the dreams at the Lohan Clinic when she was trying to make plans and put her life back together.

"Nick," she said, speaking faster now as she turned in her rocker to face him, "if you don't mind my asking, what are your plans?"

"Undecided. I've got a too-good-to-turn-down offer to train dogs for the armed forces, but it would mean a move to North Carolina. With all my experience, I feel it's my duty, in peace or wartime. These dogs would not be bomb sniffers but trackers who hunt the enemy — specific people, when we can give the dogs a scent, like what I've been doing these last two years. But Claire's my duty now, too."

"Your mother told me once that when you got the funding, you wanted to open a dog academy around here, to train dogs and their humans to search for lost people."

"True. I love this area. In a way, we're both in the finders business, aren't we? Tara, I can't thank you enough for all you've done for Claire. I know you didn't do it for me, but speaking for my entire family, gone though they are . . ." His voice trailed off again. He cleared his throat. "Anything I can do to help you — to repay — I don't mean with money. Guess you've been there, done that."

"I appreciate your support," she told him. Damn, she was resting her free hand on her belly again, almost as if she had a stomach-ache. Here she was discussing what was most important to her and Claire and she kept coming back to the fact she could not have had a baby. No! No way in all creation was that remotely possible!

"You're upset," he said, leaning toward her with his elbow on the arm of his chair, so they mirrored each other's body language. They had both stopped rocking; earlier she'd noticed how they had rocked in unison. "Even if Claire and I move across the country," he told her, "you're always welcome to visit, and we'll come see you. I doubt if the move would be permanent. Maybe just a few years. I don't mean to hurt you after all you've been through."

"Don't worry about that," she said, rising to go inside before she blurted out every-thing to him about today, not to mention the fact that she would just hate it — hate him — if he took Claire away. "Sometimes there's nowhere to go but up. I know whereof I speak."

"But all that's behind you now," he said as she started inside.

She turned back to face him. Wouldn't he be shocked if she dumped her doctor's

49

claim about a belly line and cervical dimples on a man she barely knew on his first day home? The darn doctor was right about the subtle changes to her breasts and belly, but surely all that could have resulted from her coma, too. At least, that's what she told herself before today.

"By the way," she said, "I get Claire up for school at seven, but we'll be quiet if you want to sleep in. It will be nice to have a man on the premises, since it feels a bit isolated up here, even with Beamer on patrol. I'll start looking for a new place soon, maybe in town."

"No!" Nick said, thumping his empty bottle onto the wooden deck and standing to take her arm to turn her toward him. "You do anything like that on my account, and Claire will never forgive me. Beamer will track you for us. Before you make any move like that, I'll find someplace else until everything is decided on and settled."

Settled, she thought. As she thanked him and wished him a good night's sleep, she realized she wasn't ever going to feel settled again until she proved she'd never been pregnant.

3

In her office, Tara turned on the lights and hurried to the PC she used to track down other people's kids. Finally, some time to herself. She needed answers, and she needed them now. After all, she was a researcher, a finder, a tracker of people. It was nearly midnight, but she'd never sleep if she didn't look into Dr. Holbrook's crazy claims.

Her Finders Keepers office was in the large, extra bedroom. In addition to her desk and one armchair, the office had two PCs, one of them always online, a fax/copier/scanner, and four file cabinets — fireproof ones with locks. Since Alex had taken the report on Clay from Tara's files, she was paranoid about keeping things under lock and key.

One file held her case-data sheets and time logs for payment. Also, this was where she kept her precious list of IBs — information brokers — who were always her last resort. They were expensive, obsessive, underground kinds of people she'd never want to meet in person. One of them, Marv Seymour, had been trying to hit on her via e-mail and fax, as if she'd consulted some lookin'-for-love source instead of purchasing locate info from him. Unfortunately, he did not live far away, in Centennial, south of Denver. She'd told him not to contact her for personal reasons again, after he'd claimed he "knew more than the TV and newspapers had covered about her lonely life." That was the pot calling the kettle black, since he sounded like a real loner. However much she needed a good local IB, Seymour came across like a weirdo who lived in the shadows. Colorado was one of few states that had no statewide licensing or oversight of private detective agencies, and IBs were never called to account for their actions either.

On the wall above Tara's big pine desk hung two large corkboards with a splattering of random notes, maps and reminders pinned to them. To her left was a large, white erasable marker board next to a huge calendar on which she kept track of what reports were due when. Because she juggled several cases at once, she had learned to multitask and prioritize. Once she found she could do that again, she'd known she had no lasting mental concerns from her coma. Hard rehab work had brought her through her physical weaknesses. Rather, she thought, the residual damage was all emotional.

Tara's office telephone system had three lines, one dedicated to the fax. Only one had a listed number. Tape recorders were attached to two of the three phones, because she often recorded witness interviews. Taping was legal because she always stated and then repeated that the conversation was being recorded. Her clients received a copy of the tape along with the final report — a report she would have given to Alex *after* Clay was in custody and Claire was on her way back to her mother.

Now, in Tara's zeal to learn if a comatose woman could deliver a child — maybe even a living child — she caught a glimpse of why Alex had rushed after Claire the moment she had learned her location. Like Tara tonight with Nick and Claire, Alex had chatted normally on that fateful day. She had controlled her desperation in order to hide the fact she intended to find Claire at any cost, even if it meant stealing the progress report from her friend and lying to her about where she was going.

Though Tara had told no one but her psychiatrist at the Lohan Clinic, deep down she blamed Alex for putting herself in a position to be murdered. Tara also blamed Alex for indirectly placing her in a dangerous situation that led to Clay robbing her of a year of her life. It was a miracle that Alex's rash actions hadn't pushed Clay into harming Claire, as well. Tara hated feeling so conflicted about her best friend, but she couldn't help feeling anger as well as anguish over her loss.

Tara sat down in her desk chair and double-clicked her mouse. The big, flat screen woke up, displaying the latest wallpaper on her home page. She had taken a photo of the mountains and valley from the highest safe access point above the house, an outcrop called Big Rock. But over the breathtaking view she had superimposed the headline from the *Denver Post* reporting her recovery from her coma: Comatose Conifer Woman Gets Back Life But Not Her Past. Was it possible her coma had taken something else from her?

The article had told about her memory loss, starting the day Clay had slammed her over the head with the butt of the same gun he'd used to kill Alex. It had also revealed that her husband, well-known locally through his wealthy, influential family, had left her and moved to the West Coast during her long coma. That had surely made Laird look cold and selfish, Tara thought, and the Lohans hated bad PR. They always wanted to be seen as altruistic and generous. Laird must have wanted to get away from her badly. Veronica, his mother, was the only Lohan who had seemed to sympathize with Tara in the dissolution of the marriage, but of course, Lohan blue blood didn't flow through Veronica's veins. She'd married into the clan, just like Tara.

Tara kept the headline on her screen because, in facing its brutal truth, she tried harder to live each day better and stronger. *That which does not kill us makes us stronger,* the Nietzsche quote went. Now those words might even carry a new meaning.

She quickly located an item on *comatose woman + childbirth* on the CBS News site. There was also an article from the *Cincinnati Enquirer* about the same case:

Doctors in Cincinnati say it's an extremely rare case — a twenty-four-year-old woman who was in a coma for nearly her entire pregnancy has given birth to a healthy, full-term baby . . . Chastity Cooper of Warsaw, Kentucky, has been comatose since she suffered severe head injuries in an auto accident in November, two weeks after she conceived. The pregnancy was discovered after the accident. Obstetricians said it was extremely rare that a woman could deliver a baby full-term when she was in a coma and bedridden through the pregnancy . . . Doctors said they used labor-inducing medications, but no strong pain relievers in the vaginal delivery . . .

Tara just stared at the screen. *Doctors said . . . Obstetricians said . . .* Her mind bounced back to what her own doctor had claimed today. He was theorizing, of course, that she'd had a child before her coma, possibly years ago. A comatose delivery might have been "extremely rare" but, obviously, it was not impossible. And *vaginal delivery.* Why did those words especially disturb her?

Her hands clasped so hard in her lap that her fingers went numb, she reread the article, word for word. "But this girl obviously wasn't on birth control pills," she whispered aloud as she tried to convince herself that one rare case proved nothing.

She searched further and came across a Fox TV Web site with a brief mention of a similar case. At first, because it took place in Kentucky, Tara thought it referred to the same rare instance, but it was much more current, from exactly three months ago.

We have an update tonight on a story Fox 7 first told you about in January. A comatose Webster County, Kentucky, woman has given birth to a healthy baby girl. Ashley Chaney was allegedly beaten by her ex-boyfriend and remains unresponsive in a nursing home. Chaney delivered the five-pound baby girl in late May. Thomas Matthew Yancy is charged with beating Chaney and putting her in a coma . . .

Tara shuddered. Despite the fact she had no memory of her own assault, she pictured herself being hit on the head by Alex's ex-husband. After she had come out of her coma, when she'd interviewed the Central City law officer who had found her, he'd described how she was sprawled lifeless on the wet ground. Could she have been harboring a new life within her?

After shooting Alex and attacking Tara, Clay had fled again, taking Claire with him. But he'd made the mistake of speeding and had been pulled over near Grand Junction. Ballistics later proved his rifle, found in the cab of his truck, killed Alex; it still had

Tara's hair and blood on its butt.

The law officer's exact words echoed in Tara's mind: "You were sprawled lifeless on the ground." She lay lifeless there — and for long months after that, first in a rescue helicopter, then a Denver E.R., then intensive care, and finally, at the Lohan Clinic. How could she have produced another life?

No, she still didn't believe that possibility. It was rare — extremely rare, doctors said. So what was wrong with Dr. Holbrook? Was he just looking for his moment of fame, a newspaper article or TV segment, like these quoted doctors? An article in a medical journal? No way a comatose pregnancy and delivery could have happened to her. But then, she'd been in hell all those months, helpless, lost to herself and others, except for some sounds she thought she heard, and a relentless parade of nightmares she sometimes thought she could almost recall.

All that time she'd been in the coma, could something as momentous as childbirth have occurred?

Tara jolted alert and looked at her big office clock. Too late to make the phone call to Jen now. That would be like getting a second opinion, since she'd been her obgyn for years and hadn't left the area until Tara was comatose. Though her former physician and friend had drifted away from her, she was calling Dr. Jennifer DeMar first thing in the morning.

Tara had finally fallen asleep when a scream shredded the silence of the night. She awoke instantly. Claire! One of Claire's nightmares. She used to have them every night, but now they only happened when something set her off. Perhaps Nick's homecoming had.

Tara ran for Claire's bedroom before she realized she hadn't put a robe on over her T-shirt and panties, in case Nick came running, too. But the child was shrieking, "No, no, don't hurt her!"

Tara didn't turn back even when she heard Nick thudding up the steps from his room in the basement. It was nicely finished down there with a Franklin stove for warmth, a bathroom and sofa with its Hide-A-Bed. Right now she wished it was farther away or he was a sounder sleeper.

"It's all right, sweetie," she crooned to Claire, and clicked on the bedside lamp to add to the wan night-light that was always on. "Just another bad dream. I'm here."

Tara scooted her bare legs under the covers next to the quaking child as Nick's big form filled the doorway. He was in Jockey shorts and a cutoff gray T-shirt that showed his flat stomach. Tara cradled Claire, who wound her arms tight around her.

"They were shouting," Claire choked out through such thick sobs her words were barely discernible. "He said he'd kill her. He locked me in my room. Mommy was screaming my name . . . then a big bang."

"It's over. You're here and safe now," Tara whispered, rocking her like a baby. "It's all right."

"It isn't! He's going to kill her all over again."

When Nick stepped into the room, Claire jolted. She went stiff in Tara's arms, then limp as a doll. "Oh, Uncle Nick. I thought — I thought you might be him, that you were going to hurt me, too."

"No," Nick said, his voice raspy either from being suddenly awakened or from a rush of emotion. "No, I'd never hurt you. And your dad's gone, so he can't hurt anyone now."

"I think he's hiding up in the trees outside, like when he hurt Aunt Tara. Out the window — I saw him hit her on the head by the trees. He could come back. He's in the trees above our house."

"No, no, he isn't, and he won't be back," Tara said, her lips moving against the top of Claire's head. "He's all locked up and can't get out. And I'm all right now. Both you and I are safe, especially with Beamer and your uncle Nick here."

Tara's eyes met Nick's over the girl's head. It was a new nightmarish twist that Clay could be lurking up in the trees above the house. Tara had thought Claire understood and accepted that he was in prison on the other side of the state, but, of course, it was just the bad dream speaking.

Nick stood silent, taking them both in. The big guy, who'd been living in the desert and caves, in danger of losing his life for two years, had tears in his eyes for a child's nightmare.

"Listen to me, Claire," he said, his voice steadier as he came a step closer. He gestured with his index finger as if scolding her. "He's not hiding up in the trees, and he's not going to hurt you or Aunt Tara again, ever. So you just tell yourself there's no reason for any more nightmares!" he added, his voice sounding as if that was a military order. With a sniff, he leaned closer to pat the girl's shoulder, somehow managing to tangle his fingers in Tara's hair. He gently tugged free, did an about-face and marched out into the dark hall.

He'd been in a dangerous no-man's land with Special Forces soldiers who probably survived on giving and taking orders, so for now, Tara ignored Nick's brusqueness to the child. She really didn't think his just-get-that-out-of-your-head-right-now approach would work with Claire — or with her, either. She was done with guys who came on to her like that.

A half hour later, when Tara left the sleeping girl to go back to her own bed, she saw Nick sitting on the floor of the upstairs hall, still barefoot but dressed now in jeans, long legs stretched out. Beamer lay next to him, his big head on Nick's knee. She couldn't see them well at first because she'd left the light on in Claire's room and her eyes hadn't adjusted. But Nick's obviously had. She suddenly felt naked. She crossed her arms over her breasts; at least there was no light behind her.

"I guess I'm too damned used to giving and taking orders," he whispered. "I didn't mean to sound so stern."

That touched her. Unlike Laird, this man had a heart and soul. "It's all right," she whispered, but her voice caught.

"I do know," he whispered back, "that everyone has nightmares. I've had my share, and sometimes it works for me to tell myself, 'You will not have that bad dream again.' "

"Can't you sleep tonight?"

"I'm okay. But I heard footsteps. It sounded to me like you were up late, even before this."

"I had some office work to do. See you in the morning."

"Tara." He rose lithely to his feet, forcing Beamer to lift his head. Even barefoot, Nick seemed tall. Leaning one broad shoulder on the wall, he whispered, "I wish they hadn't let her testify against Clay, telling all she saw and heard that day. It's no doubt made her bad dreams worse, screwed up her mind."

"If I hadn't been comatose, my testimony might have made her deposition unnecessary. At least she was kept out of the courtroom and the papers. They convinced your mom the deposition was the best way to convict Clay. But I, for one, can certainly see how all this has screwed up her mind."

"I didn't mean to sound critical any more than I meant to sound harsh."

"She's still very fragile, Nick."

"I hear you. We all are, all got our minds screwed up by something or other."

"Yes." She fought back the tears prickling behind her eyelids. "And I know Claire and I aren't the only ones who have been through very tough times." She reached out to touch his rock-hard upper arm, then headed for her bedroom before either of them could say or do more. She closed the door quickly but quietly. She did not want to shut him up or shut him off, but after today, she was even more scared of her own nightmares. And she was still fighting the compelling urge to tell that big stranger all about them.

At seven-thirty the next morning, Tara dialed Dr. Jennifer DeMar's cell phone number. "Nothing like caller ID." Jen's voice came crisp and clear. "Tara, how are you?"

"All right. Listen, I know it's a bit early in the morning, and I apologize for that. But I know you're an early riser, and I wanted to catch you before you went to work."

"You caught me, all right."

Her voice seemed slightly slurred. Tara hoped she hadn't wakened her. She also noted an undercurrent to her voice that had entered their recent, sporadic conversations. Obviously, Jen had been trying to gently cut ties.

"Is everything all right?" Jen asked when she hesitated. "You sound upset."

"I need to ask you a professional question and a personal one."

"You're talking in riddles, but then, you always did love puzzles. A professional medical question? Something about complications from the coma?"

"In a way. Jen, Dr. Holbrook actually asked me when I had a baby."

A beat of silence, then, "He *what?*"

"Let me back up a second. After he did my pelvic exam and pap smear, he said I showed signs that I'd been pregnant and had had a vaginal delivery. I think he meant of a full-term baby."

"Is he crazy? You mean he's implying you delivered a baby in the middle of a long coma?" Jen's voice was shaky but dripping sarcasm. "An invisible infant? Maybe one abducted by aliens?"

"So you do think he's wrong?"

"I hope you told him he's dead wrong. If he's saying your uterus or cervix is stretched, so what? Some women have larger ones, even if they haven't been pregnant. I don't know of any studies done on formerly comatose women to see if their uterus or cervix would be naturally relaxed. Do you know how rare a comatose pregnancy and delivery would be?"

Tara was glad Jen was shocked and outraged. Jen was more recently trained than Dr. Holbrook, so she probably knew much more about current medical discoveries and advances. But then, how much could have changed about how a woman who'd delivered a child looked?

"I researched it," Tara told her. "I realize a birth to a comatose mother is extremely rare, but I found a couple of such cases."

"My dear friend," Jen said, her voice quiet now, "your new doctor is not serving your needs well. He should have his license yanked, but that would take time and money. However financially generous Laird may have been with you, it's best if you just don't go back to him — the doctor."

"Would you advise I get a second opinion?"

"That's absolutely not necessary. Next year when it's time for your annual physical, get someone else. Try one of the doctors at the Conifer Medical Center on Pleasant Park. They're all good. As for the personal question — you're going to ask if I visited you while you were comatose, right? Yes, I certainly did, a couple of times before I moved. You most definitely were not pregnant, nor had you been. I'm so sorry you've had to go through this — this new trauma. Set your mind at ease, and take care of your niece. Go on with building your new life in Conifer. That's what I'm doing here

66

— both professionally and personally, as you put it. Listen — I've got a full day. Gotta go. Tara, just forget all that nonsense and have a great day and a great life."

Jen must have covered the mouthpiece of the phone, because her last few words came out muffled. Was that a man's voice in the background? Yes, very muted. Jen must have a new man in her life. That reminded Tara she had Nick to deal with today. That thought actually gave her a lift.

"Thanks for —" Tara was cut off by Jen hanging up.

As she watched the light go out on the screen of her cell, Tara thought that had sounded not like a temporary goodbye but a permanent one. However much she valued her former friend's advice, she'd sounded like Nick ordering a nightmare-terrified girl to just forget her fears, as if they were not worth a damn. She resented that Jen considered her earthshaking question nonsense.

It seemed as if Jen were shuffling her aside as a friend, but had she also done so as a doctor? Despite Jen's fervent claims, maybe she did need another doctor's opinion. But it would have to be fast, because this — unlike what Jen had counseled — couldn't wait.

4

Nick borrowed Tara's truck so he and Beamer could take Claire to school. When he returned, he found a hearty breakfast of pancakes and sausage waiting for him. Tara had laid out a bright woven place mat and a matching cloth napkin. A ceramic vase held orange and yellow wildflowers. Tara looked a bit wild, too, beautiful but exhausted and windblown. She'd evidently been outside to pick the flowers. She wore no makeup and her hair was tousled as if she'd just gotten out of bed. Nick shifted his legs under the table. The woman got to him in more ways than one.

"This looks great. I didn't mean to oversleep," he told her.

"You were able to spend some time with Claire before school, and that's what mattered. I'm sure you're jet-lagged. Is the Hide-A-Bed okay?"

Biting back a tease that he'd rather have

her bed, he dug into the pile of pancakes. "That foldaway mattress is not half hard enough for what I'm used to. I'm going to have to bring in some dirt and rocks to approximate what I've been sleeping on. It's even weird to be sitting at a table to eat."

She poured him a glass of orange juice and set it beside his coffee. She seemed to keep her distance, not physically but emotionally. Polite but careful. Kind but distracted. Lack of sleep, or worry he was going to take Claire and Beamer and leave the area, he decided. He hoped she didn't lump him with the kind of guys who took their kids and ran. It did get to him that Claire had just started second grade and liked her teacher and had friends in her class. But she'd learn to settle into a new situation if she had to. Whatever he decided was the reasonable thing to do, Claire would have to go along.

Beamer shifted his position on the floor, tipped his head and perked up one ear, as if interested in their conversation. Tara was washing dishes at the sink, banging things around pretty good. Yeah, she was upset about something.

"Great pancakes. So, how did you get into your line of work?" he asked, spearing a sausage link. He hoped not only to get to know her better, but to discuss something harmless. "Not many P.I.s specialize in tracing kids who are snatched by their dads."

"Or their mothers' boyfriends, as the case may be," she added. "Three reasons, I guess. First of all, I've always loved puzzles . . . finding something hidden in a picture, like in those old *Highlights for Children* magazine years ago. Riddles, cryptograms, Sudoku, you name it. But more importantly, my uncle snatched my nine-year-old cousin, Linc, who was my age and to whom I was pretty close. When we were about fourteen, I suppose Linc really started to question or challenge his dad about their situation. My uncle just dropped Linc back at my aunt's house, then disappeared again. But Linc was completely changed — out of control, defensive, nasty. He even felt his mother had betrayed him. He ran away when he was seventeen, and my aunt had no way of knowing what happened. We still don't know if he's dead or alive," she said, her voice snagging.

Well, he thought, wrong topic choice again. He stood with his dirty plate and went closer to put it on the counter. "Tough memories. Sorry I stirred them up."

"No, it's fine. I — That's not the only reason I started Finders Keepers. I went on

70

to get my degree in social work from the University of Colorado. Well, you knew that, of course, since Alex and I roomed together. I specialized in family relations and human development."

Damn, but he noted that tears glazed her eyes again. Was Claire's guardian this unstable? He hoped he wasn't making her uncomfortable. From the first he'd felt as instinctively protective of her as he did toward Claire.

"I worked with cases of abuse and neglect," she went on, going back to washing dishes with a vengeance. She had a dishwasher right there, but maybe she needed something to do with her pent-up energy. "I placed kids in foster care and tried to get families reunified whenever possible, especially kids put back with their biological parents."

"However draining the work was, you must have felt you were doing good — like you are now with Finders Keepers and with Claire."

"I saw some pretty bad situations," she said, nodding, "so I hated the job almost as much as I loved it. I tended to get so involved with my cases that I always took my work home with me. When I stumbled on a couple of cases that involved ex-husbands snatching their own kids and saw how tragic that was for the left-behinds — professional lingo for the mothers of the kids — I started my own specialty firm."

"Have you ever retrieved snatched kids for their fathers when their mothers took off with them?"

"You know, I haven't, but I would if the case seemed right. It's just that word about my services has spread among women, I guess."

"Did you get a lot of family support for all this?"

"Not really. When I became engaged, my fiancé didn't think that profession was appropriate for a Lohan wife, so I really had to stand firm with him."

Beamer jumped to his feet and growled. They both turned to look at the dog as he went to the double sliding glass doors and stood alert. With Beamer, that meant a stiff stance, intense expression and another long, low growl.

"Someone must be coming up the road," Nick said, and walked toward the sliding doors to the deck. He looked through the glass in one direction, then the other. "I didn't hear a vehicle and don't see one either."

"Elk come into the yard about this time

but, as I said, he barks at them, and doesn't usually growl. There's been a fox around here lately, too."

"I don't see a darn thing, but Beamer's looking up into the tree line."

He walked back into the kitchen and leaned over the sink next to Tara to look out and up through the window in front of her toward the thick clumps of pines and aspens above the house. He thought he saw a glint of bright blue in the early slant of sun. A blue jay? Or could Claire's night fear have been prophetic? Maybe she'd seen a hunter or hiker up there and translated it into a bad dream about Clay. It was hunting season, after all, deer and elk for archery, and wild turkeys and blue grouse for muzzle-loading rifles. Years ago, they'd had trouble with careless hunters too near these isolated houses.

"I'm planning to go over to a friend's house today and get my truck out of his garage," Nick told her, "but I think I'll take Beamer for a walk first. He's obviously eager to track whatever creature's up there. Be back in a few minutes. You do keep all the doors locked, don't you?"

"Always. Just habit from some of the bad scenarios I've heard about through my cases, though I know your mom seldom locked the doors."

"Be back soon," he repeated, and took Beamer's thirty-foot lead and working collar off the peg on the wall. Beamer immediately stood at attention. He'd always been eager to work, but then, he'd always been able to sense danger, too.

After Tara locked up behind Nick, she went to her office and called local ob-gyns until she found one who could see her today — thank heavens for a cancellation in just a couple of hours. She called Dr. Holbrook's office to arrange to pick up her medical records. Then she tried to get herself back on track with her caseload. Despite getting up now and then to look out her window for Nick, she forced herself to concentrate.

She always treated her open cases with respect — even keeping the folders clean, unbent and neat. To her they symbolized the heartaches and hopes of those who were missing their children. As she handled each and added more information, she knew they were trusting her to find them.

One case, which she could now happily put in her inactive file, lay on top of the cabinet she unlocked. Like Nick, her client had served her country despite great hardships at home. When Susan Getz's National

Guard unit had been sent to Iraq, the divorcée had left her three-year-old son, Bryce, for whom she'd been given legal custody, in her mother's care. Her ex-husband, Dietmar Getz — a U.S. citizen, though he'd been born in Germany — had moved to California and seldom paid child support or even saw little Bryce. But, while Susan was deployed in Iraq, Dietmar returned to Denver and snatched the boy, sending an e-mail that he could take better care of his son than that old woman, the mother of a woman who put war first.

Tara had a copy of that e-mail; the whole case had really upset her. Dietmar knew his wife was in the guard and could be called to active duty when he married her, just as Laird had known she was dedicated to Finders Keepers when he proposed. Tara was proud she'd located Dietmar. Since his passion was extreme biking, she had traced him through rally events for that sport. The result had been great for Susan, who was reunited with her son, and terrible for Dietmar. He'd paid heavy fines, had been incarcerated for a while and lost his job at a bike shop. Susan's Denver lawyer, through whom Tara had been paid, told Tara that Dietmar was furious with both his ex-wife and Tara, whose name he'd gotten off court papers.

With another sigh, Tara filed the folder in the Inactive/Resolved section of the drawer and hoped the case would remain that way.

She took out the folder of a new case, a fascinating one. The left-behind, Myra Gavin, was convinced her ex had not only abducted their fourteen-year-old son, Ryan — Tara didn't take cases where the child was eighteen or older — but that her ex had faked his own death. His car had gone over a cliff into a swollen river, and though there was no body found, the police believed the body had washed downstream, just as they believed Ryan, who had been a troubled kid, had run away. Myra wanted Tara to prove a case not of suicide but of pseudocide, as the lawyer who had hired her had called faking one's own death. And, of course, to locate Ryan so he could come home.

Though Tara took any case where she thought she could help, she liked working for law firms rather than for emotional, distraught individuals directly. Like Claire's mother, they could get in the way of ultimate success. Lawyers remained calm and controlled, mostly, and she knew she'd get paid. If Laird had not left her a decent financial settlement — as Jen had hinted this morning — Tara could not have afforded to take on some cases where she knew she'd get little or nothing for her efforts.

The other case she needed to review today concerned a biological dad, Jeff Rivers, who had kidnapped his own nine-year-old son from a couple who had adopted the boy over eight years ago. Tara was working hard to locate the man. Usually, she wanted a biological parent to have a child, but in this case, the more she learned about the skip, the more she realized he was a horrible person. So far, she'd had no luck finding him.

But she'd had great successes from other difficult cases, which encouraged her to keep going. Carla Manning, one of her first clients, whom she'd known from her old neighborhood when she was single, had not only gotten her daughter from an abusive husband, but she'd gotten her life back. Carla had returned to college and was now an attorney and child-rights advocate in Seattle. Tara would love to visit her someday, except that's where Laird had moved, and she couldn't bring herself to even be near the same area.

Tara sucked in a big breath and got up to look out the window again. No Nick or Beamer in sight. It was as if the forest had swallowed them. She crossed her arms over her stomach, feeling it cramp. It was almost time for her period to begin, but she knew it was more than that. It wasn't worry about Nick; if there was anyone who could take care of himself, it was him, though she still wasn't convinced he could take care of Claire. No, this was because of what the doctor had said yesterday. And nerves about seeing another doctor for a second opinion — actually, a third, counting Jennifer's — so soon.

Tara sat down so hard in her chair it rolled away from her desk. She had felt all uptight like this in the weeks before Clay killed Alex, almost as if she sensed something would go wrong with one of her cases. Did that mean she was sensing something like that now, or was she just getting paranoid because of how tracking Clay had ended up? No, too much was going on in her life right now, that was all.

But her stomachache had triggered a memory. A couple of weeks before her coma, she'd had what she thought was a virus, with nausea and cramping. She wasn't due for a period then, not until a week later. On the Pill, she'd been so regular. Surely she could not have had morning sickness that week! She bent over her knees, agonized, feeling she'd be sick right now. She wanted to get what the doctor had said out of her head, but it kept coming back to haunt her. It would be hard not to blurt it out to Dr. Bauman today, and demand that he disprove it.

"Listen to yourself!" she scolded aloud and sat up. "You just have a stomachache. You certainly aren't pregnant now, and you weren't pregnant then!"

But what if? *What if?*

She reached for her cell phone. Though the last thing in the world she wanted to do was contact Laird's family, she was going to call his mother, Veronica. If she had any chance of getting a straight answer from Laird's family about whether she could have been pregnant during her coma, it would be from her.

Nick saw a web of paths through the brush and trees above his property. There had been animal trails up here for years. Most were made by mule deer and elk. He saw places on the trees where animals had rubbed off the bark to mark their territories. This was probably a wild-goose — that is, wild deer and elk — chase, but Beamer was tracking something.

As far as Nick was concerned, the alert, self-confident track-and-trail breeds of dogs were one of God's great gifts to mankind. Most bloodhounds, beagles, German shepherds and Labrador retrievers could smell hundreds of different scents, sometimes from something as tiny as shed skin cells. Whereas people might enter a kitchen and smell vegetable soup cooking, tracker dogs could break that down into meat stock, celery, potatoes, even pepper or herbs. Beamer could sprint up to forty miles an hour. He had a wide range of vision, nearly one hundred eighty degrees, and could see something as small as a mouse from a football field away. He could swivel his ears in two separate directions to pick up diverse, muted sounds at a great distance. All that, and he was eager to give hours of exhausting nose time to search for anyone from lost kids to escaped criminals, just for a bit of praise and a scratch behind his ears.

Nick had no idea what trail Beamer was working so hard now, but he felt increasingly wary and on edge. The exertion at this altitude soon got him out of breath again. The Lab took him higher, slightly around the south side of the mountain toward a deserted hunting cabin he remembered. In the old days, people who lived in Denver would come up and stay in cabins on the weekends, but with better roads and vehicles, the small buildings were seldom slept in anymore. Derelict cabins were scattered throughout these mountains. He and Alex had played up here years ago in this one, pretending that the native Arapaho, Ute and Cheyenne tribes were still in the area and that the old place was their fort. He saw the cabin was still there, in more ramshackle shape than ever.

In his heart he envisioned Alex, as she used to look, with her face all smudged and a stick rifle in her hands. He bit his lower lip hard as he followed Beamer to the door. It stood ajar and askew.

Nick stopped so suddenly that he jerked Beamer's lead. For one moment, he had pictured how careful the Delta boys were when they entered a cave. Buried bombs abounded, and the Taliban could be hunkered down in the shadows, guns ready to blaze destruction and death. Or the troops sometimes cornered someone hiding, like Sadam Hussein himself. But they'd never found the big quarry, Bin Laden, and that haunted him yet. And then there was that hellish moment when they'd lost lives . . .

Nick shook his head to clear it. Stop it! he told himself. No post-traumatic stress syndrome for him. He wouldn't allow it.

Duty had called, and he'd done his duty. It wasn't reasonable to dwell on failure, so he would not. He had hold of his weak emotions, and he would do what he must to keep it that way.

His breath still coming hard and his heart pounding, he peered inside, even looking behind the door. He was surprised to see the floor was fairly clear, as if someone had swept out debris and leaves, even spiderwebs, at least with feet and hands if not with a limb-and-leaf broom. And a bed of fresh-looking moss had been brought inside and bore the slight imprint of a human form. The moss wouldn't last long in here without sunlight or water, he thought. Yes, this had to be fairly new, but then it was a hunter's cabin and it was hunting season.

His gaze snagged on a clean-looking purple, light green and white paper wrapper in the corner of the cabin. He picked it up and turned it toward the filthy window to read in the wan light: *Cacao Reserve by Hershey's. Dark Chocolate. Bright fruity notes and delicate spices.* He flipped it over. Made in Germany, no less. This wasn't your everyday hunter's candy bar.

But finally, he had an object to scent Beamer on. "Find. Find!" he ordered, and thrust the wrapping at the dog's nose.

With one big sniff, the Lab jerked his head and, nose to the ground, took off immediately, out the door, retracing the path they'd taken to come up here. The dog locked on the trail and worked it hard the whole way. Nick kept a pretty short lead on the leash so Beamer wouldn't wrap it around a tree.

Unfortunately, the dog led him to a spot just above the house. Beamer raised his hackles, then went in a circle as if he'd found a scent pool where their quarry had sat for a while or even lain.

Then Beamer growled and stood perfectly still. Picturing the enemy snipers he'd seen too often up on a rock or cliff, Nick gritted his teeth and shook his head. Stooping next to Beamer and looking through the blowing scrim of pine needles, he could see directly into the kitchen through the window over the sink, and into Tara's office and bedroom.

5

Veronica Lohan could not find her cell phone. It was ringing, wasn't it? That is, playing her favorite pop culture organ piece, the theme from *The Phantom of the Opera.* But why did it sound so muted?

The cell should be on the bedside table. She felt for it there and found nothing. Maybe she hadn't heard the music at all. Often melodies danced through her head, pieces she knew by heart or, at least, ones she once knew. She used to misplace her tiny cell phones all the time, especially when she was in detox and recovery treatment at the clinic, but she'd been good lately, so normal. No more secret stashes of Vicodin washed down with double martinis.

It was still dark, so it must be early. She and her husband, Jordan, had shared a lovely, late dinner at home last night, a meal he'd ordered from their cook for her — her favorite pasta primavera, although he liked heavier fare. "If I had one last meal to eat on this earth," she'd told him, "this would be it."

Whatever was wrong with her? It must be dark and quiet because she had her earplugs and silk sleeping mask on.

Still trying to drag herself from sodden sleep, she yanked the plugs out and pulled off the mask. Oh, for heaven's sake — broad daylight and the sun up already. Ten in the morning? How could she have slept so late? She was an early riser, always had been.

Feeling strangely light-headed, she got out of bed and went to the bathroom. Catching her reflection in the mirror, she leaned, stiff-armed, on the fluted basin and did not like what she saw.

At age fifty-six, Veronica Britten Lohan, Juilliard class of '73, knew she was still a good-looking woman, even without her usually upswept coiffure and makeup. She had great bone structure under smooth skin, a gift from God or at least genetics. She was trim, maybe too trim, but still statuesque. Her hair was raven black, as the poets used to say — with a bit of help from her hairdresser. She had rather liked the silver at her temples and the big streak of it flowing back from the center of her forehead. It was a sign of someone who had lived, someone worthy of stating an opinion or two or giving advice. But Jordan had urged her to color it.

She'd had two facelifts her family had talked her into, done right on the grounds of the Lohan Mountain Manor Clinic by a doctor Jordan had imported, just the way he and Laird had brought in a specialist for poor Tara's coma treatment. She just didn't look like herself anymore. Her eyes were tilted up a bit too exotically, and her forehead, cheeks and mouth felt tight each time she smiled. Indeed, the feel of her face was an ever-present reminder that almost everything she'd done the last thirty-four years of her life had been to please her husband or two sons, not herself.

Still, she was the same inside, still a Britten at heart more than a Lohan, she tried to tell herself as she washed up, humming a Bach prelude. She was grateful for her musical talent, enamored of her grandchildren and, of course, proud of her sons, though she was disappointed in Laird lately.

She should have breakfast in bed this morning. She could call down to the kitchen and get something brought up, especially her hazelnut coffee. She felt a bit rocky from it being so late and not eating this morning, that was all. Why, she'd slept as if she were drugged.

As she headed back toward the big bed she seldom shared with Jordan anymore, though he had an adjoining suite she could visit whenever she wished, she heard her cell phone again. Surely she wasn't hearing things this time. The organ music filled her as *The Phantom of the Opera* played those dissonant chords, *Da, da, da, da, da!*

She frowned when she saw the phone on her bedside table where she was sure she'd put it last night. How had she missed seeing it earlier? Oh, and a breakfast tray was on the table by the window, as if someone had known exactly when she got up. She could smell her favorite coffee from here. She had mentioned yesterday to her maid, Rita, that she always forgot to recharge her cell. Rita had probably done that for her when she saw she was still sleeping, then brought up this tray. Thank heavens, she had not been imagining things or hallucinating as she used to during the worst days of her dependencies. She hurried to the cell and punched the talk button while she poured herself some coffee with the other hand.

"Veronica? It's Tara. How are you?"

"Tara, how lovely to hear from you. I've been fine lately, my dear, much better than most of your memories of me when I was ill, I assure you. I believe we can both consider ourselves successful alumni of Mountain Manor Clinic. How are you and your little charge, Claire, doing?" she asked as she sat down on the edge of the bed to steady her legs.

"Fine, thanks. I'm so glad to hear you're well. Are you still on the advisory board for Red Rocks?"

Red Rocks was a huge outdoor amphitheater, set in a stunning array of mammoth, tilted sandstone monoliths. Between Conifer and Denver, it was nearby for Tara and the senior Lohans, whose home was in Kerr Gulch in Evergreen. Jordan and Veronica Lohan had long been benefactors of Red Rocks, and for years Veronica had been active in helping to select the wide range of cultural events staged there.

"Yes, a real veteran of the advisory board," Veronica told her with a little laugh. "But why do you ask? May I get you tickets for something?"

"I was wondering if we could meet there today. I've appreciated how kind you've been through everything and was hoping we could keep in touch. I haven't had a mother for years, but I've always valued your advice. I don't suppose Laird would approve but —"

"Nor would his father or brother, so let's do it!"

There was still something exhilarating, Veronica thought, about bucking Jordan, the head of the clan, or even her dyed-in-the-Lohan-wool sons, Thane and Laird, who always thought they knew what was best for her. Talk about the Kennedy women having to toe the line for their husbands' careers!

Veronica smiled stiffly, recalling she'd once overheard Tara tell Laird that he really didn't want a Lohan wife but a Stepford wife, a clone windup doll like his brother Thane's Susanne, who was a perfect and perfectly obedient wife.

Tara had always reminded Veronica of herself, back when she still thought she could maintain her career as a concert organist with the symphony. But she hadn't managed to even play a theater organ for classic silent movies in the summer or be some church's guest organist. Instead, Jordan had bought her not one but two massive pipe organs, one here at home and one in the chapel at the clinic. She usually ended up just playing for family or friends, when she'd always longed for a bigger stage — like the one at Red Rocks.

"What time shall we meet?" she asked

Tara. "It's already after ten, but we could meet near the restaurant in the Visitor Center at one."

"Would you be willing to make it one-thirty? I've got a doctor's appointment. Can you meet me out by the first set of rocks to the left of the west entry, the one with the great view of Creation Rock? You remember, where we took that walk and had that heart-to-heart talk?"

"The one with the natural table and bench?"

"Yes. I'll bring a picnic for us, then we can get caught up in private without all the people you know coming up to our table to chat in the restaurant. It's been a while since we've really talked, though I treasured your visits after I came out of the coma."

"Is there something wrong, Tara? You can tell me, and it will go no further."

"I hope not. I'll save it all for our lunch."

"I'll be there, my dear, and if something goes awry, I'll call you."

"Tara, I don't want to sound like an alarmist, but I think someone's been watching the house," Nick told her. She was madly stuffing chicken salad into pita bread; a wicker picnic basket sat on the kitchen counter. Her hands stopped; she looked up

90

at him, eyes wide.

"Did you see someone?"

"No, but Beamer found a trail to that old hunter's cabin, which has been swept out and used. I know it's hunting season, but there's a distinct spot above the house in the tree line where someone's been lying down with a clear view in through these back windows."

"Animals sometimes lie down. Maybe Beamer —"

"No. I scented him on this. Does it mean anything to you?" he asked, extending the Cacao candy bar wrapper to her.

She took it from him and read both sides. "It's not the kind of Hershey's for s'mores around the old campfire, not that campfires are permitted around here. I see it's made in Germany."

"And?" he prompted.

"Nothing, but success in investigation work is often in the details."

"Tell me about that detail," he said, pointing at the words she was frowning over.

"One of my disgruntled skips was born in Germany," she explained, going back to her sandwich-making. "But I recently checked, and he'd gone back to California. He's not pleased I tracked him down and made him pay for snatching his son. Still, that's a far stretch over a candy bar wrapper in some old hunter's cabin."

"Is he a hunter, like Clay was?"

"No, he's a biker — a mountain biker."

"I know it might mean nothing, but I always had to watch my back the last two years, and that's a hard habit to shake." He glanced out the window over the sink again. "I'm going to keep an eye out for someone up there — and Beamer will keep a nose out."

She turned to him and smiled, evidently at the way he'd worded that. It lit up her face and made her look younger. They still stood close together over the sink, and she didn't move away this time.

"I'll be careful for Claire's sake as well as mine," she promised. "And I'll recheck to be sure Dietmar Getz is still in San Jose, at least for his home base. He's not only a mountain biker but a so-called extreme biker who goes all over the West for races and rallies. Would you believe he thought he'd provide a better home for his child than a devoted relative who stays in one place?"

Nick wondered if that was a hint he should leave Claire with her, but Tara was already off on another topic as she went back to fixing food again.

"I have an appointment in town, then I'm going to have lunch at Red Rocks with my former mother-in-law, but I've made extra for you, in case you're hungry later. Or if this doesn't suit you or fill you up, please just take anything you want around here." She shoved her hair back from her face and their eyes snagged again. "You know what I mean," she added, blushing.

"Like food from the fridge or laundry soap," he told her, as he bit back a grin. "But about someone watching the house, a word to the wise." As she closed the picnic basket, he put his hand around her wrist like a big, warm bracelet. "If it's just some neighborhood voyeur or your garden-variety teenager, Beamer and I will be enough to scare him off — but you need to be very careful," he added, stressing each word. "Besides being a good-looking woman, you're in a business where you've made enemies. Just for the heck of it, as soon as I get my truck, I'm going to drop in to see Clay's brother and find out what he's been up to. If he was as upset as you said — well, you just never know."

"Thanks. Since you were his brother-in-law for years, he won't be suspicious and maybe you can calm him down. And we agree that I'll be careful, for Claire

93

and myself."

"Oh! Jordan!" Veronica said, when her husband suddenly walked into her suite from his adjoining one. "You gave me a start! I thought you had gone by now."

Despite the fact she had a terrible headache, she was dressed and ready to head out to meet Tara at Red Rocks. The coffee and breakfast seemed to have steadied her a bit. She could tell Tara had needed her and she was not canceling their appointment. She hoped Jordan hadn't planned on her eating with him here.

To her surprise, her primary-care doctor from the clinic, Henry Middleton, followed Jordan into the room. They were both distinguished-looking men, even when not attired in suits, shirts and ties as they were now. Jordan had always been handsome and had kept his good looks — full head of hair, square jaw and six-foot frame — over the years. He hardly had a gray hair amid the dark brown he kept perfectly trimmed.

Dr. Middleton, prematurely silver-haired and blue-eyed, was a good bit shorter but also had an athlete's build. A real health fanatic who often jogged the rustic paths on the clinic acreage, he had been very instrumental in her successful treatment for alcohol and drug dependence. Because Mountain Manor was heavily endowed by the Lohans, Jordan, in effect, was the doctor's — all employees' there — superior.

"Whatever is it?" she asked, putting one hand to her throat. "Thane or Laird haven't been hurt? The grandchildren? What —"

"I'm doing family intervention early this time, Veronica," Jordan said, "before this snowballs again and Thane and Laird need to be called in."

"Whatever are you talking about?"

Instead of answering, Jordan went over to her bedside table and rummaged around in the top drawer. Dr. Middleton looked so very sad, upset even.

"Here — I thought so, I feared so," Jordan said, and thrust a pill bottle at the doctor. "I won't say she's mixing booze with these again, but, for her sake, we have to stop it now. I — the entire family — can't go through all that again. 'The Betty Ford of Denver' newspaper headlines be damned."

"That's ridiculous. You're wrong," she told Jordan, facing him down as steadily as she could. In truth, she was still feeling a bit strange, but it must have been something she ate either last night or this morning. "If those are Vicodin —"

"They appear to be," Dr. Middleton interjected, frowning at the bottle.

"Then they are old ones, because I'm clean," she insisted. "Oh, yes, I want a drink now and then, but I stick to Perrier, and I have not touched a Vicodin tablet since I was admitted to Mountain Manor! Jordan, we had a long dinner last night together. You saw I was normal then —"

"On the contrary, my dear. Your erratic actions and wandering talk were what forced me to face the fact that you're having a relapse."

She gasped. He was lying. He had to be lying. She had to get away from him, get away from her own husband. Trying desperately to hold herself together, she said, enunciating each syllable so they would realize she was not slurring her words, "Excuse me, both of you. I'm leaving. I have an appointment and —"

"If," Jordan said, stepping close to grip her right arm, "you haven't had a relapse, you won't mind my looking around at your old stash locations and will agree to a few tests."

"I won't. I tell you I'm not using, and I expect you to believe me. I'm fine and —"

"Don't you realize you're denying everything, just as you did before?" Jordan demanded.

Traitor! she wanted to scream. But why? Did he want her admitted to the clinic for some reason? It was like a prison there. Did he have another woman? Or could he have somehow learned she was meeting Tara and was terrified she'd tell him about Laird's other woman?

Dr. Middleton took her left arm. "Please keep calm, Veronica. A relapse is not uncommon, and we can help you again. We'll have you tested at the clinic by mid-afternoon and admitted if there's a need —"

"No!" she shouted, trying to yank free. "There is no need! Jordan, what is the matter with you? I'm not going!"

Veronica Britten Lohan, matriarch of the most powerful family in the area, felt sicker and sicker as she was hustled off down the back stairs to a car waiting at the side entrance, as if she had no power over her own life at all.

Tara had always loved the unique area called Red Rocks, though one could feel very small and insignificant here. Such a powerful display from the author of the universe, she thought as she walked the trail. But now, again, everything had changed. Dr. Bauman had not been as forceful in his opinion as

Dr. Holbrook had but, after examining her, he had concurred with the impossible.

"Yes," he'd said, peering at her over the top of his horn-rims. "You do present some signs of having had at least a long-term pregnancy and, probably, a natural delivery. No signs of cesarean section. A vaginal birth would be incredibly unusual, since you were comatose, but it's not impossible."

She'd hardly heard a thing he'd said after that. Dr. Jen had been so adamant that she had not been pregnant during her coma. Obviously, she was trying to protect her from more grief — the loss of a child she never knew. But Veronica would tell her the truth, help her solve this puzzle. Surely her former mother-in-law would know whether Tara had borne a child, another grandchild to Veronica.

Carrying her picnic basket, she forced herself to look around, not to keep agonizing within. This awesome area had a way of putting people in their place. After all, she was only one person in the march of time. Geologists claimed the surrounding, sharply uptilted monoliths here recorded the history of the ages. Not far from the spot where she was going to meet Veronica, dinosaur tracks from the Jurassic period and fossil fragments of sea serpents were imprinted in the rocks. Jurassic Park, indeed. Yes, she thought as a shiver snaked up her spine despite the warmth of the day. She could imagine a primordial monster crashing around the corner of a cliff, ravenous for prey. She was just as ravenous for answers about her lost child, no matter what stood in her way.

A good distance from this fringe area lay the amphitheater itself. Cut like a gigantic sandstone bowl into the surrounding red, rocky terrain, it had once been listed among the seven wonders of the world. With its stone-and-glass Visitor Center, which stood sentinel over it, the vast outdoor concert venue was situated between the largest two rock formations, both standing taller than Niagara Falls. The southern massive monolith, because of its appearance, was called Ship Rock; on the other side loomed Creation Rock, which Tara could see clearly from here.

But her awe was tempered when she passed a familiar brown sign with white print, which brought her back to earth with a thud: No Climbing on Rocks. $999 Fine or 180 Days in Jail or Both.

She reminded herself that life had consequences. Putting her own panic about having possibly been pregnant aside, she wondered if Nick could be right that someone had been watching the house. If she only knew why, surely she could find out who. Worse than that worry, her desperate dilemma pressed hard against her heart again. Laird had been so understanding, so solicitous in the month or so before her coma. He had even seemed to accept that she wanted to stay on the Pill until they settled their problems, although he had fretted and fumed over that before. They had made love more than usual those last days. If she had not taken her pills religiously — she did recall she had done so — she supposed she could have gotten pregnant.

She reached the spot where she and Veronica had taken walks twice before. Tara had served as a docent here, working in the Visitor Center when she and Laird were first married. She put the picnic basket on the natural rock table with its red sandstone bench, which seemed to be carved for their use. No wonder the early Spanish explorers had named this entire area *Colorado,* their word for "reddish color."

This was the perfect place for an early-afternoon respite, because the overhanging cliff shaded it from the sun. But she felt hot, flushed. The sun was still warm for September and she'd hiked in from her car at a good clip, but she was perspiring from nerves.

Dare she ask Laird's mother if she'd been pregnant during her coma? Wasn't that not only a shocking but a stupid question? She trusted Veronica to tell her the truth, but if by some wild chance she had been pregnant, that meant Veronica's own son was to blame for not telling his wife about their child's birth and death. And both the senior Lohans were protective of their family.

Surely, Tara agonized, if she had borne a child, he or she must have died. But wouldn't Laird — or at least his lawyers who had handled the divorce — have had the decency to tell her about the loss of her own child?

She paced back and forth in the stark shadow under the rock rim, then glanced at her watch. Her former mother-in-law was late. Veronica had been through her own terrible times, and it had taken her a long while to get back on her feet.

Tara's and Veronica's stays at the clinic had overlapped, though their luxurious outlying cabins were widely separated on the hilly, heavily wooded grounds. At Mountain Manor, the individual residences were called "cabins," just the way the Vanderbilts and Astors had called their mansions in

Newport "cottages." It was, indeed, an opulent place to recover from dreadful problems. As far as Tara knew, Veronica's face-lifts and Tara's own treatment for coma were the only medical procedures done there that didn't relate to drug or alcohol dependency and recovery.

Although Tara's memory of her long treatment for her coma was a big blank, she was sometimes certain she had heard sounds during the dark depths of her unconscious hours, sounds she couldn't quite recall. Maybe voices, too. Had she hallucinated, or had she heard Veronica playing the huge organ in the clinic chapel?

Tara paced faster. Her stomach knotted tighter. What if Veronica wasn't coming? What if she couldn't face her former daughter-in-law because she'd guessed what Tara wanted to talk to her about? What if she actually had been pregnant when her coma began? And what if Nick was right that someone was watching or even stalking her? Would Nick take Claire away from her even sooner? She could not bear to lose Claire and then learn she'd lost a child, too.

Tara closed her eyes to ward off a bit of blowing dust. Then she realized it came not from the wind, but from above, like gritty rain. It was in her hair and on her shoulders.

Something scraped, then rumbled. Thunder? The entire earth seemed to shudder. She looked up and shrieked as a huge sandstone rock rolled over the ledge above her head.

6

Tara's scream shredded the air. She threw herself back against the cliff, banging her shoulder and hitting the back of her head. She cringed inwardly at the blow to her head — fear of another injury, a coma . . .

The boulder, the size of a wheelbarrow, crashed into the natural sandstone table five feet from her, just missing her purse but smashing the picnic basket and the edge of the table. Fragments flew, but the boulder's momentum kept it rolling. It disappeared in a cloud of pebbles and grit off the other side of the flat, waist-high structure, where its massive weight ground it to a stop.

She was stunned but still conscious. Sucking in dust, pressed against the solid rock behind her, Tara was drenched in sweat, yet she shivered as if she were freezing. At last, but for her thudding heart and panicked panting, there was silence.

The red sandstone dust shower burned

her eyes, making her blink back tears and cough. A sharp shadow of a man thrust itself onto the surface of the remains of the sandstone tabletop. Someone must be peering over the edge of the cliff above. She was grateful he must have come running to see what had happened, but he shouldn't be climbing the rocks.

"Did you see that?" she shouted, then fell into a coughing fit again. She craned her neck but couldn't see anyone peering over. She took a few tenuous steps out from the cliff and shaded her eyes to look up into the sun. "Hello! A rock fell and just missed me!"

No answer. No one there and no shadow now. Suddenly, she knew.

She gasped and leaped back against the cliff. Someone had shoved that rock over the edge to hit her, crush her!

Run or stay here? She should not have picked this deserted spot. She was always careful not to take risks, but she hadn't considered a picnic at Red Rocks to be one. She realized too late that this side of the cliff couldn't be seen from the road where she'd left her truck.

Tara grabbed her purse and ran. She heard footsteps spitting sand or grit above. An echo? The sounds became more muted, distant. Could her attacker — her would-be killer — be running away? The back side of this behemoth rock was an easier climb than from where she stood.

Tara tore around the side of the cliff toward the road. She spun in a circle but saw no one. If she wanted to get a glimpse of who it was, she'd have to run farther, faster. Had someone followed her here? Followed her from the doctor's office? She'd seen no one in her rearview mirror. Had someone kept Veronica from coming — or harmed her?

Tara ran farther around the rock structure, then stopped again. Out of breath, a stitch in her side, exposed . . . What if the person had a gun? No one else had evidently heard or seen what could surely be considered a natural event, an accident. She'd better get to her car, get home. She needed to check on Veronica, and she needed Nick's help now.

If she asked him for that, he would ask her who wanted to harm her and why. But however much she prided herself in finding answers, right now she had only guesses.

As she neared her truck, grateful to see it looked untouched, she saw a man jogging away toward the amphitheater from the vicinity of the fallen rock. That meant nothing, of course. Someone could have heard the noise and be going to tell a park ranger. People ran here all the time, both in the slanted aisles of the huge acoustic bowl and on the paths in the area. But what if he was the one? He was too far away to recognize.

Tara got in her truck and clicked the door locks closed. Trembling so hard that she couldn't even get the key in the ignition on the first try, she finally jammed it in. She knew she should report what had happened to the Red Rocks rangers, but she was getting out of here. She had no proof it was an attack, and most certainly not that it was attempted murder. After so much of her life had been made public, she didn't want her name in the papers again. But she had to admit that locals didn't even deface these rocks with graffiti, let alone try to harm the natural structure of the place. Nor had she heard of falling rocks here.

As she started away, in her side mirror, Tara saw a mountain biker burst from the rocks near where she had been. But he didn't follow the road or look in this direction. He was going the other way, fast. There were many biking trails in this area, not to mention thousands of avid bikers on them all the time.

She gripped the wheel and turned onto the highway. Don't speed, she told herself.

You're all right now. No one is following. Maybe that was just an accident, she rationalized. And someone nearby, who was climbing the cliff and shouldn't have been, just took off, too. Maybe he'd seen the sign about the fine or jail time. He certainly wouldn't want to be blamed for a loose boulder almost falling on someone.

Swiping tears from her cheeks as she drove, she headed toward home. But when she caught a glimpse of herself in the rearview mirror, she yanked her sunglasses off, pulled over, parked and burst into sobs. Her hair and face — even her eyes, which she'd instinctively closed in terror when the rock fell — were coated with pale reddish dust. She looked like a ghost tinged with blood, like a nightmare of death itself.

After Nick picked up his truck from his friend and got it serviced in Evergreen, he decided to stop by to check on Clay's younger brother Rick Whetstone. Luckily the last phone number he had for him connected, and he was still in Evergreen, the next town northwest of Conifer.

Marcie, a woman who described herself as "hanging out here with Ricky," said he'd be back soon from running errands. She rattled on that he had a really good job catering parties, but they were still in their small apartment above a store near Lake Evergreen. Nick knew the area. It now boasted a new library, soccer fields and an event center, but he'd always referred to the broad part of the valley between Buffalo Park Road and Meadow Drive as "old town."

Years ago, if Nick had been asked to place a bet on which brother in the Whetstone family would end up in prison, he would have picked Rick, not Clay. A real hell-raiser as a kid, Rick was about twenty-five now. Maybe he'd settled down with Marcie and a decent-paying job. Still, Tara had told him that Rick had blamed her, as well as Alex, for what had happened to his adored brother Clay, so Rick couldn't have matured too much.

"Tell him I'm going to stop by to say hi," Nick had told Marcie. "Just wanted to see how he's doing."

Evergreen was really spread out these days. Part of the old town was kept up as a historic Western town in fine fashion to attract visitors, and had gift shops and restaurants stretching several blocks on one side of the highway. Most Evergreen residents, however, lived in the northern, newer parts of town in the same valley, or in cliff-clinging homes in various well-to-do, gated gulch communities. As everyone in these parts knew, the Lohans, Tara's former in-laws, had one of the most spectacular homes in Kerr Gulch, about ten miles from the more isolated Mountain Manor Clinic they funded and pretty much ran, so he heard.

Nick found a parking place near the store where Marcie said they lived. He had always liked this area; it calmed him, despite the traffic and tourists, because across Highway 74, from the row of buildings, ran noisy, rushing Bear Creek, bouncing over rocks. He stopped and got out, taking Beamer with him for a short walk. Man and man's best friend, they stared at the bursts of foam. The sweet sound of it — damn, what wouldn't his dust-eating Delta Force buddies he'd left behind give to hear and see this? The water was so strong in places that rocks had been wired back so they wouldn't tumble in as others had.

He thought about Rick and Clay again. Surely Rick would not get caught up in crazed revenge the way Clay had. Nick hoped what had happened to his brother had put a damper on Rick's grandiose schemes and volatile temper. And he hoped he wasn't the one spying on Tara and Claire. What if he tried to snatch Claire the way his brother had or took his anger out on Tara?

Trying to avoid thinking the worst, Nick put Beamer back in the truck to wait for him. Even if that was Rick's trail the dog had been on yesterday, Beamer would not alert on him without Nick's command and an item to smell. In some instances, a kindly faced dog could diffuse a potentially bad scene. But if Rick was the one who'd been watching the house, it might take some verbal pushing to get him to give himself away. No way was Nick taking his dog into what might become a volatile situation.

"Be right back, boy," he told the Lab, and locked him in since the weather was cool enough today. Nick crossed the road, went up the back steps and knocked on the door Marcie had described.

"Hi, you must be Nick," a twentysomething bleached blonde with short, spiky hair greeted him. She had added reddish highlights, as if to match the rose tattoo she had at the top of her left breast, which her low-cut blouse flaunted. She had a big, toothpaste-ad-perfect smile. Bright red lipstick was not only on her full lips but smeared on her front teeth. "Ricky just got back from some errands, and he's taking a quick shower 'fore he goes to work for the evening. Come on in," she said, ogling him from the crown of his head to the crotch of his jeans. "Then I'll leave you two alone for the Nick 'n' Rick show."

She laughed, and Nick smiled. Leave it to Rick to attract a dim bulb, but she seemed nice enough.

"He's working for a caterer, huh?" Nick asked as he sat on the new-looking leather sofa she indicated. His knees were almost in his mouth. She checked out her appearance in a full-length mirror on the wall, scrubbing the lipstick smear from her teeth with an index finger. Then she checked herself in the mirror front and back, maybe posing for him and not herself. He saw a mop leaning against the door and a vacuum cleaner in the corner. He wondered if she'd hurriedly been cleaning the place for his visit; it looked pretty immaculate, especially for a small place, where clutter could quickly build up.

"Yeah, he's working for a real deluxe company," she said. "They do a lot of fancy parties for houses of the you-would-not-believe type. He gets big tips, too, and we're going to get a house real soon, more new furniture."

She bent toward a chair to grab her purse and a denim jacket sewn with sequined stars. Her stonewashed jeans were so tight they looked painted on. He noticed her new-looking, tooled Western boots.

"But he still says I need to keep my hostessing job at the L Branch down the street, 'cause what would I do all day but get in trouble, if ya know what I mean. Hey, you just come on into the L Branch sometime. You'd love the taste of the food, I will personally guarantee it," she said with a hooted laugh, but she lowered her voice instantly when a door banged open from the other room. "Well," she added, throwing out an arm as Rick came in from what appeared to be the only other room in the apartment, "heee-re's Rick. By, hon!" She opened and darted out the door with a wink and wave at Nick from behind Rick's back.

Rick had obviously just showered, because his hair stuck tight to his head. He wore jeans but was bare chested. Nick had forgotten how much he looked like his brother Clay, whom Rick had always admired so much: olive skin, solidly built, curly, dark brown hair with a beard shadow even after he'd shaved. Nick stood to shake hands; he was almost a foot taller than Rick.

"Surprised you looked me up," Rick said, walking away to lean a slumped shoulder on the frame of the window overlooking the street. Jamming his hands in his pockets, he looked both ways as if he was expecting someone else. "What's the occasion, man?"

"I just got back from overseas, working with the army in Afghanistan, and thought I'd drop by."

"Yeah, you missed all the family action."

"Action!" Nick spit out, then checked himself again. "You mean the tragedy. I regret I wasn't here. I'm back in Conifer, staying with Claire and her guardian, Tara Kinsale, for a while." Nick saw Rick's jaw tighten at Tara's name, but that was all. "I can speak for Tara, too, when I say we have no hard feelings — toward you, that is — about what happened."

"Claire's my niece, too, much as she's yours," Rick blurted, frowning. "You're just lucky I didn't put in for her custody, 'cause I was around."

Nick stopped himself from stating the obvious: it was highly unlikely a murderer's brother was going to be given custody of a young girl. But if Rick was angry that Tara was caring for Claire, wouldn't he have harassed her sooner than this? It seemed unlikely he'd been spying on her all this time without making some kind of move — unless Clay had put him up to it lately.

"Have you been to visit Clay recently?"

"Off and on. If you're here to run him down, don't start," Rick said, his tone hardening. "Too many people mixing in, it just got out of hand."

"Oh, yeah, I'd say it did," Nick said, clenching his fists at his side. He fought to keep from launching into a harangue against Clay for snatching Claire in the first place, let alone killing Alex. Clay's claims of self-defense and accidental death had been pure bull.

Rick kept bouncing his right leg like he had the shakes. For the first time, Nick realized he'd miscalculated in coming here. He had told himself he wanted to psyche Rick out and now all he wanted to do was punch him out. Rick repeatedly wiped his palms on the hip bones of his jeans as he frowned out the window again. Maybe he did have someone else coming. Nick had that prickly-back-of-the-neck feeling he used to get — just like the dogs he was training in the desert — when he scented the enemy nearby. Still, he had come to make a point, and he meant to say his piece.

"I'm glad you've got a lot going right now," he told Rick. "Take care of yourself, because it wouldn't look good if you harassed others who had suffered from Claire's abduction and Alex's death."

Finally, Rick's dark eyes narrowed and met Nick's. "I'd never hurt the kid," Rick muttered. "But maybe you didn't mean Claire. After all, you moved in with Tara Kinsale fast enough."

"So you're implying what?"

"I'll tell you what I'm implying if I need to spell it out, but you know what I mean. Didn't catch enough bad guys playing G.I. Joe, so you've got to pick on me?" Rick goaded as he thrust himself away from the window and stalked across the room to yank the door open. Nick could see they'd passed the point of no return. "You're back trying to make up for it," Rick plunged on, "talking about me doing something wrong?"

Hell, at least he got that part of the message, Nick thought, wanting to pretend Rick was Clay and beat the bastard to a pulp. But then he would have sunk just as low, striking out at someone who — maybe — wasn't to blame at all.

"Just keep clear of Claire and Tara," Nick said, and started toward the door before he bounced this guy off every wall in the room. He'd always prided himself on maintaining control at all times, prided himself on doing his duty and being reasonable. He'd expected it of himself, as had the amazingly strong Delta Force units and the Rangers he'd worked with. Even when they'd lost two dog handlers in an ambush and he blamed himself, he'd stayed stoic because he had to. But now it really scared him how powerfully the passion to protect his girls pounded in his ears and roared through his veins.

The moment Tara got back to the house, despite the fact she was still deeply shaken and dust coated, she looked out the back window toward the hiding place Nick had pointed out to her. When she saw nothing unusual, she washed her hands and face at the kitchen sink. Before she leaned out the front door to knock more Red Rocks dust off her purse, she looked both ways out all the front and side windows.

Damn, this was no way to live! She'd never been one to take risks, except for marrying Laird, which she'd thought at the time was a sure thing. For the first time in her life, she felt that even stepping outside was hazardous. She felt almost under siege.

Stepping back into the house, Tara dug in her purse for her cell phone. It was coated with a layer of grit, but it still worked. Feeling in control enough to call Veronica now, she scrolled to her number. It rang five times, then a recorded voice came on asking if she'd like to leave a voice-mail message.

She ended that call and tried the house phone number at the Lohans. Unfortunately, her former father-in-law answered. The old saying "like father like son" was sadly true in the Lohan clan. Both Thane and Laird not only resembled their father physically but had inherited or imitated his worst traits.

"Jordan, it's Tara." No way was she calling him *Dad* anymore, as he and Laird had wanted. "Veronica and I were to have lunch today, but she didn't come. She said she'd phone me if anything came up. Is everything all right?"

"Tara, great to hear from you."

She just rolled her eyes.

"She doesn't feel well, that's all," he went on. "It was rather sudden, and she's being taken care of. I'll tell her you called, and I'm sure she'll want to reschedule later when she can. How's little Claire?"

She couldn't help being touched he'd asked and surprised he'd remembered the child's name. "She's doing well, really likes school. Her uncle, Alex's brother, is back from working with the troops in the Middle East, and he's not certain what their long-term plans will be."

"Have you started your social work P.I. firm again, after everything?"

"I certainly have. It gives me a tremendous sense of purpose and helps a lot of women, when the men in their lives insist that everything revolves around them, instead of being willing to form a partnership."

There, she thought, she'd said it. Nicely, calmly.

"I believe you're old enough to know, Tara," he replied, his voice still silky smooth, almost patronizing, "that it takes two to tango in a marriage. A failure is never one person's fault. Maybe you could better spend your time counseling women to be good wives, so it doesn't come to some sort of sad situation where a man would actually feel driven to divorce."

She should have known not to butt heads with Jordan Lohan. He was the ultimate master of the brilliant put-down.

"Please tell Veronica I wish her well," Tara said simply. She would not degrade herself by shouting every insult and accusation she could think of. After all, it was Lohan money and power that had taken such good care of her when catastrophe came calling.

After the call, she made sure all the doors and windows were locked and went to take a fast shower. The screech of the rings of the black-and-white shower curtain across the rod reminded her of fingers scraping across a blackboard, and of something worse — the screeching background music during the shower murder scene in *Psycho*. Like an idiot, she'd watched the old black-and-white Alfred Hitchcock classic on TV last week. Lately, though it was better with Claire and Beamer and now Nick in the house, she'd dreaded taking showers. She wished at least one of them were home right now.

In the movie, Marion Crane had made a big mistake when she'd embezzled money and fled, but she was trying to make it right. Then she'd stumbled into a creepy, isolated motel run by a psychotic murderer, one wearing the worst sort of mask and disguise. Trapped and stabbed in her shower, with black blood running everywhere on the white tiles . . .

Despite the warmth of the water, Tara shuddered to the depths of her soul. Why had a vision of crimson blood just flashed through her brain, as if the movie had been in full color? She fought to get her mind back on track with her own life, where no one was trying to kill her, she hoped. Tara wasn't sure which was worse, trying to talk to a Lohan man or having a boulder nearly flatten her.

She changed the showerhead to jet spray and let the water pound on her. She'd always done some of her best thinking in the shower, but she was still very upset by the idea that she'd been pregnant and lost a baby. She was almost coming to believe it was true. Jen had obviously decided to lie to protect her; somehow, she'd ended up in cahoots with Laird. Maybe Laird had paid Jen to keep the terrible news quiet. The revelation of a comatose birth and lost baby would put the Lohans back in the media again and make Laird look even more callous for deserting her.

No way was she crawling to him for information, not unless it was a last resort. She wanted nothing to do with the deserter. A little, broken ditty tormented her: She still had no absolute proof, still wasn't sure of the truth. Two doctors said yes, but Jen said no, and Veronica just didn't show. She didn't trust the Lohan men, but should she tell Nick or not then?

"Damn!" she sputtered into the spray of water. She wanted to trust Nick, to confide in him. But, in a wrenching way, he could turn out to be another Laird. Granted, she was very attracted to him, yet she was fearful that he might take Claire away, a child she loved. Would that be worse than losing one she'd never held in her arms?

After she shampooed and rinsed her hair, Tara turned off the water and got out to dry off. She pressed her hands over her flat belly and looked down at herself. With a fingertip, she traced the light *linea negra,* as Dr. Holbrook had called it. She did have stomach stretch marks she didn't remember from B.C. — before coma, as she and her physical therapist had always called it. But after her days at the clinic, even after Laird left, none of the staff who had cared for her had said a thing about a pregnancy. She had the feeling that, if she were to ask them, like Jen, they'd say she was crazy. They'd blame the aftereffects of the coma and insist she get more counseling than she'd already had. Was it a conspiracy against her?

She toweled herself off and pulled on slacks and a sweatshirt. Blowing her hair dry on high blast, she was still fuming over talking to Laird's dad. He'd obviously cut her off when Laird did. She knew Laird had told his parents she didn't want to start a family right away. To Jordan Lohan — no doubt to Thane and Susanne, too — that was black sin from the very pit of hell.

She paced the living room waiting for Claire. Tara could see the school bus out the front picture window, releasing children below, then lumbering upward. For one moment, she wished it was just her and Claire against the world, without having to worry that Nick would take the child away. And yet she felt so much safer with Nick around, safe from everything but the jumbled emotions she felt for him.

Tara started out to meet the school bus. Perhaps she and Claire would have a few minutes alone before Nick came back. In the driveway, she skidded on a loose stone and looked down to watch her footing. There she saw, running parallel to the driveway but evidently coming down from the tree line above the house, the distinct tracks of a deep-tread mountain bike.

7

Nick got home shortly after Claire did. Tara waited until Claire greeted him and let the two of them go out on the deck while the girl told him about her day. Neither of them had said anything to alarm Claire, but Tara saw Nick move the porch rockers around to the front of the house, rather than sit where they could be seen from the back tree line. With another glance up into those very trees, she went out with mugs of cider for all of them, then pulled a rocker around the corner for herself.

"Why are we changing the chairs, Uncle Nick?" Claire asked, after a sip of cider. "I know this is really your house, but —"

"I just felt like getting a little more sun," he said as his eyes met Tara's over the child's head. After Claire's nightmare about "Daddy hiding up in the trees," they'd decided not to tell her their suspicions, at least not yet. "The breeze is a little cool today," he added, "so the extra sun feels good."

"Oh, yeah," Claire agreed, ever ready, it seemed to Tara, to go along with whatever Nick said. "By Halloween last year we already had three snows! But you look nice and tan, Uncle Nick."

"I guess you'd just say I'm used to warmth. I bet I fade fast in this autumn mountain sun compared to where I've been."

"Aunt Tara has real pretty skin and it looks real white, maybe because of her pretty red hair. Don't you think she's pretty?"

"Claire Louise!" Tara said. "Do not put your uncle on the spot like that."

Claire thrust out her lower lip. "I just want you guys to get along."

"We are getting along," Tara said.

"But I think you been wanting to cry, or maybe you been crying."

Tara tried not to burst into tears. She was worried Nick would think she was too emotional to raise an already disturbed child. But before Tara could compose a comment, Nick said, "To answer your question, honey, yes, I think Aunt Tara is *very* pretty, and it's really rare to having coloring like hers."

"But," the child plunged on, "when she

125

gets upset, she gets pink in the face, too. See?"

"Yeah, I do see," Nick said, and quickly gulped his cider.

Tara could fully understand why Claire was matchmaking, but she'd have to talk to her about that. She hoped Nick wouldn't think she'd put the girl up to it. But right now, she had more important things to take care of and that included getting Nick off alone to tell him about the bike treads and about what had happened at Red Rocks today.

"Do you want to watch your princess video?" she asked Claire. "I need to talk to your uncle."

"No, I'd rather — Well, yes, oh, okay. Are we all going to a Red Rocks concert this weekend, or do you guys just want to go alone and I can stay at Charlee's house?"

"This is a family weekend, my first one home," Nick put in. "I say all three of us stick together and do something fun tomorrow and Sunday. Go on in now. Want me to set the video up for you?"

"Oh, no, I know how," she said as, smug and grinning, she headed inside. She shot them a long look out the picture window before they heard the video come on, much

too loud with its *Once upon a time* beginning.

"I'm *sure* you put her up to all that. Very
subtle," Nick said with a chuckle. "I'll
apologize for her crazy —"

"Nick, I do need to talk to you, but not
about that. And I need to show you something," she added, pointing toward the
driveway. "I found what I'm sure are mountain bike tracks, coming down from the tree
line."

He put his mug on the deck and stood.
"In other words, Herr Getz might have
come calling? Show me."

He followed her down the wooden steps,
then stooped to look at the tracks, turning
his head up toward the trees, then in the
direction the tracks seemed to go.

"Assuming this distinctive V-and-bar pattern points in the direction he was going,
I'd say the biker was heading downhill from
the tree line, and pretty fast."

"That's what I thought. I don't suppose
Beamer could track that?"

"Not unless the biker was dragging his
foot all the way. I didn't see anything like
this when we were up on the path or near
the cabin yesterday, so this must be some-
what fresh," he said, standing.

"There's an old bag of plaster mix in the

back of the garage. Do you think we could mix some up and make a cast of this tread, right here where it's the clearest?"

"We can try. You looked upset by more than Claire's shenanigans when I got home, so I didn't tell you I'd seen Clay's brother Rick. He seemed pretty jumpy, but said nothing to implicate himself, even when I served him fair warning about leaving the two of you alone."

"Actually, it's not just this tire tread that's got me on edge," she admitted, and wrapped her arms around her waist. "Today at Red Rocks, while I was waiting for Veronica, who never came because she suddenly took sick, I just missed being flattened by a boulder."

He stood and took both her shoulders in his big hands. "You — You look all right — more than all right. An accident?"

"I don't know. I saw two men at a distance, leaving the scene — one on a mountain bike — but then I got out of there as fast as I could. Yes, it could have been an accident. I honestly don't think I was followed there."

"A couple of glances in a rearview mirror doesn't mean a thing. Maybe your cell phone call to set things up with Veronica was picked up by someone nearby. The army does that all the time in the Middle East."

"Yes, but this is the American live-and-let-live West. I don't know. I did specify where she and I should meet."

"And Rick was supposedly out running errands," he muttered. "Maybe that's why he was so shaken when I showed up and said I was staying here. Maybe he'd followed you to Red Rocks and taken his shot at his warped idea of revenge or justice or whatever the hell he's thinking."

He must have felt her trembling, because he took both of her hands in his, then pulled her to him in a hard hug. As she wrapped her arms around his waist, she turned her cheek against his neck and felt his pulse pounding there. It was the safest she'd felt for years, and yet the very forests here seemed to have eyes watching them.

No, she thought, as they finally stepped away from the embrace. Maybe it was just Claire. She saw the little girl peeking out the window, thinking her attempts to make them a family were working like her happily-ever-after video.

Turning, spinning, drifting. Where was she? Not in her own bed . . .

Through a scrim of fog, thick as soup, it

came back to Veronica in distinct detail. In the clinic. She was in her old cottage at the clinic. Jordan and Henry Middleton had admitted her. When she'd fought them, they'd restrained her arms, strapped her down. How could she be expected to reach the organ pistons this way?

At least she'd felt safe here at the clinic before, where the drugs and drink couldn't find her. But how had she gotten back on Vicodin? She couldn't recall taking any, yet there was hydrocodone and acetaminophen in her system. She'd seen the test, she knew those dreaded words.

Jordan said she'd get liver damage, worse than before, if she didn't stop — no, he'd said, *if she wasn't stopped,* right now. He'd said something to someone, that she *must* be stopped. And she could feel she was on something again. She needed a pill right now, right now, but she knew better than to ask.

When she found she couldn't raise her arms, she forced her eyelids up. Dim in here. There had been a nurse sitting by the bed, one she didn't know, but she'd evidently stepped out. Oh, yes, the same cabin she'd lived in during her detox and rehab, a silken cage, beautifully decorated. But oh, dear God, not the nightmares of detox again, not the shame of letting her family down.

And then she remembered Tara. Poor, poor girl. A picnic by herself at Red Rocks. She had to tell her . . . tell her where she was, tell her . . . something else, but what was it?

Slow music crawled through her head, Felix Mendelssohn's "Consolation," sad, sonorous, the way she felt. Someone needed consolation. Yes, she could hear the crescendo of the piece, punctuated by the dripping of the two IVs beside her bed and someone's footsteps.

She heard the nurse come back in. It hurt her to move her eyes. No, not the nurse but someone she knew. That meant she was still thinking, still remembering, didn't it? She knew this woman, didn't she? Something about music . . . as if she needed more music than what she already had in her head and heart. Veronica Britten Lohan's organ music was born through her dancing feet to make the chords on the keyboard pedals, flowing from her flying fingers on the manuals and stops. Stops . . .

Stop. Stop and think. There was something she was trying to remember. Something she had to tell someone. Not Jordan. Without her sons this time, he had done an intervention about her drugs, just as he had always intervened in her life. Something about Laird?

An angelic face hovered over her. Pale, blond, straight hair. Is that what angels looked like in heaven?

"You look like an angel," Veronica said, but her words were slurred.

"An angel? Yes, you used to call me your angel of music. Veronica, it's Elin. Elin Johansen. Remember me, the music therapist here at the clinic? I used to go with you while you played the chapel organ at night, all those classical pieces. Remember, you played *Phantom of the Opera* for me because I thought it was so scary and romantic?"

"I remember," Veronica tried to say but it was hard to form her thoughts and words. Damned drugs. Why had she started using again? Was someone using her? Could she use this woman?

"I'm so sorry we had to meet again here," Elin said. "I'm not supposed to be in your cabin, but I thought I'd pop in for a sec when I saw your nurse had stepped out for some fresh air. You just have the doctor let me know when I can help. I think it helped you last time to play for hours. I still have all those *Phantom* songs in my head. My favorite was 'Masquerade' and yours was

'Think Of Me.' Do you remember?"

Remember. Yes, she had to remember something. "Think of Me." Something about Laird? Or was it Tara? Yes, that was it.

"Call Tara Kinsale," Veronica whispered, but it came to her ears in the blur of one hissing sound. She wanted to speak clearly, but she had to whisper, too, so no one else would hear. "Tara Kinsale."

"Oh, sure. Tara. But she's been gone from here for a long time — you remember, don't you? I overheard Dr. Middleton tell them at the reception desk that you might be kind of — well, distracted for a while and wouldn't be getting visitors, so Tara can't come to see you right now."

"Call her. Say, Jen's not in Los Angeles."

"What's that? I'm having trouble hearing you," the angel said, pulling her long, straight hair back and leaning closer. "It's all right though. You'll be here for a while, so don't worry about —"

Veronica tried again, but her speech still sounded slurred. It was just something they must have given her, but she had to try. "Jen's not in Los Angeles," she whispered again. She had more to add, but that was all she had time for now. She heard new footsteps.

Another voice in the room. "Dr. Middleton says she's not to be disturbed, Ms. Johansen. She's on heavy meds for a while because she was so distraught they thought she might hurt herself or someone else."

The angel stood up and turned away. "It's only that we worked closely together last time she was here," she told the nurse. "Mrs. Lohan is a fantastic organist, classical performance level. I was just assuring her we could work together in the later stages of rehab."

"Right now, it's just the sedatives talking until we can get them all calibrated."

"Sure. Well, I know her doctors will let me know when I can help get her back on her feet again and all."

The angel-faced girl moved away, and the sour-looking one took her place. Now, who had that angel been? Veronica wondered, and finally surrendered in her battle with heavy, heavy sleep.

"This used to be my bedroom, when I was a kid," Nick told Tara as she sat at her desk and he took the only armchair in her office, with Beamer flopping instantly next to his big feet.

Her insides cartwheeled to think that she, too, had spent hours in his room. "Oh, I didn't know. I could move my office down-stairs, and you could come up here if you want it back."

"No, this is fine. If — only if — I decide Claire and I are moving east for a while, I thought you might want to rent the place — at a great price. But I'll find and stop that lurker first," he promised, with a glance at the back window. If he was surprised she'd lowered the blinds, he didn't say so.

Nick's promise to find the lurker seemed a small consolation prize for losing Claire, however upset Tara was about someone watching the place. But she nodded and turned away before he could see she was tearing up. She did not want him to think she was as fragile as she felt lately, or he'd really question her ability to look after Claire.

As hard as she fought accepting the idea, she was becoming obsessed, absolutely haunted, by the possibility she had borne a child of her own and the child had died. She prayed that at least, if she *had* lost a baby, it had been early in the pregnancy. But, two to one, the doctors didn't indicate that. And Jen — she would have known about a pregnancy, but she could have been bribed to lie. She had to know the truth, but Veronica had been taken away from her.

She was getting so desperate she was considering asking Jordan Lohan — or worse, Laird — and she wanted nothing to do with either of them. And she kept coming so close to blurting all of that out to Nick.

She forced herself to get down to business. They had just put Claire to bed together and then come in here so Tara could try to trace Dietmar Getz online. They wanted to know if he was in the area. The candy bar wrapper wasn't much, nor was a bike tread, not in an area where so many people biked. Coloradans were hiking and biking crazy. Cyclists enjoyed everything from slightly uphill pedaling to extreme biking in body armor, crashing up through the woods, then careening down the mountains. Still, other than trying to find out more about Rick Whetstone, the disgruntled Getz was the best candidate for their lurker right now.

Before dark, they had made two six-inch plaster molds of the best indentations of bike tire treads. They were going to let them dry overnight before trying to pry them out. Tara was betting she might find something else online to implicate Getz, or at least put him in the area. Motive, means and opportunity, the police always said. Getz had the motive. And a mountain bike taken up and down Black Mountain or Shadow Mountain could be the means. If he was traveling out of California again, would that mean he had the opportunity?

She went to the mountain bike Web site she'd used to find Getz in the first place.

"Yes!" she said.

"Yes, what?" Nick asked, and came to lean so close over her shoulder she could smell his tart aftershave. It was something fresh and free, like the pines in the alpine forests here. Yet it reminded her of some secret scent hidden deep within her memory, a smell sharper than that. Something close, clean, astringent — but her brain would go no further. It was like her deepest fears roused by *Psycho,* the black blood that seemed scarlet to her.

"What is it?" He repeated his question so close to her ear that she startled, and came back from her agonizing.

"He's definitely in the area," she said, pointing at the monitor screen. "He's on the competitor list for an Extreme Bike Rally — tomorrow, no less — just about fifty miles from here, see?"

Nick leaned closer and read aloud:

"X-Treme MB Race and Rally
Conquer the Divide

At the Continental Divide
Loveland Pass, Colorado
SW of Denver
Join us at the Loveland Pass S of Route
70, Arapaho Basin Entrance to Grays
Peak Park. 10:00 a.m. till 4:00 p.m., race
at noon. Vendors, food, money prizes,
sponsored by —

"That's a long list of sponsors, so there
must be some good money to be won," Nick
went on. "But where's his name?"

"Here," she told him, scrolling down the
page, "under the maps of the location and
the layout of the race."

"Which I see is through mountainous,
wooded terrain. Getting up to and then
down from the land above this property
would be a piece of cake — German chocolate cake — for this guy."

"Here's his name — and what's evidently
a nickname," she said, pointing.

"Yeah," he said, so close that his cheek
brushed the hair along her temple. "Dietmar (Whacker) Getz, San Jose, CA."

"I hate that nickname, Whacker," Tara
said, sitting back a bit. She had the strangest desire to turn her head and rub her lips
against the light gold stubble on Nick's face.

" 'Whacker' doesn't mean what it does in

cop and mafia lingo here," Nick told her, "not a hired gun or sniper. To extreme bikers it's short for bushwhacker, which means somebody who pushes ahead through the worst risks, whether on or off the marked trail. I had a couple of college friends who were into X-treme, as they called it. The opposite of a bushwhacker is a backtracker, somebody who's supposedly more sensible and rational."

"Like me — once," she whispered.

"I was going to say, like me, despite the fact I learned a lot living with some of the best, most skilled fighters I've ever seen. They almost always got their man. They were efficient, purposeful and disciplined, not mavericks or rebels. I was proud to be a part of their unit, even if . . ."

His voice trailed off.

"If what?" she asked as she hit the print button to run off the race information.

She saw him shake his head as if to clear it. He straightened up, towering over her again. "I think I'm off to the races tomorrow morning," he said, in an abrupt change of topic. "The X-treme races. One thing I've learned is that the best defense is often a strong offense, so — like with Rick — I'm going to have at least a chat with Herr Dietmar Getz, alias Whacker."

"Not without me there, you're not," she said, standing to face him as the printer hummed the material onto paper. "And you promised Claire an outing for all three of us. If you'll go with me, I want to face him down, to let him know we're onto him. After all, what's he going to do with all those other people who know him standing — riding — around? We need to cart one of those concrete impressions of the treads with us and see if his bike tires match."

"You're something," he said with a tight smile as his gaze went over her like a firm caress.

"I will *not* be threatened by another one of the despicable moral cowards who snatch their children. Lately, I've come to understand a bit more how Alex could have been so obsessed with getting Claire back, even if she had to lie and steal from me and face Clay alone."

"So that's what's been eating at you. Coming to terms with all that, not just worries about a possible stalker."

She gazed into his sky-blue eyes. They seemed to bore deep into her. Desperately, she wanted to share her burden with him, ask his advice. But she didn't want to break down in front of him, for fear he'd really want to get Claire away from her, too.

Too? she thought. Too, as if you now accept that you had a baby and lost that baby? Do you believe that now? she asked herself.

Nick was saying, ". . . so I guess mother instinct is that strong. My mother once dove into an icy cold stream after me when I was screaming for her."

Tara felt jolted into some other dimension. "Icy cold," he'd said. "Screaming for her." She recalled herself being so cold . . . in the snow . . . screaming for someone . . . some child. But where and when?

His deep voice went on. She nodded. Her eyes were still locked to his laser-blue gaze, but she wasn't thinking of his mother. She was thinking of herself. She felt pregnant with the deep, driving need to find, not some stalker who hid outside, but the child she might have carried within.

8

"Are we there yet? What does the constant divide divide, anyway? Will we see a big line on the ground?"

Tara was tense and she knew Nick was, too, but Claire was having the time of her life, asking continuous questions from the backseat of his truck.

Driving in fairly heavy traffic on I-70W, Nick had let Tara do most of the talking, but he answered Claire's last question. "It's an invisible line that marks where rainwater and rivers flow in different directions on the Con-tin-en-tal Divide, not the Constant Divide. If you had a rock and you poured water on top of it, the water would slide off in different directions. To the east of Continental Divide," he went on, gesturing broadly so she could see from the backseat, "water flows into the Gulf of Mexico or the Atlantic Ocean. To the west, it goes toward the Pacific. This pretend line goes through five different states."

"Colorado and what else?" came the clear voice from behind them.

If Claire didn't have a seat belt on, Tara was certain she would have tried to crawl up into the front seat so she could keep an eye on every nuance of her and Nick's facial expressions. All of a sudden, the child was not only into matchmaking but gauging how well her aunt Tara and uncle Nick were getting along at any given moment. As if it wasn't enough, Tara thought, to have a possible watcher outside the house, they had one in their midst.

She could almost read Nick's thoughts. Beamer, however excited about their outing today, was content to be a quiet backseat companion. That was what Nick had been expecting from Claire. Nick McMahon had a lot to learn about rearing a child. He'd been successfully training dogs for years and giving or taking orders working with the military. But that did not translate into dealing with a little girl, and he was probably going to have to learn that lesson the hard way.

Tara saw she was resting her arms protectively on her belly again. When she realized what she was doing, she forced herself to put them on the center and door armrests while Nick dutifully recited the other Continental Divide states. "Montana, Idaho, Wyoming and New Mexico. We're going to be really close to one part of the line near the Arapaho Basin at Loveland Pass. And, no, we're not there yet."

"Loveland Pass?" Claire cried with a whoop. "That's a good name, right? Maybe the biker guys will want to bring their girlfriends there, and other men who go there will fall in love, too."

Nick gave an imperceptible shake to his head and darted a sideways glance at Tara, who was biting back a grin. "Nothing like comic relief," she told him, "even in the midst of a grim mission."

She saw Nick's smile go taut, then disappear. His lower lip almost quivered, and a frown crunched his forehead and narrowed his eyes. She could grasp why he might be a bit exasperated with Claire, but what had she said? Grim mission? She was starting to think she wasn't the only one walking around with a hidden trauma, where an innocent remark could set off an explosion.

In his college days, Nick had been to a couple of X-treme mountain bike rallies with his buddies, but this was a big one. It might be really tough to find Dietmar Getz here, despite the fact Tara had printed an online picture of him from the Denver paper. It was a small, grainy photo, taken when Getz had been indicted for snatching his son. The other one she'd found online was of Getz, alias Whacker, winning an X-treme race trophy in California. But he wore his helmet and body armor and looked like a dust- and mud-speckled storm trooper from an old *Star Wars* movie. They'd probably have to ask around to find him.

"Okay, we're going to have a few ground rules today," Nick announced to Tara and Claire as they walked through the parking lot. It was loaded with vans and cars with bike carriers attached to the tops or back bumpers.

"Rules for when we're on the ground, but not if we go higher up?" Claire asked.

"No," Nick said sharply. He realized he was sounding testy, but the kid had not let up. "Ground rules means basic rules."

"Sir, yes, sir!" Tara said, and gave him a mock salute and a look that he read as *lighten up.* Didn't the woman realize this was serious stuff today?

They had a good hold of Claire's hands as she bounced along between them, and in Nick's outside hand he had Beamer on a leash. The dog knew the difference between being on a working lead, though he sniffed at the mingled smells and still stayed out in front as if pulling Nick along. As the crowd got thicker, Nick said, "Beamer, heel," and the Lab instantly fell in behind him.

Tara wore big sunglasses and had pinned her bounteous, distinctive red hair up under a Denver Broncos cap, so there'd be no possibility Getz could spot her first. Despite her desire to face the guy down, Nick didn't want her talking to Getz, not unless they could confront him together. He was going to try to locate and ID him first. Locate and ID: it was starting to sound as if he worked for Tara's Finders Keepers.

In his backpack, he carried a small piece of plaster with the reverse impression of the mountain bike treads they hoped to compare to Getz's. Mountain bikes were expensive and often customized. Though Whacker could certainly have more than one set of tires, or could have changed them, the X-tremers Nick had known had been picky about their bikes. A lot of them were superstitious. They might like occasional new gear, but they were almost sentimental about keeping what had won races for them.

Despite Tara evidently siding with Claire about Nick making rules for the day, he went on. "We're going to buy some lunch, then put our blanket in a good place to watch the bottom of the race course, the end of it. I may go up a little higher, but I'll come right back."

"Why can't we go up with you?" Claire asked. "You mean that part's not for girls?"

"Every part of watching this race is for girls," Tara put in, "though it is only guys in the race today. Still, there are women racers at other meets I've read about. In America, girls and women can do whatever they want and need to do."

Nick lifted both eyebrows, but said only, "That's right. But it will really be fun for you to see the end of the race, and I won't be gone long. Now, let's get something to eat."

As they walked deeper into the grounds, men pushed bikes everywhere, hemming them in. Nick and Tara tried to scan faces, most of which might as well be masked. Some already wore big, scuba-diving-type goggles or helmets with attached mouth guards that hid the lower halves of their faces. Those still barefaced had daubed black paint under their eyes to cut sun glare or wore green/brown camo face paint like some of the Special Forces guys did.

In the center of the area, from booths or tents, vendors sold water and energy drinks, and high-carb food. Tara got a pasta salad and Claire some mac and cheese, but Nick went for a good old American cheeseburger with onion rings. Again, he thought of how much his Delta unit — even the dogs — would love to bite into this instead of MREs. He'd been cautioned about the devastating results of survivor's guilt after what had happened on their first mission. He supposed he had that in common with Tara, maybe even with Claire. Unlike them, he figured he didn't need counseling.

They passed another row of tents as they walked with their food to find a good place to eat. Here men and women bent over the tasks of selling or repairing goggles, body armor and pads, tire tubes — but not the tires themselves — bike saddles and something called rescue indexes. Then, bingo! Nick thought, and pointed out to Tara a booth selling granola and candy bars, including expensive, dark chocolate ones.

"I'll take one of those Cacao Reserves," Nick said, and passed the money over to the man for the purchase of a candy bar with a wrapper identical to the one he'd found in the old hunter's cabin. "A lot of X-tremers like this kind?"

"Oh, yeah, man," the vendor told him. "That stuff's full of good antioxidants and good vibes. Dark chocolate's just another kind of vegetable 'round here."

They found a good place to lay out their blanket. Nick put Tara against the trunk of a big aspen so no one could see her from behind. They not only had a great view of the last couple of meters of the race from here, once the riders broke out of the stony, heavily treed terrain above, they had a stunning view of the mountains. They could clearly see Grays Peak and Mount Evans, two of the so-called fifty-four Fourteeners of the front range of the Rockies, which stood over 14,000 feet. Though it was a fairly clear day, both snow-topped mountains had snagged massive cumulous clouds.

Later, at Tara's urging, Nick walked Claire over to watch the bikers start out on the uphill climb of the race while Tara stayed with their things. Fingering the wrinkled photocopies of Getz's photo in his jacket pocket, next to the candy bar, he turned around to check on her. He could see her on the blanket with Beamer, who wasn't pleased that Nick had walked off without him. Hell, was everyone he loved mad at him today?

Loved? The word echoed in his thoughts. Everyone he *loved?* He loved Claire, sure, out of family duty, affection and his need to protect her. In a way, he loved all the dogs he trained, Beamer most of all. But he hardly knew Tara, though he wanted to, in all kinds of ways.

And then, as they got close enough to see the start of the race, it hit him. Riders were going off three minutes apart in groups of four while a man with a bullhorn was announcing their names alphabetically. And they were already to the *E*'s.

Wishing he hadn't given in to bringing Claire with him, he held tighter to her hand and scanned the faces of the racers waiting to go next, then the four after that. Tara had given him some ID indicators that didn't involve having to see the racers' full faces. She'd said Getz had a goatee and hair almost to his collar. He was thin and lanky, but that was hardly a distinguishing feature with X-tremers. Their heights might vary, but they all looked gaunt and rangy to him. He could not pick the guy out.

But the man with the bullhorn looked familiar. Nick startled, not because the man resembled Getz, but because he reminded him of Tony Morelli, who had been one of the first Delta handlers Nick had trained to work with a trail dog in Afghanistan. Tony, who talked about his mom's Italian cooking until they all wanted to chuck their MREs in the dirt . . . Tony who had a terrible voice but like to sing opera . . . Tony who had been killed because Nick decided to let the men take a wrong turn to make a point — and then . . . boom!

He jolted, jerking Claire's hand. That bull-horn again. Damn, they were almost to the *G*'s. "Dom 'the Cannon' Iocono!" the announcer shouted. "Chuck Isaly! Lou 'the Flyer' Gardner! And Dietmar 'Whacker' Getz!"

Yes, that bastard, all in bright yellow and black on an all-black bike. With the other X-tremers around as those four took their places at the starting line, he'd never be able to match the treads with the piece of plaster he'd brought along. But the race was supposed to take around two hours. He hoped Getz lost, but win or lose, he'd be waiting for him at the end.

"Claire, will you wait on the blanket with Beamer?" Tara asked. "You have to promise to sit right here. Nick and I are going to talk to someone who just finished the race. We'll be real quick."

"Did he win? Can't I go, too?"

"Don't argue. You'll be able to see us and we'll be able to see you, too. And we don't know if he won, because that depends on how long it takes each rider, and there are lots not finished yet."

It had come, Tara thought, to the moment of truth. She and Nick had decided to confront Getz and tell him to keep clear or else. About ten minutes ago, after he'd finished the race, Nick had sidled up close behind him and managed to match their piece of concrete to the tire itself. The V and bars seemed identical, although he'd noted some other riders had the same tire tread.

What really got to Nick was the shirt the guy wore. It was a metallic yellow with a black, double-headed eagle on it, like some kind of old German flag he'd seen. "A double-headed eagle, like the two-faced bastard I'll bet he is, pretending to look one way in his own life, but spying on you," he said to Tara. "At least, I don't think my time under fire in Afghanistan has made me so paranoid I can't put two and two together."

Getz was sitting near other sweating, exhausted racers who had just finished their brutal uphill then downhill, but it seemed each rider was pretty much keeping to himself.

"Beamer, stay," Nick told the dog as they started over to confront the man.

"Claire, stay," Tara said with a tight little

smile as she dropped a kiss on the girl's head. "See, we're only going over there."

Taking the piece of plaster with them again, they hurried to where Getz was sitting beside his bike. His helmet and body armor lay nearby in a pile. He was like a knight of old after a joust on his steed, Tara thought. With a backward glance to be sure Claire was all right — she had her arms around Beamer's neck — she stepped up to Getz first, as they had planned.

She evidently caught his eye immediately, though he seemed not to recognize her. He rose, planted his legs far apart and crossed his arms over his chest. Though she couldn't see Nick, Tara sensed that he had stiffened his stance.

"Hey, babe, you like X-treme ridin'?" Getz asked, flashing her a smile. Though he'd lived in the States for over twenty years, his German accent was distinct. He whipped off his wraparound aviator sunglasses, which reflected her distorted image. His eyes, pale gray, went thoroughly over her.

She pulled off her sunglasses and her cap, spilling her hair down to her shoulders. "What I like is for X-treme riders to stay way clear of my property."

He frowned. "You live around here? What's your problem?"

He actually seemed confused. If he'd been spying on her, surely he would recognize her instantly. Or was he that good an actor?

"Our problem, Whacker," Nick put in, aligning himself shoulder to shoulder with her, though he'd said he'd give her more time, "is that an X-treme biker's been spying on Ms. Kinsale here, whom I think you know from your checkered past. And the bike treads, which we've made a cast of for the police, suggest that the trespasser might have been you — someone who obviously has a beef against her."

Nick thrust out the six-inch piece of plaster, then pulled it back, holding it, one-handed, at his side. "And next time you leave one of these with your fingerprints on it," he added, pulling out the Cacao Reserve candy bar from his shirt pocket in pure bluff, "we're not even going for a restraining order, but straight to the police."

"I don't know what in hell you two are talking about," Getz blustered, shoving his glasses back on, but he was starting to show less bravado. "Okay, I get it now, who you are, lady. But I got rights, too. I don't care what you and that bitch of an ex-wife or her mother say! Rights to my kid, rights not to be dissed by some chick and her boyfriend when I'm minding my own business, miles away from your property."

"So you do know where her property is?"

"I don't need this. Get the hell out of my face."

"We're doing you a big favor, Getz," Nick insisted, leaning toward him and punching a finger in the middle of his chest. "We're warning you to keep clear and keep clean, because I'm sure there are no X-treme races in prison."

"You're both nuts. Besides, there's nothing says a biker can't ride mountain paths anywhere. Any biker, anywhere!" he insisted, thrusting Nick's hand away, though Nick quickly caught the man's wrist. Tara noticed that several other bikers were looking their way. A couple of them stood and started shuffling over.

Nick swiveled his head. He saw them, too, but he went on, his voice low and menacing. "Tell you what, Whacker. We wish you good luck on the race here, but we're the ones who are going to win if you ever set foot anywhere near where we are. Got that?"

"I'm going to call the police over."

"Do that," Nick countered, loosening his grip. "We'll fill them in on everything. Tara, could you go get one of the officers we passed coming in?"

"Forget it, man! Just back off and leave

me alone."

"Deal," Nick said, his face inches from Getz's. "That's the deal. You leave us alone, too."

Tara started away, thinking Nick would follow, but the two men stood frozen, glaring at each other. She was afraid Nick might ignore the threat of the other bikers and have it out with him, or all of them, but he spun on his heel, took her arm and they walked back to Claire and Beamer.

Later, Tara, Claire and Nick applauded when the winner's name was announced, because it wasn't Dietmar "Whacker" Getz.

Tara's spirits lifted even more when they got home. On the side deck lay a box of crimson roses with a flamboyant yellow bow and a card.

"Oh, look," she cried, stooping to lift the box in her arms and smell the roses. "One of my former clients, who's now a lawyer in Seattle, sends me flowers once in a while, but the delivery man never leaves them here."

When she opened the card, it was signed by Marv Seymour, the creepy, online information broker who had been trying to interest her in a date. The note read, *"I see you everywhere . . . I'll be seeing you."*

9

That night, over their second glass of red wine, Tara and Nick sat a few feet apart on the leather couch before the gas log fire in the living room. Claire had been exhausted from their day's excursion and had fallen sound asleep after dinner, so Nick had carried her to bed. The drumming of the rain on the roof should have lulled everyone, Tara thought, but she and Nick were both on edge. Before it had gotten dark and the storm had started, a huge cloud seemed to have slid down Shadow Mountain to press itself against the windows, sealing them in together.

"When it rains, it pours," she said, "in more ways than one."

"Yeah. Maybe I'm bad luck. I show up, and you've got a whole list of idiots who could be spying on you, or worse."

"Worse? What could be worse?"

"Someone out to harm you as well as

scare you."

"Like someone trying to roll a rock on my head?"

He sighed, put his stockinged feet up on the wood-and-glass coffee table and leaned back into the soft leather cushions. Beamer lifted his golden head, then put it down on his paws again.

"Here's a wild thought for you," Nick said, rubbing his eyes with a thumb and index finger. "Maybe whoever's been watching this place from the trees above the house is after me, and the Red Rocks incident was just an accident."

"Oh, right, someone after you. Maybe some of the Taliban followed you here from —"

"Never mind. You're right, it doesn't make sense. Despite the roses, I think it was Getz. Hopefully, he'll steer clear of you now. Unless Clay swore his brother to some sort of vendetta, Rick's got other things to keep him occupied, namely a woman who's a handful and a decent job, evidently with good perks. But it's obvious this information broker you've dealt with is off the wall."

"I've never met him, but the weird vibes come right through the laptop. My life and face have been pretty public during the last few years, so he clearly thought he knew me even before I started using him. He's one of the best IBs I've ever worked with, so it's too bad I have to cut ties. Too bad about those beautiful roses, too."

Thank God, she thought, Nick had been here to help her during all of this. After making sure the roses weren't bugged, he had taken them up to the old hunting cabin. He'd laid the box, note and all, on the moss bed while Tara tried to answer Claire's questions about why they weren't keeping the flowers. Tara had e-mailed Seymour that she would not consider "seeing him" or accept any gifts. She also made it clear that she wouldn't use him for locates anymore.

"Let's do something nice and calm tomorrow," Nick said. "I'd like to thank the pastor who did Alex's funeral service. We could go to church, then visit her grave. You said you and Claire had done that without Claire having bad dreams. That is, if you don't mind hanging out with the two of us again tomorrow."

"I'm grateful you're still including me. I know the two of you might not be in my life much longer."

"Don't say it like that," he said, sitting up and putting his wine goblet on the table. He turned toward her, bending one leg up onto the couch. "This is a good transition period for me and her — and I hope for you, too. I know she'll do what she has to when the time comes, but it really helps me to see how you handle her. I guess I have some things to learn."

"It's not quite like being a dog handler, Nick — sit, heel, stay."

"Yeah, I hear you. I'd forgotten how women think," he said with a low, raspy laugh that sent shivers up her spine. He stretched his arm out on the back of the couch and tugged at her hair. It was a light moment, yet tension hung heavy between them. "I'd forgotten," he went on, speaking slowly, his deep voice rougher than usual, "how a woman feels in my arms, until you let me hold you yesterday."

Their gazes met. She nodded, and that seemed to unlock something in both of them. He moved first — or else she did. Arms around each other, hips touching, sliding together, they leaned in unison back on the deep, soft couch. And then the kiss.

It had been years for Tara but it felt like eons, and she wanted it to go on forever. His mouth was taut and firm at first, but it softened, coaxing her to relax. Yet every nerve in her body went on alert; she could feel the kiss and caress down into the pit of her belly. It made her curl her toes until her calves almost cramped. They bumped noses as they tilted their heads to deepen the kiss. His arm moved lower to clasp her waist and lift her slightly toward him while she hung on to stop the tilting of the couch, the room, the entire mountain.

Maybe the coma had made her forget how this could feel. Laird must have been a great kisser, because he'd absolutely seduced her, but she couldn't recall that, and she didn't want to. This was the first time anything had been this magical and powerful, at least where the power was hers, as well. It was hard to believe that this was only Nick's third night here, yet this emotional whirlwind with him made everything else seem so muted and distant.

And from somewhere — damn — in some other galaxy, a phone was ringing, ringing.

When Nick pulled slightly away, she realized they had been breathing in unison through their open mouths.

"Won't that wake Claire up?" he asked.

Tara didn't care if it woke the dead. "No, once she's asleep — except for the bad dreams — she's out. That better not be Marv Seymour," she added, her voice shaky. "It might be a desperate client or Veronica."

Reluctantly, she took the cell from Nick when he picked it up from the end table.

With one hand in the small of her back, he steadied her as she sat up. It wasn't unusual for the mother of a snatched child desperate for news or a new client still in shock at her loss to phone at odd hours. Sometimes Tara still used her social work counseling skills and was glad to do it. Now, she tried to clear her mind, so she could make sense.

She cleared her throat. "Tara Kinsale here."

"Ms. Kinsale? Formerly Mrs. Lohan, right?" A young woman's voice, slightly nervous.

"Yes, formerly Mrs. Kinsale-Lohan. May I help you?"

"This is Elin Johansen from the Mountain Manor Clinic. I'm the music therapist there. I don't suppose you know me."

"No, but Veronica Lohan has spoken fondly of you."

"Oh, that's just it. Do you know she was readmitted yesterday?"

"But — I just talked to her yesterday morning, and she seemed fine."

Nick ran his fingers through his hair and took the empty wineglasses into the kitchen to give her some privacy. Or maybe he was just relieved that it wasn't Marv Seymour.

"You mean she had a relapse?" Tara asked. "I appreciate your calling me, Elin." Especially, Tara thought, since Jordan Lohan had obviously stonewalled her. What Jordan Lohan wanted around the clinic, he got, despite the fact he was a financier and not a medical mind. "Have you seen her?"

"Briefly. I wasn't really supposed to, but she asked me to tell you something, not that it made sense. She's heavily medicated right now."

Tara kept nodding. Yes, she knew how that felt. Even when she was finally being weaned from the coma, she was sometimes sedated. "What did she say?" she prompted the woman.

"Okay, here it is, word for word. She said, 'Tell Tara Kinsale, Jim's not lost, Angel.' She nicknamed me Angel, you know, because she said I looked like an angel painted on some Baroque organ she'd seen in Belgium."

"So her message to me was 'Jim's not lost'? That's what she wanted you to tell me?"

"I said she wasn't making much sense, but I would have felt terrible if I hadn't told you. I'm sure the powers-that-be around here would think I'm meddling, but Veronica is a musical genius, and I think the world of her."

"You know, Elin, despite all I've been

163

through with the Lohans, I do, too, and I thank you for telling me where she is and what she said. Do you think she's referring to Jim Manning, the clinic groundskeeper? He's the only Jim I can think of that both of us know."

"She could have meant him, I guess. He's always joking that he'll get lost on that huge acreage he tends. You know," she went on, lowering her voice as if someone could be listening, "I heard Mr. Lohan has him working on their land in Kerr Gulch off and on, too. Veronica always appreciated Jim's sense of humor. She told me once no one else but him around the clinic had any."

"He was kind to me, too, brought me wildflowers more than once when I was in rehab. . . ." Tara's voice faded. How different she'd felt about receiving scarlet mallow from that kind man compared to those stunning roses from Marv Seymour.

"So, are you feeling all right these days, Ms. Kinsale?"

"Better and better, physically. For the rest of me, I'm a work in progress. And please, call me Tara."

"We're all always a work in progress, Tara."

"Thanks again."

"Sure. I — I don't know if they'll let me work with Mrs. Lohan again, but if they do,

I'll let you know how she is. With the wonderful music she made on the pipe organ in the chapel, especially my favorites from *Phantom of the Opera,* she was as much help to me as I was to her."

When they said goodbye, Tara's heart was thudding, harder than the rain that pounded on the windows as if some monstrous mountain beast wanted in. Staring at her knees, she sat still a moment, feeling so sad for Veronica and puzzling over the strange message. Well, Veronica was doped up, so her mind might have been wandering. Yet, even if she were out of it, could the message have meant more than it said on the surface?

But besides all that, Tara was desperately trying to recall how she knew Veronica had played on the chapel pipe organ late at night — even that very *Phantom of the Opera* music — when Veronica had left the clinic months before Tara came out of her coma.

Tara was walking through the thick, dark fog in her heart and head. It crept down from Shadow Mountain and coiled around the house, crawled into her bed and her brain. Was she still hidden away in a coma? Voices, bright lights! Someone shone a bright light in each eye. "Is she alive?" someone shouted.

Was Alex dead? Where was Claire?

Though the air was thick with grief, she slogged on. Her feet were cold, so cold. The rain made the tree limbs slump and brush together, washing her with icy water. But she had to know. She had to find Alex and Claire, find Veronica, too. Mostly, she had to find herself, find what it was she had lost. Finders keepers, losers weepers.

"Jim is not lost," someone whispered.

But she was lost, not sure which way to turn in the trees. In this darkness, she might slide off the edge of the cliff, and then the pain would break her in two, into two Taras, two people . . . She wanted to hide from the pain.

The sound of sharp barking. She was lost, but Beamer would find her. Barking, barking . . . deep barking, like thunder . . .

Tara sat straight up in bed. Oh — she'd been dreaming, but Beamer's barking was real. A storm with lightning and thunder! The alarm clock read 5:04 a.m. She and Nick had talked more after Tara's phone call last night, then gone to their beds about midnight.

Tara jumped up and pulled on a robe as she ran down the hall. Claire's door was still closed; when she slept, she slept, but Tara peeked in to be sure she was all right.

Yes, sprawled across her bed, breathing deeply. When she heard Nick's voice, telling Beamer to be quiet and to sit, Tara closed the door and went to the top of the stairs.

"What is it?" she asked. "Is it the storm?"

"He never used to bark at storms," he said, his voice low. "It's still thick as pea soup out there. But I think I heard footsteps on the deck and Beamer sure heard or smelled something."

"Maybe a big, human rat," she said. "Hit the outside lights."

She ran down the stairs as the exterior lights came on. She supposed they should leave them on all the time now, but what good did it do in rain and fog? There had never been a need to have lights on all night anywhere near Conifer.

Nick, in sweatpants and a T-shirt, was barefoot. He pulled the curtain open farther and they peered out. The lights only pierced about three feet into the gray, swirling mist. But that was enough for them to see a dozen roses had been beheaded and their blood-red petals strewn across the deck. Twelve stems had been stuck upright between the deck boards as if to make a thorny barrier for anyone who stepped outside.

"He must have just been here," Nick muttered, and unlocked the sliding glass door as thunder echoed from the mountains. "Seymour, Getz, the boogeyman or whoever. I'm going out after him."

"No," Tara cried, and grabbed his arm. "Whoever it is, he could have more than a trap of thorns waiting, maybe even a gun. Nick, I'm so sorry about all this. Please, don't go out there."

He nodded once and locked the door again, yanked the curtain closed, then pulled her to him. They stood, holding each other tight, in the dark house while something infinitely darker ruled the night.

Although the sermon was a good one, Nick had to fight nodding off. He'd hardly slept last night, too keyed up after kissing Tara, then too angry about someone tormenting her. He hadn't even gotten over jet lag yet, which was throwing his internal clock off.

" 'If a man has a hundred sheep,' " the pastor read from the Bible, " 'and one of them goes astray, does he not leave the ninety-nine and go to the mountain to find the one that is straying?' "

He should have run out onto the mountain after the trespasser last night, Nick told himself. But Tara might have been right. It could have been a trap. If it was meant to lure him out, he didn't want to leave her and Claire alone. He was starting to think that if he took the Fort Bragg job, he should insist that Tara come, too. She could run Finders Keepers from there, though he knew she wouldn't go. Not unless she was going *to* something instead of running *from* something. She was scared here, but then, so was he. The truth was, he'd been running scared and guilt-ridden ever since the day they'd lost Tony and Superman.

Superman's name was really Clark Brent, so he'd always lived with being teased with cornball questions like, "Hey, Clark Kent, where's Lois Lane?" or "When do you dart into a phone booth to change into your tights?" But Clark, who was from a little Ohio town called Sunbury, took it all with good humor and had some clever comebacks. "Just hope those Taliban SOBs don't have Kryptonite in those caves," he joked the day he and Tony were lost . . . the day they died. The new dog had taken them the wrong way and then the rocket-propelled grenade hit the two men . . .

"And from the book of Luke, the same message of our Lord seeking straying sinners, with a different illustration," the pastor was saying as Nick gave a sharp sniff. " 'What woman, having ten silver coins, if she loses one coin, does not light a lamp, sweep the house, and search carefully until she finds it?' "

They'd found their bodies, or what was left of them. Ironically, the dog had lived and was still working, searching caves in the mountains . . . maybe finding the head mullahs like Hezbi Islami or other remnants of the Taliban.

Man, Nick thought, forcing himself to think of something other than the bloody scene that still haunted him, Tara ought to be loving this sermon. It sounded custom-made for her P.I. firm. But she was frowning. Was she even paying attention, or was she lost in her own thoughts? He knew she was puzzling out the cryptic message from her former mother-in-law.

As for Claire, she seemed to be listening, though she was drawing a picture on the program, one of a mother and daughter, stick figures with skirts and hair, holding hands. It reminded him he'd said they'd go to visit Alex's grave after church. This afternoon, he intended to go with Beamer up on Shadow Mountain to trace the scent on those rose stems, if the rain and fog had not washed it all away. Sometimes, it seemed Tara's tormentor, like the Taliban, had simply vanished into thin mountain air.

■ ■ ■ ■

For several reasons, Tara had always loved Evergreen Memorial Park just off North Turkey Creek Road. The cemetery seemed so natural, with its lakes and what appeared to be spacious meadows, which were actually three burial areas. The Garden of the Pioneers provided a history lesson about the area, with its Indian fighters' and women settlers' tombstones near an original log cabin and artifacts from earlier times. Besides the usual cemetery buildings of the chapel and crematory, the park had a wild game preserve and a pet cemetery. Only in the area called the Garden of the Cross were there upright grave monuments, so most of the grounds looked pristine with flat markers. Events and weddings were held at the center of the park in a historic barn with stunning, stained-glass windows.

The park was Alex's eternal resting place. Tara's parents were also buried here, in the Garden of the Pines. She had happy memories of them here; when she was a child, her family had often visited at dusk to watch elk emerge from the forest to feed on the meadow grass and drink from the ponds. Today, as Nick drove them in, she remembered there was a section where babies and children were buried.

"I'm going to let you go over to Alex's area, while I take a walk the other way," Tara told Nick and Claire. "Then I'll meet you back at the car."

"Aunt Tara's mom and dad are here, too," Claire told Nick, as if this was just the expected place to visit parents.

"Sure, that's fine," Nick said, and took Claire's hand as they headed in the opposite direction. Again, Tara noticed that he was not only distracted by his own thoughts — understandably, since he hadn't been to see his murdered sister's grave before — but he also seemed disturbed. It was, she sensed, something that went deeper than their current troubles with a trespasser, or perhaps even than the harsh reality of seeing Alex's grave.

Tara knew where she was heading, and she knew why. The small area beyond the western lake drew her, an area she'd never set foot in before. The ground was still wet from last night's rain, but she didn't mind. The grass smelled fresh, despite the cool air. Soon, too soon, this would all be cloaked by late-autumn and winter snows.

With her hands clasped between her breasts as if to steady her heart, Tara walked the neat rows of infant graves, reading the flat markers. Little lambs were carved into some of the simple, flat stones. She thought of the sermon today. People were driven to search for a lost coin until it was found . . . for a lost lamb until it was recovered. Only then, could they rejoice.

She had a lost lamb of her own to look for.

So sad, these lives cut short, she thought as her eyes skimmed the names and dates. *Beloved baby . . . our pride and joy . . .* Some died the day they were born. A few had plastic-coated pictures embedded in their stones, those stiff, just-born hospital photos parents used to use for birth announcements before so many people had digital cameras. Just as her clients had lost their children, these parents had lost theirs, only this was forever, a tragedy one would never get over.

It was still difficult to believe that she had borne and then lost a child. It must have been because she was so ill no one had told her. Those who knew about the miscarriage or stillbirth didn't want her to suffer more. Laird, who had desperately wanted children, had been heartbroken and moved away. Perhaps people didn't want to answer questions about how the baby had died.

So she could have had a child, but if the Lohans weren't talking, they would not have laid the baby to rest in such a public place. She could easily check cemetery records for the entire area online. She could become her own client for Finders Keepers. Sometimes, she never found the child of a grieving mother. She kept those files separate, revisiting them from time to time. She never gave up.

Tears blurred her vision. The cool September wind lifted her skirt and ruffled her hair. She turned and looked across the lake to see Nick and Claire, holding hands, heads bent, standing beside Alex's grave. It helped, she knew, to have a place to mourn, a person to mourn.

She must learn whether she had borne a living child, and, if so, how he or she had died. She vowed she wasn't going to rest until she had the entire truth.

10

"You take the lead," Nick told Tara. "That way you can get the feel of how Beamer tracks."

They'd just put Claire on the school bus Monday morning. It had rained again Sunday afternoon and evening, so Nick had not tried to track their Saturday-night visitor. Without Claire around now, they could talk and walk more freely. The child had been told that someone was trespassing and had left the flowers for the wrong person, but she'd been assured that the unwanted visitor was not her father. It must have worked, at least so far, because there had been no repeat of the nightmare where she'd dreamed he was lurking above the house.

The storms yesterday had put a crimp in Tara's plans. She'd hoped to spend time online looking through burial records for a baby, last name Lohan, but with all the lightning she'd kept her PC unplugged. Before Claire and Nick awoke this morning, Tara had thoroughly searched all local cemetery records for such a burial and had come up with nothing. Surely, Laird would not have used cremation, because he didn't believe in that.

All these dead ends — though she didn't like to think of it in those words — meant she was going to have to interview people who might know something. If she got nowhere that way, she would have to confront Jordan Lohan or even phone Laird.

"Oh," she said as she took Beamer's taut leash from Nick, "he's raring to go."

"That's my boy. Okay, now since he got no scent off the soggy rose box or the stems, I'm going to re-scent him with the candy wrapper to see if the original trail is washed clean or not."

"Aren't fog and rain bad news?"

"Very, but these tracker dogs surprise you sometimes. I've seen them follow a trail over bare rock in a dust storm."

"Has Beamer ever done something to protect you? He feels so strong."

"Yeah, once when he was young. In downtown Denver after dark, Beamer tripped a guy who tried to rob me. I think the thief thought I was blind and Beamer was my guide dog. Anyway, he knocked the guy into a brick wall and my would-be mugger ran off like a flash before I could even react. He's a hero in all kinds of ways, more than I'll ever be."

As if he knew what was being said, Beamer wagged his tail during that story, but jerked his head when Nick let him smell the wrapper. "Tell him, *f-i-n-d*." Nick spelled it out as if the dog were a child.

"Beamer, find!" she told the dog, and they were off, down the deck stairs, in circles under the deck — no doubt where their unwanted visitor had been lurking — then up into the tree line with a long stop at the matted-down area where Nick had showed her someone had lain or sat for long periods.

"This is what you called a scent pool," Tara observed. "If it survived all that rain, it must be fairly fresh. Which means our lurker is fanatical enough to be out in a lightning storm on a mountain with tall trees."

"Yeah, I know. But on a happier note, your partner found this. Scratch him behind the ears as a reward, and repeat the command. He's not resting on his laurels here."

Like Beamer, Tara was following the orders of her handsome handler. Nodding at Nick, she suppressed a smile at that thought. "Beamer, find!"

The dog circled the scent pool, then pulled her onward, though he slowed down at times. The fact the trail toward the hunter's cabin was partly mud and bare stone did not stop him. Nose almost to ground, he plowed ahead on the path through thick, wet trees and piles of pine needles and aspen leaves. But he was discerning about it; he ignored narrower deer or elk trails that darted off at odd angles.

When the lodgepole pines above them shook in the wind, dousing them with drops, Tara experienced a strange foreboding. It was just a little water, for heaven's sake, she told herself and fought the feeling of déjà vu. What was it that she was on the verge of remembering? She pulled herself back together; it was important to her to show Nick and Beamer she could do this.

"Give him a little space, but not that much slack in the lead, or he might wrap it around a tree," Nick said, coming close behind her. "Don't distract him. When he stops, you stop. Keep your distance."

Keep your distance. The words stayed in her mind. Nick had asked her last night if she wanted him to keep his distance. He would probably be leaving in the near future and he didn't want her to have any more emotional losses beyond missing Claire.

She'd told him to keep his distance only if he wanted to, and he'd given her such a devilish smile that she'd giggled like a girl.

But that little exchange had also made her decide to tell him about her search for her own child. She was tired of trying to hold Nick at a distance about her growing obsession. Maybe after she shared that, Nick would want to keep his distance. She knew that when she tried to pin people down on the possibility of her having been pregnant and delivering while comatose, they might think she was crazy. Or they might peg her as the embittered, deserted wife, snatching at straws, wanting to get back at her wealthy ex-husband. But she'd reached the point where none of that mattered now.

She stubbed her toe and hit her shoulder on the branch of an aspen tree. Wet leaves cascaded around her. She accidentally jerked Beamer's lead, but the dog did not stop. Nick was there instantly, steadying her, giving Beamer a bit more slack in the lead.

"I can't imagine training a new dog to do all this, let alone teaching a handler," she told him.

"It's a partnership that kicks in at a certain point. They learn each other's habits, and the intensity of the quest bonds them. The handler has to stay in charge and yet let the dog do his part, too. Okay, looks like he's taking us back to the cabin. Hold him here and let me look inside first. Tell him to *s-t-a-y*."

"Beamer, stay!"

"Don't shout. Just use a low, steady voice. Besides, the woods might have ears, and I don't mean deer and squirrels."

So he was feeling it, too, she thought, that something was wrong or that something living — even evil — was out here somewhere.

She watched Nick produce one of his father's old carpentry hammers from his jacket pocket and hold it ready as he pushed the door inward, then looked behind it.

"Oh, yeah," he said, "Seymour or someone was here Saturday night. I see a few rose petals from one rose that's been ripped to shreds."

"But there were a dozen of them on the deck. Who buys thirteen roses?"

"Either the florist was selling a baker's dozen, or the guy's intentionally giving you a so-called unlucky number," he said as she followed him to the door. "You like puzzles, so try to puzzle that one out."

She saw Beamer wasn't budging without permission. That was all right, because the cabin gave her the creeps. She peeked in to see a single rose had been beaten to death.

Its petals were strewn all over and its broken stem, which looked as if it had been trampled, lay on the floor.

"There's a lot of anger here," Nick said, his voice a whisper.

She nodded. "I wish we could get the police to ID the blood type or get DNA off the thorns, if he broke the stem with his hands," she said. "But I know better. Sometimes you can't even get a restraining order until there's an actual threat of physical violence, and I don't think a massacre of roses counts. I just hope it is Seymour who was here. IBs usually seem like personalities who are all bravado but not much action. If only Colorado licensed and sanctioned P.I.s and IBs, I could file a complaint against him, but we're still the unregulated Wild West in that regard."

She realized she was rambling, but it helped to talk to Nick. He put a hand on her arm. "Let's see where Beamer takes us from this cabin, because I don't think Seymour or Getz parked a vehicle down by the house. Maybe we can find more of Getz's X-treme tracks, but I doubt it with the rain. Here, scent Beamer with this wrapper again and tell him to you-know-what."

"If you weren't here would he even take orders —"

"Not orders, commands."

"Commands from me?"

"Tracker dogs are loyal to one master, but they are bright, working dogs, so yes. I think he's especially eager to please you because he sees us as friends, though I'm still the alpha male in the relationship. Maybe he's smart enough to realize I want us to be more than friends."

Despite the breeze, she felt herself blush. Both Nick and the dog were looking at her alertly, as if enjoying her emotional rush. What was wrong with her? No man had ever gotten to her so deeply with so little said. And she didn't want Nick to know that, at least not yet.

"Find, Beamer," she said, and let the eager Lab sniff the wrapper again. He went in a tight circle, then gave the lead a tug, and they were off again, uphill on the twisting path around Shadow Mountain.

Beamer led them higher to the location where the gravel road called Greening Drive became a narrow dirt one. At a tight turn-around point, they found lots of car and truck tracks, all churned together, but none that they could be sure were from Getz's bike. Only two footprints stood out: one from a running shoe, another of a Western-style boot heel. Tara and Nick were both out of breath in the thin air, and Beamer was panting with his tongue out.

"Whoever it was probably got in his car or truck here," Nick said, walking around a mud puddle. "But since your partner got us this far, give that lucky dog a scratch behind the ears again. Praise him, but no baby talk. Once they are out of puppyhood, I always teach that as part of respecting the dog."

Baby talk, she thought. They needed to have some talk about a baby.

As she scratched his ears, Beamer wagged his tail and looked ecstatic, almost as if she'd dumped an entire sack of dog food in front of him. It was amazing how hard he worked for some TLC and a few kind words. "Good dog, Beamer. You are a handsome, smart, good boy."

"I know I'd work hard for praise and petting like that," Nick said. "I think we're at the end of our line for now," he added with another glance into the trees and both ways on the narrow road. "Let's go up on Big Rock and rest before we head back down."

Big Rock was a massive stone outcrop from which they could view the entire valley between Black and Shadow Mountains. They climbed up carefully, making sure the dog didn't slip.

"Spectacular!" Nick said, looking at her, then back out over the broad panorama of sites. To their left, toward the north, they could see distant Denver. On a clear day like this, Pike National Forest could be seen to their right beyond and above the little town of Bailey. Nick sighed. "I can't tell you how many times I thought of this view when I was in the Hindu Kush Mountains in Afghanistan."

"Did you get homesick?"

"I tried to keep on task, stay busy, do my duty. It wasn't reasonable to get down over what I couldn't have right then."

That was him in a nutshell, she thought: duty and rationality. But there were chinks in that tough armor. They sat side by side on a slight rise of the rock, as if it were a natural seat made for them. Tara looked back up over her shoulder to be certain no rock could roll down on them. No, no way.

Still panting slightly, Beamer lay down beside her instead of Nick. That touched her deeply. Did this wonderful dog think he belonged to her instead of Nick now?

"There's something I've been wanting to tell you," she said in a rush, afraid she'd lose her courage. Her voice broke. "Something I only learned four days ago, a few hours before you got home. It's been haunting me since."

His big head snapped around toward her. "Claire said you'd been to see a doctor that day. You're not ill?"

Blinking back tears, she shook her head. "It was a regular checkup. I hadn't had a full physical, except by a clinic doctor, for about three years, with the coma and all. Nick, I know what I'm going to tell you might sound crazy, but I got a second opinion — a third, actually," she added, not wanting to explain everything about Jennifer right now. She knew of no other way to get this shocking news out but to tell him the bottom line.

"Nick," she said, bracing herself for his reaction, "my two new doctors — they said I showed signs that I'd had a child."

He looked confused. "You had a child, but hadn't told them?"

"No, sorry. That's not what I mean. To my knowledge, I have never had a child, but then there was that long coma. I — I don't want to go into the details of my broken marriage, but I was on birth control pills when Clay's attack caused my coma. Still, one doctor said that the pill is not one-hundred-percent effective. There are even some contraband ones that are duds. Of course, it's rare that someone delivers a baby while comatose, but I'm starting to believe that has to be what happened."

"But wouldn't your husband's family have told you? Or could they have done that and you forgot, when you were still coming out of the coma?" Frowning, he fumbled for words.

"Maybe they wanted to spare me — or just be sure I didn't make waves for how they handled it. I don't know. The Lohans are a breed unto themselves and are, evidently, not to be trusted." Rhythmically hitting her fists on her knees, she plunged on. "Nick, I'm going to investigate what happened to my child. I have to do this. He or she must have died, and Laird evidently did not want to add to my woes. He was leaving me anyway. I called my former doctor, whom I'd had for years — once a good friend — and she said there is no way I was pregnant. She visited me twice before she left for California, while I was still in a coma, and she said I was not pregnant nor had I been. But the Lohans could have bought her off. I can't let it go — it won't let me go . . ."

"You need to just ask Laird, face-to-face."

"He's living outside Seattle. He's only been communicating with me through Lohan lawyers, which is fine with me. The last person in the world I want to talk to is Laird Lohan — and his father's the next-to-last. I might have been comatose, but, one way or the other, they'd probably make it all my fault."

"But you like and trust Laird's mother? And you said she didn't show up at Red Rocks and is now in the same clinic you were in?"

"Yes," she said, nodding. "She was the first one I wanted to ask but I can and will track down others. I do know the clinic and its expansive grounds well. If I could just get in there to see her."

"Get in there how? I need to leave this afternoon to meet with the people who made me that great job offer at Fort Bragg. I was hoping you had somewhere to go, too, or could just lock yourself in the house while I was gone."

"I'm not making my — *your* home a forti-fied camp! I'm just going to talk to a few people, that's all. For starters, the clinic's groundskeeper. Maybe my former sister-in-law. I'll be fine."

"Famous last words," he muttered, reach-ing over to take her hand. He unwrapped her tight fingers and stroked her palm.

"Thanks for not saying I'm crazy. I did research this possibility. It's rare but women

187

have delivered babies while comatose."

"Babies that died?"

"Ones that lived, too, but that's impossible in my case. Legally, they would have had to tell me that. Laird was so anxious to have kids, he might even have wanted to stay married, if I was the mother of his baby. It was a cardinal sin to him that I wanted to wait to have a family until we settled our differences. Laird Lohan is into creating a dynasty, and his brother Thane is three kids ahead of him," she added, gently pulling her hand back and glaring out toward distant Denver. She crossed her arms as if hugging herself, her hands thrust under her armpits.

"So, if he'd wanted to keep you, would you have wanted that — another chance?" he asked, leaning closer again.

"No. His leaving me and leaving the area are about the only good things to come from my coma. I want children, but not with him."

"If I can help in any way — you know what I mean."

Their gazes met and held. "You already have helped," she said with a deep sigh as she leaned back, stiff-armed, not breaking eye contact with him.

When they shifted closer together, Beamer

188

scooted over and put his muzzle on Tara's thigh, right next to Nick's big hand.

Veronica awoke to see Jordan sitting at her bedside, going through a sheaf of papers. Had he said her name, or was that the drugs again?

"Ah, you're back among the living," he said, putting the papers aside. "I thought it best to let you sleep. We've got to get that Vicodin out of your system again, darling, let alone the other sedatives the doctor used to calm you down." He leaned forward and took her hand. She was grateful her arms were no longer restrained. "You really don't recall taking the pills again? I found them several places in your suite and in the sunroom."

Was she going mad? Had she somehow gotten back on drugs? Was she lying to herself or losing her memory? She could not bear to believe what she had feared at first — that Jordan was lying about everything.

"I brought you a new robe, imported silk," he told her, and lifted a golden, embroidered garment from the foot of her bed with his free hand. "Flowers fade, but not my love for you, no matter what."

She wet her lips; he instantly dropped the

robe and released her hand so that he could lift a glass of water to her lips. As she drank, he pushed a bedside button to lift her bed so she could more easily sit up, then took the glass from her. That was how attentive he'd been that last night they'd dined together, she thought, whenever that was. She remembered Tara telling her how kind Laird had been in the weeks before her coma — and he'd deserted her while she was desperately ill.

Drat, Veronica thought, if she remembered that, surely she'd recall taking Vicodin again. She used to buy them through her maid, Rita, who got them from her brother, but Jordan had never known that. To save Rita's job, she hadn't told him. Could Rita have put Vicodin in the food or the coffee on her breakfast tray that last morning or the day before? But just because Rita had been her source for the drugs, the woman wouldn't want her dependent again, not after she'd covered for her with Jordan.

"What day is this?" she asked.

"Monday, September tenth, around noon. You've been resting for about forty-eight hours, so perhaps it's time to get to work again with rehab. Thank God, we have the best of facilities and can care for you here."

"I wouldn't mind working with Elin Johansen."

"I think you need some basic counseling and group therapy before that. I hear she popped in to see you."

"Oh, yes, that's right. I — it was nice of her, but I was rather out of it."

He seemed to be waiting for her to say something else. When she didn't, he told her, "By the way, Tara called the house. You were evidently going to meet her. Is there anything you want me to pass on to her?"

"If I can have visitors, I'd like to see her."

"Not for a while, I think, or, at least, family only, and she's no longer that," he said, standing. "Thane will stop by tomorrow, and Laird sends his love." He bent over to kiss her forehead. "I told them you had a little relapse but that they're not to worry. I assured them you will work hard and go along with doctor's orders."

"Jordan," she said, summoning the remnants of her courage, "shouldn't we tell Tara about Laird?"

"Were you intending to?" he asked, frowning. "Tara's busy rebuilding her life, she told me, back to that social work she does with her P.I. firm, and rearing her friend's child. I even sensed she might have a new man in her life, the child's uncle. Remember, darling, we decided, after all she's been through, it was best to cause her no more pain."

"But doesn't she have a right to know, especially because she thinks Jennifer is in Los Angeles?"

"Why should she have to deal with what she might consider a friend's betrayal? Until she's really back on her feet and gets more objective distance from the past, you'd do her a favor by your silence. We're not lying to her, just protecting her. Besides, do you really think any woman would get over losing a man like Laird, not to mention forfeiting the power and wealth of the Lohans? Tara's been given a generous settlement, and we made a family decision to let sleeping dogs lie. So that's that."

11

"Nick, thanks for driving in to meet us," John Radcliffe said, thrusting out his big hand. The white-haired U.S. Army major was attired like a civilian businessman. "Damn, we had no idea the Denver airport was so far out of town. Sorry if we're late. Can't stand people who are late. This is my aide, First Lieutenant Garrett Granton."

Neither man wore a sign of their branch of service or their ranks. They shook hands, then followed the hostess into the restaurant and took the corner table Nick had reserved. He was really uptight and not just because Tara was out on her own. He knew these men could put a lot of pressure on him to move to North Carolina immediately, and he wasn't quite ready. Claire, too. After his being home only four days, he and Tara needed more time together before he could possibly ask her to move across the country with them. She'd never go with the problems she'd be leaving, nor could he desert her. But he was really starting to realize that Claire needed her, even more than the child needed him.

"I give you credit for putting in time over there," the tall, ramrod-straight African-American lieutenant told Nick when they were seated. "I'd trade my stateside briefcase for another deployment with my old PSG-1 semiauto anytime."

A former sniper was an aide to a veteran Delta Force commander? Hell, that fit. Nick knew they both had their sights set on getting him under contract again.

They ordered steaks and made more small talk. Both men were assigned to The Ranch, the Delta Force training area at Fort Bragg, North Carolina, but they were frequently in and out of Iraq and Afghanistan. Major John Radcliffe, a crusty veteran who was still in fantastic shape at forty-something, had overseen the insertion of the Delta team Nick had been with. This 'old man,' as the D-boys called anyone in charge, also had a string of degrees in psychology. Nick kept waiting for them to get down to business. Over the first course, they did.

"We realize you left one tough situation and returned to another," Radcliffe said, salting his salad while focusing his laser gaze

194

on Nick.

Nick almost told them he couldn't leave Tara right now, but decided not to. What she was facing didn't compare to the life-and-death situations they had all been through, at least in scope. Maybe his feelings for her and Claire made someone spying on her seem worse than it was; maybe the rock that almost flattened Tara was strictly wrong-place, wrong-time. Had he made things worse for her by being paranoid? He wanted to phone her again, but he'd told her to call his cell if she needed him in any way.

"So how're you adjusting?"

"I'm handling things well," Nick insisted. "Of course, I'm more worried about how my niece is adjusting to her parents' loss, but — do you know all that?" he asked, his fork halfway to his mouth as Radcliffe kept nodding.

"This new dog search program is important to me, so you are, too," Radcliffe admitted. "Let's just say I'm current with your dossier."

"I had thought Claire could benefit from a change of locale, but she's very attached to Tara, the woman she's had living with her."

Radcliffe nodded again. "Any chance, if

you moved to the Fort Bragg area for a while, you could bring both of them?" Radcliffe asked. "I'm not suggesting something permanent, but having a familiar caretaker for the child could be a bridge over troubled water, so to speak."

"It has crossed my mind, but I haven't brought it up yet. Tara could move her business for a while, I guess, though I have no right to ask her without having something more than mothering Claire in mind. But I've got to admit, she's much better with the child than I am. Neither of us would like to leave this area — I'm a Coloradan at heart — but a stint to train more tracker dogs would be doing my duty to my country. I just don't want that to conflict with my duty to my niece."

"I've got two young kids," Garrett put in, buttering a roll. "The Carolinas make for great living. Families are in and out of Bragg all the time. They stay a few years, leave their house, move back to their home bases — you know what I mean. We could facilitate your finding housing for three instead of two."

"Tara loves Claire very much, but it would still be a lot to ask."

"I've people who could show her the ropes there, introduce your little girl and Tara to schools, shopping centers," Garrett went on. "More trail dogs are needed fast, not just the bomb sniffers we've had for years. Training them on site in the mountains must have been tough, but we wanted to try it, and you are a mountain man."

"There was a cost," Nick said, frowning. "Too damn steep a price. Both KIAs were young, good men."

"Ambushes are a big part of this war," Radcliff said. "No one blamed you."

"*I* blamed me!"

Both men stopped eating. "Frankly," Radcliffe said, leaning across the table toward Nick and speaking in a low, soothing voice, "that's one thing I wanted to ascertain — how you felt about that loss. You're also dealing with family losses. Two family members died when you weren't there — two comrades when you were right there. Nick, I know you turned down counseling after the debriefing. Is this still affecting your day-to-day? Listen to me. The D-boys don't blame you. They blame themselves for not giving you more training, just like I bet you're down on yourself because those dogs weren't quite ready."

As if they were a tag team, Garrett jumped in. "You know the D-boys pride themselves on making things happen. And they bravely face the fact that the price of failure can be death. They accept that."

"Yeah, when *they* screw up, but not when it's someone else's failure."

"Nick," Radcliffe said, his voice calm but strong, "that was a tough day. All of you were without sleep except for field naps in a kill zone we didn't know was there. Guys with one hell of a lot more combat training than you came home with PTSD."

Post-traumatic stress disorder, Nick thought. The scourge of the modern army in terrorist times, a mental disorder Nick refused to accept as his own diagnosis. After all, he wasn't a soldier. He'd been there to train dogs, not kill the enemy. He'd carried a gun only in self-defense. And he'd come home intact, at least physically.

Realizing he was slumping, Nick forced himself to sit up straight again. For the first time, he felt back in military mode, though he'd always acknowledged the gap between him and the others. "Sir, the dog turned the wrong way, evidently following some cross-scent. I suspected it, but I let him go a little ways with the men following, because I was going to use it as an example of what not to do. And then the RPG hit and all hell broke loose. After that, I did okay, as long as we could see the enemy. But when they were just lurking out there, it really made me nuts."

"I know. Believe me, I know," Radcliffe said.

"You were doing your duty, man," Garrett added. "And that's all any of us can do. So, can we rely on you to at least consider training more dogs? It's a chance to train them completely before they're sent over this time."

Nick sat back in his chair. He hadn't touched his salad and here came their server with the steaks. "To tell the truth, though I know you can't swing it," he told them, "the dogs would be better off being trained in this area with the mountains, though we'd never approximate the heat or dust — or danger."

"Here's my card," Radcliffe said, as a sixteen-ounce T-bone steak and smothered baked potato were set in front of him. He extended a business card across the table to Nick. "Those phone numbers will get me day or night if you want to talk — hopefully, so you can tell me to set you up at Fort Bragg ASAP. Also," he went on, as Nick took the card and two other plates with big steaks appeared, "I want you to know that some very powerful people appreciate your work and are willing to almost double your salary if you will move east to train the dogs for us."

Nick stared at Radcliffe. If he agreed to their offer, he could help compensate Tara for the move, if she'd go.

"Is my benefactor on the Fort Bragg staff or someone in D.C.?" he asked.

"I'm not at liberty to say. Let's just leave it at this — a powerful and patriotic American knows the best interests of others can be in his best interest, too."

Tara parked her truck but didn't get out right away. For some reason, she was extremely reluctant — scared, actually — about getting out and walking up to the house. Yet there was nothing to fear from Jim Manning, the longtime head caretaker of the extensive grounds of the Mountain Manor Clinic and, according to Elin Johansen, now the caretaker of the Lohan estate in Kerr Gulch. Tara wasn't sure why she didn't just park in front of his house, but she had the strangest feeling she was being watched, and not just at home. If someone was following her car, she didn't want to get anyone else, like Jim, in trouble.

She tried to throw off the déjà vu feeling of unease that clung to her like a wet, cold sheet. She was relieved that Claire had been happy to stay at her friend Charlee's house after school and that Charlee's mom, Heather, had been such a good friend. Nick had phoned Tara before his business lunch, but not since. If he got home before her, he could read the note she'd left on Beamer's collar and go get Claire. All that planning felt as if they were parents trying to keep up with their child's schedule. She was going to feel doubly devastated when he took Claire and left.

She finally convinced herself to approach Jim's house. After all, he'd been kind and considerate when she was recovering at the clinic. He'd made certain that nearby snowy paths were cleared for her first forays outside on a walker and then a cane; he'd given her little nature talks to get her brain cells working again. And there were the early purple columbines that had appeared at her cabin door from time to time. Jim was about sixty, but had a boyish face. A childhood accident of some sort had given him a permanent limp, but he got around on a golf cart to oversee the planting, weeding, raking and cutting in the woodsy atmosphere of the clinic. He'd never married — he was married to his work of taming the wilds, Veronica had once said.

Claire hoped he was home. She recalled

he went to work at the clinic at first light. Just after lunch he usually went home to tend his own yard, then returned to work until sunset. She hoped she was hitting his schedule about right. As she walked to his driveway, then up toward the small stone house, she saw his truck was there.

His small yard took her breath away, for it was planted with mountain wildflowers of every kind: blue-bonnets and lupine, Aspen daisies, and an array of others she couldn't name. The place reminded her that Veronica once said Jim created paintings like those by Claude Monet, but alive and "fraught with fragrance."

Tara didn't even have to knock. As she lifted her fist, the door opened as if by magic.

"Ms. Kinsale, what a surprise!" Jim extended his hand for a hearty shake. His leathery face crinkled into a web of lines as he smiled, showing uneven teeth. "Do you have something for me to take Mrs. Lohan? She's back at the clinic and restricted," he added, lowering his voice as if someone would hear.

"Actually, I wanted to ask you something else. I heard she's been readmitted. Have you seen her?"

"No, ma'am, but then, I didn't see hide

nor hair of you either, for months. If you want me to landscape something, the Lohans got me pretty booked up. Been loyal to them for years, and they treat me great. Now, where's my manners? Come on inside. Got a few minutes till I head back. You know me, set in my ways."

Tara stepped inside a tiny, flagstone foyer. The living-dining area was filled with old furniture and flowers, crocks of them. She could see, through a double sliding glass door, that the backyard fell steeply away.

"Want to look out back?" he asked her and led the way.

His back deck was on tall stilts above rock gardens and a profusion of flowers running riot in what she'd call an English garden. It was so late in the growing season that most of them looked leggy. He walked her down the stairs. Bright bushes with flame-red leaves grew under and around the deck.

"They get good morning sun here," he told her.

"It's beautiful, Jim, all of it. You certainly have the touch. How kind you were to me when I was recovering. That moved me deeply."

"You had a hard time of it, in more ways than one," he said, not looking at her but off into the distance, down the steep spill of flowers to the road below. "Glad to help. Glad to help any Lohan."

"Which I'm not any longer, but you could help me now. I'm going to level with you about why I'm here. Can I ask you first if you actually saw me anytime during my coma, from late May of 2004 through April of 2005?"

"Saw you?" he said, shifting from one foot to the other. "Naw, I'm not medical staff."

"I realize that, but you're everywhere on the clinic grounds. A glimpse through a window, an overheard conversation . . . Jim, I know this might sound a bit off the wall, but a doctor has informed me I was pregnant when I began my coma — that I must have had a baby while I was comatose. Did you hear or see anything that might make you think that could be true?"

Wide-eyed, he looked at her before his gaze darted away again. He wiped his palms on his jeans. "Word of that would have gotten out for sure," he said, shaking his head. "Can't be."

"So you never even caught a glimpse of me?"

"Only that night late in February in all the snow, when you got out."

"I got out? Out to where? It was early April before I really woke up from the coma. Are you sure it was February?"

"You must have come to for a while, 'cause I found you in at least four feet of snow just outside the chapel. See, Mrs. Lohan was inside playing the organ real loud. She came out with Elin Johansen. The three of us got you back to your cabin, but mostly I carried you."

"And I — I wasn't extremely pregnant, because you would have known."

"I may be a lifelong bachelor, ma'am, but I would have known that. You were in just a nightgown and a robe, not even shoes. You left some bloody tracks in the snow. Your feet and legs were scratched and cut from walking through bushes or thorns, but it could have been much worse. You could have lost some toes to frostbite or froze to death."

Tara shuddered, reaching in the dark for those memories. Icy cold — she felt icy cold right now. She stared at the flame bushes all around them, seeing instead her crimson blood in the snow. "Did I say anything?"

"I think you said you were lost. Mumbling, not making much sense. It was a while ago, but I think you said something about looking for the hiding place."

"Hiding place? They never told me I'd been out like that," she whispered, leaning back against the tall post that held up the deck. Her legs were still shaking. She was trying so hard to remember that her head hurt. "And I have no memory of that, even if I was walking and talking. No wonder they sedated me and weaned me off meds slowly after that. Jim, is there anything else you can tell me about any of this? Maybe an exact date?"

"Not rightly sure," he muttered, looking down the hill. "Only that it was in the dead of winter."

When Nick called Tara about his job offer, that further upset her, because he said they were really pushing him to accept. Tara phoned Claire, who was happily watching CDs with Charlee at her house, and told her she was going to stop to see an old friend, though that was a bit of a lie. Her former sister-in-law, Thane Lohan's wife, Susanne, had never been much of a friend. The woman had seen her as competition for the affection and fortune of Jordan and Veronica Lohan. If the family knew that she had been pregnant and lost the child, wouldn't Susanne want to rub it in?

Just as Tara and Laird used to, Thane's family lived only a few blocks from the senior Lohans. Tara had called Susanne to ask if she could pop by to see the children, whom she and Thane were always willing to show off, their winning cards in the game of Lohan dynasty poker. At first, Susanne declined Tara's offer to visit, saying that the children were at lessons of various kinds after school. She acquiesced when Tara said she'd like to come over anyway. Maybe she was testing Tara or wanted to surprise her, because Tara was certain she'd heard kids' voices in the background. Maybe Susanne had meant they were going to their lessons, but, as Tara remembered it, mother hen Susanne always took great pride in personally delivering the children to their various destinations, including plenty of grandparent visits.

Thane Lohan's house was only slightly larger than the house Tara had once shared with Laird. Of timber and stone, it boasted a huge rec room, a gourmet kitchen overlooking a great room and dining hall and an indoor pool pavilion. As she got out of her truck, she recalled the driveway had a snowmelt system.

Looking as striking as ever in beige linen cropped pants and a jade silk shirt, Susanne greeted her at the door with an air kiss and something approaching an air hug. "It's so good to see you, Tara! Isn't it sad about

Mother?"

"I can't believe she got back on anything like that after her first struggle. Was it alcohol or sedatives?"

"Big, bad Vicodin again. Thane couldn't believe it. Come on in, then. Sorry the children aren't here."

As ever, walking in, they passed the two-story wall of numerous, ornately framed color photos of Lawrence, Lacey and Lindsey, all under ten years of age, formally posed, nothing casual or natural looking. Tara noted that one big picture had been taken off the wall. Its hook had been removed, but the slight discoloration on the woven wallpaper around it suggested where it had hung. Tara recalled that spot had always held the annual Lohan three-generation photo. She wondered if it had been taken down so she didn't have to see Laird in it without her. No, that would be too thoughtful for Susanne. She'd be more likely to have it on the front door.

"Sit and have some coffee," she said, indicating a tray she had already laid out on the glass coffee table, which was surrounded by an oversize, horseshoe-shaped, ivory leather sofa. "I know you would have loved to have seen the children. I'm going to have them make get-well, we-miss-you cards for their grandmother the moment they get back. So, why have you graced me with a visit after all this time? Oh, I know it works both ways, but three children and a husband and social duties — well, you remember some of that, don't you? I often wonder what you can recall."

"Too much sometimes and not enough other times," Tara said.

Susanne shifted in her seat as if she were poised on something hot or sharp. "It's so lovely," Susanne said, pouring two cups of coffee from a sterling silver carafe, "that you have a daughter of sorts now."

Why, Tara scolded herself, did everything Susanne Lohan say annoy her? Even when she was playing the perfect hostess, smiling and chatting, it was as if a chilly mountain breeze blew from her.

"It's been a wonderful experience to have Claire, especially after my personal loss," she told Susanne.

"You mean losing Laird."

As she took a sip of coffee, Tara leveled a long look at Susanne over her coffee cup. The woman couldn't sit still. Which meant nothing too dire, of course. Lowering her cup on her knees, Tara said, "I mean Laird and the other."

"The other? Oh, little Claire's mother."

Susanne so obviously heaved a sigh that Tara almost reached out to shake her. Why had she seemed relieved to come up with that? Was there something else she didn't want to reveal?

"Claire's mother, yes, but my other loss, too," Tara said as the awkward silence stretched out between them.

"Whatever are you talking about?" Susanne's cup rattled in its saucer and she put it down. "Tara, I hope you didn't come here so we could play Twenty Questions. Are you fishing for answers about how Laird's doing?"

"Knowing Laird, he's doing just fine. Hale, hearty, happy and hellishly self-centered." The words burst from her. She'd realized she was hurt and upset and angry, but she hadn't come here to unload on Susanne, for all that. Tara put her cup down, too, and rose to leave. She couldn't stay another minute. This was a bad idea, all around.

"You know, don't you?" Susanne asked.

Rather than ask what she meant, Tara decided to take a risk. "Yes, Susanne. I know."

"It just happened. You can't blame them," she blurted, her hands fluttering in her lap. "You didn't really want to devote yourself to Laird anyway — I could never understand that, and neither could she. I know you feel betrayed, but don't take it out on me! So how did you find out about him and Jennifer?"

"Is he bankrolling her now? He tried to buy her off, didn't he?" she demanded, before the real import of the words sank in.

"What?" Susanne cried, clasping her hands around her neck as if she'd choke herself. "I thought you meant you learned that Laird married Jennifer DeMar, your doctor — that's all."

Tara sank back onto the sofa. "That's all?" she heard herself echo. For a moment, all the fight drained out of her. She felt like a fool. Betrayed but stupid. Laird had bought Jen off, all right. He'd done more than bankroll her to keep her silence about a dead baby — he'd rolled her in the hay!

She'd called Jen more than once since she'd been out of the coma, and the witch hadn't let on. Everything fell together now, how Jen had politely tried to distance herself . . . even the man's voice in the background on the phone. And no one had told her. Or had Veronica tried to? *Jim's not lost, Angel? Jen's not lost?* No, not lost at all, but with Laird, whom she'd always had her eye on and now had her claws in.

"Tara, I'm sorry to spring it on you like that, but I thought you meant you'd figured out that Jen's not in Los Angeles, but Seattle."

Jen's not lost, Angel . . . Jen's not in Los Angeles?

Tara had always felt a certain sense of triumph in putting puzzles together, but this one had turned tragic. She stood up and walked toward the front door with Susanne scurrying behind her. Tara was so shocked, so hurt, she wanted to strike out. The Lohans might claim they were trying to protect her fragile feelings about a lost child, about her health, but it was all to cover for Laird and his new wife. If the first wife couldn't deliver a live child, maybe the second one would.

"I hope you won't lose Lohan points for having told me about Laird and Jen," Tara clipped out. "You'd better hope she doesn't have a boatload of sons to split your and your children's cut of the Lohan fortune. My good fortune is that I'm out of here, in more ways than one."

Before Susanne could get to the door, Tara opened it, then slammed it. But she knew what she'd just said wasn't true. One way or the other, she still had Lohan doors to kick open and not just about Jen and Laird.

12

It seemed so natural for Tara to hug not only Claire but Nick when she got home. She was still shaking.

"What's the matter?" he whispered.

"Later."

"No, now. Claire will be okay with Beamer for a sec." He turned around and raised his voice, "Honey, will you play with Beamer since he's been alone all day? I need to talk to Aunt Tara for a minute."

"Oh, sure," Claire said with a little smile. "Can we go outside?"

"Not right now. Stay in here, and we'll be right back."

They went into Tara's office and closed the door. Her phone message light was blinking, but that was not unusual. She ignored it.

"What happened?" he asked.

"Just a surprise — a shock. My former sister-in-law let spill that my former husband ran off to Seattle with Jen DeMar, my ob-gyn and once-upon-a-time friend. They're married. I'm assuming that's what Veronica was trying to tell me — Jen's not in Los Angeles. She probably thought if she told me that indirectly, her husband couldn't blame her and I could track her down."

"They ran off together while you were comatose?" he asked as he put his hands on her shoulders as if to prop her up. "Hell, it sounds like they deserve each other. Did the caretaker say anything about that?"

"No, but he said that sometime in February, when I was supposedly in the depths of the coma, he found me wandering the clinic grounds in the snow. And that I told him I was looking for a hiding place."

"It's not much, compared to keeping the lid on a secret pregnancy, but maybe the clinic's trying to cover up that you got out when you were under their care, or that you were not actually comatose as long as they claimed."

Her head snapped up. "They did use sedatives freely there. They said it was to delay my coming out of the coma too soon to recover well. I've always accepted that, but does that make sense? Maybe it was to protect Laird and his lover, give them time to clear Colorado — or time for me to recover from a miscarriage or bad birth outcome."

"Did your sister-in-law say anything about your having been pregnant?"

"No, but I didn't ask her directly. I was going to, but when she blurted out about Laird and Jen, I lost it and walked out."

"I can imagine."

"Besides, maybe she didn't know everything. Maybe I was lucky to have stumbled on that much. By their acts of omission — not telling me about delivering a child — the Lohans could all be lying. Nick, I just don't know what to think. Maybe after my baby died, Laird hated me even more, so he turned to Jen . . . oh, I don't know, but I'm going to find out."

She burst into tears. He pulled her to him. "Sorry," she murmured against his shoulder, trying to get control. "I — if you and Claire leave soon, I don't know what I'll do. Except," she said as she pulled away from him and got a tissue from the drawer, "I'm not letting up on the Lohans until I get more answers. I'm going to get in to see Veronica. I don't care if they have that place locked up as tight as Fort Knox. If that doesn't get me answers, I'll go to Jordan and to Laird. If I bore a child, I have every right to know all about it — whatever pain it causes Laird or me. I have every right to visit my child's grave over the years!"

"Of course you do. If they've kept something like that from you, it's wrong — warped."

"Somehow that sounds just like them."

After dinner, when Claire had been put to bed and Nick was walking Beamer outside, Tara finally got some time in her office. She checked her e-mail and was relieved to see she had no return messages from Marv Seymour. Good, she thought. He must literally have gotten the message. But had he been their lurker?

She also checked online to try to trace Dietmar Getz's movements. His Web site stated that he'd come in fourth in the race where they'd confronted him. His next race listed was in Utah next weekend. That could be to throw her off, of course, because he was still the front-runner for her stalker. And that left him time to still be hanging around here. She typed up a quick list of why she felt Getz was more likely than Seymour to be after her. She was going to leave keeping an eye on Rick Whetstone to Nick.

She turned to her phone messages. The machine was still blinking behind her and she hadn't thought to listen to them first. Two were from clients desperate for updates, one from a possible new client, whom she'd call tomorrow, and the fourth one —

"Ms. Kinsale, Jim Manning here. There's one thing I thought I'd better tell you. I forgot about this. I think the reason you might be mixed up about your having a baby — 'sides the fact you seemed pretty out of your head that night in the snow, and you know how some of those meds they give out screw up people's minds — is there was a rumor kinda like that."

Tara bolted straight out of her chair. She leaned on her desk, staring at the answering machine.

"I mean," Jim's message went on, "not a rumor about you, but you probably overheard it and got mixed up. I heard a nurse say that people hear things while in a coma sometimes. So, anyway, I heard from a custodian sometime that winter that a wealthy patient had delivered a child that died somewheres on clinic grounds, and the clinic wanted it all kept hush-hush. I didn't see nothing myself, but you know them and their clients — no publicity. 'Sides, the clinic could get themselves sued, I s'pose, 'cause the baby died. You know, like they didn't take the person to a regular hospital in time. Anyhow, thought you should know that's prob'ly where you got so mixed up . . ."

Tara sank back in her chair, put her face on her knees and grabbed handfuls of hair. *You got so mixed up . . .* That could be part of it. Maybe she did overhear something like that. After all, she thought she recalled hearing organ music in her coma, and now she knew why. So maybe she thought she heard something about a baby. But what about two doctors telling her she'd been pregnant, possibly to full term, and had had a vaginal delivery? And why did those last two words haunt her? Had she heard someone tell her she was going to have a *vaginal delivery?* Or was she going completely crazy?

She went to the front door to call Nick in to hear the phone message, but she heard voices. A woman's shrill tones? Someone shouting, as if she were hearing her own inner screams.

Tara saw a car had pulled up in the driveway. A woman got out. It was dark, but in the wan glow of houselights, Tara could see spiky blond hair and the glitter of something bright on her back. And Nick was holding her, or at least, the stranger was hugging him.

His arm around the woman, who leaned against him as if she could barely stand, Nick brought her up toward the house; they went in the door to the lower level. Tara closed the front door and hurried down to meet them.

"What is it?" she asked him. "Who —"

"Marcie Goulder, a friend of Rick Whetstone's. You know, who I visited last Friday. She says Rick committed suicide this morning."

Tara's hands flew to her mouth; she gasped. "That's terrible! I'm so sorry," she told the woman, who merely nodded. *But,* Tara mouthed to Nick behind Marcie's back, *why is she here?*

Nick just shook his head and led Marcie up the stairs into the great room. Tara noticed she was really built and might be pretty; her face was so ravaged with grief that Tara couldn't tell. Her running mascara had made dark half-moons under each eye. She wore tight jeans thrust into boots and a denim jacket embroidered with a starburst of gold and silver sequins on the back. One of the threads had broken, and an occasional sequin dribbled off as if she left a trail of glitter. Nick sat her on the sofa where she put her head into her hands and moaned.

"Marcie has no family, and Rick had only Clay," he told Tara. "Since I had stopped by to see him and was family, she thought I should know. She tracked me down through my last name in the Conifer phone book."

Tara was thinking that the woman could have called, but the poor thing was obviously distraught. In Marcie's condition, it was amazing that she'd found her way safely way up here in the dark. Tara had comforted many bereft women, but this one had loved the brother of the man who had killed her best friend, Claire's mother — and Nick's sister — so why did he have to be so solicitous?

"I'll get her some water," Tara volunteered.

"Yes, that would be good," he said. "And Beamer's still outside. The crazy dog jumped in her car, so I closed him in there rather than letting him run loose."

Tara brought Marcie a glass of water, and, with a nod of thanks, she sipped it.

"Sorry to crack up like this," she choked out. "I just couldn't stand being alone in the place where he did it. He overdosed on pills I didn't know he had. No warning. I thought things were good. He was earning money, we had plans. Left me a note on my computer, which the police took — the whole PC, I mean. And it's brand new. Gotta check out suicides, I guess."

"Yes," Tara told her, "that's standard procedure. But if he left a note, they'll just take a look at the computer, then give it back."

"I read the note," Marcie said with a sniff. "It said he was gonna kill himself, but not exactly why. Just overwhelmed, nothing to live for. Damn, ain't that a kick in my pants. They're gonna do an autopsy — regulation, they said. Hate the idea of that. Ugh!" She took a big swig of water. "I blame myself in a way, 'cause I had no idea — no idea he was so shook to do something like that. Listen, I'm sorry to bust in like this, but I had nowhere else to go. Couldn't go to the L Branch where I work, not with everyone talking, and Nick seemed so nice when he dropped by."

At that, Tara decided to shelve her own quandary for a few minutes. Heartfelt feelings for hurting women stirred. She sat down beside Marcie and asked in a gentle voice, "Do you have anyone you'd like to call, even if they can't be here? Or do you have a pastor or church to —"

She shook her head hard; the spikes of

stiff white-blond hair hardly budged, but her hoop earrings bounced. "Came here from Santa Fe, met Rick. We hit it off — talked marriage too. But he was always moody and nervous. I don't know, maybe since something was wrong with his brother, it ran in the family."

Ran in the family, Tara thought. The Lohan family had circled the wagons, but there might be a way into what they knew. Family . . . then she remembered Beamer was outside. "We forgot Beamer," she told Nick.

"I'll go get him. Maybe you can fix Marcie something."

"How about some herbal tea and soda crackers?" Tara suggested.

"Oh, I couldn't eat. But if you got any hot chocolate mix, I'd like that. I'd love a stiff drink but I can't drink and drive, and I've gotta go home to that apartment, where I found him. . . ."

Tara and Nick looked at each other. She frowned; he narrowed his eyes and tipped his head. "You can stay here tonight if you want," he said. "I'll sleep up here on the couch, and you can have the run of my place in the lower level. But shouldn't you call the cops so they don't think you've taken off, in case they need you?"

"I can't thank you enough. I can't sleep

there, I know that. I'll call the officer who gave me his number and tell him I'm here. I gotta make a call to our — my — landlord after that. And I've got to call Clay tomorrow . . . sorry," she said with a loud sniff and blew her nose hard. "Didn't mean to mention him here, not after what he did."

"Be right back with Beamer," Nick said. "I've still got your key, Marcie. Beamer was really misbehaving, Tara, rubbing against her. He almost knocked her over. When he doesn't have his work collar on, he turns back into a spoiled pet."

"You've made a friend in Beamer," Tara told Marcie, as Nick went outside. "In the morning, after breakfast, when we get our girl — Nick's niece — off to school, we'll be sure you get back home safely."

"You've both been great. Is it okay if I use your bathroom? I'm — I'm a mess."

"Sure. Up those steps, first door on the right, then there's one downstairs, too. There are extra towels on the far rack. I can loan you a T-shirt to sleep in if you want. But one thing. If you see Claire in the morning, don't tell her why you're here, all right? Rick's her uncle, and she's already had some terrible losses. Rick might remind her of her father, Clay, and she's had nightmares about his coming back to hurt her. She even thought he was hiding up in the tree line above the house."

"No kidding," Marcie said, her bloodshot eyes widening. "Poor little thing. I sure sympathize with her now, having to live with something like that, losing someone in such an awful way."

And then it hit Tara. Maybe she had a devious mind because of all the terrible situations she'd heard of with her clients. Maybe it was Laird and Jen's betrayal that made her want to trust no one. But what if, through Rick, Clay had somehow gotten to this woman and hired her to snatch Claire again, or something even worse?

As Marcie took her purse and went up to use the bathroom across from Claire's bedroom door, Tara feared they'd made a terrible mistake to allow the woman to stay here tonight. Had they let a sort of Trojan horse into their safe haven?

Beamer interrupted her agonizing when he bounded into the room. He sniffed the floor and the couch, which Tara saw was dusted with a few gold and silver sequins. Then the lab hustled up the steps and sat outside the bathroom door until she called him and the dog came back downstairs.

"Nick," Tara said, keeping her voice low, "I'm sure she's telling the truth, but with

Claire so close here —"

"I was going to suggest you go online to read the local papers. Even though she said he killed himself this morning, it should be online by now. I'm thinking the same thing, since Rick mentioned that he had as much right to Claire as I did. But she's obviously distraught. And don't worry. The reason I'm going to be awake on this couch all night and she's downstairs is because I'll be between you and Claire, and her."

Nick and Tara were thankful their suspicions about Marcie were wrong. Nick, who muttered something at breakfast to Tara about being used to no sleep at night the past two years, said Marcie hadn't budged from the downstairs area, but he'd heard her pacing and sobbing at times. After Tara had verified that Rick Whetstone, brother of a "convicted murderer," had indeed "committed suicide in Evergreen on Monday morning," Tara had sat up half the night with Nick while they discussed Tara's problem. He didn't want her trying to get into the clinic without permission, but he admitted that Laird's running off with Jen De-Mar was another reason she couldn't trust her former husband for a straight answer about a possible dead child, even if she did phone him.

Marcie didn't even appear until Claire was off to school, and then she looked wan and subdued. "I should never have crashed in on you like that," she told them. "I can't thank you two enough for welcoming and tending to a stranger. You don't need to go back down the mountain with me. Your kindness and a little sleep got me settled down. And Beamer sure took to me. I guess it's 'cause I got cat hairs on me from the live-in pet at the L Branch. Well, back to real life today, back to being alone without the man I thought would work out. Back to getting over another big loss."

Tara's heart went out to the woman. She knew exactly how she felt.

13

Veronica Lohan paced the sitting room of her cabin at the clinic. Rain rattled against the roof and smeared itself down the windows. Not only was she feeling claustrophobic, but she thought walking — ten paces over and ten back — might be a good way to make the desire for those damned drugs leave her system. She must have been mad to take them again.

But she knew she wasn't mad. And that left only one conclusion. Someone had slipped the pills into her food or drink. It could be Rita, who had sold her the Vicodin for a pretty price when she truly was abusing drugs and alcohol. Perhaps she hoped to get her hooked again. Or, obviously, it could be someone else. Who that someone else might be scared her to death.

"Hello, darling," Jordan sang out as he came in the door. He didn't look a bit wet from the rain. The nurse, who had just popped into the bedroom, evidently heard him and came back out from the bedroom.

"Is it all right if I take my break now, Mr. Lohan?"

"Fiddledy-de-de!" Veronica said with an exaggerated, pseudo-Southern drawl. "Mr. Lohan is not the doctor or the overseer of this here plantation, though he does sometimes act like Simon Legree. And I do declare, I realize that's not from *Gone With The Wind,* y'all."

"Yes, fine," Jordan said to the nurse, waving a sheaf of papers. "I see Mrs. Lohan's feeling more herself this morning."

"Papers to have me committed to the insane asylum, dear?" Veronica asked as the nurse gladly vacated the premises, and Jordan sat in an armchair by the hearth. "Not needed, since I'm already a prisoner here."

"I rather thought you'd like to see these cute get-well notes from Thane's three," he said, ignoring her dramatics and tossing the papers onto the end table.

She snatched them up. "I was hoping you didn't have to tell them. And, yes, I am feeling better. But just like last time," she said, shuffling through the darling drawings and large-print notes, "I'd be helped immensely by being able to play."

"Tag? Hide-and-seek?"

"Very funny," she said, glaring down at him. "The chapel organ. You only paid one-point-eight million dollars for it, so it might as well be played by someone who knows what they're doing."

"Like last time, just go in there and play alone?"

"You are welcome to come or to bring the entire current clientele."

"You'd need to have the nurse with you."

"How about Elin Johansen?"

"Maybe. Let's make a deal, Miz Scarlett. By the way, how in the world did you get onto that old chestnut of a movie?"

"I suppose I was thinking about Tara. Her mother named her for the plantation in that book, you know. What deal?"

"When Susanne dropped off those notes for you, she said Tara's been asking around about things, and Susanne blurted out about Laird and Jen."

Veronica's insides cartwheeled, and she sank into the other chair. "Poor Tara. I mean, I thought she would discover it herself, that she should know all of it eventually, but —"

"Not from us!" he said, and smacked the table with his fist so hard that the lamp rattled. "But," he went on, his voice controlled again, "she's good at getting things out of people, always was. It's that social work background of hers, along with that sordid P.I. practice. That's one reason it wasn't a good idea for you to go off to some picnic reunion with her. But here's my proposal," he said, leaning forward with his elbows on his knees. "You play that little five-thousand-pipe organ to your heart's desire, and I'll handle Tara."

Since she'd gotten one thing she desperately wanted, Veronica kept her mouth shut. She'd considered saying, *Frankly, my dear, I don't give a damn* to his attempt to control her life — Tara's too — but if he was going to tell more lies to Tara, she actually cared a great deal.

Sitting in her truck down the street from Jim Manning's house in the rain, Tara waited for him to emerge. She didn't intend to question him further, nor get him involved, at least not directly. She planned to follow him back to the clinic after his midday break at home, then dart in on foot before the service entry electronic gate swung shut. Hoping he didn't look in his rearview mirror, she vowed not to look in hers anymore. However terrified she was to learn the truth, it was full bore ahead from here on out, no matter what.

She turned her cell phone to mute, then just turned it off, so it wouldn't give her away. And so Nick couldn't call to try to stop her. She had told him she had some errands to run and that she might stop by to see how Marcie was doing on the way home. All that was true. She just hadn't told him that, despite the windy, rainy weather, she intended to sneak into the clinic grounds to talk to Veronica.

Nick had gone to see a buddy he used to train dogs with; he'd admitted he was looking at all his options before he signed another government contract. The fear he'd take Claire and leave sat in Tara's stomach like a big, cold lump, but she had something else to worry about now. Even if she lost Claire, she could visit her. But if she'd lost her own child, she had to know where the precious mite was buried. Whether the little grave was nearby or in Seattle or in Timbuktu, she was going to find out and find it.

She had finally abandoned her policy of no risk taking and plunged into the bleak, black land of desperation. After Claire and Nick had left this morning, Tara had replayed Jim Manning's phone message over and over. Surely, that rumor he'd recalled was about her. It was like that old kid's game of telephone, where you whispered a fact into someone's ear and, as it went around the circle, the message got slightly skewed. She had even gotten back online to reread those articles about the two women who had given birth while comatose. Those babies had lived, of course, but she was certain hers had not.

Laird had probably seen it as a miracle that she'd gotten pregnant on the pill and had gone — at least almost — to full term, despite her coma. He must have been devastated when the child died. It had been the last straw in their rocky relationship, and he'd turned to Jen for comfort and for a new marriage and a future family. Oh, yes, Jen would gladly toe his Lohan line, Tara thought as she hit her fists rhythmically against the steering wheel.

The rain drummed on the truck roof and provided a screen for her when Jim drove by. Still, she slumped in her seat. Once he was past, she kept up with him without getting too close. She took a side street and sped up near the clinic so she could be on foot when the gates opened for him. How she'd get back out, she wasn't sure. But she was sure that if Nick knew what she was doing, he'd be frantic and furious.

"Can't help it, can't help it, have to, have to," she recited to herself as she locked her truck and stood back under the trees near the service entrance. No umbrella today. It might catch someone's eye.

This compulsion to risk anything and everything was what Alex must have felt when she had slipped into Tara's office and rifled through her papers, then sneaked them out of the house. This was how driven Alex must have felt, facing down her dangerous ex-husband to get her child back.

The gates swung outward, and Jim drove slowly through. His truck's wheels sent small waves across the pavement, almost as if the place were surrounded by a moat. When the tall iron gates with the entwined initials MM for Mountain Manor began to slowly swing closed, she darted in.

The entire area, which wrapped around the side of a mountain above Evergreen, had once been the estate of a local cattle baron. But the old family mansion had fallen into disrepair and now stood, a roofless hulk, far into the acreage. Tara had walked through the skeleton of the old mansion once, admiring the remnants of fine stone craftsmanship on a single fireplace that still stood, imagining the family that had once walked its spacious rooms and gazed out its now glassless windows. Much of the woodwork had been pirated for the interior of the clinic reception room and Jordan Lohan's office. But it was the isolated cabins and, now, strangely, the chapel, since Jim had mentioned her strange journey there, that haunted her more than the bones of that old building.

Distant thunder rumbled as if the whole mountain shuddered. Using the trees for a partial shelter, Tara moved quickly off the road onto a path. The trees and foliage were thick here. She hoped there was no lightning with the thunder. The narrow walkway was familiar territory from her weeks of rehab within the iron, spiked fence. Today she would move about like a ghost until she located Veronica. She had her red hair pinned up under a black baseball cap and wore khakis, old running shoes and Nick's too-big camouflage jacket. Pulling up the collar and hunching her shoulders, she told herself that the weather was a blessing, since not many would be outside today.

But even the dripping trees bothered her. They loomed over her like dark, faceless monsters from a fairy tale. Despite the fact that she was sweating, raindrops dripping down her neck made her shiver with foreboding at some sort of misty memory she couldn't quite recall. She hugged herself for warmth and comfort as she crossed a humpbacked bridge over a rushing stream. She glanced down, mesmerized by the foaming white rapids that beat themselves against the rocks.

As she strode farther into the hilly clinic grounds, the path wound its way through denser vegetation. The needlelike fingers of pines and blue spruce snagged her clothes and scratched her. Deep in the heart of the clinic forest, she was surprised to see pine beetle damage, a common Colorado blight that turned the ponderosa and lodgepole pines a dry, deadly brown. The unseen devourers had devastated forests westward toward Vail, but many once-green trees were also dying here as if they'd been cursed by a powerful hand.

To get to the cabin she assumed Veronica was in, she would need to pass what had been her own cabin, then traverse the more public areas near the large central lodge that housed the welcome center, meeting rooms, classrooms and offices. The staff psychiatrists, therapists, doctors and adjunct staff had offices in the maze of corridors, as did Jordan Lohan, the driving financial force behind all this. Everything was regulated here, everyone's schedule planned and controlled, from seven in the morning wake-up to lights-out at eleven. Appointments, classes, group therapy, assignments, meditation time, rest and relaxation. Her schedule had been different, since she was a unique patient here, but, during her weeks of rehab, she'd learned the daily drill from the staff, most of whom seemed to regard her with a mix of fascination and pity — the outcast Lohan, the woman about to be exiled from the bounteous hand of the family behind Mountain Manor's largesse.

She hesitated when she reached the trees circling the cabin where she'd spent so much time, both comatose and then recuperating. Sadly, the pine beetle blight had withered the trees here. The lights were on; some other patient was inside, and she wished him or her well. But what could the cabin say if it could talk? Could she have been pregnant there? Had a baby? And had that dearly beloved child both come into the world and departed from it there?

She tried hard to recall living there, before those days in April when she began to really live again, to venture outside into the world. She'd been told that the specialist who had tended her was on a three-year leave of absence, traveling in Europe. If she could access some contact information, she could call or write him. But why, as she stared long and hard at that cabin, so rustic on the outside, so luxurious within, did the memories she needed elude her?

But one memory stabbed at her: the Lohans had actually asked her psychologist to break the news to her that her marriage was over, and only then because she'd kept asking where Laird was. He'd left the area . . . he'd gone to start a new life . . . he was sorry, but all communications with him from now on would be through the Lohan lawyers.

Biting her lower lip hard, Tara forced her feet off the path, cutting through the trees toward the lodge and Veronica's previous cabin, the closest to the lodge. But what if they'd changed her locale? If she had to search the grounds for her former mother-in-law, it could take hours. It was so dark that she kept forgetting it was only midday, but she still didn't have that kind of time.

The rain hadn't let up, and the wind moaned through the limbs. She hoped she didn't get sick from being out here like this, for she felt chilled to the bone. At the next rumble of thunder, she hugged herself again to stop her shaking. How would it have been to hold her baby in her arms?

Yes, through the trees, the main clinic building, which looked like a spacious lodge with its sprawling log and stone exterior.

Lights were on today; wan squares of amber shone through the gray slant of drifting mist. No one would expect someone out in this, threading their way through trees, camouflaged to blend in, on a mission. She remembered how Nick's expression had darkened when she'd merely mentioned the word *mission* to him the other day. She guessed he must have been on a mission that went bad. She prayed this one would not.

As soon as Claire arrived home from school, which was early because of a half-day, district-wide teachers' meeting, Nick took her and Beamer for a walk down their long driveway to get the mail. He listened to Claire's chatter, but he was worried about Tara.

She wasn't answering her cell phone. She wasn't at Marcie's, because he'd just phoned there. Marcie said she was checking with a funeral home for when she got Rick's body back. The coroner had phoned to tell her Rick's death was being ruled a suicide. She also said the police would soon bring her computer back. But Tara hadn't called her.

At least he knew Tara hadn't gone to face down the senior Lohans, because Jordan

Lohan had left a recent phone message that she should call him and they could meet at the house. He wanted to update her on Veronica and talk to her about some family matters. Nick hoped Tara would forgive him for playing her messages, but he was getting downright scared about where she was. The worst scenario was that she'd taken a flight to Seattle to confront her ex and his new wife.

"I said, can you read this *Highlights Magazine* with me, Uncle Nick?" Claire said, flourishing a brightly colored cover she'd found in the mailbox. "There's a really neat drawing in here where you have to find hidden things. Aunt Tara and I love to do it."

"Sure, but shouldn't you wait for her, then?"

"Can we read 'Goofus and Gallant' then? See, one guy always does something nice and polite, but the other messes up all the time."

"Sure, fine. But let's take Beamer for a little stroll first."

"You can get a hidden picture minibook too, and we could all do that together, the three of us. There's all kinds of things you can't see real easy and have to look and look, 'cause things are hidden —"

"Yeah, good."

"You're not listening, are you?" she demanded, one hand on her hip, her tone that of a grown woman. "You don't want to read with me or Aunt Tara either. Why are you so mean today?"

"Claire, I'm not mean. I just have a lot of things to think about, like where I'm going to work, where we should live."

"But can't we live right here, with Aunt Tara too? See, if you're my uncle and she's my aunt, it would be just right for you two to get in love and get married, and I could be in the wedding, so —"

"Honey, I've only been home five days!" he said, staring down at her and trying not to look as upset as he felt. "You don't fall in love and make plans to get married with someone you've only known five days!"

"But what about love at first sight, like in *Cinderella* and *Snow White*? I can tell you're mad at me, and maybe at Aunt Tara too. You want to take me away from her! You don't want her to be with us."

"Yes, I do, and right now!" he roared.

Claire thrust out her lower lip. When she blinked, tears flew onto her cheeks. Even Beamer cocked his head. Nick never shouted at his dogs, but these women were getting to him. He gritted his teeth. He wished he could give Claire an order to stop all this fluffy-feelings, female stuff.

"Claire," he said, speaking slowly, calmly, "you're going to have to learn to give this time."

"But what if time runs out? In *Cinderella,* the clock struck, and everything went back the way it once was — real bad, too. I mean, I'd like to go back to when Mom was alive and my dad was nice, but then I'd lose Aunt Tara, and I don't want to lose her."

That last word dissolved into sniffles and bigger tears. The child was actually quivering. Nick knelt and hugged her to him. As her thin arms wrapped around his neck, even Beamer cuddled closer. But, like Claire, Nick felt a big hole in their little circle.

Where the hell was Tara?

As Tara gave the lodge a wide berth to head toward Veronica's old cabin, she saw the lights were on in the chapel. Though attached to the main building, the addition with its peaked roof was off to the west end. And — was she imagining this? — muted music drifted from those windows.

Could this be near where she was standing when Jim had found her wandering in the snow in the dead of winter? But she'd just walked that way now from her cabin.

Even if her legs had been bare that night, she was pretty sure they would not have been so cut up that she'd bleed. True, today the pine needles had caught her pants and might have given a superficial scratch. Maybe if she were out of a sickbed, staggering, she could have fallen and cut herself that way. But to leave bloody footprints in the snow?

She felt lured on toward the chapel, by the music and the possibility Veronica was playing. The melodies were beautiful, haunting. Jim had mentioned that Veronica was "restricted," which meant she was closely monitored, but who else could play that well?

Glancing up and down the driveway that circled the lodge, Tara sloshed through the puddles and darted to the stone wall of the chapel. Pressed against the exterior of the building, she was certain she could feel the music as well as hear it, like a memory that was still so vivid she felt she was living it again.

Other than that night she could not recall, she'd only heard Veronica play for the family, mostly classical, but she'd remembered this piece. It was from *The Phantom of the Opera,* her former mother-in-law's favorite musical. She closed her eyes to try to picture being here in the snow, bleeding into the snow. But all she saw in her mind's eye was that white mask the Phantom wore in both the stage production she and Laird had seen, and the movie, which she'd seen again this year on TV. Something contorted and grotesque was behind that mask in her mind. This tune was "Think Of Me"; why couldn't she remember?

The music segued into another, louder song from *Phantom* called "Masquerade." Tara jumped as distant thunder rumbled, reverberating off the stone building, as if it blended with the organ. She couldn't look in the windows because they were too high. Despite the fact Veronica must be accompanied by a clinic staff member, who would surely report Tara if she showed herself, she edged closer to the back door. The main entrance was through a hall that led to the client reception rooms. She could only pray that, somehow, this back entrance was open. If she could get Veronica's attention, get her away for a moment, or at least have a few minutes before someone could be summoned to throw her out . . .

She tried the heavy door. It pulled out toward her. Using both hands to open it wider, she darted in and braced it while it swung silently shut.

Tara moved into the shadows in the back corner of the high-beamed room, which rang with the reverberating notes of the song. At the front, across the rows of ten pews, the chancel was well lit, but it was darker here. Her heart fell when she saw two women sitting in the front pew with their backs to her. From Veronica's descriptions, she was pretty sure that one was Elin Johansen; the other was dressed like a nurse in the pale peach the medical staff all wore.

Feeling like a fool or a felon, she dropped to her hands and knees and crawled along the outside, carpeted aisle toward the front of the chapel. Once she showed herself, she might not have much time to talk to Veronica and she needed every precious second.

14

Could Tara have had an accident on a slick road?

Nick was starting to panic. When any of the Delta Force guys didn't report in on time, it had been alarming, but this was worse. Though it was early afternoon, it had gotten dark outside because the weather was degrading. He didn't approve of snooping, but he went into Tara's office and played all her phone messages again, even those before Jordan Lohan's recent one. She'd left Jim Manning's on, one he'd already heard. The guy sounded totally believable. But he was recounting a rumor that could have actually been about Tara.

Of the other messages, only the new one from her former father-in-law seemed significant, so Nick replayed it. At least, he thought, if Jordan Lohan was inviting her to their home, maybe the family was finally going to provide some answers. He didn't think she could have gone there already, because this message had been unplayed when he first heard it. But maybe Lohan had contacted her some other way.

Nick could hear Claire playing with Beamer in the other room. He paced, fists jammed in his jeans pockets, shaking his head. Of course, he had no right to tell Tara what to do or to order her not to go somewhere. Even if, as in Claire's fairy-tale dreams, he was her husband, he wouldn't do that. They'd be a partnership, comrades as well as lovers and spouses.

Damn, what was the matter with him? Had he fallen this fast for a woman he hardly knew? And yet, he felt he knew Tara as deeply as he'd ever known another woman. And needed her much more, not only to be with Claire but with him.

Continuing to pace, he made a second call to Marcie. She still hadn't seen Tara; he could hear the rain and thunder over the phone, so it might even be worse near Evergreen than it was here.

"Where are you?" he asked. "I can hear the storm really loud."

"Sitting outside in my car, with my laptop. It's wireless, and I paid a bundle for it, can't get it wet. I got it back faster by picking it up instead of waiting for the cops to bring it back. I'm going inside the apartment, but I have to psych myself up for going in. Can't stand to go into the bathroom where I found him, and it's the only one in the place. I'm moving out as soon as I can. Rick's funeral is Thursday morning at ten at the Corbett Funeral Home in Evergreen. It won't be much, unless we get some gawkers, but I'm hoping you and Tara will come."

"Sure. Of course we will."

"When I called Clay at the prison to tell him, he was real shook. Blamed everyone but himself for Rick's depression. Don't tell Tara, but he said not to trust her. I do, though. She's been great."

"Did Clay actually threaten Tara?"

"Just said he bet she was going to be extremely sorry. That's what he said, 'extremely sorry.' And then he said something kind of strange. He said he'd heard she was an extreme risk fan — something like that."

Bingo! Nick thought. Not only was Rick off the list of those who still might be spying on Tara, but Clay must be ultimately to blame. Somehow he must have contacted Dietmar 'Whacker' Getz, or vice versa. Maybe they'd made a deal that, when he wasn't doing extreme mountain biking, Getz would watch or harass Tara. So that meant Marv Seymour, computer tech and

247

online guru extraordinaire — despite his "I'll be seeing you" gift of thirteen red roses — was probably in the clear. But had Seymour or Getz ripped up the roses and stuck the thorny stems between the deck boards in some sort of perverted warning?

"You're sure Clay didn't say anything else about what he meant by 'extreme risk fan'?" Nick asked.

"No, but it's pretty obvious. She took a risk that day she went after your sister at Clay's place. He probably meant she'd do something again to get herself in trouble. But don't worry about Clay, because he's not going anywhere to get anyone in trouble ever again."

Maybe not, Nick thought, but Whacker Getz was still out there somewhere, and who knew what Clay had paid him to do. Had those two men, ex-husbands of women Tara had helped, sworn some sort of mutual vendetta against Tara? And, if she wasn't careful, could she soon have her own ex on her tail?

Near the front of the church, when she almost had a side view of the three women, Tara rose to peek at them. As the music swelled and soared, Elin and the nurse seemed entranced, but Veronica looked transported. Her eyes closed, she swayed slightly as her hands skimmed the keys. Her feet flew over the wooden pedals as if she danced. Music engulfed the room, reverberating from the banks of silver organ pipes pointing skyward at the back of the chancel.

Tara realized she'd need to be almost on top of Veronica to get her attention, but the other two women would see and stop her by then. She didn't want to alarm Veronica; she was here to be helped, not to receive any sort of shock treatment.

Tara decided to wait where she was, crouched on the dark blue carpet, until Veronica paused or looked up. Besides, this beautiful chapel calmed and strengthened her. She must face up to losing her child, but she had to know what had happened.

Veronica stopped playing, though the last notes hung suspended in he air. The woman Tara was certain was Elin Johansen applauded and the nurse joined in. Behind them, Tara stood. Gripping the pew in front of her with both hands, she called out, "Veronica, that was beautiful. I walked all the way in from the back entrance. I need to speak with you. I need your help."

The nurse gasped, craned her neck and rose. Elin turned her head, then stood too. The nurse started to protest — Tara ignored that — but Elin cut the woman off. "It's all right, Anne. This is Mrs. Lohan's former daughter-in-law, Tara."

"It isn't all right," the nurse cried. "I have my orders."

But that was all background buzz as Veronica's clear blue eyes met hers and held. She looked fine to Tara, though her hair was wild compared to her usual precisely put together appearance. No, there were darker shadows under her eyes and more wrinkles on her high brow. And not only surprise lurked in her troubled gaze but fear.

"Tara, my dear, however did you get through the gate?" she asked as Tara rushed toward her. Veronica stepped down to the floor from the organ; her hand hit some keys, and dissonant notes blared from the pipes.

They hugged each other. Elin was arguing with the nurse, who had a cell phone or beeper in her hands. Veronica was perspiring from her performance; heat seemed to radiate from her to warm Tara's ice-cold skin.

"I know about Laird and Jen," Tara told Veronica, her voice low so only she could hear. With her back to the other women, speaking fast, she held Veronica at arm's length, staring into her eyes. "But I have to know the truth about when I was comatose. Did Laird and I have —"

"Oh, my dearest girl, I'm so sorry," Veronica interrupted and hugged her hard again. She whispered in her ear, "About that — I'm so sorry. Please don't blame any of us that —"

A door banged open. Maybe the nurse was going for help, but a man's booming voice cut off all thought and words.

"Tara! I'm so glad you tracked us down here. So you got my message that I wanted to see you? What luck I was just down the hall when Veronica's nurse buzzed me that you were visiting."

Jordan Lohan strode at them from the side door into the hall. It swung shut behind him.

"Such a surprise, right, Veronica?" he asked, and hugged both of them as they held tightly to each other. One arm around each of them, he somehow pried them apart, though they still grasped each other's hands. "Tara, you understand she's had a relapse. I had her admitted because she wasn't making much sense — the drugs talking, as Dr. Middleton says."

"I came to ask you both for the truth."

"Absolutely. I hope Veronica told you that

we feel you're strong enough now to hear some sad news."

He was going to tell her? And he'd sent her a message. She should never have turned off her cell phone.

"I think I know what it is," she said as tears blinded her to make two Veronicas, two Jordans. "You should have told me before — right away."

"Anne," Jordan interrupted, turning away, "would you please take Mrs. Lohan back to her cabin? It's pouring out there — Elin, perhaps you can assist?"

Both women jumped to attention as if God Himself had spoken. But at least Tara had forced the Lohans to tell her the truth now. Yet, suddenly, she felt more afraid than ever.

"However did you get into the grounds?" Jordan asked Tara as they entered his spacious clinic office down the hall from the chapel. The masculine room always smelled of rich leather and pine. He went to a coat rack made of steer horns behind the door and took down a coat. "Here, let's wrap this raincoat around you for warmth. I'd build a fire, but I want to make this quick, then be certain you get home safely before the storm gets worse. You'll catch your death of cold."

"My car's parked outside the back service entrance," she told him. "I waited until someone drove through, then hurried in on foot. I want the truth right now — all of it."

Her teeth were chattering, which she hated, because it made her sound weak and nervous. She'd disliked and distrusted this man for so long she wondered if he put his raincoat over her like a blanket to warm her or to keep her from dripping all over his beige Berber carpet. How had she ever managed to call him *Dad?* And what did that or anything matter now? He'd gone too far to draw back from finally telling her what had happened. He sat in the brown leather armchair opposite hers in front of the empty hearth.

"Jordan, just tell me the truth. It might have shocked me once, but I'm ready for it. Did I have a child when I was comatose?"

He nodded solemnly, then blurted, "Don't blame Laird, or me either. He was devastated and, believe me, the two of us grieved for you, as well. His loss was as great as yours when you lost the child."

When you lost the child.

So, he'd said it. There had been a child, her child! But she gritted her teeth as she noted how he'd worded that. *She'd* lost the child.

"And Veronica," he went on, "had her own problems, bad ones, so she didn't know you were pregnant. You may recall she only visited you after you came out of the coma. She probably just thought you were asking about Laird and Jennifer. We kept you pretty much secluded, but for your doctor, of course."

"Who is conveniently out of the country. And my coma — did the doctor extend that for me?"

"It was for your own health and protection, a professional decision."

"Really? You do like to play God, don't you? You and Laird didn't even tell Veronica about the child?"

"We thought it best," he went on, ignoring her sarcasm, "to leave her to her own cure without burdening her with the loss of our grandchild."

"Oh, of course," she said, her voice so bitter it surprised her. "If you don't tell the mother, why in the world would you bother to tell the grandmother?"

"Tara, I know this is hard."

Desperate to know everything, she decided not to antagonize him more. She gripped her hands together so tightly in her lap that her fingers went numb. Dear God in heaven, it was true, it was true. To hear it admitted

— though she'd thought she was ready — staggered her.

"But I was on birth control pills," she protested.

"It surprised Laird. Delighted and excited him, however upset he was about your condition, of course. A miracle child, a very special child."

"Oh, of course. Not 'away in a manger,' but 'hidden away in the Lohan Mountain Manor Clinic.'"

He glared at her. "Tara, Laird was the one who wanted a child, not you. But the doctors we consulted — specialists, I assure you — told us you'd probably never make it to full term."

"And no doubt my ob-gyn, Jennifer De-Mar — Jennifer Lohan, now — was there to hold Laird's hand and whatever other part of him she could grab."

"I'm not here to defend that."

"Because you can't. Go on. What — what went wrong?"

"As you may know, such a delivery is highly unusual. It just went wrong, a stillbirth at the end, maybe because you weren't able to push, maybe —"

"That's ridiculous! They could have done a C-section! I have researched two other cases of comatose births where the babies lived. You shouldn't have had me in a clinic cabin or kept me in a coma if it was medically induced or extended! Was Jen there when it happened? Maybe she didn't care, since she wanted Laird."

Who, Tara thought, was the woman who was screaming? She wanted to throw herself at this man, to tear him apart.

"I *said* I am so sorry, Tara. Tragedies happen — you certainly know that from chasing after your friend Alex without Laird's knowledge or approval. We left no stone unturned to have good medical help for you at the birth, though I realize we may have mishandled telling you. But with the loss of your friend Alex and then Laird, you had been through so much."

"So, in the end, the miscarriage is all my fault, right? I was dead to the world, but we can all just blame my coma for a dead child."

She felt nauseous, but she wasn't going to get sick in front of this man. Under his coat, she pressed her hands against her lower belly, where she had carried a child she never knew. At least Jordan Lohan was telling the truth about one thing: he regretted the loss of the baby. Like Laird, Jordan coveted Lohan heirs. But she wanted to curse him, hurt him.

"A boy or a girl?" she asked, her voice suddenly wan and listless.

"A girl."

"What was she named?"

Frowning, he shook his head.

"She wasn't named? I wasn't there to hold her, and no one so much as named her? Where is she? I searched the records of all the local cemeteries. You didn't just dispose —"

"Of course not! She's interred in the Lohan crypt in a private cemetery, on land my parents once owned. We had her cremated privately — as a favor, actually, to you so that the birth didn't smear all of your previous tragedy through the papers again."

"Cremated? Laird never liked the idea of cremation, so you really must have been in charge at that point. And as a favor to me? I can't imagine why I'm not grateful to the lordly Lohans."

"I know that's pain and grief talking. We have been nothing but good to you. As I said, you never wanted his child. Laird told me."

"Not until we had a decent marriage during the day and not just at night! Oh, he was warm and understanding that last month —"

She stopped shouting and frowned. Why

had Laird suddenly been so sweet? Was he feeling guilty because he'd already taken up with Jen? Maybe even the Lohans didn't know when Jen and Laird really got together. Jen had known Tara wasn't happy; Tara had realized Jen thought Laird was the ultimate prize. Could she have put herself in his path — and then that woman had attended to her when their baby was born? A child to adore and rear together might have, at least temporarily, patched up their marriage. But if things went wrong, Laird would need comforting.

"Was Jennifer there when my baby was born?" she asked.

"Yes, but so was your specialist and Laird. I was in and out, mostly in the next room."

Tara threw the raincoat off so she could get up to flee this place. They'd let her daughter die, all of them.

"Sit down!" Jordan ordered, and pushed her back into her chair. "I'm going to call someone to drive you home. I'm sure your girl Claire will be a comfort to you. Her uncle, too. A new family, Tara."

"Nothing and no one can replace a lost child," she whispered, shaking her head so hard that her long hair flew free from her cap and whipped her face. "I want to visit the Lohan crypt," she insisted, shoving her hair back behind her ears.

"Of course," he said as he rose and pressed buttons on his telephone. "Yes," he said into the mouthpiece. "If Dr. Middleton's not with Mrs. Lohan, send him in to see me, with his bag. And find Jim Manning."

Tara jumped to her feet. She wanted to see her daughter's resting place right now, not be sent home. She was going to lose control; she could feel it coming, fury and regret rampaging through her.

"You turned her into nothing!" she screamed. "No name! No grave! No bones, even. I want to see her, hold her . . ."

For the first time in her life, she fainted.

Nick stood, horrified, as Jordan Lohan explained everything to him on the phone.

"Who is it?" Claire asked, coming up to him and tugging at his sweatshirt. "Is it about Aunt Tara? Is that her? I want to talk to her."

Nick gestured for her to keep quiet and turned away to look out the window. "How could someone be prepared for that?" Nick asked the man. "She had found evidence, but it's still a terrible shock."

"I think the fact that she exhausted herself walking a couple of miles in here in the storm contributed. She was soaked to the bone. She's awake now. We've given her a sedative and hot tea, and Jim Manning and Dr. Middleton will have her and her vehicle home to you soon. I've assured her that she can visit the child's resting place when she feels stronger, though she's insisting it be right now. Mr. McMahon, we may have handled this wrong, but we were only doing what we thought was best for her after all she'd been through. It would have set her back —"

"More than now?" Nick challenged.

He heard Jordan Lohan clear his throat. "It's wonderful that you and Claire will be there waiting for her. If only she could get away for a while, or even leave the area completely, it would surely be best. Our son Laird was so distraught to lose his child that he left —"

"With his new wife," Nick cut in, "while the woman who had delivered his dead child was still comatose. Look, I appreciate your getting her back to us. I'll be coming with her as soon as possible to visit her daughter's grave," he said, trying to sound decisive and strong. He wanted to say much more to this man, who was corrupted by his absolute power — actually, he wanted to beat him to a pulp — but Claire needed him, so he kept his mouth shut and ended the call.

"Aunt Tara got caught in the storm today," he told Claire, squatting to her level. "She was taking a long walk and got cold and wet. She fainted, so a doctor and an old friend of hers are bringing her home. We'll just give her time to let her tell us what happened her own way, okay?"

Wide-eyed, looking older than her years, Claire nodded. "Fainted. It isn't as bad as a coma, is it, like she was in before?"

"No, she's awake and just fine," he assured her. But he realized that Tara might never be just fine for a long, long time. And he was astounded by how damn much it mattered to him.

Footprints in the snow . . . bloody footprints in the snow. She'd obviously been hemorrhaging that night, no doubt from childbirth, Tara told herself. At least, they didn't let her die, but then, they couldn't have simply had her cremated and stuck away in some old family crypt without a lot of questions.

Frowning, she stared out the passenger window into the rain as Dr. Middleton drove her truck up Shadow Mountain Road. At the clinic, he had rushed in and broken an ammonia capsule under her nose. Now

Jim Manning was leading them in his truck, his taillights blinking in the rain so they could follow. But her mind was following her own thoughts. In fainting, she'd hit her head. Had it jarred loose some memories of her daughter's birth? Surely, Jordan Lohan had not told her everything. She remembered bright lights — flashes in her eyes. Yes, twisting pain and crying, crying, crying . . .

But was that her crying or the child's or Laird's sobbing, or . . .

"Not feeling faint again, are you, Tara?" the doctor asked. He was Veronica's doctor and seemed nice enough. He wasn't someone who had ever attended her — she'd asked. If he had, right now, however bad she felt, she would have been interrogating him as she never had any other witness. She almost said, *I'm okay,* but that would have been such a lie. To answer his question, she said, "No," and looked out the side window again.

Maybe, just as they'd forced her to wake up today, they had brought her out of her drug-induced coma when the labor started. Maybe they thought she could help deliver the child. Then, after the miscarriage, when they were all focused on the baby, she'd gotten away somehow, run out in the snow bleeding. They'd thought she'd still be comatose, but she'd been aroused and agonized by a *vaginal delivery*. Just like today, she'd made it to the chapel where Veronica was playing the organ. Jim had found her and called for help, so Veronica knew something had happened. Still, she did believe that Veronica had tried to tell her that Laird had married Jen, but that her former mother-in-law had not known about the child.

Her thoughts tied themselves in knots and twisted like spiderwebs. She was never so happy to see home — that is, Nick's home — than she was when it appeared through the rain.

She would see her child's resting place tomorrow, hold the urn, then try to build a new life. Somehow, she must go on, even if she lost Claire and Nick and Beamer.

Nick opened the car door and lifted her in his arms. Over his shoulder, through the slant of rain, she saw Claire waving from the lit doorway with Beamer at her side. Nick's touch was so strong and sure. Exhausted, beaten, grieving, she buried her face against him. Cradling her, he strode inside with her close to his heart.

15

Nick fixed dinner and fed Claire while Tara took a shower and fell into a deep sleep. All she'd told him was, "It's true. I had a daughter. I'm going to see where her ashes are tomorrow. If you can come . . ."

"Of course I can. I'll be right beside you through this."

She had shaken her head. "Don't make promises," she'd whispered, still not meeting his eyes, but staring off toward the blank wall behind him. "Because it will take me forever to get through this."

After Claire was ready for bed and Tara was awake, the child went in to see her, then darted right out and told Nick as he was wiping the table, "She says, can you come in too."

Tara was in bed, in a white terry-cloth robe, with the covers pulled up to her hips. She reached out to pat the bed. That must have been some sort of sign, because Claire lifted the corner of the covers and got in beside her. Tara put her arms around the child.

"Sit, Nick, please," Tara said, nodding toward the bed. "I want to tell you both something."

He sat, about at her knee level, feeling almost like an intruder.

"I just found out today," she said, looking down at Claire, "that when I was in my coma, I had a baby, a little girl, but she died right when she was born."

"Oh, no!" Claire cried. "That's as bad as losing a mom!" She lifted her head from Tara's shoulder to look closely into her eyes.

Nick thought Tara looked like a ghost of herself, pale, mournful, almost ethereal. Her voice was a whisper nearly muffled by the wind and rain. He ached to hold her.

"I had an idea it might be true," Tara went on, "but it was still a big shock. To learn there was a child and to lose that child all at once — and that she's been gone for two-and-a-half years."

"But you still have me," Claire told her. "At least, unless Uncle Nick takes me away."

"Claire, this isn't the time for —" he started to protest, but Tara held up her hand.

"I will always love you as a daughter," she

told Claire, "and I wanted you to know why I'm so sad."

"And I'll bet you're mad too," Claire said, "that she died and they didn't tell you sooner!"

That outburst made Tara feel as if she herself had spoken. But she felt so bereft, so exhausted that she couldn't handle that right now. "If Uncle Nick will put you to bed, I need some sleep," she said, kissing Claire's forehead.

With a big bear hug, Claire kissed Tara's cheek and scrambled out of the bed. But as Nick rose to go tuck her in, Claire asked, "What was her name, Aunt Tara?"

"Her name was — is — Sarah Veronica Lohan-Kinsale. Sarah for one of her grandmothers and Veronica for the other. But we will call her Sarah."

"It's a real pretty name, and even though I never get to meet her, she's kind of my sister now."

Nick saw that Tara, fighting to hold herself together, was ready to burst into tears, so he scooped Claire up and put her in bed. A few minutes later, when he left her room, he saw that Tara's door was still open with the light on. From his earlier night-watchman forays to check on the place, he knew she slept with it closed and her light off. He tiptoed back to close the door.

"Nick?"

"Yeah. Just going to close your door."

"Don't, okay?" she called to him. "I can't stand to feel closed off, closed out right now."

He peeked in at her. She was still huddled in her robe under the covers. Leaning one shoulder on the door frame, he said, "I understand. It doesn't help to be alone in times of loss."

"You know whereof you speak. Feel like talking?"

"Sure, but you need sleep."

"Feel like holding someone, then — just for a little while?"

He covered the space to her in four quick strides, sat on the edge of the bed with his back to the headboard and reached for her. At first he cradled her as he might Claire, but then he stretched out next to her, shoes and all, outside the covers, and held her hard.

She clung to him, her face pressed against his neck, wetting his throat with her tears. The pillow they shared was soaked.

They didn't move for what seemed to him like minutes but was hours. He could see her bedside clock. As he felt her eventually relax against him, he settled into a more

267

comfortable position. Shifting his weight, he heard her sigh as she turned over, her back to him so they lay spoon fashion with his chest and thighs cradling her back and bottom.

He wanted her. But he wanted even more than that to make the agony of her loss, mingled with guilt and anger, go away. It didn't work to try to bury losses. You had to face them, feel them, work through them. Through Tara's struggles, he was learning that about himself. Post-traumatic stress disorder was something they, unfortunately, shared.

"Nick?" she said, startling him from dark dreams of mountain caves and the bright bang of an explosion.

"What, sweetheart?"

"Claire's right. I'm sad, but I'm really mad. I want to go to the Lohan estate today and then see where they put Sarah's ashes, but I don't trust that man or my former husband any farther than I could throw this entire mountain."

"You've got a bodyguard with you now, Tara. All the way."

Holding a bouquet of white calla lilies in her lap, Tara frowned out the front window as Nick drove them through the neighborhood of Kerr Gulch where she and Laird used to live. Today she was not nervous, not distraught, just deeply hurt and angry. She kept telling herself she was under control.

"Quite a place," Nick observed as they passed through the Lohan monogrammed gates that had to be buzzed open from the house. "Exclusive privacy, great views and huge lots."

"This estate is about twelve acres and worth about three million dollars, I guess," Tara said, her voice a monotone as if she were reciting the alphabet. "The house Laird and I had was on a five-acre lot, but it would have been better for us to be in a hut and happy. Pull up under the porte cochere."

A dove-gray Lincoln Town Car was parked there, but Tara had no intention of riding with Jordan to the site he'd mentioned. She actually wanted to go just with Nick, but she didn't know where the crypt, as Jordan had called it, was. Knowing him, he'd have the place locked up.

Before they rang the bell, Rita, Veronica's plump, middle-aged Mexican maid, opened the door for them. With Veronica away for treatment again, Rita was probably filling in at different jobs.

"Rita, it's good to see you again," Tara

said, extending her hand.

Looking surprised, then grateful, Rita took it. "So sorry for your loss, Ms. Kinsale. Mr. Lohan told the staff, and he's going to tell Mrs. Lohan today. So very sorry for you and Mr. Laird and —"

"This is my friend Nick MacMahon," Tara said as Rita eyed Nick, then gestured for them to step inside the huge stone house.

"Mr. Lohan will be right with you," she said, and led them past windows that overlooked the covered courtyard pavilion into the hand-hewn beamed great room. The room had panoramic views of the gold and green valley and blue-gray mountains. The rain was over; it looked to be a clear day. All the furniture in the spacious room was oversize; it had always made Tara feel as if she were Alice in Wonderland and she'd eaten something that had shrunk her.

A silver tray on a low table held a coffee carafe and a porcelain plate of pecan rolls. "May I serve you?" Rita asked.

"We're fine. Thanks, Rita," Tara said, so the maid left them alone.

Nick poured himself coffee, then went over to study the impressive array of pictures of Jordan with powerful politicians, from state senators to the governor and even the vice president. Tara knew the Lohans had always been big political contributors on both the state and national levels, but she was long past being impressed with anything they did.

She drifted around the room, ignoring the power photos in lieu of the personal ones in carefully arranged clusters on the grand piano and the walls. Of course, there were plenty of Thane's three children, and old family photos of Laird's family when he and Thane were small. All of her photos had disappeared, but, Tara noted, there were none of Laird and Jen either. Perhaps Jordan and Veronica were ashamed of how quickly he'd dumped his comatose wife for another woman. Or, like Susanne, had Jordan had some removed so they wouldn't upset her more than she already was?

Tara looked for the yearly, three-generation Lohan photo, but found it missing. Unlike at Susanne's house, there was no bare spot on the wall over the massive stone mantel where the current one had always hung. Instead, she saw, there was one of the family of four when Thane and Laird were about high school age. Tara noted the photos were all by the same photographer, Robert Randel, the man who had taken pictures she'd been in during the two years of her marriage. If Rita came back in, she'd ask her about that, because —

"You are not only prompt but early," Jordan said as he strode into the room, rubbing his hands together as if he were washing them. "Nick, I'm glad to meet you and thank you for lending support to Tara. I see Rita has offered you something," he said with a jerky gesture at the tray. "I was just phoning to check on Veronica this morning. I'll be heading over there to explain everything to her after our visit to the crypt. I know she'll be greatly grieved too. How I wish I could have protected both of you from such dreadful news, Tara."

Tara thought he was on edge, which was unusual. He was trying to fill the air with chatter. She was tempted to ask him the location of the current family photo, which surely must include Laird and Jen, but he'd have some slick answer for her. No, she'd find out about that another way, from someone more likely to tell the truth. She hadn't learned to be a P.I. and a skip tracer for nothing. Once she'd seen her baby's resting place, she just might do a little research on Laird and Jen. It shouldn't matter to her when they fell in love, when he decided to desert her, but somehow it did.

Tara cringed every time anyone, including

herself, said the word *crypt.* It conjured up images of haunted Halloweens or old horror movies. She expected to see a decrepit, spiderweb-covered hulk with a creaking door.

After going twenty miles down the valley toward the west, they drove Nick's truck onto a narrow paved lane behind Jordan's car. He'd pretended to be surprised that they would follow in their own vehicle; Tara thought he was secretly relieved. She craned her neck to look all around. At least it was lovely here. She should have known it would be since it was Lohan land. Jordan had said his parents had once lived in a "starter house" here, but, unless it was hidden by the grove of quivering aspens just ahead, it must have been long gone. At the back of the acreage, she saw a fenced-in area with old gravestones and a single larger structure.

"Is everything the Lohans own fenced and gated?" Nick asked.

"It's even the way they like to treat their women. At least this is protected. And pretty."

"Like Lohan women. That it is."

A mountain stream ran nearby; they couldn't see it, but the sound floated to them as they got out and closed the car doors. With the whispering of falling leaves, the lilting sound was almost like a lullaby, Tara thought.

The three of them walked toward the six-foot-high, spiked iron fence, and Jordan fitted a key in the gate. It screeched as if in protest when he opened it. Tara's heart was thudding. The bouquet of lilies shook in her hands. She wanted to cling to Nick, but she didn't.

The crypt looked much too grand for this rural, isolated site, especially set among the smattering of old, rough headstones. The two-pillared edifice looked carved from imported stone — maybe marble — with its dull pinkish tint and small black flecks. It wasn't polished but it looked sturdy, eternal. Under its peaked roof, on the flat lintel, in big, heavily incised letters was carved simply, *LOHAN.*

"I had it built over their original grave sites, so there are no real vaults above-ground in it," Jordan said. "Except, of course, for the niche for the child's urn."

"Her name," Tara told him as they went up the two steps into the crypt itself, "is Sarah Veronica."

She saw Jordan's hand quiver as he inserted a smaller key into what appeared to be a small, bronze door, about two feet high by one foot wide.

"All right," he said. "If you'd like, I can have her name carved right above this little door and etched on the urn, with the dates."

"The date," Tara corrected.

As he opened the small, grated metal door, she held her breath. Morning sun slanted into the crypt through the doorway behind them, throwing stark shadows and illumining the niche. She could not believe it even now. For one moment, she imagined she'd seen a tiny face staring out at her.

But there was only a polished, bronze urn within with the words on it, *Baby Lohan, beloved child.* Nothing else but dust that had sifted through the keyhole and a spider's web, which Tara brushed away before she lay the lilies beside the fancy foot of the urn.

"I want to hold it," she whispered. She felt Nick step closer to her, edging Jordan away. Nick's hand came lightly to the back of her waist.

"Of course," Jordan said, stepping away. "Be careful. It's heavier than it looks."

But it didn't seem heavy. It was light. And so cold to the touch. Tara stared at it, at the words, *Baby* and *beloved,* then cradled it in her arms. She stepped away to sit down on the single stone bench and held the urn in her lap. Neither man said anything. Jordan stepped farther way, though Nick hovered. The wind sighed and the stream rattled on.

"I want this. I need to have it," Tara told them.

"N-need it?" Jordan blurted. "For what?"

"For me. Just for a while."

"Tara, it belongs to Laird and the family, too," Jordan protested.

"I also have a family. And this precious part of it has been taken from me in more ways than one. She should have a birth certificate, and a death certificate, too. You've made it like she didn't exist!"

"I told you, we did all we could. We were trying to protect you — yes, and Laird —"

"And Jen!"

"— from having everything dragged through the media again. You being attacked by a killer and being comatose with the danger of brain injury was bad enough. We didn't need this, too."

Tara had tried to keep calm, but she couldn't help herself. She didn't shout but raised her voice so that the interior of the crypt echoed with her words. "As usual, you didn't need or want bad publicity. But I needed and would have loved this child! Don't blame me or the coma for her death, because I wasn't really there, and you and Laird and Jen and your doctors were. I might not have wanted a child until Laird and I solved our problems, but I would have cherished this child."

Tara stood, the urn still in her arms. It was warming to her touch. She could not let it go. Nick looked as if he was going to round on Jordan and tell him off or worse. She was learning to read the telltale throbbing at the side of his throat. It pleased her to note that her former father-in-law looked more distressed than she'd ever seen him.

"Will you promise me," Jordan said, "that as soon as I have the stone cut with her name and date, you will bring the urn back? All of us should be able to visit it here."

"Then have keys made for me, to the gate and this little door," she countered, stepping closer to him and looking up steadily into his face. He met her gaze, but a slight tic at the corner of his left eye jumped.

"All right," he said, clearing his throat. "That seems fair enough. Tara, I'm doubly distressed to see you suffering so — you can only imagine how broken up Laird was — and I'm dreading telling Veronica this afternoon."

"Tell her I honored her as best I could with Sarah's middle name," she said, nodding to Nick and starting away from this place and this man.

Nick quickly came behind her. "You were great," he said, after a few steps, keeping close, shoulder to shoulder, but not touching her. "So strong. Do you think he will really make you the keys?"

"If he doesn't, I'll never give this back," she vowed, the urn clutched against her breasts. "Besides, I mean to find my own keys to whatever it is he's still hiding. I've never seen him so shaken. He's no more grieving with me than that marble crypt is. I think Laird and my old friend Jen probably had an affair from way back. I've got to find out if Daddy Dearest agreed to let them keep me comatose — which killed my baby — until Laird could be free of me to run off with Jen. Or if Jen did something to make sure my baby was stillborn, because she was afraid then Laird might have had second thoughts about running off with her. One way or the other, someone snatched my child from me. Finders Keepers has a new desperate but determined client, and it's me."

16

With the urn holding her daughter's ashes on her lap, Tara worked like a madwoman on her own Finders Keepers case that afternoon, evening, night and the next morning.

After all, in a way, her child had been snatched away by her ex-husband. He had taken little Sarah without telling her where the baby was — or even that she had existed. The case was the most consuming she'd ever had. Though she had no hope of getting her child back, how much more deeply she felt the desperation of women who had asked for her help.

During Sarah's birth, Tara had been completely at the mercy of her doctors and the Lohans. Laird had allowed a doctor near her who had every reason to want their baby to die, so that she could comfort and run off with Laird. On the Internet Tara found Laird and Jen's marriage license in Seattle court records. It was outrageous that they were married just a few days after the divorce. And she'd traced the transfer of Jen's license to practice medicine to the state of Washington, though she could not locate where she was practicing in the Seattle area. Perhaps she was just enjoying the good life with Laird, hobnobbing, putting down business and social roots.

What a gullible idiot she'd been to trust the woman she had once considered one of her two best female friends. Alex — dead. Jen — the worst sort of Judas. It was horrendous that a physician who had taken the Hippocratic Oath to do no harm might be, at least indirectly, a murderer.

Tara also researched the various levels of coma, especially drug-induced ones. Previously, she had avoided reading anything that touched on that terrible experience; now she devoured information on the chemical means to produce a medical coma to aid in treatment and recovery.

One fact repeated by online experts and verified by several long-distance calls she'd made this morning seemed important: *Some patients seem to recall very distinct events while they are in a coma; others seem to remember as if through a mist.*

"I know I heard Veronica's music," she

said aloud to the empty house. Claire would be at school for hours, and Nick, after hanging around all morning, had finally been convinced to take Beamer for a walk. "And I heard someone tell me I was going to have a 'vaginal delivery' — Jen's voice, I swear it." She also recalled someone crying, not a newborn's wails, but an adult's. Yes, someone crying, crying, perhaps herself, from the pain of labor — or loss.

Maybe she'd been so deeply incapacitated by drugs she couldn't help deliver her child. She studied amnesiac drugs, ones that could have kept her out of it, even if her medical coma were lightened for the delivery. For some reason, one called Versed sounded familiar to her.

Used for various procedures, Midazolam, more commonly called Versed, induced a short-term, twilight, semiconscious state in which the patient could follow basic orders, even respond, but would recall nothing of a painful experience afterward.

But she'd gasped to read that if Versed were used during the last few days of pregnancy, it could cause drowsiness and slow the mother's heartbeat — and *cause troubled breathing and weakness in the newborn infant!*

If Tara could prove malpractice or malfeasance — or worse, intent, at least on Jen's part — that resulted in her child's death, she'd get a lawyer and go after Jordan, Laird and Jen. She'd get Jen's license revoked at the least, see her go to prison at best. Whether Tara won or not against Lohan power and money, at least she'd make them pay with their precious reputations. How dare Jordan claim that *she* had lost her child? Not she and Laird. Not a doctor. Not all of us. He'd intimated it was all her fault. No, her miracle baby's death was not her fault! And she was going to uncover something better than misty memories to prove that.

She carefully placed the urn back on her desk and began to pace, raking her hands through her hair. Of all that she'd read, one thing haunted her as if some specter whispered over and over in her head, "Locked in syndrome. Locked in. Locked . . . in."

She had memorized the words from a Web site about the Glasgow Coma Scale: *Some coma patients suffer from "locked in" syndrome in which they are awake but unable to react or act upon their environment . . .*

Locked in syndrome . . . locked in . . . She was locked in until she could prove the Lohan doctors had used drugs to control her while she was pregnant and then botched her baby's birth. She spent hours reading about other drugs that could induce deep comas for someone with head trauma: lorazepam, or Ativan, were the drugs of choice for patients requiring long-term sedation. Pentobarbital induced comas for patients with head bleeds . . . On it went in a maze of possibilities.

She jumped when a knock sounded on her office door. The familiar surroundings came back to her from whatever dimension she'd been in. "Nick?" she called.

"Can I come in?" he asked and cracked the door open. "You skipped breakfast. I made us some good old peanut butter and jelly sandwiches." He carried a tray with milk, sandwiches, potato chips and apples.

"Thanks, but I couldn't eat."

"You have to keep your strength up. Doctor's orders — mine."

"I've been researching doctors, some I trust — and then, on the other hand, Jennifer DeMar Lohan, ob-gyn."

He set the tray down on the end of the desk. Beamer padded in with a bone in his mouth and flopped on the floor to gnaw at it. "Tara, where would be a good place for that?" Nick asked with a nod not at the tray but at the urn.

"A nice way of telling me I can't carry her

ashes around with me day and night? I know that. But Sarah's my client, too — both of us."

"You need to take a break."

"I know. All right."

"I thought I'd show you the other aspect of tracking with Beamer — the human aspect. The dog can only do so much of the work."

"Is that a ploy to get me outside, get some exercise, Dr. Nick?"

"It is, but a tracker like you should know some of the tricks of a tracker like me. After Claire's gone to bed tonight will be time enough to get back to all your research."

"I have to admit, my eyes are ready to cross. Even when I close them, I still see lines of print from the screen — and her face. Sarah's. You know, what she might have looked like. I've read that some parents who lose newborns take photos of them to keep the child's memory alive. I don't think that's morbid. She would have been two and a half. Since I never saw her, I keep picturing her as looking like my old baby pictures."

He reached out and cupped her cheek with his big, warm hand. "Could be. That's logical. Beautiful, red-haired with forest-green eyes, just like her mother."

She turned her head and kissed his palm. She heard his sharp intake of breath. His eyes narrowed, his nostrils flared, but she could tell he held himself back from seizing her. "You've been so wonderful to me," she whispered. They stood there, frozen in time, staring into each other's eyes as if mesmerized.

Then he frowned and broke the spell. "Tara, the army's pushing me for a quick answer about training dogs at Fort Bragg. I got a phone call this morning, and they've sweetened the pot again. I'd love for you to come with Claire and me. You could work your case and others from there, maybe with more objectivity and security than here."

"I can't," she told him as she stepped away and looked down at the urn again. "I need to actually question some people in person, and that's too far away."

"Laird?"

"Not yet, at least. When I do, it will probably be with legal help. Besides, he'd only lie or blame me. He and Jen would obviously both spout the Lohan line. I've got to have some ammo when I finally face them. Don't worry — I'm starting with a family photographer when he gets back in town. No danger there."

She surprised herself by not breaking

down in sobs. Her pain was now too deep for tears. She knew Nick would go east with Claire and leave her here. Last week that realization would have almost killed her, but now she was dying inside anyway, dying to know all of the truth about what had happened to her baby.

The day after Jordan had told Veronica about Laird's lost child, she finally managed to stop crying. Her nurse, Anne, thought she was in the depths of drug withdrawal and, in a way, that was true. Since Jordan had confessed that Tara had borne a baby who had died — and whom he and Laird and Jen had cremated and told no one else about — Veronica Britten Lohan realized she had indeed been drugged by Jordan's twisted version of family love and loyalty.

Tara's words kept clanging in her ears as if set to Tchaikovsky's dirgelike melody, "None but the Lonely Heart."

"I walked all the way in from the back entrance," Tara had said. Imagine that, walking by oneself, against rules and regulations, despite fences and gates, through storm and distance, defying Jordan Lohan all the way. How inspiring! Tara had always reminded Veronica of her better self, of what she should have been, and she vowed right now to resurrect that self as soon as possible.

Veronica had decided, whatever the price she would pay, she was withdrawing from the Lohan clan.

However Tara had gotten in, Veronica had hatched a plan to get out. Of course, that would involve theft, threats, lying, flight and a new life of her own choosing, but if her despicable son Laird could do all that, so could she.

Nick had scented Beamer with one of Claire's flip-flops, and now he and Tara followed the eager Lab on a trail Nick and Claire had laid down the previous day. Tara tried to enjoy the crisp, sunny September weather, but it just made her heart heavier. A two-and-a-half-year-old child should be by her side, toddling along, chattering, taking in the sights, sounds and scents.

She knew Nick was doing his best to distract her with a change of scene from her office. It scared her that she found it hard to concentrate. Maybe she did need a break.

"In a way," he told her, "trackers have to be what we call fence walkers. They need to walk the line, to stay rational, not emotional. As a tracker, you might have demons within, but you've got to react like a battle-hardened veteran on the outside."

"That sounds like army lingo — like what you might have told the guys you were training with the dogs," she said as they followed Beamer's lead down to the mailboxes and then uphill again. "And I get the personal point, because you know how obsessed I am with my own hunt for answers. If the shoe fits . . ." she said, pointing at Claire's flip-flop, which he had jammed in his jeans pocket.

"I was also thinking of myself," he admitted, frowning, as his longer strides easily kept up with her and Beamer. "I can preach rationality all I want, but I was ready to fall apart in the Middle East, not only from losing Alex and my mother, but two guys I was training."

"Nick, I'm sorry. That must have been terrible for you. Did you blame yourself? And did you fall apart?"

"To the latter question, no way. Not in front of heroes who face that sort of tragedy all the time."

"But now that you've been home and left your buddies there, it's still bothering you — maybe even more."

"Tara, we're out here to learn some tracking skills, and that's it, okay?"

So close but so far away from what he had

buried inside, she thought. She'd finally shared her problems with him. Why couldn't he just open up to her? But she knew enough to answer her own question. Because he was a man, of course. She understood at least that much about the male sex. But he had chinks in his macho, duty-bound, rationality-at-all-cost armor. He had admitted he'd been too brusque with Claire and her, and she thought he was finally realizing that rearing a kid was not like training a dog.

Tara wished she could help Nick fight his pain, but she was trying to build all sorts of walls against her own demons right now, and the effort was draining her.

"Beamer, halt," Nick commanded, and the dog obeyed. "Here, Tara," he said, pointing ahead as if eager to get out of the hole he'd dug himself into. "See my tracks next to Claire's small ones? Besides the different sizes, what else can you tell about the man walking with the child — just from the prints?"

Tara bent over to study Nick's footprints, impressed in the soil between two small rocky outcrops. Loving puzzles as she did, this challenge would ordinarily have intrigued her, but she just wanted to get back to her office.

"The adult is a big man, probably not more than middle-aged," she said. "His weight is mostly in muscle and height, not girth, because the prints seem quite deep but not wobbly, like a fat or older man might walk. And the strides are long but the prints aren't blurred, so he probably wasn't walking too fast. In short, he must not know I'm after him."

"I bet he'd walk even slower if he knew you were after him," he teased. "But from the prints alone, how do you know it's a man?"

He had her there. She's the one who had overstepped. "Depth of the footprint, especially around the heel?" she ventured.

"Many men put their heels down first, but so do some women."

"I get the hint. These adult prints show someone who walks with his or her weight quite evenly distributed, not to one side or the other. And the person, probably a man, must not have been in too much of a hurry."

"Better. Now you're studying pressure points. Such close observations can reveal weight and height, but also hesitation, indecision, confidence or fear. So soon you're into the realm of emotions and personality as well as physical traits."

"But such close observation will give you

a sore neck and back," she said, straightening. "And you won't look ahead to see what's coming up next, such as maybe your prey, hiding around the next tree, waiting to get you."

"Good thinking. You need to be especially careful if you're dead tracking — that is, following your prey faster than he or she is moving, trying to catch up."

"Dead tracking. It's a scary term, let alone a scary idea. So, besides watching what the dog's doing, you have to balance your time between studying the tracks and keeping an eye out."

"Roger that. Besides, if you stare at tracks too long, you start to lose depth perception and can get not only neck and backaches but eyestrain or a headache. After a while, you can be affected by what's called ground surge, where the earth seems to be moving in waves. You can almost get nauseous from it."

"I've already been suffering from ground surge, ever since I fainted in Jordan Lohan's office. It's as if the earth is going to rise up to smack me in the face or swallow me right up."

"Yeah, well, I've been feeling I'm lightheaded, at a high emotional altitude, since I laid eyes on you six days ago. Tara," he said, turning her to face him, "I can't promise much right now, but I'm asking you to go with Claire, Beamer and me to North Carolina. I can't leave you here, and I want to protect you. I need to do my duty — my mission — to train those dogs for the troops. But I also need to be a parent to Claire, and I could really use your help. Tara, in all kinds of ways, *I need you!*"

She longed to throw herself into his arms and agree to anything he wanted. To keep Claire — to be with Nick! Though he had most certainly not proposed marriage — and, even for her, it was far too early for that — she wanted to scream out, *Yes! Yes!* It was her happily-ever-after dream come true, just like in Claire's favorite fairy tales.

But he was asking her to leave her own mission. She could not do that, not for anyone, until she'd settled how little Sarah had died and somehow found a way to make the child's short, short life worthwhile. When Nick had come home, she'd briefly seen him as her enemy because he might take Claire and leave. Now, he was asking her to go with them, but he'd become her enemy again, tempting her to leave her quest. She cared deeply for him, was starting to love him. She admitted that to herself at least, but she could not give in.

"Nick, I'm sorry, but the timing's wrong now. I'm sure you understand why. I have to do my duty, too. I'm on a mission, in a way, tracking someone who's dead."

Jaw tight, he nodded. He seemed so stoic, but that telltale vein on the side of his throat throbbed. She could tell he wanted to say more, maybe wanted to grab and shake her.

"I understand," he whispered, not looking at her now but down the trail. "Well, hey, there's not much more of this exercise left. Beamer's really getting too old for long treks, so this won't take long. Beamer, find."

With Nick walking behind, either hurt or fuming, Tara followed the dog along the path above their closest neighbor's house and finally, toward their own. She couldn't bear to look at him again right now. Soon they'd be at the spot where someone had sat or lain to spy on her or on them. How that had upset and frightened her at first, and now it seemed like nothing — unless she could tie her watcher to the Lohans somehow. Could they have hired someone to alert them if she caught on to their scheme? No, that didn't make sense, because just watching the house would not tell them if she was trying to expose them from her actions within.

At least she knew they had no worries

from Rick anymore, and she'd checked on Dietmar Getz earlier only to find he was back in Germany for an extreme biking race there. Marv Seymour seemed too weird and weak to do more than leave roses, and she hadn't heard a thing from him since she'd cut ties.

"You took Claire to the scent pool?" she called back to Nick when she saw where Beamer was headed.

"Yeah, we went this far, but not up to the old cabin. The trail ends here."

"Maybe it does and maybe it doesn't," she said in a shaky voice. She'd seen something small glitter in a wayward shaft of sun through the scrim of pine branches and thought she recognized it.

"What?" he asked, as she stooped and pointed. "Damn!"

On the ground, surrounded by dried pine needles and fallen aspen leaves, lay two sequins, one silver and one gold.

17

When Tara went back to her office to check her calls and e-mails, Nick followed, still arguing.

"Two sequins doesn't automatically mean Marcie was the one watching the house," he insisted. "What's her motive? I guess it's possible that she just stepped out for a walk that night she was here, and I didn't hear her. Distraught, she wandered around, sat down for a while above the house, losing the sequins off her jacket, then —"

"Oh, you would defend her. Maybe she was fixated on you and was up there stalking you before she dropped in when Rick died — ran right to you for comfort, which you quickly gave her. She said you were 'so nice' when you visited them, and she sure hung on you that night."

He muttered something she luckily didn't hear. Beamer sat in the middle of the room, his head turning from one to the other as they raised their voices. Hands up, palms out, Nick said, "Okay, okay, let's look at this a different way."

Despite his strident tone, she turned away and played her messages. One was from Robert Randel, the longtime Lohan family photographer. He'd be back in the office tomorrow, and she could stop to see him about having a picture taken with her niece, the pretext she'd used to get an appointment without tipping him off, just in case he was on the Lohan payroll for more than his photography.

"Look at it what different way?" she asked, scrolling through her e-mails. Two from clients, none from Elin Johansen at the clinic, whom she'd taken a chance on e-mailing. That pretext was that she wondered if Elin could give Claire private piano lessons; the real reason was to see if Tara could jog her memory about the night she was found bleeding in the snow.

"You're not even listening," Nick said. He spun her to face him. Thrown off balance, she sat back on the corner of his desk with him leaning over her between her spread legs as if to pin her there. "Let's say," he went on, "that Rick was the one who was up there spying on you, maybe the one who was at Red Rocks that day the boulder just

296

missed you. So he told Marcie what his deal was with Clay, and she agreed to help him with it. When he was busy, she came up here to keep an eye on you."

"For Clay?"

"That's my guess."

"That's possible, I guess. At least we can question Marcie tomorrow after Rick's funeral," she said, pushing him away, though he helped her up.

"Or maybe," he said, crossing his arms over his chest, "when Rick killed himself, she picked up where he left off, to keep the money coming in. Working at the L Branch tavern, she can't have earned much on her own, and then there are funeral expenses."

"I agree with you that Clay could have a vendetta against me, but the man's in prison and most of his funds must have gone to lawyer's fees. And I think Rick and Marcie would have been living higher on the hog if he hadn't been strapped for cash in the first place."

She faced him squarely, hands on hips. "Nick, haven't you ever heard the saying, 'Follow the money trail'? It's more or less what you're doing, working for the army until you can build your own dog-training business here. I mean, I know duty calls, but you also need to support yourself and Claire."

"True. So?"

"So Clay *might* have some money stashed somewhere, but if I had Beamer's nose, I'll just bet I could follow the stench of big bucks to Jordan Lohan. He probably wanted me watched to be sure I didn't . . ." Her voice wavered and trailed off.

"Didn't what? Put a big banner up outside saying the Lohans lied about your child? What could Jordan get out of having someone watch the house?"

"I — I don't know. Maybe to see how you and I were getting along?"

"What the hell does he care, as long as you leave his little Laird alone — Oh, now I see where you're going."

"You said some big shot with power and money, some local person, has upped the ante again for you to take the Fort Bragg job. Maybe someone besides Claire was hoping you'd take me with you — get me out of this area, out of the Lohans' hair, so to speak. You took a good look at those power photos of Jordan with local and national politicos in their house. He could have pulled some strings to get your army contacts to push you to go and take me, too. I mean," she said, her voice dripping sarcasm now, "it wouldn't be the first time someone in political office did something illegal and immoral."

Now he sat down on the edge of her desk, looking suddenly shell-shocked. "Both of my contacts urged me to take you east. They even offered some help setting that up."

"See? Think the worst of the Lohans, and you're probably only scratching the surface of what they're capable of. If they can make a dead baby just disappear in this day and age, they can probably abracadabra anything."

"But what possible tie could someone like Jordan Lohan have to the likes of Rick Whetstone and Marcie Goulder?"

"I don't know. But if we can just put these pieces together somehow . . . I admit that the Lohans usually deal with lawyers and power brokers, not small-time, off-the-wall people like them. And why watch the house from outside," she said, sinking in her desk chair, "when what counts is what's going on inside the house, though we did hug each other outside? On the one hand, I could see Rick hiding above the house, thinking he could snatch Claire, but surely Marcie wouldn't want her now, and Clay's in jail . . . Sorry if I sounded jealous about Marcie."

"That part, I liked."

"I suppose the one she's been watching has to be me."

She stood and looked out the window, up toward the scent pool. Remembering she had the two sequins in her shirt pocket, she took them out and attached them to a sticky note on her desk. Nick came up behind her and put his arms around her shoulders; with a sigh, she leaned back into his strength before turning to face him again.

"Nick, Beamer's another part of the puzzle, at least his behavior the night Marcie was here. Remember how he freaked out around her, and she tried to pass it off as the fact some cat at the L Branch had rubbed against her?"

"You're a genius. I should have thought of that right then."

"Maybe you were blinded by the glitter of sequins or big boobs."

"I've been a boob. Maybe it was always her up there and never Rick. That time I thought I saw a flash of blue — it could have been her denim jacket. And you've said that big truths are always in little details. Right away, I noted that old hunter's cabin had been swept out, and, when I was at their apartment, I noticed it was really clean. But the key thing is that the candy bar wrapper was hers, so Beamer had tracked her before, and he remembered her scent."

"She didn't want me to fix her tea, but asked for cocoa. She loves chocolate. Maybe we've been on a dead-end trail with Whacker Getz, and that's why he looked so shocked when we confronted him. I mean, the guy hates me, but those bike tracks could have been from anyone mountain biking around here."

He pulled her to him and held her hard; she clamped her arms around his waist. His mouth close to her ear, he whispered, "You're good at what you do, sweetheart. As you said, Marcie's a captive audience at the funeral tomorrow, so let's take her out afterward and carefully, cleverly interrogate her."

When Jordan went into the kitchenette of the clinic cabin to speak quietly with the nurse, Veronica quickly jumped up and felt in his raincoat pockets. Yes, his cell phone. Praying he wouldn't miss it before he left, she took it and pushed it down between the cushions on the couch.

Breathing hard, she sat on top of it and strained to hear what they might be saying. Something about doses of her medicine.

Veronica recalled a classic scene from the

old movie, *One Flew Over the Cuckoo's Nest,* where Jack Nicholson was stuck in an insane asylum. Yes, she thought, though it was hardly a luxe environment, it was rather like this place, with the Lohan version of that controlling Nurse Ratchet from the film. When the woman had insisted Nicholson take his pill that doped him up to stay cooperative, no doubt, he managed to keep it under his tongue. Yes, some version of that would do.

"Darling, I've got to run," Jordan told her as he came back out into the living room and scooped up his raincoat. She prayed he wouldn't look for his cell, but he just came over and kissed her cheek. She had an urge to turn and bite him, but then he might have her restrained again. And she couldn't have that, because she'd soon be going for a nice, long walk — in this case, a freedom march.

Tara and Nick entered the Corbett Funeral Home in Evergreen just before ten the next morning. The cloying smell of flowers and of some sweet chemical — cleaning fluid or worse — hit Tara in the pit of her stomach. Like Beamer, she was sensitive to scents. Suddenly, she was certain she had smelled sharp scents at the same time she'd heard the words *vaginal delivery,* the same night she'd heard someone crying and then later, the organ music. Smells from a makeshift delivery room in her clinic cabin?

"Isn't Ms. Goulder here yet?" Nick inquired of the hovering funeral director, Ralph Corbett, who had just introduced himself.

"Not yet, though she said she'd be here a half hour ago," Corbett, a rotund, dapper man told them, glancing at his watch. It looked strange to see someone nattily attired in a suit and tie around here, where most people dressed Western casual. "And we've had no other calls inquiring about the time of the service, since that wasn't in the newspaper obituary," he added.

"No one from his workplace — a caterer here in Evergreen?" Nick asked.

"No one on his or on Ms. Goulder's side. It's almost as if the poor man didn't exist."

Hair on the nape of Tara's neck prickled. That was the way she'd described what the Lohans had done to her little Sarah: it was as if she had never existed. Here she was attending a funeral for a man she barely knew and yet she had not been able to formally mourn her own daughter.

In the pearly lighting from two torchère lamps, Corbett escorted them up to the closed casket. On it lay a single spray of white carnations, dyed red around the edges. The white ribbon tied around it bore no words. Recorded organ music played in the background. It made Tara miss Veronica again. Despite her growing loathing of the Lohans, Veronica had cared for her, and somehow they had been kindred souls.

Nick paced while Tara sank into a wooden chair in the front row of a neatly arranged semicircle of them. "What if Marcie doesn't show?" she asked Mr. Corbett.

"I'm not sure. It's most unusual. No minister is coming. She was going to do a reading or two, as I understand it. I do have permission and payment to inter the body. My, I hope nothing has happened to her. She seemed such a nice, sincere young lady."

"Yes, didn't she?" Tara said with a pointed look at Nick.

"This whole thing is so sad," Mr. Corbett went on. "I understand the deceased's only living adult relative is in prison, and here his significant other seems to have deserted him."

"I believe," Nick said, "we will go look for her, rather than phoning. Perhaps, when it came to really saying goodbye, she became despondent and needs help. Mr. Corbett, if we don't call you by noon, go ahead with the plans to inter Rick Whetstone. He was once my brother-in-law, so perhaps I'm the closest one to him right now — if Ms. Goulder has left, for some reason."

As soon as they were outside in their car, Tara said, "But if the reason she's missing is that we're onto her, how could she know?"

In the bathroom of her cabin, with the shower running to cover her voice, Veronica sat on the closed toilet seat and whispered into the phone. Even if Anne, her own Nurse Ratchet, was listening at the door, Veronica was quite certain she could not hear. She'd managed to avoid swallowing her medicine and, later, to dump her coffee into the orchid plant Thane and Susanne had sent her, just in case it was laced with something.

"Rita, this is Mrs. Lohan. I don't want you to indicate in any way that you are talking to me, at the price of your job — or even more, considering my source for the Vicodin. Do you understand?"

"Oh, yes, ma'am," her maid said. "What is it I can do?"

"Listen carefully to me. You realize that I did not tell Mr. Lohan the source of my drugs before and how devastating his knowledge of that could be."

"Oh, yes."

"Here's what I want you to do. Do not write this down, do not repeat it except to your brother, if you need help. And, Rita, don't think you can tell Mr. Lohan what I'm asking, because I have left a way for you to be arrested if you do, even if I am still locked up at the clinic. You managed to keep things quiet before, and I want my requests now kept the same way."

"Yes, I understand."

The woman's voice kept getting weaker and shakier. Ordinarily, Veronica would have pitied her, but this had to be done decisively and quickly.

"Tomorrow night at ten o'clock, I want you to park your vehicle where it cannot be seen outside the west service entry gates of the clinic grounds. I want you and your brother to bring two extension ladders about fifty yards south of that gate where there is heavy vegetation, placing one ladder inside the fence and one out. You are to wait there. Are you with me so far?"

"We can do that for you."

"Excellent. And I'll need money from under my everyday jewelry box in my second drawer. I believe there are several hundred dollars there. Bring all of it and two casual changes of clothes for me. The other thing I need you or your brother to get me is a rental car in another name — not mine, not yours. After I climb the fence, you will drive me to where you have left that car. Do you understand all that, Rita?"

"Yes, tomorrow night."

"I am relying on you, just as you rely on me to keep the secret of your and your brother's drug dealing. And bring no one else in on this. As I said, there is someone who knows your secret, and it's not Mr. Lohan — yet. If anything goes wrong in any way, you and your brother will be arrested."

Breathing hard, Veronica cut off the call and hid the phone under the extra towels until she could place it by the door behind the chair where he'd put his raincoat. She'd love to phone Tara right now, but she couldn't push her luck. If Jordan found his phone and checked the log of who had been called when, he might be tipped off anyway, but she had to risk that. If he did check the log, she hoped to be long gone by then, until she had all the answers she needed — and a way to make sure Jordan never locked her up again.

Marcie was not at her and Rick's apartment, nor was her car parked anywhere in the immediate vicinity. Tara and Nick talked the landlord into letting them in to look around. Like the rest of the place, the bathroom where Marcie had said Rick had killed himself was immaculate. Her clothes were still there, as if she were coming back.

"That laptop of hers that meant so much is nowhere in sight," Nick told Tara as they walked back out onto the street. "Let's go down to inquire about her at the L Branch where she was hostessing."

The place was called a tavern, but it was more restaurant than bar. Western music — Kenny Rogers crooning an old hit — and Western ambience seeped from the place. Nick asked to see the manager, who turned out to be a burly, bearded guy in a plaid flannel shirt with his graying hair tied back in a ponytail.

"Marcie Goulder?" he said when Nick asked if he'd seen her. "Not for a couple months. She worked here for a while, then split, I think, when she met some guy with dough."

He knew nothing else about her. As they started out, Tara turned back to ask, "Do you have a cat that hangs around here?"

"No way," he told them. "Dogs, I like, but I'm allergic to cats. I just set rat traps, if it comes to that."

"Good advice," Nick told Tara as they

went out on the street again. "I think we'd better find a way to set some traps for our own kind of rats."

18

After calling Ralph Corbett to tell him they couldn't locate Marcie, Nick and Tara hurried home. They were hoping Tara could find some sort of information about Marcie online, some hint about where she might have gone. Since Marcie's new laptop had seemed so important to her, perhaps she had some sort of online presence, though they didn't trust her to be using her own name. If they got any leads, they were going to look for some link between her and the Lohans.

As Nick drove Tara's truck into the garage and killed the engine, he realized something was wrong. "Beamer's not barking," he told her.

When the Lab was left alone, he'd always given them a loud welcome home, though not the big display he had the day Nick had returned. That was only one week ago, though it seemed like a year. Now Nick felt the same ripple of fear as he had in the desert before everything exploded.

"Wait here a sec," he told Tara, taking the house key from her as she got out to unlock the garage door to the house. With all that had happened, could someone have hurt or taken Beamer? Thank God, he thought, Claire was at school.

He fought down his instinct to prepare for a frontal assault and pulled Tara from the garage and around the corner of the house where they huddled under the deck. "Get out your phone and be ready to call nine-one-one," he said. "I'm going up into the trees in back to see if I can spot anything. Beamer would not keep quiet on his own. You stay put here."

"No!" she whispered, grabbing for his wrist but missing. "The trees are where someone would hide."

He ignored her protest. Keeping low, he darted up into the trees. It took him only a second to see the back window over the kitchen sink had been completely broken and that a wooden ladder lay on the ground under it.

"Call the cops!" he yelled to Tara. "Tell them someone broke into the house. I'm going in."

"No, Nick, wait!" she cried, but then he

could hear her on the phone. The fact that the ladder lay on the ground made him believe their invader had come and gone. Whatever had been taken from inside, it was Beamer he was most worried about. The dog couldn't be lost, too, not like Clark and Tony in Afghanistan and Tara's daughter here.

He jammed his key so hard in the back door he almost broke it off. "Beamer? Beamer boy?" he cried as he slammed the door open and thudded up the stairs. No sounds whatsoever. The dog evidently wasn't locked up somewhere. If someone had tried to take him, Beamer was used to obeying commands. The doors had been locked, but that didn't mean someone hadn't just gone in the window then out a door, dragging the dog.

Nick tore through the great room, scanning the floor, then into the kitchen where glass, glittering in a shaft of afternoon sun, lay shattered over the countertop and floor. Below the sink, in a smear of blood, Beamer lay unmoving.

Tara's panicked call to the police surprised her, and not just because they answered immediately and were on their way. With adrenaline pounding through her, and with the house and trees nearby, she suddenly recalled phoning the police for help when Clay had held Claire and killed Alex. The sight of her friend tied to a chair in the kitchen leaped at her. Others had told her about that day, but she saw it now, even as she tore around the house to follow Nick inside.

She rushed in, expecting to see the place vandalized or torn up. But the main room looked normal, untouched. Was this just a warning to them to lay off their search for answers about her baby? But once again, how would anyone know for sure she had been driven to avenge her baby's death?

She gasped when she came into the kitchen. Nick knelt in shards of glass on the floor with Beamer in his arms, trying to hold him up so his dangling feet hit the floor. The Lab looked limp and lifeless.

Her feet crunched glass; she almost slipped as she ran to them, and then saw blood. "Has he been shot?"

"Cut by glass, drugged. I thought he was gone. Can you help me? He's got to move."

"Thank God, he's alive!"

But Beamer was dead weight at first. Tara moved his legs while Nick held him up. The dog's tongue lolled from his mouth, and his eyes were dilated. He breathed in shallow rasps.

"Nick, we've got to get him to a vet."

"I know one who makes house calls, but I'll need the phone book. Maybe I can get him to drop everything and come up here."

"I'll get the number," she said and stood. "Oh — there's a gnawed bone with icky-looking meat on it over here. Not ours."

"That must be how they — Marcie, whoever — took Beamer out of commission. I swear, I'm gonna kill somebody."

"She may be unaccounted for, but she did know we'd be in Evergreen this morning — at her request."

"Don't touch stuff. Maybe the police can take fingerprints."

As Nick dialed the number she read him, Tara could hear the distant wail of a siren. For the first time, she feared for her work in her office and went down the hall to check, peeking first in Claire's room. Nothing amiss there. But in the bathroom, the medicine cabinet door gaped open and the shelves had been shoved clear. Boxes of bandages and plastic bottles cluttered the floor, as if someone had been madly looking for drugs. Drugs, when they'd drugged poor Beamer?

In her office, things looked intact, her file

drawers not jimmied, her PCs in place. She'd have to check her bedroom for the extra cash she kept there. Surely, someone hadn't broken in just to hurt Beamer.

"You'll have to let the cops in. I'm not leaving Beamer!" Nick shouted to her as she darted into her bedroom. It also looked normal, but the extra cash she kept in her top drawer under her lingerie was gone. Her small leather jewelry box had been dumped on the bed, but there was nothing of great value there. Maybe it just was a break-in for cash and drugs, not a warning. Living in the mountains used to be so safe, but urban life was intruding. She started out to meet the police, who had shut down their siren just outside. She heard car doors slam.

But she ran back into her bedroom, to the cabinet at the bottom of her bedside table where she'd left the urn with Sarah's ashes. Shaking, she fell to her knees on the floor by her bed and opened the cabinet doors.

The urn still sat there, but she knew it had been moved. The small, framed baby picture of herself she had placed behind it had been shoved back into the cabinet, and the urn itself had been slightly rotated. She was sure of it.

"Ms. Kinsale!" came a man's voice from the front with a rapping on the door. "Evergreen Police, Ms. Kinsale!"

She banged the cabinet doors closed and raced to let them in.

That night, after putting Claire to bed in Tara's room, since she was disturbed by the break-in and didn't want to sleep alone, Nick and Tara sat on the living room floor with a drowsy Beamer between them. The Lab's head was heavy in her lap as Tara stroked his silken ears. Nick gently rubbed his back, as if, Tara thought, he were their baby. The vet had come and gone, observing that it was good Beamer had not eaten more of the sedative-tainted meat that must have been heaved through the broken window. Two big cuts on the pads of his feet, which had made the blood in the kitchen, had been bandaged.

"I don't care if the police say it has all the earmarks of a break and enter for cash and drugs," Tara said, "I think it was Marcie or a Lohan lackey looking for something about my search for information about Sarah."

"But you said your office didn't seem to be disturbed, and no one knows your password to access your online work."

"I know, but I'm telling you the urn was moved. I don't put it past Jordan or Laird to be so ticked off I took the urn that they hired someone to switch it with an identical one, so I wouldn't even have her ashes."

"Tara —"

"I know, I know. I'm starting to sound over the edge. Well, maybe I am. The police may have fingerprinted some spots, but I didn't want that black graphite dust all over the urn. Besides, of course, it would have had Jordan's fingerprints on it anyway."

"It's ironic, after all you've been through, we end up bringing in the police because of a break-in."

"I thought of that. I would have loved to be calling them in because we proved something against Marcie, or better yet, the Lohans. But I'll need to really lay the groundwork for that. I have a lawyer friend in Seattle, a former client. After I traced Carla's ex and she got her daughter back — Annelise is about Claire's age — Carla got her law degree and specialized in child advocacy. At least I'd know she's not tied to Lohan money and power."

"Okay, a lawyer and law enforcement — I can see we'd need that, which is why it was good we told the police we think Marcie's been casing the house for days and may have conned us to get inside to look it over. But I don't want you personally going up against Jordan or, worse, Laird."

"So far I've never been able to stomach researching anything to do with Laird. I couldn't bear to see his face or even read about him online. I've wanted even less to do with him than he evidently does with me. But he's betrayed me in more ways than one, and I'm at the point I'm going to have to force myself to look into his and Jen's life, just as I have so many other victims' exes."

"Long-distance research or working through that Seattle lawyer, fine."

"No, maybe more. Nick," she said, turning to face him, though she slightly jostled Beamer's head, "I think I'm going to have to go to Seattle to do some on-site, pretext work on Laird and Jen. I'll see my lawyer friend before I go to the police. Maybe when you and Claire head east, I'll drive to Seattle and —"

"You're not facing them up close and personal, and definitely not alone. We can't be separated. Not yet, not now anyway. Duty may call me, but it's going to have to wait. I'm with you on this. Whoever is behind everything is willing to hurt those who are innocent, and that's my definition of real evil. They've harmed Beamer, maybe your Sarah. They've harmed you, but I still don't want you taking them on face-to-face.

And it's going to take both of us to protect Claire, so —"

As if that declaration was doomed, from down the hall, Claire shrieked once, then again. Tara started to move the dog's head off her lap, but Beamer's body tensed, and he sat up as if on alert.

"Stay. Beamer, stay," Nick told him. As Tara ran down the hall, she could hear Nick racing behind her. She shoved the bedroom door, which stood ajar, all the way open. Light from the hallway spilled in. The child stared vacantly into the shaft of hall light.

"Claire, I'm here. It's just a bad dream, sweetheart."

Claire knelt on the bed, pressed against the headboard, clutching her pillow. "She's dead with dark eyes!" she cried. "She's in the hall!"

Tara sat on the bed, pulled Claire to her and held her hard. Nick came in and sat close, rubbing Claire's back. "No one's in the hall," he said, his voice gentle. "We're both here, and no one is going to hurt you."

Tara had feared the day's events might disturb the child, when she'd been doing so well. It had been an entire week since she'd had one of her screaming nightmares, but with the house broken into, police around, reminding her of terrible times, and Beamer harmed . . . Sometimes, Tara wondered if Claire didn't just subconsciously absorb her own fears, even when she tried to act steady and strong around her.

Finally, still holding tight to Tara, Claire quieted to sniffles. For once, Tara was not hoping she would simply fall asleep and forget the dream. Tara had learned the hard way — Nick had, too, she thought — that it was better to recall and face nightmares rather than trying to ignore or bury them.

"Claire," she whispered, "don't worry about anyone coming back into the house. Robbers don't return once they've hit a place, especially not with people here and the police knowing all about it."

"But I heard you tell the police it was maybe that lady Marcie."

"I didn't know you overheard that."

"Yes, after I got home from school. They said they would look for her. But she came back a second time after she was in to the hall and your office."

"No, that was just in your dream," Tara said. "She was in our bathroom and down-stairs, the night she stayed here, but not in the hall or in my office."

"I saw her," she insisted, nodding. "She had bad, black marks under her eyes that night. Beamer sat outside the bathroom door, then you called Beamer. Then she went quick and quiet down the hall and in your office. I was peeking out of my door at her."

Nick scooted even closer on the bed. "Honey, why didn't you tell us before?"

"I didn't remember till the dream tonight. If she was the robber today, she came back a second time. I guess in the dream I kind of thought she was Mommy's ghost come back to find me, crying with dead eyes."

"No, no," Tara crooned, rocking her again. "Mommy's not a ghost, and she's not coming back that way, but she'll always be in your mind and heart." With wide eyes, Tara looked at Nick. So, Tara thought, Marcie wasn't in the bathroom all the time. But what was she doing in the office? Deciding they had to know more, she said quietly to Claire, "I didn't know you saw Marcie that night."

"I guess I forgot. See, I had to go to the bathroom, but I heard someone crying and was scared it was you. So I peeked out and saw a strange lady with dark, dead eyes go in the bathroom. Then, when Beamer went downstairs, she came out of the bathroom and ran down the hall to your office. I didn't know if it was one of your sad ladies you help or not."

"No, sweetheart," Tara cried, squeezing her harder. "Marcie's not one of my ladies, and her mascara was smearing under her eyes from her crying about losing a friend. What else do you remember? Did she have her pretty jacket on with the gold and silver sequins in a star pattern on her back?"

"No, I think a T-shirt is all."

"Well, it's good you remembered now. You were just woken out of a deep sleep that night and saw someone you didn't know."

"But since you took her in, you know her, right?"

Nick spoke. "We thought we knew all about her, but we didn't. Just remember, Aunt Tara and I are both here to take care of you, so — so nothing else bad is going to happen."

Tara heard his voice waver. Like her, he was waiting for some other, awful shoe to fall. But what could be worse than losing little Sarah and Nick's beloved Beamer getting hurt?

"I'm sleeping in Aunt Tara's bed tonight, and you can, too, if you're scared," the child told Nick.

"A great idea," he said, "but some other time, because I'm going to sit up with Beamer to make sure he keeps getting better."

"I'm glad you put boards over that kitchen window that got broke," Claire told him with a big yawn. "You know, even if we had a robber, I still don't want to leave this house, Uncle Nick. I won't be afraid to keep living here, really. I like it way better than somewhere called North Carolina and Fort Bragg."

"You just get some sleep," he said, his voice tense again. "We'll be right here so just call out if you want us."

Tara knew what she was going to do. She was horrified that, as an investigator who was paid to find people, she hadn't even thought about locating listening devices in her own house. She kissed Claire good-night again, then Nick did, too. At least, she thought, trying to buck herself up, they finally had the answer to how someone had known their every thought and move, even from inside the house, maybe even from inside her computers.

At 9:40 p.m., Veronica jimmied the bathroom window of her clinic cabin with a nail file and climbed out while the shower was running full tilt. The past three nights, she had taken long showers and told her nurse that she thought the heat and steam were helping her. Veronica had taken it as a good sign that Jordan had come back for his cell phone and found it exactly where he had thought it might have fallen out. When she'd said goodbye to him earlier this evening, she had forced herself not to add, *And good riddance.*

Still, it really did pain her to leave her old life behind. Thane and Laird might disown her and turn the grandchildren against her. But she was leaving. She had to do this, had to desert not so much Jordan as the old, obedient and weak Veronica. She must find herself again.

It was chilly outside, especially in just a nightgown, robe and slippers, but it felt bracing, she told herself as she hustled along, first down the path and then off it. Her nightclothes would have to do because she dared not take anything else out from under the eagle eye of that nurse. She soon felt warm from exertion and excitement. The tiny, puffy clouds of her breath seemed to lead her on.

She prayed that Rita would be waiting. She thought she would, for Veronica had been in the Lohan lair long enough to know how to put clipped command in her voice. Once she finally escaped, she could become just Veronica Britten again, whatever the cost of her ruined past.

As if standing shoulder to shoulder against her, the pines and firs thickened here, but she pushed on. Yes, outside the fence, someone with a flashlight, playing it upon a ladder! She prayed Jordan had not somehow found out. Surely he had not bugged their home's phones, the way she'd overheard him boast he had that of a financial rival several years ago. He was good at having people watched and at setting traps, and she could only pray Rita had not betrayed her.

If she'd not been panting so hard, Veronica would have held her breath in anticipation. Two ladders over the fence, the lofty doorway to new beginnings. That is, after she checked on Laird and Jennifer. She had to know one thing, and, however long it took her to drive to Seattle, she wasn't turning back.

"Rita?" she whispered. Then louder. "Rita!"

"Yes. Here. Me and Carlos, we here."

Hiking up her robe and nightgown with one hand, Veronica grabbed the highest rung of the ladder she could reach and started to climb.

In the hall outside her bedroom, Tara wanted to scream, but, leaning against the wall with Nick, she whispered to him, "I feel like a complete fool. That night we took a supposedly hysterical, grieving woman in, I'll bet she planted bugs in my office, then had to break in to get them out."

"I shouldn't have let her stay, but I felt sorry for her."

"Don't blame yourself. She would have gotten in somehow — maybe like she did today."

"Damn her for almost killing Beamer. And who's to say she didn't kill Rick for some reason?"

"I know. How convenient he typed a suicide note on her laptop. I'll bet she got all the bugs ripped out of my office, but let's search anyway."

Not saying another word, Tara looked under her desk and behind her file cabinets while Nick got down on floor level and looked under her chair and in the closet. He reached up and ran his fingertips along the top of the molding on the doors and windows.

"I think the coast is clear," Tara said in a normal voice.

"At least in here. If you find one of those bugs, I'll buy you a diamond ring."

That off-the-wall remark stopped her for a moment, but she grabbed a flashlight out of a desk drawer and searched on. He might have meant the comment as a joke, but it was strange he seemed to have that on his mind.

"And if I don't find a bug, no diamond ring?" she asked, hardly believing they were talking like this. If she thought a listening device was still in here, she'd stage a little play where they gave out all kinds of disinformation to whoever was listening. Maybe that's what he was doing, because he was sure confusing her.

"Diamond ring or not," he said, "I'm still thinking the four of us make a good team."

The four of us, she thought. Ah, yes, Beamer, too.

Her light caught something far back under the knee space of her desk. "What do I get if I only find the tape one of the bugs was anchored with?" she asked, and pulled off the small piece of black duct tape. Eager to show it to him, she bumped her head when she came back up.

He reached to take it, but it snagged their fingertips together.

"You get my solemn vow I won't go east until we find out who's behind all this, and I don't just mean Marcie. If you're still listening, Jordan or Laird Lohan," Nick declared with bravado as if he were speaking into an invisible microphone, "you're soon going to be toast."

She wanted to laugh at that. Laugh in defiance, laugh in joy that Nick now believed her about the Lohans, laugh that he would stay to help her and wanted her in his life even after — after whatever befell. She wasn't stopping until she solved her own Finders Keepers case.

"I've got to check my PCs for spyware," she said, "the sophisticated kind that's downloaded directly and doesn't come in online, because my anti-spyware programs would have sniffed that out. I'll bet all she had to do that night was pop a CD or disk in and out."

"I'd be shocked if Marcie is the brains behind more than installing that. You know that precious, pricey Wi-Fi laptop of hers? It was probably given to her so the data coming out of your computers went directly to hers and then she reported to her employer."

"Maybe she was reading what the bugs picked up that way, too — or just by hanging out above the house with some sort of audio receiving equipment. You mentioned the army using that, and I know people's cell phone calls can be picked up by a receiver in the vicinity. I'm thinking we owe

Dietmar Getz a couple of new tires or something, though he's still a jerk."

She was excited now, on a roll, as if they were really getting answers. And that could mean finding out what had happened to her little Sarah.

"You know," she went on, giving her main PC commands to search her hard drive, "computer spyware has shown up in several cases I've had. One ex-husband installed something called Lover Spy on his former wife's PC. Yes — yes, Nick, here it is!" she cried, leaning closer to her screen.

"What?" he asked, bending over next to her. "How can you tell?"

"See this encryption message? It's reporting a specialized spyware called a key logger, which records a victim's keystrokes and sends images of the computer's screen to whoever installed it. Maybe she didn't have time to uninstall this today, or just thought I wouldn't catch on — which I almost didn't. I feel like I've been conned by the Lohans all over again! This stuff tells everything. Nick, they now know I've researched sedative drugs to keep a patient in a coma and that I tried to track the specialist they hired for me at the clinic, the one I'll just bet they sent, all expenses paid, to Europe."

"At least, if they wanted to get rid of you,

they could have by now."

"How about that boulder that just missed me at Red Rocks?"

"I'm still hoping that was an accident. But maybe they have some strange loyalty toward you, since you were once a Lohan."

"It could be. After all, they figure that Laird's leaving me is already a fate worse than death. I just don't know. I used to love puzzles, solving things, tracking people, but I'm just so lost in all this!"

"Can you remove that crap from the computer?"

She tried to get hold of herself again. Thank God she had Nick to keep pushing her on, keeping her on course. She forced her fears down again. "I've advised others not to until they contact a lawyer or law enforcement. I'll check to see if it's on my older PC and, if not, just use that. We may even be able to use this to throw them off, because it's evidently still functioning. Since the ladder was left outside, maybe our arrival caught Marcie, or whomever they sent, before they could remove this."

"Or it was helping them track your moves so well they decided to chance leaving it. After all, they tried to cover the real reason for the break-in with the money and drug motives. But won't your keystrokes show them you've found it now?"

"I don't think so — only that I might have checked my hard drive. It's worth a chance. Besides, spyware and a seemingly random, anonymous B and E is hardly enough to confront the Lohans with. If we could only find Marcie and make her talk!"

She got her main computer back to its screen saver and turned to her other. Its hard drive looked untampered.

"Nick," she whispered, and motioned him to follow her down the hall to Claire's empty, dark bedroom. She pulled him into it, then into the closet among the short, hanging clothes where the two of them sat on a shelf among stuffed animals. Desperate just to hide out, Tara slid the closet door closed.

"What in hell are you doing?" he asked.

"I don't care what we found and figured out tonight, I'm still paranoid. Who knows where Marcie put bugs that night we were being so nice to her, but going by what Claire recalls, I don't think she was in here."

"Definitely not in the closet," he muttered, sounding suddenly amused. "And here I was hoping you just wanted to be sure Claire didn't watch us make out and have some sort of dream about it later."

She felt herself blush. How ridiculous at

331

her age and in the dark. No man had ever affected her like this one, not even Laird. Yes, Nick impacted her roller-coaster emotions and hormones, but her ties to him went deeper. Nothing was the ultimate escape but being in his arms.

Thank heavens, it was pitch-black in here, because the heat started at her throat and climbed clear up to her ear tips while her skin tingled. She had meant to ask him in private what it would mean to his job offer to delay going east, but he reached for her and nuzzled her throat, then trailed wet kisses down it.

Trying to sound normal when her heart was beating as if there were a set of drums in there, she whispered in his ear, "Nick MacMahon, I've fallen hard for you, but I've got to go after Jordan, Laird and Jen, using any ammo I can. And I'll understand if you're not along for that part of the battle. You know what I mean, I think . . . don't you?"

Whenever this man touched her, she lost her train of thought. What had she just said?

"I'm in it all the way, in all the way," he murmured as the tip of his tongue plundered the hollow of her throat while his hand slid up the inside of her thigh.

Right now, that vow was better than a

diamond ring, she thought, better than the standard promise of *I do.* She relaxed under his kiss, slanting her mouth sideways to get closer to him. Stuffed animals gently thudded off the shelf as they sprawled out together. They heard the padding footfalls of their real animal, pawing at the closet door.

"It's Beamer," she murmured, though that was obvious.

"Hell of a tracker dog, even when someone doesn't want to be found."

Nick slid the closet door open. Beamer stepped in and flopped among the displaced array of stuffed animals, putting his head down on a big yellow tiger. A wan silver glow from an outside floodlight gilded his golden coat.

"He won't tell what he sees," Nick murmured, running his hand along her bottom to lift her hips into his lap. "You can trust Beamer and you can trust me for the utmost discretion."

Amidst the chaos of all the losses in her life, she smiled deep within as his mouth covered hers again.

19

The next morning, using her spyware-free PC, Tara tried to trace Marcie Goulder. Dead ends all the way. Was that even her real name? she wondered.

The house was quiet. That had pleased her once, but now she longed for the sound of Claire's voice, Nick's heavy tread and Beamer's barking at elk and deer. Nick had refused to let Claire take the bus this Friday, but had left to drive her to school himself, with Beamer riding shotgun. After he'd dropped Claire off, he'd gone to check Marcie's apartment again, but had called to say she hadn't shown up. He'd said he'd be back soon, but he was going to get a piece of glass to replace the broken window.

Tara sighed, remembering how wonderful it had been to be with Nick last night. With him she felt so safe and yet so tense, as if she could explode. Once she'd settled everything with the Lohans, she couldn't wait to have days with Nick where they weren't afraid of or angry at what could happen next. Only one week with Nick, and she was ready to give him her body and her life — but she couldn't completely, not yet.

She shook her head at her wandering thoughts and tried an online search site to locate anyone named Goulder in this immediate area. Could Marcie be a nickname for Marcia?

Outside, something bright caught her eye. She looked out and up toward the tree line. Nothing amiss, but what had caused that flash?

It darted by again, piercing her eyes so she blinked. A reflection from the trees. She gasped. A square piece of glass? Was Nick back and had carried the new window glass up there?

Under an aspen, something moved. A booted foot, not Nick's.

"Damn!" Tara yelled, and stood so fast she hit her chair with the backs of her legs and it rolled away, bumping a filing cabinet. "She's out there again with her laptop!"

She grabbed her cell phone, dialing Nick's number as she ran through the house. The gall of that woman to come back here like this!

"Pick up, Nick, now!" she muttered as she

jammed shoes on her feet and ran to the side door. Her gut instinct was to chase the woman, grab her and that laptop, but what if she bolted into the trees? Without Beamer, she'd never find her in the thick forest if she took off running. But maybe she was heading toward the hunter's cabin and Big Rock.

Nick's voice on the phone. "Tara?"

"Marcie's outside again!" she cried without preamble, as she dipped her head to look out the great room window. She wished the kitchen window wasn't boarded up, because that was probably the best angle. "She was near the scent pool with her laptop, but I don't see her now."

"Call the cops, and I'll be there as quick as I can. Stay put."

"She's moving away. She'll get away. I'm going after her."

"No! It may be a trap. Stay put and call —"

She hung up. Turning off its ring, she jammed the cell phone in her pocket, though she knew there were dead spots where it didn't work in the mountains. She grabbed her jacket and went out the front door. No use charging out the back and spooking her. Mommy's ghost, indeed! She had a lot to settle with that woman, and she wasn't getting away. Man, she could use

Beamer, but trekking mountain paths right now might open up the poor Lab's cut foot pads. And Nick had said the dog was getting too old for long, hard tracking.

Tara took time to lock the door. She had the Evergreen police on her speed dial, so she knew she could summon them if that really was Marcie. She'd only seen her jeans, boots and laptop, but it had to be her. Tara figured she'd head for the old hunter's cabin and she was sure where she must have left her car. She'd stop her somehow and get the answers they needed to link Marcie to Jordan or Laird.

Tara's heart thudded as she quickly climbed to the tree line, passing the scent pool. All around her, the aspens shook their golden leaves; it looked as if they were trembling.

Tara looked for tracks. Yes, Nick would be proud. Clean boot sole prints. And what, he might ask, can you tell about this person?

"That she's a lying Lohan lackey," Tara muttered as she stretched her strides, trying to keep an eye on the footprints and the path ahead. Dead tracking, Nick had called this. She should have brought some sort of weapon, a knife from the kitchen or one of Nick's father's hammers, but it was too late now.

She caught a glimpse of the woman up ahead. Yes! Marcie for certain, with that spiky blond hair. Carrying her laptop and something else. What if she was armed?

Once Tara never would have taken such a risk. Laird wouldn't have allowed it, and it wasn't in her nature. Until now. Now almost any danger was worth it if she could just get some answers. Follow the evidence trail, follow the money trail — follow . . .

Tara pressed her hand to a stitch in her left side, right under her rib cage. She was used to the altitude, but felt as if she couldn't get a deep breath. The hunter's cabin lay just ahead. As if the trees had devoured the woman, Marcie had disappeared. Inside? Could it be a trap, or could Tara herself lay one?

She stepped off the path and circled around behind the cabin through the trees. It had rained hard two days ago, and the ground up here was soft.

She halted when she saw a grimy window on the mountain side of the cabin. Perhaps no one could see out, but she couldn't see in, either. Still, she could throw a shadow; she'd have to duck and get under it fast. If Marcie had not gone inside, she could not afford to let her slip away in a car parked below Big Rock.

Hunched under the window, Tara froze to listen. Thank God, no engine started on the road nearby. She heard the wind soughing through the spikes of pine needles, and her own thudding heart. How long could she stand there, waiting for Marcie or Nick? Nick might have called the cops, though she wished she'd told him to hold off on that until she had some time with Marcie. And would he tell them to come up here or would they just wait at the house?

Again, she had a flashback: she'd called the cops, but not soon enough. Outside his house, Clay came up behind her, stomped on her wrist and sent her cell phone flying. Then he hit her head so hard he knocked a year of life out of her, ruined her chance to know her baby . . .

Trying to keep so much as a twig from snapping, Tara tiptoed around to the front of the old hunter's cabin. Just as before, the door was ajar and askew. She was the hunter now, and she had to look in. Lifting a solid branch from the ground for a club, she peeked in the door.

Dirty but deserted. She'd wasted too much time, just the way she'd wasted time trusting Laird, wasted time not knowing she was a mother.

Still holding the branch, she started down

toward the road where she and Nick had surmised their stalker had parked, though they'd still thought they were looking for Dietmar Getz then. So misled, but, she was certain, that's exactly what the Lohans wanted.

Yes, a car was parked there, but not the dark-colored one Marcie had driven to their house the night Rick died. No matter. Money could buy a thousand new cars, a thousand new spies, a thousand new wives for a Lohan.

Could Marcie be up on Big Rock? It made sense, in a way. From that high, open vantage point, she could surely send or receive cell phone messages that crags or outcrops interfered with below.

How long before Nick could get up here? she wondered. Surely he'd know this was where she'd come. She wasn't sure if he'd use Beamer to track her. It would take him at least twenty-five minutes to get home from Evergreen, and she'd probably been out of the house for at least fifteen now.

Tara quietly climbed the bulbous outcrop that was Big Rock. Careful where she put her feet and the branch she carried, she inched up, trying to avoid so much as a gasped breath. She slipped once, scraping her knuckles and knees, but went on. More sky came into view, then the valley.

And the spiky top of Marcie's head! She was sitting, facing away, looking out over the vast expanse. She seemed to be on her cell phone. But the wind was wayward, and Tara could not tell what she was saying. She'd have to wait until she was finished, for if she was reporting to someone dangerous, Tara didn't want her to call for help. Besides, this would give Nick more time to get here.

But it was hard standing half down, half up the steep, smooth slope. Her calves began to cramp. She thought of calling the police from here, but Nick might have done that. Besides, she needed to question Marcie before they read her her Miranda rights and let her call a lawyer, probably funded by a Lohan. She'd never get information out of her then.

Tara ducked when Marcie turned her way, still sitting, talking on her phone. For the first time, her words came clear: "I'm outta here, outta this deal. And don't think you can risk any more faked suicides. I've got enough goods on you, too!"

Marcie evidently ended the call with that. When she stood, almost her whole body popped into view. It was now or never, before Marcie saw her and took off. Tara knew she'd have to block her against the steep drop-off side of the rock to make her stay and answer questions.

"So," Tara yelled, and scrambled up onto the slightly slanted surface, "how does it feel to be stalked and to have your conversations overheard?"

The shock on the woman's face showed she had not known she was being followed. Marcie's wide eyes darted past her, around, down the rock.

"You're — you're alone?" she asked, taking a step back. Her shiny black laptop lay on the rock a few feet from her, next to a small gray case. A camera case? No, probably some sort of listening device.

"Hardly," Tara brazened. "Your old friend Nick's down at your car to be sure you don't get away, and the cops have been called — the same ones who want you for B and E. Soon, I'll bet, they'll want you for collusion in a faked suicide."

"You're crazy. That's pure hearsay."

"Oh, I'm sure you'll have an excellent lawyer to object, when I testify against you in court. The best that Lohan money can buy."

"Whose money? I just — I fell for Nick MacMahon the first minute I saw him and want to get him away from you, that's all.

That kind of stalking, nothing else."

"Oh, so bugging my office and my PC helps you to keep track of him? Marcie, you're wanted for stalking, harassment, criminal trespass and burglary, but I won't testify against you for any of that if you just tell me who hired you, who you were just talking to."

The woman's face went whiter than the clumps of clouds behind her. "Get out of my way, Tara. I admit I've been distraught since Rick died. I'm not responsible for my actions. I — I couldn't even bear to go to the funeral home, and I'm sorry for that."

"But no better time to drug our dog and rip out all evidence of your spying. So, was Jordan Lohan's initial offer to Rick or to you? However did he find you in the first place?"

"Get out of my w—"

"You've been in mine too long! The Lohans are dangerous if you cross them, don't you realize that? If Rick's suicide was really murder, they obviously needed him out of the way. You can testify against the Lohans, make a plea deal. Otherwise, don't you think when they're done with you, they'll eliminate you, like they did him? You're expendable, Marcie! I was a Lohan wife, one who bucked them. I know them. Now answer my questions and then clear out of here fast, because they'll be after you next."

When Marcie stooped to grab her laptop and the case — whether to throw them off the rock or at her — Tara rushed her with her wooden weapon raised. She hit her arm. Marcie yelped and drew it back, then tried to race around Tara to get off the rock. Tara swung the branch at her feet and tripped her.

"Answer me!" she shouted, straddling the prone woman as she pressed the end of the branch into her chest.

Tara couldn't believe the violent surge that rose in her. This woman had answers she wanted and needed. If Marcie or Rick's illegal actions could be linked to the Lohans, she had some leverage. She would go to Seattle, get Carla Manning's legal advice, tell the police what had happened and fight to avenge Sarah's death.

The strange sound was distant, a whining at first, like a buzzing fly, but it quickly got louder, came closer. *Whap-whap-whap.* A helicopter lifted from the valley far below. Oh, thank God, Nick had called the police, and they'd sent a chopper to land up here and arrest Marcie. But she needed answers first. She needed . . .

The chopper was shiny ebony with a black

bulbous window over the cockpit. No police insignia, like she'd seen before. No number on the chopper's tail, nothing . . .

As the deafening aircraft hovered lower, the wash from the rotors kicked up dust and skittered tiny rocks into her. Blinded, Tara tried to motion the chopper to back off. Marcie kicked her branch away. The blast of air took Tara to her knees, then flattened her to the ground near where Marcie lay.

But she was gone.

Tara crawled in the direction she was certain the laptop had been, but she must be disoriented. Stop! she told herself. Stop before you roll off the edge of the slanted rock, or before Marcie jumps you or you get blown off.

She couldn't move, couldn't breathe. But then, through the flying scrim of debris, she saw Marcie scramble for the chopper as it hovered lower like some flying beast coming in for the kill. Its treads were only a few feet from the rock. Marcie was going to climb in! Not the police but a rescue for her? Yes, she passed the black square of her laptop into the plane, then heaved the gray case inside; black-jacketed arms with black gloves reached out for her.

"No-oooo-o!" Tara screamed, but she choked on grit and dust.

She tried to belly crawl backward, in case the chopper tried to knock her off. The rock began to slant down behind her. She scraped her stomach and chin; opening her arms wide, she tried to find something to grab in the hurricane from the chopper. If she wasn't crawling toward the road, she could slide off the edge to her death below. She was disoriented, so dizzy. Could she have hit her head? No coma, no living death, never again! It terrified her that Claire's face, Nick's, her own as a child — Sarah's — flashed through her brain in that awful second.

And then the chopper lifted and tilted away, taking Marcie with it. Beamer's distant bark! Nick's voice called from behind her somewhere . . . Nick coughing, now kneeling over her, shouting, "Marcie's car's on the road below! Where is she?"

Her voice came out in a rasp. She coughed and hacked as the chopper climbed the face of Black Mountain. She pointed toward it, choking out, "That — rescued her when I — had her cornered. It came fast, just after she threatened — whoever sent it — and I — know who — did."

"Jordan? She threatened him about what?"

"She — didn't say his name. Said she'd tell about Rick's — fake suicide. But if she thinks she's safe . . ."

They gasped in unison as, kneeling and hugging on the hard face of Big Rock, they watched in horror as a small, blond figure cartwheeled from the chopper and fell into the jagged mountains far below.

20

Every time Tara closed her eyes, she saw Marcie dropping through the clear Colorado sky to her death. After searching from the air for hours, the local Civilian Air Patrol and a Denver Police helicopter still had not located her body. The police said that in that rough terrain, they might never. It was as if she had disappeared into oblivion, just as Tara's own little Sarah had.

"Nick?" Tara murmured.

"Hmm? What?"

They lay side by side on the long couch as daylight dusted through the darkness outside. Neither of them had gone to their beds last night, but had been talking, planning, until they had fallen asleep here.

"Even if they found her body and located the black chopper," Tara said, picking up where they'd left off, "and it led straight to the Lohans, they'd just claim she was despondent and had jumped. Of course, they'd say they tried to save her, like they tried to save my baby. They'd be so sad — what a shame." Her voice dripped with sarcasm. "Marcie told me she wasn't herself and couldn't face the funeral. I think she was lying, but I'd have to testify to what she'd said. They'd get away with murder again. They'd haul in made-to-order doctors claiming she was of unsound mind — unsound mind, just like me."

"You can't let this keep eating at you. The Lohans are not invincible," he insisted, sitting up and rubbing his bloodshot eyes with a thumb and index finger.

"In other words, you think I'm turning into one of those crazy conspiracy freaks."

"I didn't say that, but Jordan's got to make a mistake sooner or later. Your ex and his bride may have already made one, if they didn't take all precautions when you had your baby. You said you were going to try again to track down the specialist who attended you and see if you could get him deposed by a lawyer over there in Europe."

"Yes, but I've got another rock around here to overturn to see what's under it first."

"I don't see what a photographer's going to get you, now that you already know Laird married Jen. She's in the photos, so they hid them." He stretched his arms high over his head. "I'm going to make some coffee and feed Beamer. At least it's Saturday, and we don't have to let Claire out of our sight, even at school." He hugged her once hard and got to his feet.

"I do feel safer now that Marcie's not lurking outside," she admitted, rising, too, and following him out to the kitchen. The clock on the oven said 8:04 a.m.; that meant they'd had about four hours' sleep. She felt as if she hadn't slept forever. But she had things to do, including dropping in on the Lohan photographer in Evergreen at ten this morning.

Nick was right — that lead was a long shot. But the fact that both her former sister-in-law and father-in-law had hidden pictures from her — even, in Jordan's case, *after* she knew about Laird and Jen and *after* she knew she'd had a baby — indicated something important was in those latest photos. She knew better than to think it was just that they wanted to protect her feelings. They were only into protecting Lohans.

After her escape from the clinic, at a nearby gas station restroom, Veronica had changed into a set of clothes Rita had brought, then she'd driven her rental car out of the Denver area like a woman possessed.

Hours later, she had stopped at a Mc-Donald's to eat an early breakfast. Imagine Veronica Lohan changing clothes in a dirty gas station restroom and eating an Egg Mc-Muffin at Mickey D's. Well, she'd better get used to it, but then, as generous as Laird had been with Tara, surely Jordan would not dare to cut off his wife of so many years with a mere pittance. He might be furious, but he wouldn't want outsiders to know anything that could sully his philanthropic reputation. Even his sons might draw the loyalty line at Jordan cutting her off financially.

Exhausted, she stopped at an out-of-the-way motel, slept the sleep of the dead — but without clinic pills and shots in her blood — then pushed on at mid-morning. Weekend traffic was heavy. As usual, not only tourists but the natives were heading for the hills to hike or bike.

Spending cash whenever she stopped for anything, she carried on toward Seattle — and freedom.

Nick insisted on driving her to the photographer's, which was fine, but Tara asked him to wait in the car. He readily agreed, since he had Beamer and Claire to deal with. Tara was already nervous and didn't want to spook Robert Randel by Nick hovering like a bodyguard. And Claire might blurt something out if she heard Tara lie — which she would no doubt have to do: *pretexting* was just a clever investigator's word for that sad reality. Her visit to Evergreen Photography had to seem like business — important, but not a matter of life and death. So why was she suddenly seeing it that way?

A bell jangled overhead as she entered the shop. She'd never been here before, since Robert and his lighting assistant had always come to the Lohan house for the yearly photos. She recalled how thrilled she'd been to be included in the annual shoot done just before her wedding. Sad to think that the two times after that her smiles were forced and insincere. She'd never managed the stoic grace her one-time mother-in-law had always displayed.

The decor here was Western Victorian, with overstuffed chairs, fringed lampshades and a thick, patterned carpet. The mood was enhanced by blowups of modern-day people in old-fashioned Wild West garb, in color, though posed stiffly like tintypes. Thank heavens the shop was clear of clients, because she needed to finesse this. Her pulse picked up, and her insides twisted.

The maroon velvet curtains separating the

shop from the back work area parted, and Robert came out. He had a tanned, leathery face, probably from doing so many shoots outside over the years. Tara guessed he was in his late fifties, though he'd never married. She'd heard he was a man-about-town with local ladies. He wasn't handsome but striking, with his black hair and sleek eyebrows accenting his aquiline nose. He wore khakis and a navy sweater and moved with a silent stealth that must have come from his part Indian heritage, which was also echoed in his high cheekbones and dark, narrow eyes. Maybe it was just the photographer in him, but those eyes were really looking her over.

"Ah, Ms. Kinsale," he said, holding her hand a beat longer than necessary, "as lovely as ever. With that face and hair, you should have done some modeling. So sorry about all your troubles. It must be an adjustment not to be a Lohan."

She bit back a sharp retort, telling herself she had one mission only here. Forcing a small smile, she tugged her hand away. "Though I'm no longer a Lohan, I consider your fine photos heirlooms I'll never part with. Besides discussing an outdoor photo shoot of my foster child and me, I was wondering if I could get a copy of the current Lohan family photo."

She almost fell over when that popped out of her mouth. She was indeed desperate if she thought she could carry off that in-your-face ruse; it was not one she'd rehearsed or agonized over.

"Ah, the current photo or the last one you were in?"

"Veronica Lohan and I are still very close, and I can hardly hold a grudge against such generous people. Yes, the current one, for old time's sake."

"It's my property," he said, hand on his chin as he tapped his mouth with his index finger, "but technically theirs, too, with the current privacy laws and all. Why don't you have Mrs. Lohan just call me with permission then?"

"You likely haven't heard, but she's back in the clinic and rather incommunicado right now, though I've been to see her. And I'm sure she wouldn't mind."

"Tell you what," he said, reaching out to pat her upper arm, "let me just print a photo of Veronica for you — I still do everyone in smaller family groups and separately, too, of course — and you can call me when you get permission for the multigenerational one." He turned toward a huge keyhole desk, sat at it and rolled out a bottom drawer with neat-looking files. "Everything's digitized today. Got to keep up with the times. No negatives to care for anymore, everything on CD. Ah, here it is. I'll be right back."

His white teeth flashed in his brown face as he waved a CD labeled in black marking pen and disappeared with it into the back room.

Her hopes crashed. This wasn't going to work. She was finally going to have to force herself to research Laird online to get his and Jen's address in Seattle and any other information she could. And then she was going there to . . . To what, other than to see her lawyer friend? Nick would have a fit if she tried to confront Laird and Jen. But she was starting to fear she'd never get answers any other way. If Nick refused to let her do that, she just might have to sneak out on him.

Tara could hear the photographer in the back room. How long would it take him to insert a CD and print a picture? And what did it matter, since the photo was only of Veronica?

She sighed and glanced down at the manila folder he'd left on the desk. The shiny silver curve of another CD protruded. Holding her breath, she slid it out. In bold, black marker, it was labeled *Lohan/Spring 2006/Seattle.*

This held last year's family photos. But Seattle? Had everyone gone to Seattle for them? Why, when they were always taken at Jordan and Veronica's home, with the view of the picture window and mountains in the background? Or would this CD just be of Laird and Jen?

She could hear a printer from the back room. He'd be back soon. This CD wasn't what she'd come in for, but maybe it was better than nothing. At least she could throw darts at the photos of Laird and Jen, she thought perversely. They'd already been married for over a year when these '06 photos were taken. It would be wrong to take it, but so much was wrong. What else was she capable of, to get answers and justice for herself and little Sarah?

Praying Robert wouldn't miss the CD, which she intended to somehow return, she pocketed it just before he came back in. If only she could swap this one for the one in his hand. Surely Susanne and Jordan were hiding the most recent photo from her, so would the CD she'd taken even help?

Her next thought staggered her: perhaps Laird and Jen had a child of their own. That could be it. Because Tara's child had died, and the family felt guilty about that — or feared she'd discover that and prosecute them — they had hidden from her the photo of Jen and Laird, not only happy with each other but with their own baby. That would explain why Jordan had taken down the current family photo when she already knew of Laird's marriage and of her lost child.

Tara leaned against the desk to steady herself. It took every shred of self-control not to run outside. If her theory were true, Jen must have been pregnant when she and Laird were married. And that was proof positive that they'd had an affair, maybe even before Tara's accident. No wonder they were wed just a few days after he divorced his comatose wife!

And that would explain why the Lohans risked damaging PR when it got out that Laird had divorced a helpless woman in a coma. Worse, perhaps it was a coma their doctors intentionally induced or extended so she couldn't contest the divorce. How shocked Laird must have been to discover that his injured wife had also gotten pregnant, despite being on birth control pills. Having her own child was another reason that Jen might not want Tara's child to live.

Somehow she managed to calmly take the five-by-seven photo Robert extended to her.

She had to get hold of herself, keep up the charade, but her voice came out much too shrill. "Oh, that's a lovely photo of her." Tara tried to focus on it. It seemed blurred, wavy. She must not faint again as she had when she'd learned she had a child. Think, she told herself.

In the photo, Veronica wore a lavender suit and a pristine strand of pearls. Her smile was lovely, but a haunted look lurked in her eyes. Her former mother-in-law had never been like the others, gung ho for anything that profited the family. If Tara's new theory about Laird and Jen was correct, perhaps Veronica had more to feel guilty for than her own alcohol and drug problems.

"Careful," Robert said. "It's barely dry. I'm so sorry to hear she — she's ill again. Please give her my best. Let's set a date for our session with you and the child, then. And, Tara, if you're ever in town and just want to talk, please call me. I know a great new restaurant just down the way."

In other words, she thought, maybe if she let him date her, she'd eventually get the evidence she really wanted. But she might already have that, on a CD, one that felt as if it was burning a hole in her pocket and in her heart.

■ ■ ■ ■

Veronica had driven like a bat out of hell until she was clear of the Denver area. As she headed northwest on Route 19, she drove slowly and carefully. She could not afford to be stopped for speeding, because she had not a shred of ID on her. With all her planning, she had not thought to ask Rita for that. Just as well, she told herself, because she had no intention of being traced until she did what she had to do. Besides, she was a new woman now.

Despite the fact she was going to speak with Laird about his "lost child," she savored her freedom. Except for Thane's children, she didn't miss anything she'd left behind. And the scenery was breathtaking, with its alpine lakes reflecting the surrounding jagged, blue-gray peaks topped by clumps of clouds.

Not used to long drives, she planned to stay one more night in Colorado, but by tomorrow, she'd be in Wyoming. Yes, she'd stop for the night at the little town of Walden, just twenty miles from the border. Henry David Thoreau had said, in his paean called *Walden,* that he went to the woods because he wished to live deliberately. When it came time for him to die, he'd written, he didn't want to find out he hadn't lived. Yes, she understood that now. Her very own Walden, it would be.

As if she were a tourist with all the time in the world, she went into the Walden Ranger District Office to pick up information and maps. They kindly called ahead to book her — Alice Marvel; she'd picked the name of a girlhood friend out of the blue — a room at one of the small inns in town.

Despite the fact her cozy, wood-paneled room had a kitchen and eating area, she ate at a small, down-home restaurant on Main Street, reading brochures about how this area used to be a favorite Ute tribe hunting ground. Fine, she thought. She would officially begin the hunt to find her own, real *Walden* self here, and that meant finding an organ.

She checked her brochures for churches and took a brisk walk to the Catholic one. Weren't they more likely to have an organ than the Baptists or Methodists or that defunct-looking movie theater on the main drag? At least Saint Timothy's was open; the parking lot of the small church was crammed with trucks and cars. Oh, yes, she should have known: a hand-lettered sign read BINGO NIGHT.

She followed the buzz of voices to a large, multipurpose room labeled Fellowship Hall, where people were bent over rows of bingo cards. Up front, a woman spun balls in a metal basket and called out numbers into a microphone. Just inside the door, a long table was set up with cakes, cookies and coffee urns. Veronica wound her way around the room to the smiling young priest and asked him if they had an organ.

"Indeed, we do. Mass is tomorrow at ten, if you'd care to attend. We welcome guests in the house of the Lord. And you are?"

"Alice Marvel. Father, I know this sounds strange, but I was wondering if I could rent the use of the organ, right now, just for an hour or so. I would only play religious music, of course."

He wouldn't hear of letting her pay, he said, and led her into the dimly lit sanctuary where two young women were dusting the wooden pews.

"We have a guest organist, just for a while," the priest told the women. "Don't tell Rhoda that I let anyone else touch her organ," he added, and the ladies laughed as if he'd made the most hilarious joke.

In the corner of the room, near the baptismal font and overseen by a wooden statue of the Virgin Mary, sat not a pipe organ, but an electronic one she would have spurned years ago. It was well-worn, its sustain pedals scuffed, and two of the keys on its manuals were split. Worse, its stops stuck. But Veronica turned it on with anticipation. The ladies kept dusting, and the priest hovered, probably thinking that some poor woman was about to make a fool of herself. "We've a songbook or two around here if you'd like," he called out from the back door, evidently eager to return to his bingo-playing parishioners.

"Thank you, Father, but I'm fine."

She began to play and paid no more attention to her tiny audience. She let the music soar, to help and heal her. First, "Jesu, Joy of Man's Desiring," with all its running notes, then "Ode to Joy" from Beethoven's *Ninth Symphony.* On and on, until she happened to glance up and saw the pews were filled with rapt people, many of them with their bingo cards still clasped in their hands. She remembered then they were Catholic and segued into Schubert's "Ave Maria," then played the version by Gounod and Bach.

When she finished, she was astonished that everyone stood and applauded, some with tears running down their cheeks. She saw the priest wipe his eyes. Then everyone rose, clapping, clapping until they finally went silent, still standing.

Although Veronica had wanted to be alone with her music, broken keys and broken life, it was suddenly the best performance she had ever given.

21

"You think Laird and Jen had a child, too?" Nick asked, wide-eyed. "Sweetheart, maybe you're just baby-conscious. You know what I mean," he insisted as he followed her at a fast clip into her office.

"Baby obsessed — baby haunted, more like," Tara admitted, dropping into her desk chair, while Nick hovered over her.

Though they'd just gotten home, Claire was on the phone to her friend Charlee already, so Tara had taken the opportunity to tell Nick her new theory.

"The point is," Tara plunged on, booting up her spyware-free computer, "they had an affair stretching back who knows how far? Every time I think his — and Jen's — betrayal can't be worse, I find out it is." She inserted the CD with the 2006 photos. "Maybe they kept me comatose to hide not only the death of my and Laird's child, but the birth of their own. This could also mean

Jen, one of my attending physicians, has an extra motive for not wanting my child to live. She didn't need competition for her own Lohan baby, the gold digger."

"Was she really that kind of person? You knew her."

"I've learned the hard way I didn't know her at all."

She used some commands to bring up the pictures on the screen. Her hands were shaking so hard she missed a key and had to backtrack. Claire's laughter floated in from the other room.

"Nick," she said, not taking her eyes from the screen as photos popped up in neat rows, one after another, "I don't want Claire anywhere near me until this is settled — because she might get hurt, if they really come after me. And, she can't lose you, too, after she's lost so many. But, whatever it takes, I have to get to the bottom of this."

Standing behind her chair, he grasped both her shoulders. "She won't lose either of us, but we are going to stick together. I am not going to let them harm you the way they did Rick and Marcie. The high-living Lohans are starting to remind me of the lower-than-scum Taliban, laying ambushes or shooting at us from caves where we can't see them. The Lohans don't get their own hands dirty but hire others to do it, then eliminate them when they know too much."

"Finally, you see them for what they are!" she said, leaning her head back against his hard chest and grasping his hands on her shoulders.

"I just didn't want to believe it could be this serious." He dropped a kiss on the top of her head. "I figured, when I got home from that hellhole of war with deceptions and death, innocent kids and women being hurt, nothing could be that bad — but in a way, it is."

She hunched forward to stare at the screen again, blinking back tears to keep it from blurring. At least a hundred, postage-sized photos must be on this CD, some of many people — yes, the entire Lohan clan, she thought, squinting to see who was who. Some were of Thane's family: him with Susanne, then with all three of their children. She knew how Laird had seethed over his brother's brood. Laird was the firstborn, with no children, while his brother was building a dynasty.

She scrolled down to ones that must be of Laird and beautiful, blond Jen, and yes — yes — a child in blue on Laird's lap! She gasped and pointed at a small picture on the screen. Nick swore under his breath.

Trying to decide which picture to enlarge, she double-clicked the first one of Laird's trio.

It opened full-blown, immense in its impact. Elegant, dark-haired, handsome Laird, his chiseled features tilted slightly by a smug smile. Jen, so blond, glowing, leaning into him, looking like a million — no, like a billion — dollars. And a golden-haired toddler, all in blue, evidently a son.

"Damn them!" Nick whispered, leaning closer. "You're right!"

His hands tightened on her shoulders. At first, she couldn't speak. Alternately leaning over her keyboard, then sitting back, she enlarged picture after picture of Laird and Jen with their baby in varied poses. As usual, in Lohan style, each one was formally posed. With each photo, Tara felt a fresh stab of longing and grief.

The child was darling, of course. She had to admit that. Wide-eyed, almost cherubic, with curly, bright blond hair and blue-green eyes. He had Jen's hair and pale skin coloring, but with the slope of Laird's head and his ears set tight to his head. As if she had been there, Tara could sense the little boy had had trouble sitting still. He wanted to squirm out of their grasp, get down and toddle about, check out the clicking camera at close range. He wanted to free the little fist Laird was holding, maybe so he could suck his thumb. She could almost feel what he was thinking and feeling.

For the beautiful — living — child, Laird had decided it was worth moving to Seattle, worth a hasty divorce and quick marriage, and evidently worth burying another baby and consigning her to oblivion. But what was killing Tara was that this boy must have been similar in age to her Sarah. One lived, one died. For this precious baby's sake, she should leave Laird and Jen alone, but she could not.

"Once," she said aloud, startled at the sound of her own voice, "I thought I could not be more hurt than by his leaving me when I was so ill, despite the fact I could honestly say good riddance to a bad marriage. But then the idea that he might have kept me comatose so he could court Jen hurt more. Next, that he hadn't told me of our child, then, that he had just made her disappear when she died. But now, it's worse than that."

"Sweetheart, you've had so many losses, and I can understand how you feel — I can share that much. Let me go check on Claire, get her busy with something so we can talk."

"And plan. I have to plan. Yes, go take care

368

of Claire."

She closed out the array of photos and went online to an expensive, client-only database to locate Laird's address. She could not stomach doing this before; it made her almost nauseous now. The site gave her both his home and business address. They were in Medina, Washington, a suburb east of Seattle on Lake Washington. She learned from several sites that it was a very well-to-do area, as she would have expected. Microsoft's Bill Gates was a neighbor.

Aware that Nick was back with her, she went to Google Maps and selected satellite views. Then, when a partially wooded lake-front area came in view — Laird's estate clearly marked — she zoomed in on it.

The house was clearly sprawling, with a U-shaped driveway in front and a free-form deck and patio in back. On the spacious rear lawn leading to the lake, besides an L-shaped, fenced-in swimming pool, was what appeared to be a child's small, round inflatable pool and a large play set with slides and swings. That's right, she thought. The baby in the pictures would be over a year older now, not a toddler anymore.

The front, landscaped lawn led to a curved street. The houses all appeared to be gated, some even fenced in from the lake. Tara reversed the zoom to get a wider view, then pulled the camera back again.

"It's huge," she told Nick, pointing as he leaned closer. "A gated front, but maybe not fenced-in back on the la—"

"You're not planning to go there in person, not directly to the house." His voice was commanding, not questioning.

"I'm going to phone Carla Manning in Seattle, tell her I'm coming and that I want to ask for her legal advice. Then, somehow, with or without her, I'm going to question Laird and Jen."

She went back to the closest zoom of the area and hit the print button. She stood, turning to face Nick while the printer hissed the aerial view onto paper. "I think you and Claire should head east and take that job," she said, trying to sound calm and strong. "God willing, I'll see you after —"

"No! I meant it when I said that we are not splitting up. If you have to do this, we'll put Claire somewhere safe, maybe with Charlee and her mother, and I'll go with you."

"You can't. You can't keep putting off Fort Bragg. I'm starting to think Jordan has been matchmaking for us through the army officers, hoping you'll get me out of their way."

She startled at the way she'd put that. Her own words echoed in her head and heart: *Jordan has been matchmaking for us . . . hoping you'll get me out of their way . . .*

Nick. Faithful, fearless Nick, always near. Often knowing what she was thinking, what she was going to do next. She'd come to trust him so much. No, the Lohans could not have hired him, like they evidently had Rick and Marcie. Tara told herself that she was just getting crazier, more paranoid, seeing a Lohan behind every tree. She was coming to rely on Nick, to love him. But that was, no doubt, just what the Lohans wanted. Could she trust him, or should she refuse to let him come with her to Seattle? She'd already proved she was terrible at knowing whom to believe, but with Nick it was different — wasn't it? He wanted money to open a tracker dog training school. Had he really decided to stay around here because he wanted to help her, was maybe falling for her? Why hadn't he jumped at that offer from a private donor the moment he heard it — unless he had the promise of more money for doing something else?

"Nick, I don't know where Claire would be safe if the Lohan powers-that-be decide to go after her to control me. I've seen too many kids snatched by too many people.

We can't really hide her, so I think you've got to take her with you and head out to —"

"No way. I'm not leaving you alone, here or in Seattle. All right then, how about this? I call my Fort Bragg contacts to say I'm coming east with all three of us — driving and making a bit of an educational trip of it for Claire. In case we're still being watched around here, we pretend to pack some boxes, load them in my truck and head east just out of Denver, then turn around and head northwest for Seattle."

"But you'd be burning your bridges with them, then."

"If they're on the Lohans' payroll, fine. If not, I'll explain when I get a chance. If they want me as badly as they should, to train more dogs — even though I lost two of my human trackers . . ."

Tara was surprised to see Nick tear up, but she loved him the more for it. She stared straight into his eyes. The impact of the man always stunned her. So did she believe that he was her protector and not a danger? Laird had fooled her. Jen, too. But it was now or never to lean on this man. Yes, she needed him, trusted him and loved him.

"Thank you!" she cried, and threw herself into his arms. "Yes, we need to keep Claire with us. That might work. It will give us a couple of days to get things done in Seattle while we're supposedly heading cross-country to North Carolina."

"I'll set it up then."

She hugged him harder. "I don't know what I'd do without you. After I settle things with the Lohans, I'll really go to Fort Bragg with you and Claire, if you want. The only thing is," she said, stepping back from his embrace, "I don't know if I can bear to send Jen to jail or get even with Laird now — not since I've seen that little boy of theirs. A child without its mother, father, too . . ."

Tara gasped when she realized Claire had come into the room.

"I see you been crying," the child said, looking wise beyond her years. "Were you talking about me, 'cause my parents are gone? Or about your little Sarah 'cause she's dead and doesn't have you either? Is someone else's dad going to jail?"

"Let's all sit down together," Tara said, pulling Claire into an embrace which Nick completed by putting his arm around both of them. "We have some things to talk about."

After what Nick called their "family meeting" ended, Tara fixed dinner, and Nick went to call Fort Bragg.

Tara felt bad that they hadn't told Claire much more than that they were taking a week's trip to get to North Carolina. They were afraid to admit their real destination, because she might let Seattle slip to someone when saying goodbye, and they were beyond trusting anybody. Despite Claire's sadness to leave her friends, she was so relieved that Tara was going that she accepted it. And, Nick had told her, they weren't selling the house, because they would come back after he got the school going for trackers like Beamer. "And Beamer," Claire had said, "is happy riding in the truck, so he will like the trip okay."

A loud knock resounded on the front door. Before Tara could get out of the kitchen or Nick come up from the basement, Claire cried, "Bet it's Charlee and her mom! They're gonna be sad when I tell them!" She opened the front door.

Tara yelled, "No!" but too late. It wasn't Charlee and Heather at the door. Jordan Lohan stood there, casually attired, looking furious.

"Claire," Tara said, running to her and pulling the girl back, "go tell Uncle Nick we have a guest. Now."

"Is she here?" Jordan demanded, stepping

inside and looking around. Tara assumed he had come alone. His big sedan was parked in the driveway.

"Is who here?" Tara asked.

"Don't play dumb with me. Veronica's missing. Thursday night, she evidently walked out of the clinic grounds, just the way you walked in, and we've looked everywhere else. You helped her, didn't you?"

"No, but if she had asked me, I would have. Don't you recall, you pried us apart as quickly as you could the night I saw her in the chapel? We barely had time to hug each other, let alone lay some sort of plan. Do you — do you think she's all right?"

"I know no one else she would come to," he said, as if he hadn't heard her. "If she's not here, have you helped her get somewhere else?"

"Jordan, I find all this absolutely impossible to believe. Why would she run away from a great husband like you, who let her pursue what mattered to her, like her dream of playing the organ professionally? Why would she try to escape from the wonderful way she's always been treated at the clinic? So well taken care of, just the way I was there. . . ."

She wanted to scream all her suspicions and accusations at him, but that would mean she'd never get to Laird. He'd stop her. He'd warn Laird. He'd demand Sarah's ashes back. No, she had to pretext this as she never had before, but she was right on the edge of losing control.

"You always were ungrateful!" Jordan said, his voice rising. "A beautiful but spoiled and self-centered woman, after all the family did for you. You had Laird's love, and you weren't happy."

"Tara!" Nick said, coming up behind her. "To what," he said, facing Jordan squarely, "do we owe this honor?"

"My wife's missing from the clinic."

"Could it be," Nick said, "that she's run off with one of her attending doctors? Maybe she'll get a quick divorce and head for the hills."

"You son of a b—" Jordan clipped out, then cut himself off, evidently when Nick stepped forward and flexed his fists at his sides. Jordan took a big step back, outside the threshold.

Tara had to stop Nick before he blurted out too much. How stupid she'd been to think he could possibly be involved with the Lohans. No way this confrontation could have been staged. Money could buy almost anything, but that didn't include Nick. He didn't need some local political pull or funds to get his dream of training dogs or having his own tracking business someday.

Though he now stood outside, Jordan stared around Nick at Tara and said, "If Veronica's left in some sort of misguided protest, I blame your influence."

"Really? I'd say you were the one who did even more than just influence her. You as good as corralled and branded her, so if she's turned into another terrible maverick like me, God bless her!"

She stepped forward around Nick and slammed the door in Jordan's face.

By Monday morning, they had closed up the house, sent in a hold on their mail, told the neighbors they were moving to North Carolina, written an explanatory letter to Claire's school and packed Nick's truck with mostly empty cartons. Tara had phoned Carla Manning, who had insisted she had room for the three of them and that a visit — even in sad circumstances — was long overdue. And yes, she'd do anything legal she could to help.

They drove east into the rising sun on the outerbelt until they hit Route 6 E. Then Nick pulled off into a huge service station near the airport, which was full of cars in front and trucks getting diesel out behind.

He got a fill-up, then drove behind the station where the monster trucks were idling.

"Okay, mirror," he said, and Tara handed him her big mirror with a handle she'd jammed in her purse.

"What's he doing?" Claire asked, and even Beamer peered out at Nick as if he thought he was crazy.

"He just wants to check under the truck to make sure it's ready to take the trip," Tara said. They'd decided not to tell her that they had checked the vehicle several times to be sure there wasn't some sort of homing device on it. They had finally both become not paranoid but practical.

"Touchdown!" she heard Nick call out. He stood up to lean in the window and grin at them. Tara saw he had a small black box in his hand, attached to some sort of large magnet. "Excuse me, ladies, while I just go wash my hands and chat up a trucker or two," he said, handing the mirror to Tara. They watched as he strolled back to the diesel gas pumps where trucks, both in-state and out, waited while their drivers chatted or paid their bills.

"He's talking to people," Claire reported, twisting around to look out the back window, "but he hasn't washed his hands."

Nick was learning to pretext, Tara thought.

She could help Nick train tracker dogs someday, and he could help her pretext, if and when she ever got back to Finders Keepers.

He soon returned, looking smug. "I have a surprise for each of you," he told them as he got in and started the engine. "Tara, your surprise is that Jordan is getting a dose of his own medicine, because the device I found on the bottom of my truck is now on a sixteen-wheeler that's en route to Virginia — close enough to North Carolina. And, Claire," he said, interrupting what was an obvious spate of questions from the girl, "your surprise is that we are going to Seattle, Washington, instead of to North Carolina, at least for right now. It's a lot closer. They have a neat aquarium you can visit."

"But I told Charlee and her mom North Carolina for our trip. And that's what it said in the note to my teacher! Is this a surprise envelope, and we're all running away so you guys can get married?"

"You mean elope?" Nick asked with a chuckle, then started to hem and haw his way out of his predicament.

Tara bit her lower lip so she wouldn't cry. Laird and Jen had run away to Seattle and had gotten married. Now, finally, she was running after both of them. They were welcome to each other — but they had a lot to answer for.

22

Early Tuesday morning, after taking turns driving all night, Tara and Nick made it to Carla Manning's neighborhood in the Seattle suburb of Bellevue, only about three miles from Laird's neighborhood of Medina. While Nick drove, Tara had studied local maps with her flashlight until she thought her eyes would cross. Claire had been asleep for hours, curled up on the narrow backseat while Beamer sprawled on the truck floor beneath her, gently snoring.

"I can't believe we're here," Tara told Nick. "I'm finally going to face Jen and Laird and get answers."

"But," he said as they scanned mailbox numbers in the beams of their headlights, "we're consulting with Carla first. If she advises against confronting them, no rash moves, no jumping the gun. There, that house," he said, and turned in the driveway of a contemporary frame home with a big blue spruce in the front yard. In the pearly predawn, they got out and stretched. Tara felt wobbly on her feet. Despite the familiar trees, the area seemed alien, with its relatively flat terrain and the smell of the sea. Even with the early-morning chill, the air seemed moist, not thin and crisp.

A porch light popped on, and a face appeared at the window next to the front door. Tara hadn't seen Carla for almost four years, but they had always hit it off well, and Carla had been so grateful when Tara located her daughter, Annelise. Almost six feet tall and thin, with long black hair, Carla was a real Amazon who could tackle anything in life — until she'd married a man who almost did her in.

"I'll carry Claire," Nick told her. "Go ahead."

Dressed in baby-blue sweats, Carla met her halfway up the walk with a big hug. "I've always hoped for a way to help you," she told Tara. "I may not look like an attorney-at-law right now, but we're going to get your ex one way or the other for what he's done. I've taken the morning off, so I can get you breakfast and you can get caught up on some sleep."

"I've been dozing off and on. The only thing I want to get caught up with is you —

and then Laird," Tara told her, stepping back to face Nick as he hefted Claire out of the truck. "Carla, this is my very good friend Nick MacMahon and his completely unconscious niece, Claire."

"Nick, great to meet you," she said, patting him on the shoulder since his hands were full. "I've got a bed ready for her. And this must be Beamer. He's beautiful. I had a black Lab once, and it will be great to have a pet around for my girl."

"You're a godsend," Tara told her as they went up the walk arm in arm.

"As you were to me. Come on in. Consider this your home away from home."

"Oh, no!" Veronica cried when she saw rows of red headlights pop on ahead. As the thick lanes of traffic slowed to a crawl, she hit her fist on the steering wheel. Not only was everything at a complete standstill, but she saw the blinking lights of emergency vehicles up ahead. Drat! She was between exits and, at least temporarily, trapped.

It had been stop-and-go driving as she followed 90 W into Seattle. She should have waited until later in the day when commuters weren't coming into the city, but she'd already taken too long to make the Denver-to-Seattle drive. The escape part of her journey was over, and she was anxious to deal with Laird. Unfortunately, that meant today was the day that he or Jennifer would call Jordan and tell him where she was. Well, there was one Jordan she would be happy to see, and that was little Jordie. But maybe little Jordie was the problem.

Though she feared she'd get a blast of car exhaust fumes as everyone began to idle their engines, Veronica rolled down her driver-side window and took a big breath of morning air. Yes, she could smell the ocean here. It reminded her of happy childhood days on the shore of Lake Michigan, visiting her grandparents' cottage near Traverse City. But the shrieks of seagulls overhead and the occasional boom of a distant ferry horn also reminded her of the times she and Jordan had spent here visiting Laird and his new family.

But that's what was bothering her now. Her family had not told Veronica that Laird and Tara's baby had been born and lost. They had not even told her about Laird and Jennifer's baby until she was completely recovered.

So she was also going to use the element of surprise. She wasn't phoning ahead to find out if Laird was home today. Besides, she figured she'd do better taking on Jennifer, poor pretty girl, so eager to please the Lohans. But above all, she didn't want Jennifer or Laird to be prepared for her or to tip off Jordan right away.

Somehow, Veronica was going to get the answers she needed, and not only to help Tara. Such knowledge could very well serve as ammunition to blast her way out of the Lohan prison she'd been locked in for more years than she'd like to admit.

Finders Keepers, that was the name of Tara's private investigating firm. *Finders keepers . . . losers weepers,* the old rhyme went. But the official Lohan rhyme should be Humpty Dumpty. After all, as high as he was sitting, he had a great fall, and not even the king's men could put him back together again. One way or the other, Jordan — maybe Laird, too — was about to topple off his great big wall.

By the time the sun came up, Claire was still in bed and Nick was in the shower. Tara and Carla sat over a cluttered breakfast table, drinking coffee, talking about old times and new.

"Now about today," Carla said. "I figured you and Nick would want to be out and about this morning, and I've got to go into the office about noon for a while. So my mother's coming over to stay with Claire and Annelise. I don't usually let her miss school, but having a visitor near her age is special. Mom's still bemoaning the fact that Annelise is in school, since she used to take care of her all the time, so she's in seventh heaven. If you want, she can take them downtown to the aquarium after lunch."

"Claire would love it. Nick kind of promised her that."

"Then that's settled. Now back to the legal aspects of all this," she went on, leaning her elbows on the table and cradling her coffee cup in both hands. She'd been taking notes on a long, yellow legal pad as Tara had explained everything to her. Like Tara — maybe like all women — Carla was good at multitasking and never missed a beat when they switched topics.

"I'm listening," Tara said. "You're part of the reason I was brave enough to come here."

"I still don't think you can force Laird and Jennifer to give a deposition under oath, and one look at a lawyer with you and they'd clam up for sure. Or they'd just get a lawyer to block us, unless we can get some sort of incriminating admission out of one or the other of them. Misleading and lying to you in the past won't be enough. Of course, the best thing would be to prove foul play and have them indicted."

"What about a civil suit, if we can't find evidence for a criminal one?"

"Possibly, but probably not just on grounds of having your deceased child cremated without your knowledge or permission. It was Laird's child, too, and you were obviously incapacitated. Proving they induced or extended your coma will be tricky unless you can find that Dr. Givern, whom they've obviously spirited off to Europe."

"What about the fact they never registered the birth and death of my child? That's got to be a crime."

"That might work, but the fallout would be minimal with their army of lawyers and contacts. The other drawback is that I don't have a license to practice in Colorado. You might be better off with a local lawyer for that, but you said you don't want a Denver-area attorney."

"Even if I could get them on that or win a civil suit decision, making them pay millions would be like me having to cough up a hundred bucks. Still, the publicity would hurt them. They're paranoid about the Lohan reputation. I did have a wild idea there could be some sort of genetic testing on the ashes in the urn, but I think they've been tampered with."

"You mean Jordan Lohan only let you take the urn from the crypt because it *didn't* contain your daughter's ashes?"

"I'm not sure. When the house was broken into, I know the urn was moved, maybe even exchanged for another — oh, damn, I don't know!" She lifted her arms and rubbed her aching eyes with the heels of her palms. "What I do know is that I need to talk to Jen first, alone somehow. She's much more likely than he is to slip up and say something. And I do think I can get enough information to go after her physician's license, although she may not care right now, since she's wallowing in Lohan wealth and has a son to raise."

"Strange, isn't it?" Carla said, rolling her coffee mug between her hands. "Money, position — none of it means a thing if you're not married to the right person. But throw a child into the mix, living or deceased, and then it gets hard. It doesn't take long to learn what really counts in life."

"Sad but so true," Tara agreed, hunched over her hands, now clasped on the table as if in prayer. "How sad too many women learn that the hard way."

"Nick seems wonderful, a real blessing in

your life, and his little girl has obviously become yours now. When this is all over — I mean, just don't get hurt here, because you have a great new life waiting for you."

"But I can't have that new life until I settle the old one. For Sarah's sake, as well as mine."

By late morning, Claire had set out for the Seattle Aquarium with Annelise and her grandmother, Lillian Manning — Carla had taken her maiden name back after her divorce. Nick and Tara were en route to the nearby suburb of Medina with Beamer sitting on the seat between them as if he were the kingpin on their team.

As they talked over possible ploys to get onto the Lohan grounds, they tried to ignore the gray day spitting rain against the windshield. Hoping that Laird was at his office, Tara's pretext to Jen was going to be that she was desperate to know about Sarah's birth and death. She would convey no suspicions, bring no accusations. As her former physician and friend, at least Jen owed her an explanation of her daughter's death.

But that scenario meant they had to get past the front gate and perhaps even a guard. If this frontal assault didn't work,

Tara was going to have to convince Nick that trespassing onto the property was absolutely necessary. No way had they come this far, Tara told herself, not to question Jen and Laird. And if that meant arguing with or defying Nick, it had to be done.

"Damn, the Lohan house isn't even one of the biggest ones around here!" Tara whispered as they drove past it once, turned around and slowly circled back.

Of redwood and stone, the sprawling house suited its setting in a breathtaking landscape of mature trees and free-form flower beds bursting with late blooms. A small bridge arched over what appeared to be a koi pond. Tara craned her neck, trying to glimpse the back deck and playground area to see if she could catch a glimpse of Jen or her son, but at this first pass, all she saw was a thin man bent over a rose bed.

At least a truck going by slowly was hardly suspicious in this area. They'd seen all sorts of service vehicles: heating and cooling, plumbers, yard care. Other than a few BMWs and other upscale cars with residents on morning errands, the streets were fairly deserted.

"It's really hard to grasp the Lohans until you see their houses," Nick said, staring wide-eyed at Laird's home as they made the second pass. "They say you can't take it with you, but Laird probably thinks having a son and heir is the next best thing — like King Henry VIII who moved heaven and earth to have a son, divorcing one wife after another."

"And beheading a couple of them. Look!" she said, pointing, as Nick slowed the truck in front of the yard next to the Lohans'. "Their gardener's even working in the rain."

"You said that Jordan's gardener, Jim, is totally dedicated. Maybe that's what it takes to work for the Lohans."

"Tell me about it. Nick, stop here. I have an idea. Can I take Beamer out in the rain for a minute? I'm going to find out who's home."

"Sure, but be caref—"

She had the dog's leash attached to his collar and was out of the truck in a flash, ignoring the fact she should have grabbed the umbrella. "Beamer, heel," she said, and he did. It always gratified her when the Lab took commands from her.

"Hi!" she called to the man as she strolled up to the Lohan fence. Then louder, "Hello!"

He looked up and turned her way. Would he think she was just a neighborhood woman walking her dog? He was quite young, with a Seattle Mariners cap on his head. He studied her as he walked toward the fence. It had been a long time since she had used her looks to get information. She wished she wasn't so exhausted and strung out. She forced a smile. He had big hedge clippers in his hands, not electric ones but an old-fashioned-looking pair.

"Can I help you, ma'am?"

"I hope so. I'm from the dog breeding company, Pets for Kids, and I need to check out the yard and house before one of our golden Labrador retrievers — not this one — is allowed to be adopted by the Lohans. It's a gift from the little Lohan boy's grandfather in Denver, so it's a bit of a secret. We just can't allow our puppies to be taken in unless a sort of adoption check is made, you know." Too much information, she told herself, but sometimes what just came out sounded better than a rehearsed script.

"Oh, for little Jordie? Man, he's got everything else, so why not, huh?"

Jordie, she thought. For Jordan? Of course, Laird would have named him after his father. He'd even said once that if he had a son he'd name him that, but that he wouldn't name a girl something as old-fashioned as Veronica, because he wouldn't want people calling her Ronnie. No, he'd said, he'd name a daughter Alexandra, so she was glad she'd named her Sarah instead. The way Laird had handled her death, Sarah was more her child than his!

"The thing is," the gardener went on, "they're not here right now. They gave the housemaid the day off, too."

Her insides cartwheeled. All this distance and they weren't here, not even Jen.

"Do you know when they'll be back? I must have mixed up my scheduling."

"I could let you walk around the yard, but I don't have house keys. It's a great yard for a dog, as you can see," he said with a sweep of his hand. "Hope he won't be burying bones, though. The Lohans are at the other house in the woods, up by Robe Valley. That's 'bout ten miles past Granite Falls off the Mountain Loop Highway, if you need to talk to them."

"Oh, I didn't realize they had a getaway. That might give a dog even more room to run."

"Yeah, their hiding place, Mr. Lohan calls it," he said, looking her over intently. "I do have the keys for there. I look after it when they can't get up there."

Smiling up into his face, she leaned on the fence and flipped her hair back. She was wet, but the sprinkles of cool rain had turned to a fine mist. At least, she thought, if she started to cry in disappointment, he might not be able to tell. "You are being so helpful," she said. "What's your name, by the way?"

"Todd Lawrence, groundskeeper here. Yeah, well, they like to head up there now and then when he takes a few days away from the office, and I think Mrs. Lohan's been feeling a little sick lately, so it may help her. Still, if I had this spread —" he thrust his arm out again to encompass the grounds he was obviously proud of "— I'd be set for life."

"You sure do great landscaping. You know, I really should check out that getaway residence, too. It isn't set in a place where a puppy could fall down a cliff or ravine, is it?"

"It's pretty rough territory up there, but breathtaking." He smiled down into her eyes. "They're on Pine Crest Lane, which backs up to the Mount Baker-Snoqualmie National Forest. If you don't know the area, it's a little ways past the Pillaguamish Country Club, where Mr. Lohan plays golf. I love to camp and hike around there, and I did the grounds for their place there. Fantastic view of the Cascades. It's probably raining up there, just like here. That's why they call them the Cascades, of course."

She forced a laugh at what must be a stale joke around here. But he'd told her where to find the Lohans. And if Laird's so-called hiding place was out in the wilds, maybe it wouldn't have a gate and fence.

Tara managed to get rid of Todd by telling him she'd just reschedule the visit and hoped to see him then. When he pressed her for a phone number, she made one up on the spot and hurried back to the truck, parked down the road.

"So?" Nick said when she got in. He added, "You should let Beamer shake him-self outsi—" as the dog sprayed them and the inside of the truck with water.

Ignoring that and hugging the dog, she said, "They're not here, but I know where they are. And we're going to get close enough to question them. I'll call Carla to tell her where we'll be. Head for the hills, driver."

She felt suddenly hopeful, stronger. Though Laird called the other house his hiding place, no way could he escape her now.

23

"This is going to work. I can just feel it," Tara told Nick as they drove into the small, historic town of Robe Valley. "It's not raining here, and the sun's peeking through. Things are finally going to go well," she added, sounding more confident than she felt.

He frowned, but as he took the truck around another turn, he conceded, "At least I'm used to Colorado driving, and this increasing altitude's not going to bother either of us."

Her heart beat harder, not from the thinning air but from finally getting close to facing Laird. She'd still like to confront Jen first, but she would take whatever chance she got. Considering that most of the homes tucked back up in these foothills of the Cascades looked accessible to someone driving or walking in, Tara was becoming more confident there would be no barriers to the Lohans. Surely that was another good sign.

But the thing she had been silently steeling herself for was not as much facing Jen and even Laird as seeing their son in the flesh. Sarah had died, and Jordie lived. He was a beautiful child. Yes, she was envious, but she had loved to look at him in the photos, to study his little face, those blue-green eyes and bright blond, curly hair. He must be even more appealing in person. She'd like a son just like that someday, with Nick.

"Okay," Nick said, jolting her from her agonizing, "there's the country club you said the gardener mentioned, but this town looks really small. I'd better get gas. I've only seen two stations here, and the road's got to be even wilder the farther we go."

While he filled their tank, Tara phoned Carla again as she watched Nick chat up the guy in the adjoining gas station bay.

"Pine Crest Lane is only a couple of miles farther," he told Tara when he got back in. "He said you can't miss it, which usually means you can. And I got the phone number of the local police — unfortunately, not in Robe Valley but in Granite Falls." He recited it, and she punched it into both their cells. "But the bad news is," he went on, "the guy says cell phones often don't work up here because of the mountains and the lack of cell phone towers, just like at home. On a nicer note, how's Claire?"

"Carla says the girls had a great time at the aquarium. Their favorite animals were the seahorses at the Myth, Magic & Mystery exhibit, but they thought the sharks were 'awesome and way scary.' "

"Good that they enjoyed themselves."

Just past a sign pointing to Mount Pilchuck, which seemed to hover over the valley, lending a stark, snow-tipped backdrop, they came to a fork in the road. One way headed up into the deep, dense forest fringing the foothills; the other was marked by a carved signpost for Pine Crest Lane. Nick slowed and turned onto it.

"You sure you're ready for this?" he asked.

"Never been more determined."

"Don't let them get to you."

"One way or the other, *I'm* going to get them."

When they approached the first house on the winding lane, Nick pulled off to the side and killed the engine. "That's got to be it up ahead," he told her, pointing at a chalet-style house peeking through the pines. "I don't see a car, but it could be around the other side or in the garage."

A jagged memory flashed through Tara's mind. Parked at the bottom of a driveway, she was looking for Clay's house, trying to find Alex. Grateful for the camouflage of trees, she crept onto Clay's property. No, she told herself. Stop remembering that now. This isn't like the day of that tragedy at all.

"Are you going to stay with the car?" she asked as she got out. Her legs were trembling.

"I know we agreed I wouldn't get in the way of your speaking to either of them. But I'm going to try to find a location where I can see you, or at least be in earshot if you need me." He got out the other side and put Beamer on his leash.

With the Lab sniffing at everything, they crunched through the crisp leaves along the roadside. Bare-limbed deciduous trees as well as pines rattled and shifted in the brisk breeze. On the drive, she'd seen the foliage change from a rain-forest mix to subalpine. See, she told herself again. This isn't like that day Clay went berserk, when Alex died and I almost did. Nick and Beamer are here with me, so I can put that memory out of my mind. After all, what's more important, the past or the future? Or, in this case, just surviving the present.

As they walked up the curving gravel driveway — for the Lohans, this A-frame cedar building was really roughing it — Claire glimpsed a swing set and sandbox out back. "I hope they keep a good eye on Jordie when he plays outside," she whispered. "I'll bet all kinds of wild animals are in these parts."

"Including the human kind," Nick muttered, but she forced herself to keep walking.

They started toward the front door, then stopped. The house had huge glass windows, front and back, so that they could see into the main living area. A woman sat within, slumped over a kitchen counter or bar. Despite some reflection on the glass, her silhouette was stark against the trees out in back.

"Is that her?" he asked. "Can you tell?"

Tara grabbed his wrist. "I think so. And alone, I hope."

"If you get in, stay in that area of the house so I can watch. I think I'm going to go around back. If you need the cavalry to rush in, just wave an arm over your head or shout."

She nodded, but she was thinking that was the way Marcie had watched them. They had become the stalkers.

Nick squeezed her shoulder, then he and Beamer moved quickly to the side of the house as Tara forced herself to walk up to the front door. She felt suddenly alone and afraid. The day she'd gone looking for Alex, the day her coma had begun, she'd looked in the kitchen window and seen her friend slumped over, tied in a chair and now Jen . . .

Standing directly in front of the door to avoid appearing to be staring in, she rapped hard on the wood with her knuckles.

No sound at first. Nothing. Hadn't Jen heard? What was taking her so long? Had she spotted them and was refusing to answer the door? Or was Laird here? Would he be standing there if the door opened? Dear God, what if, just like Alex, Jen was dead?

Then movement, a shuffling sound inside. Jen looked out through the glass. Her eyes went wide; her lower jaw dropped. To Tara's relief, the door opened, but so wide and fast it banged into the inside wall.

"A ghost early for Hall'ween or a blasht from the pasht?" Jen asked and hooted a shrill laugh.

Of all the greetings Tara could have fathomed, this was not one of them. Her former friend looked like a ghost herself: pale, hair wild, her slender body almost gaunt. Tara smelled liquor on her breath; she must be drunk, and in mid-afternoon. Her blouse was rumpled, her usually immaculate mane of white-blond hair looked flattened, her eyes bloodshot. With shaking hands, she hugged herself as if to keep warm.

" 'Mon in," she said. "I can use some comp'ny, true confessions and all that." She almost fell over from the momentum of sweeping her arm in a welcoming gesture. "Guessed you'd show up sooner, later."

Tara followed her in and closed the door, resisting the urge to help Jen walk. She couldn't stand to touch her. "Where are Laird and your son?" she managed, still astounded. Jen had liked a social drink as well as anyone, but she'd always seemed to handle her liquor. The curse of the Lohans, Tara thought, first Veronica's abusing drink and pills and now this.

"Laird out for a golf lesson at the club, gone wi' the wind," she said, and plopped back onto the high bar stool where she had been before. "Took Jordie 'long, give me a break for once."

Amazed that anyone could resent one moment of taking care of the little boy, Tara sat on the metal-and-leather stool beside her. If Jen really was inebriated — she'd learned to trust almost no one — maybe she'd tell her things she needed to know. And since she had no idea when Laird would return, she had to get Jen talking. But she looked so bad. Surely Laird didn't allow this, especially not when she had a son to care for.

"I didn't know you drank, Jen. The question is, why?"

Jen turned to her, leaning one arm on the bar and bending over it as if she would go to sleep on the polished wooden bar. "You, of all people, certainly don' have to ask why," Jen said. "Wanna hear a good one? Yeah, you'll like this. I don't care if he gets mad or gets another wife."

She took another gulp of whatever amber liquor she had in the cut-glass tumbler. Tears trickled from the corners of her eyes and tracked down her cheeks, but she made no move to wipe them away. "Crying in my beer . . ." she whispered, "but this stuff's harder than beer, harder than . . . than I ever thought it could be . . ." Her voice and gaze drifted off into vacancy.

A movement out in back caught Tara's eye. Thank God, not Laird but Nick up in the tree line, squatting with Beamer at his side. She had the oddest urge to wave, but that might bring him running. For once, she was grateful to be spied on.

"Jen, what were you going to tell me? You and Laird had a fight?"

"Mmm. Over kids. More of 'em. Jennifer DeMar Lohan, M.D., specialty ob-gyn's having trouble having kids. It's even in our prenup that I get an extra fifty thousan' a year in my pers'nal account for each child we have. Ha!"

"But you gave him a son."

Jen narrowed her eyes and seemed to sober a bit as she drew herself up to a sitting position. "You should not be here, Tara. You have to go."

"He wants more children, but you're having trouble conceiving?"

"Don't give me that social worker, do-gooder, I-care look!" Jen shrieked so loudly Tara jumped. "You hate me, an' you should! But I couldn't help wanting him, an' you didn't."

Tara jerked as Jen heaved her glass against the wall next to the wide glass window. Glass shattered, ice and liquor flew, streaking the pine paneling. Tara had the urge to pick up the glass shards; the little boy could cut himself. But she forced herself back to business. She'd rehearsed a hundred things to say. Now she wanted both to beat Jen to the ground and to put her arm around her. She'd spent too long helping women whose men had hurt them. But, above all, she needed to know about her own child.

"Jen, please tell me about my baby's birth. What went wrong? I just need to know — for closure, as they say. You understand that."

Jen propped her elbows on the bar and pressed her face in her hands so her words came out muffled. "Hell of a night. Lots of snow. Cold. Your primary-care doctor lightened your medicine so you could help push. I tried to help, to be there for you. Honest."

Maybe it was the doctor training coming out, but Jen didn't sound drunk anymore. "Go on," Tara whispered when she paused. Jen put her hands flat on the bar as if to prop herself up and just stared off into space. Tara had to fight the urge to ask about the medicine they gave her to keep her comatose, but this was more important.

"Jen, go on," she prompted.

"Never thought you'd go to full term, of course. Pretty rare. Laird was ecstatic."

For himself, not me, Tara almost blurted, but she controlled her voice to ask calmly, "So, for the birth, you needed me more conscious?"

"We used different drugs that night from the ones being used to give your brain time to heal. For labor, you were in a kind of twilight, lighter coma," she said, her voice sounding as if she were reciting something in a formal lecture. "Years ago, they used to put women out entirely to deliver. I tried to tell you that we were going to do a vaginal delivery. That you had to help. And you did."

Silence. Wind outside, a clock ticking somewhere inside.

"Then what happened?" Tara asked.

Jen cleared her throat. "Umbilical cord around the neck — her neck. In the delivery, strangled. She got wedged — that's it."

Tara sucked in a sob. "Which a cesarian section could have avoided?" she blurted.

Jen shook her head so hard she almost tilted off the stool. Tara pushed her shoulder to keep her on it, then pulled her hand back as if that touch had burned her. "Happened too quick, too late," Jen said in a rush. "The thing is, when we tried to revive the baby in the other room, then had to — to prepare her — Laird went berserk . . ."

Tara saw it all. The panic and confusion. A comatose woman, a dead child for Laird — and Jordan. Jen, guilty, horrified, yet pregnant herself with Laird's child. The entire nightmare leaped back into this room now.

"And then," Tara choked out, "I got out

and wandered the grounds."

"Yes, I forgot. Someone found you and brought you back. Hemorrhaging, but I stopped that — maybe saved your life."

"Saved it after you let me wander out into the snow to bleed to death in the first place. Maybe," Tara said, getting right in Jen's face, "I went looking for the child you were preparing to secretly get rid of. Or maybe I was out of my mind with pain and grief and was looking for whoever let her die."

Jen burst into tears. "I'm so sorry, so sorry," she sobbed, putting her head down on her arms. "Sorry I got into any of this."

How could she say that when she had a beautiful son? Tara wondered, unless she meant getting mixed up with Laird.

"Then help me find the other attending doctor — Dr. Givern — now, Jen. Get me his address or phone number or e-mail. I know he's in Europe. To have some sort of closure, I need to speak with him, just to know what happened."

"It was all wrong, not to tell you, but you'd been through so much — and then Laird and I — it just happened. And then he started to turn against me when I want children just as desperately as he does. I'm seeing a fertility specialist, the best, but that's not good enough for him, and I want so much to have his baby . . ."

"You have, Jen, a precious Lohan son!" Tara cried, feeling furious again. "Just give it time. Hell, I even had one when I was on birth control!"

"You weren't," she said, fumbling for a tissue in the pocket of her slacks and blowing her nose. Her eyes were swollen; she looked unsteady again. Would Laird lock her up in the clinic until she got off booze? Who would care for little Jordie then? But what was that she'd just said? *You weren't on birth control?*

"What do you mean?"

"What?"

"What do you mean I wasn't on birth control? You yourself prescribed and even gave me the tablets."

She shook her head so hard, tears flew. "Sugar pills. Laird asked me to substitute —"

Tara didn't hear what else she said. She wasn't sure if she threw herself off the stool or fell off in shock, but she grabbed the edge of the bar to steady herself. Laird had set her up to get pregnant, despite the fact she'd told him she wanted to wait until they'd solved their problems! All that sudden understanding and sweetness those last months, all that sex. Suddenly, it hardly mattered if he was sleeping with Jen that early or not, because either way, such deceit was the ultimate betrayal of their marriage vows. Laird had impregnated Tara, then — maybe as a backup — seduced and impregnated Jen, too. She wanted to hate this woman, but she only pitied her, another Laird Lohan victim, even as little Sarah had been.

Yes, the one she really hated, the one she wanted to suffer, was Laird Lohan. And suddenly there he was, coming in the front door, in the flesh, with his son in his arms.

24

"Tara!" Laird exploded, so loudly his son cringed. "That's your truck down the road? What in hell are you doing here? Why didn't you just call?"

Tara crossed her arms over her chest. "Because you never would have invited me to your hiding place for the inquisition I have planned."

"Mommy, I back," Jordie said with a wave at Jen standing behind her. Tara's insides cartwheeled; it looked as if the child waved at her. Laird did not put him down. "I hitted a ball with a long stick," the little boy said proudly, now openly studying Tara. Chocolate ice cream or candy was smeared on his upper lip. Despite her building rage at Laird, she smiled at the boy.

"That's good, Jordie. Really good," was all Jen said, still making no move to go to Laird or her child.

"Mommy crying?" he asked.

"Mommy's all right, Jordie," Laird clipped out. "She's just tired."

"She's just tired," Jordie repeated, but his lower lip thrust out as if he would pout or cry.

Laird looked as strikingly handsome as ever, but he had noticeably aged. More silver hair at the temples; frown lines etched deeper on his chiseled face that now, compared to Nick's open, rugged countenance, seemed hard and haughty.

"I needed to speak with you and Jen to settle some things," Tara said, keeping her voice calm.

"You came alone?" he asked, again loudly.

She decided not to answer that. "You're upsetting your son. He's a great-looking kid. Was our little Sarah, too?"

"Dad said you had named her that." He walked around Tara to Jen and started to hand Jordie, who was now sucking his thumb, to Jen. Evidently, when he smelled her breath, he drew the child back. Frowning even more, he kept such a tight hold on the boy that Jordie winced and fidgeted.

Jordie's face drew Tara's gaze. Unlike in the photos, where his eyes looked bluish-green, she saw their color was the clearest emerald, just like her Irish grandmother's eyes — and hers. Tara's hair had been curly, too, when she was young. As Laird had tipped the boy down to hand him to Jen, Tara had noted that his hair looked strangely reddish at the roots. Why would they dye a little boy's hair unless . . . unless . . . And why had they moved so suddenly far away when the Lohans were such a tightly knit clan and when she knew Laird would love to flaunt his son and heir in his brother's face? Had Laird and Jen even been back to Colorado since they'd left or had everyone kept coming here, even for family photo shoots?

Could she have had twins, one who died and one who — No, that was impossible. Yet, she was dealing with the Lohans.

Tara trembled as she tried not to stare at the child, tried not to reach out to touch him. It couldn't be that Jordie was hers.

"Daddy, put me down," Jordie said, squirming. "Put me down!"

But Laird gave him a bounce and kept him in his arms.

"If you're here with that Special Ops guy or whatever he is," Laird said, "you'd better find him and get going."

"He's a civilian who served with them," she said, not giving ground, unlike Jen, who had retreated to the bar to pour herself another drink. Tara wondered if Nick could see all of them from his vantage point, and if he'd stay outside as he'd promised until she gave him a sign. "But *you,*" she said, emphasizing each word and pointing at Laird to punctuate her words, "are the real special ops guy."

"I don't know what the hell you mean. My wife and I need to talk, so I'm asking you to —"

"You'd rather my attorney just contact yours, and that I go to the Denver and Seattle newspapers to get sympathy for my civil suit?" she brazened. She was getting more frustrated and furious by the minute, but she didn't raise her voice so she wouldn't scare the child. She was almost afraid to look at him again, because all the other questions she had to ask were beginning to fade next to the new obsession growing inside her. Jen was blond with blue eyes. Did someone in the Lohan clan have green eyes and red, curly hair?

"Don't try to threaten me," Laird said, finally putting the little boy down on the beige rug next to the sofa and blocking her view of him, though Jordie peeked around Laird's legs at her.

"I realize you and Daddy Dearest are masters at that, Laird, but all the things you've been throwing at me are starting to stick — not to me, to you. The police are in on it since your father's lackey Marcie Goulder took a header out of the helicopter. Could Jen please take Jordie into the other room?"

Laird sank onto the couch and said, "Jennifer, take the boy into our bedroom and don't drop him again, or so help me, God . . ."

"You're the one who needs help from God, Laird," Jen said, smacking her glass on the bar and stalking over to scoop Jordie up. "But I doubt if He wants to have anything to do with you, either."

Tara watched as Jen carried Jordie from the room. She continued to stand so that Nick could still see her, but her gaze was on those wide, green eyes of the little boy. His thumb in his mouth, he was looking at her, too, over Jen's shoulder, until they disappeared down the hall, and Jen slammed a door.

"All I have to say to you, Tara, is that you're babbling nonsense!" Laird insisted. "I have no idea what any of this is about. No one's out to hurt anyone, including you."

"You may not be directly behind the Whetstone and Goulder deaths, but your father certainly is. Ask him about a boulder

414

that just missed me at Red Rocks when I was meeting your mother there, just before she got stashed incommunicado in the Lohan Clinic again."

"Calm down. Sit. Please," he said, patting the seat beside him.

"I'll stand."

He leaned away from her, arms stretched along the back of the sofa, one leg crossed over the other knee, obviously trying to look nonchalant and cocksure of himself.

"Tara, I can understand that you're distraught over the fact I didn't tell you about our daughter's death."

"Or her existence. For which you are fully responsible, since you had Jen tamper with my birth control pills."

His head jerked a bit. "My, my, you two *have* been having a heart-to-heart."

"But you know what?" she demanded, ignoring his sarcasm. "Even though I didn't want a child, I at least cherish her memory. And if she hadn't been taken — *stolen* — from me, I'd have been a great, loving mother. But you already had baby-maker number two lined up, didn't you? Divorce one, marry the other. Keep me comatose to suit your schedule so I won't get in your way, just cremate Sarah's body, stash her ashes in a rural crypt, and don't even tell her mother or grandmother, let alone legally register her birth or death!"

"Leave my mother out of this! I'm worried sick that she's gone missing somehow, and Dad says he thinks you know where she is. Get out of my house and leave me and my wife and child alone."

He'd said those words with control but also with menace. Yet she wasn't backing off. "Jordie's chin looks like yours, but I don't see a resemblance other than that," she went on, propping her fists on her hips. "Green eyes and hair the color of —"

"Of Jennifer's," he interrupted, leaning forward to cross his arms over his knees. "I was only trying to protect you from more grief by keeping silent about Sarah's death. I'm sure we can come to some sort of suitable financial arrangement for your loss, set you up for life with your P.I. firm, get a dog training school going for your friend so that —"

"How did you know about that? Let me guess. The other Mr. Special Ops, Jordan Lohan, got that intel from the two officers from Fort Bragg or from the politician dangling on his strings."

His swift move took her unawares. He vaulted off the couch and leaped at her. Seizing her shoulders, he shook her so hard her head snapped back and forth.

"Why can't you leave well enough alone?" he shouted. "Do you have to ruin everything?"

He threw her to the floor. Her head hit the corner of the bar. Then he stormed away, down the hall, where she heard him open, then close, a door. Low, angry voices came instantly from the bedroom, Jen's, his. Then Jordie crying. Nick was pounding on the back glass window.

For a moment she'd stayed down, fearing unconsciousness, even the blackness of coma. Though her head hurt, relief raged through her. She was fine: no dark tunnel, no nightmares but the living ones.

Shaking her head to clear it, Tara scrambled to her feet. She fumbled with the back door to let Nick in, with Beamer right behind him. Nick looked more angry than she felt.

"I saw him attack you," he said, tipping her face up to look into her eyes and examine her face. "Where is he?"

"Probably calling Jordan to have some goons get rid of me once and for all."

He swore under his breath and started in the direction he'd obviously seen Laird run. "I'm taking him to the police," he threw back over his shoulder. "Citizen's arrest for assault, though I may just accidentally be pretty rough about it."

"Nick, Nick, wait. They'll charge you for assault then, and they didn't let you in here. But did you see Jordie? I swear that he looks more like me than he does either Laird or Jen."

"What are you saying?" he asked, stopping and turning back.

"She's saying," came a woman's voice from the front door Tara had not heard open, "that my son and my husband are guilty of a new kind of child snatching." Veronica. Veronica here! "I suspected it," she went on as she came closer, "but couldn't believe it. Yet with everything that's happened lately, including the desperate measures someone we both know all too well has gone to, to keep us from so much as talking to each other . . ."

"Is Jordan here?" Tara cried.

"I came on my own, and that's why I can say this," she said, nodding to Nick, then taking Tara's hands in hers. "Whatever you've asked my son and new daughter-in-law about, you've probably asked the wrong questions, my dear. What they're really all hiding is that they had Jen's dead baby girl cremated and little Jordie — who has your eyes and hair, Tara, underneath that stupid hair dye — was taken from you to be reared as if he were their child. Isn't that right, Jennifer?"

Nick and Tara turned to see Jen standing in the entrance to the hallway, seemingly stunned, with a huge, red welt blooming on her left cheek. She looked beyond tears.

"Not exactly," she said, staring at the carpet and wavering on her feet. Nick took her by the elbow and helped her into the room to sit on the sofa. She gripped her hands in her lap and looked from one to the other of them, yet it was as if she saw no one. "Sarah never existed," she said in a quiet voice. "I — I recently learned I can't have children. I promised Laird a big family. Jordie was born to Tara that night at the clinic. And in case she — you — ever found out she'd had a child, we staged the rest, Jordan, Laird and I."

Veronica gasped and sat down on the sofa. Tara grabbed Nick's arm and held tight. Sarah hadn't died, because she'd never lived! And here, they'd made her grieve for nothing, tortured her over a dead daughter who was a vile lie! Tara wanted to scream, but she also wanted to shout in triumph. That green-eyed, red-haired little boy was hers!

"Finally, the truth," Nick said. "But what's

Laird doing in there?" He didn't wait for an answer and started at a full run down the hall. They heard him pound on a door, shout Laird's name, rattle the knob, then break in.

"He's gone," Jen intoned, wrapping her arms around herself. "Out the sliding glass doors from our bedroom. He slugged me, took Jordie and ran."

"Ran where?" Veronica asked.

Tara pulled out her phone and hit the instant dial.

"If you're calling the police, a cell phone won't work here," Jen went on, looking up, "but you can use the wall phone. I wouldn't though. He said to tell you, no cops or else."

"Or else what?" Tara demanded.

Jen shrugged. "He's desperate. He won't be caught. If I were you, I'd stop fighting him because," she said, fingering the bruise on her cheek, "one way or the other, it isn't worth it."

"It is to me," Tara insisted. "Where has he taken Jordie?"

"He knew he could be stopped on the regular roads, so he's gone into the forest."

"That's a national park, hundreds of square miles!" Tara cried. "Gone where, exactly?" She bent down to seize Jen by both shoulders.

Jen didn't try to shake her off, but grabbed Tara's wrists. She was ice-cold and trembling. "Tara, can't you just say good riddance, like me? If you do as he says, he won't hurt Jordie. He adores him, even if he's yours."

"He's gone!" Nick shouted as he ran back into the room. "Gone with the boy. Beamer tracked him down to the road where he must have been parked."

"Jen says he's gone into the forest. Where?" Tara asked Jen again. The woman looked as if she were in a trance, a living coma.

"He's hunted up in there. I don't know," she whispered. "There's only one dirt road from here, but then, who knows?"

"Nick, that cutoff road back by the turn," Tara said. "It has to be that road. With the truck, maybe we can catch him. Jen, what did he drive?"

"A Humvee we leave here," she said, her voice a whisper. "I'm supposed to call his father to send a helicopter to some place where they hunted. But I won't call Jordan, and I bet Veronica won't, either. He'll have to find a place his cell works and call him himself. Tara, if you can catch him, he's all yours."

"I don't want Laird. I want Jordie! Veronica, did Jordan say anything about where they hunted, anything at all?"

She shook her head. "I knew they hunted around here — once even overnight, but I never knew where. He did mention a beautiful waterfall somewhere, pounding down on rocks, where you could hide under it. I think he might have said they had the elk they shot airlifted out of there."

"That's got to be it! Veronica, if you'd stay here with Jen, Nick and I will get going. I'm not letting Laird take my son and disappear. On Lohan money, they could be missing for years . . ."

A chill snaked up Tara's spine. She'd turned down a case where a Syrian father had snatched his son and had taken him back to his homeland, because she had no idea how to begin to trace someone who'd fled abroad.

"Does Laird have a gun with him?" Nick asked, getting in Jen's face. "Think, Jen. Does he have a gun in the Humvee, or did he take one with him?"

"In the Humvee, I'm not sure. He could. He didn't run out with one. It wouldn't even work for me to count his hunting rifles here, not sure how many . . ."

"Let's go," Nick said. "Beamer, heel!"

"Go with my prayers," Veronica said, and

got up from the sofa to hug Tara hard. "I'm ashamed Jordan and Laird are mine, but I'll stand by you any day. Jennifer," she said, "did Laird take warm clothes for the baby? What about food?"

"Clothes, but no food unless he had something in the Humvee."

That was the last thing Tara heard as she and Nick sprinted for the truck with Beamer right behind. Thank heavens they'd gotten gas and had Beamer as their secret weapon. Maybe, even if Laird got out of his vehicle and went on foot, they had a chance.

As Nick pulled into the driveway to turn around, Veronica ran toward them with a bulging plastic sack. Tara rolled down her window.

"Here," she said, thrusting the sack at Tara. "He never did think of anyone but himself, so that's food for Jordie and both of you. I'm so sorry. Whatever I can do to help, just —"

"You have already, Veronica!" Tara called out the window as Nick backed up, shifted gears, and they roared away.

"Get Beamer's lead on him, in case Laird sets out on foot," Nick said, as if he'd read her mind. They sped down the road, spitting gravel from under the tires. She could tell Nick was in full combat mode now, but then, so was she.

"If — *when* — I get my son away from him, I'm legally changing his name from Jordan to Daniel, survivor in the lion's den. No way is that innocent little child going to be named after Jordan Lohan."

"I can't believe their gall, playing God with people's lives."

"I thank God that Veronica turned up, safe and strong. We'll find Laird. We have to!"

At the fork in the road, Nick hit the brakes and swerved into the other lane. The back of the truck fishtailed, but he straightened it out and accelerated. No gravel now, just dirt, but they left no dust trail behind them. Too much rain around here. This was like one of those chase scenes she always hated in the movies, Tara thought, as she twisted around to get Beamer's leash off his collar and the long lead on. Beamer seemed to come to attention as he always did when he was going tracking.

"What if Laird made Jen lie to us?" she asked. "What if he's gone out on the Loop Road, the highway?"

"I think she was beyond lying for him."

"Or lying with him. Once he found out she could not have children, he turned on her."

"I can see tire tracks, but that doesn't mean anything. Lots of hunters could have been back in here besides Laird and Jordan."

"Veronica mentioned a waterfall and a stream or river."

"Like in Colorado, there could be a lot of those around here. There's snow melt from the Cascades, and this area gets a lot of rain."

"We don't have the right map for features in the national forest. Nick, it's such a huge place."

Trees blurred by. The woods on both sides seemed to close in on them. Everything was darker, denser, and they were climbing now. Tara could not believe it had come to this.

They passed open ground where a subalpine meadow full of wild, reddish heather had been blasted by an early frost. The coppery corpses stood and nodded in the wind as they passed.

"Since we're out in the open, should I try to phone the police?" she asked.

"As usual, Laird probably has pull here, and they might just say so what if he's gone off into the forest with his son. Maybe Veronica will get them, explain things. Just like you, she's a hell of a woman, not a victim, though I guess it took her longer to

425

decamp."

Soon the narrow road plunged into deep forest again. "I can't imagine Laird would ever hurt Jordie," Tara said, trying to assure herself, "even if the police came, even if he was trapped, even if it was by us. Look!" she cried, pointing through their windshield. "Nick, look, off the side of the road, the Humvee! Could he have run out of gas or hit something?"

"It's a dead end. See, the road ends there. He obviously knew that, so he must have somewhere else to go. Maybe he has a hunter's cabin or campsite where he thinks he can wait for his father's people — the place Veronica mentioned. Maybe he's got a cell phone on him that works at a particular place, like Big Rock above our place."

Our place, he had said. What would she do without Nick's know-how and courage? And his love. Though he hadn't exactly said so, she was pretty sure he was coming to love her, just as she was him.

"Lock the doors. Stay put with Beamer, in case it's a trap," he ordered, and stopped the truck about ten yards behind Laird's Humvee. "For all we know, he could have a gun."

"Be careful!"

Nick got out and, on the side of the narrow road away from the Humvee, ran in a half crouch from tree to tree to approach Laird's vehicle.

This can't be happening, Tara thought, again. None of it. She had a son, a Lohan son. And now this, Laird desperate, maybe cornered, always dangerous. Her heart thudded. Despite what Nick had said, she got out of the truck, keeping low, leaving only an annoyed, jumpy Beamer in it.

When she crept closer to Laird's abandoned vehicle, she didn't see or hear Nick. She started to panic. She wanted to scream his name but knew not to, at least not yet.

She peered in the Humvee. Immaculate inside, but for a child's book on the backseat floor under Jordie's empty car seat. No doubt, Laird had pulled away so fast he hadn't strapped him in. And he must have ditched the Humvee quickly, because he'd left the keys in the ignition. Did he know they would try to follow him? Could he, as Nick had feared, be setting some kind of a trap? No, surely even he wouldn't hurt someone in front of his son.

Tara reached in and took the keys. A stick cracked behind her. She spun around and gasped.

"Oh, Nick, thank God."

"I told you to stay put. Go get Beamer.

Laird's gone that way," he said, pointing toward the northwest. "He's trampled through the ground cover, and his tracks are deep, since he's carrying the boy."

"My boy."

"Then let's go get him. I'm betting if he had a gun, he would have made a stand here and just gotten rid of us. And bring that sack of food. He probably knows where he's going, and we don't."

"Can Beamer trace him from the smell of the car seat or these keys?" she asked, holding them up.

"Yeah, but I took this from their bedroom, just in case." He pulled a man's white sock from his jeans pocket. "He's got at least a ten-minute head start, so let's go. For once, he's not getting out of this. I think about any court in the land will award your son to you if —"

"If what?"

If we can get him back hung in the brisk breeze, unspoken between them. *If a tracking dog as old as Beamer, with his feet still healing, can find him in this vast, deep forest.*

"Let's go," Nick said, his expression determined.

Tara tore to the truck to get Beamer, who was in the front seat with both paws on the dashboard, looking out.

"Yes." She whispered the words skyward, like a little prayer. "Let's go."

25

Nick left a scribbled note on the dashboard of their truck that they were tracking Laird and Tara's son with a dog, in case Veronica sent the police after them. Tara got both their jackets and checked out the bag of hastily gathered food Veronica had given them. She'd obviously grabbed random things from Jen's refrigerator or larder: a box of gourmet crackers, a package of deli luncheon meat, two small cans of V8 juice and a small gold sack of Godiva chocolates. Under all that, a half loaf of bread and jar of peanut butter with stripes of grape jelly, which were perhaps Jordie's favorites.

"She's packed us a picnic for the wilds, but this isn't going to be a picnic," she told Nick. "We'll probably have to feed Beamer the luncheon meat that's here."

"I hope the rocky ground doesn't break his cuts open again," he said, tying the arms of his jacket around his waist. Despite the chilly breeze, they were both sweating. He jammed a flashlight from the truck into his belt and said, "Let's roll. I want to find them before the sun sets. It's going to be cold out there tonight, and I don't have a match for a fire."

"Wouldn't that be illegal in a national forest?"

"There will probably be campsites, maybe even people we can ask if they've seen him."

At the place where the tracks went into the forest, Nick scented Beamer with Laird's sock. "Beamer, find!" he commanded, and the dog, head down, took them right along the path of the trampled vegetation.

"Can we talk, or should we be quiet?" Tara asked, stretching her strides to keep up.

"Laird's got a good head start, so it's okay to talk for now. If we get into some soil or mud he's been through, I may be able to gauge how far ahead he is."

"We're dead tracking, trying to move faster than he can."

Nick nodded. They emerged from a line of trees to another meadow. The flowers, weeds and heather had been blackened by frost, but it made the tracking temporarily easier: Laird had cut a path through the dead and dying vegetation that even Tara could have followed. The plants were almost

431

thigh-high, but Beamer bulldozed his way through them.

They startled several deer, which bounded off. "He could easily hide in here," she said.

"I hope to hell he tries it, not knowing we have Beamer."

Bless Beamer, Tara thought, as the sack of supplies she carried bounced at her side. She prayed they'd find Laird soon. Little Jordie was no doubt being jolted as Laird walked or ran. Would the child think it was just some grand game with Daddy, or would he pout or cry? Suck his thumb? Ask for his mommy, who was not his mommy at all?

As the sun sank lower behind them, they went even faster. Tara was out of breath and fighting to ignore a stitch in her side. But that pain was nothing compared to that in her heart.

A tree line loomed ahead again, and she thought she could hear rushing water. It didn't sound like the roar of a waterfall, but maybe it was just too distant. They came down from a little rise at a good clip, and Nick fell — straight down.

"Oh, Nick!"

"Damn — ankle."

With his left leg, he'd stepped into a hole to his knee. Tara knelt beside him, then called, "Beamer, sit," since the dog had stretched out his lead.

"I think it's broken," Nick told her through gritted teeth. "Even heard it snap."

"Nick, no!"

"Ah-argh! Can you help me pull it straight up?"

His tanned face had gone amazingly white. Beads of sweat stood out on his forehead and upper lip. She got on her knees to put her shoulder under his arm, then, with his help, lifted him. They managed to pull him out.

"Rabbit or marmot hole," he grunted. "Tibia broken above the ankle. I'm sure of it."

"What can I do?"

He flopped flat on his back and seized her arm, pulling her down to him. "I can't go on, can't go back, at least not on my feet. If I could get a stick, maybe I could drag myself."

"I can't leave you, but —"

"Tara, I can't let you face Laird alone. Try calling for help for me with your cell. Police or rangers can hike in from our car with your general directions, or even a chopper could fly in."

She nodded, seeing once again Marcie's flailing body as she fell from the chopper into the mountains. But if she didn't chase

Laird right now, she might lose her son forever. And if he saw police or rangers, even a chopper — one that wasn't sent by his father — he'd think they were after him. He'd said no cops, or else.

"Nick, could you call them? Describe where you are, or they could track you on a GPS signal from your cell? I've got to go on. I know you can take care of yourself, but Jordie can't."

"I can't lose you," he said through gritted teeth. "The Lohans will obviously do anything to get their screwed-up way. You've been an obstacle in their path, but not as much as you are now. You've turned into their worst nightmare."

"I know Beamer can't take much, but I can track with him. I have to try before Laird gets away. I've come so far, with your help, but I have a son. Please, if you love me, let me try."

"I do love you," he said with a grimace when he lifted a hand to cup her cheek, "but I can't let you get hurt."

"Laird only said don't call the cops to come after him. They can rescue you. If you ask me to leave Beamer here, I will, and go on alone. I love you, too, Nick. We've had only twelve days together, but that's enough time for me to have found the love of my life. Still, I have to do this, or I'll never forgive myself — or you, for not letting me go."

He pulled her harder against his chest; she thought he meant to hold her there. But he thrust her away so she sat back on her heels.

"All right," he said. "I understand that and don't want you living with regrets. You know the commands, you've tracked with Beamer and read pressure points. But don't let that bastard do you in. Come back with your son, and we'll move heaven and earth to be together, to raise him — Lohan lawyers, lies, whatever we have to take on. But remember, the Lohans are lethal."

"I've learned that the hard way. Forgive me for leaving. I know you love Beamer."

"As I said, sweetheart, I love you, too. Get going. And if it seems you're getting close to him, look ahead, slow up, approach him round about, read the signs. Here, take the flashlight. It won't be light long, and don't make yourself a target by shining it after dark."

She kissed him hard. Tears pooled in his eyes. She was terrified, but she had to go on.

She stuck the flashlight in the waistband of her slacks, then carefully coaxed Nick's cell phone out of his jacket pocket and put it in his hand. She left him the crackers and one can of juice from Veronica's sack, then wrapped Beamer's lead around her wrist. She turned away before she lost all courage.

"Beamer, find!" she called to the dog, and they were off again. Finders keepers, she told herself, blinking away tears. She had never loved Nick more than when he let her go, but she did not look back.

When the rustling of Tara and Beamer's moving through the dried plants died away, Nick lay still, trying to bargain with his physical and emotional pain to make the call. He had to get help before dark. He didn't want to spend a night out here incapacitated, unable to protect himself if a bear or mountain lion came calling. His stomach twisted at that thought, because that meant Tara and her child could face deadly danger, too.

But if he did phone now, the police or rangers would ask questions. They'd go after Tara and Laird, and that might push Laird over the edge. Who knew what the cornered and desperate man would do with Lohan fortune and future on the line? Kill Tara to shut her up for good? Harm his own son? Maybe he should just endure this night, then call for help in the morning, give Tara time to do what she'd asked, what she was risking her life to do.

He recalled that he'd told her once that trackers must be "fence walkers," rational, not emotional. On her own, in charge of Beamer, could she keep her wits about her? From deep within, he felt his own buried demons clawing to get out, his emotions taking over. He sniffed hard and fought to keep control.

He put his cell phone back in his jacket pocket, trying not to move his leg because that shot red-hot jolts of pain through him. That hole, just a few feet from here, had ruined everything. Staring up at the darkening sky, he remembered the day his novice dog trainers had stepped into the hole that hid the trip wire for a bomb. The IED didn't go off — a dud, or somehow diffused. He'd started feeling lucky then, feeling invincible for all of them, but that very afternoon the horror happened.

Nick shuddered as his thoughts ran rampant. Why had he let Tony and Clark go on when they made a wrong turn? Because the bomb hadn't detonated, did he think they were home free? Home free — how he'd like to be safe at home with Tara and Claire, a family, like Tony and Clark would never have because he screwed up and they got blown to bits. Had he made another mistake in letting Tara go on without him? Even though she had Beamer . . . what if he lost them both? It would be his fault again, again . . .

He started to sob in great, wrenching heaves, causing agony through his leg. He had not cried at all, not when he'd lost his men and blamed himself, not when he'd seen Tara grieving for the lost child that had turned out to be a lie.

"Take care of her, Beamer," he whispered, as if the dog could hear on the reach of the wind, " 'Cause I can't now."

Tara almost screamed at a sudden roar. Oh — a covey of ruffled grouse burst into flight from the field. Damn! Nick had told her to watch for signs. Maybe she could tell Laird's location by such things as startled animals on the run or in flight. All that locate work she'd done from the safety of her desk, all the times she'd stayed home and searched only online, all that was behind her now. She had to find and face her own child-snatcher in person.

They were almost to the trees edging the huge heather meadow where Nick lay. She felt torn in two, not to be with him, to have left him. But Nick injured was surely safer than Jordie, even when the child was hale and hearty. And the boy was now in the arms of a desperate man. She believed Jen when she said that Laird wouldn't hurt the boy, yet hadn't he already hurt him by taking him from his real mother? By letting someone with a drinking problem take care of him? By carrying him into a huge forest where anything could happen?

Through another dense stand of spruce with wind sighing through their branches, she heard a bubbling stream again. If only it could be the one feeding the waterfall Veronica had mentioned, but she heard no telltale booming sound. She pulled Beamer back on a shorter lead. Thank God, the scent must still be strong because the dog never wavered.

Tara felt even more hopeful when they came across a marked trail and turned down it. The going was so much easier here, and she might meet hikers or hunters. On another train of thought, her jacket and slacks were tan, which might help to camouflage her from Laird's eyes, but she'd heard of hunters mistaking people for deer or elk. Was it hunting season here, like at home?

She saw and heard no one on the trail. It soon led to a wooden boardwalk over a soggy piece of ground. A sign read Crooked Creek Trail. She almost cried in relief to see any hint of civilization. Maybe Laird was taking Jordie to a campsite with shelter for the night; maybe she could catch up with him, reason with him, use all her skills of dealing with distraught parents to convince him to give Jordie to her. Then he could escape and she'd send no one after him, tell no one what the Lohans had done.

But she knew she'd already said too much. She'd accused him and Jordan of complicity in two murders, as well as stealing her child.

"Beamer, sit," she whispered, and, panting, the dog obeyed. Up ahead she saw a small, slant-roof shelter built above the narrow, rocky floodplain of a stream. The water was white with small rapids as it bounced over boulders. All around, shadows were long, but the stream's foam stood out in the dying rays of sun, reflected from the tops of the trees.

She caught up to Beamer. Remembering Nick's hurried advice to her as she set out, she took the dog off the trail and approached the site through the trees. It looked deserted, but someone could be in the small shelter house above the stream bed. It reminded her of the day she'd followed Marcie and mistakenly thought she might be in the hunter's cabin.

Should she send Beamer in alone? If he tracked Laird to the shelter, did that mean he and Jordie were inside? Or would that just show he had been inside but had come back out?

Feeling like a fool, wishing desperately Nick was with her, she took Beamer back onto the trail, unhooked his lead from his collar and scented him again with Laird's sock, which she had stuffed into the sack. "Beamer, find."

Feeling bereft and alone as the dog went on without her, she hid behind a tree to watch. The Lab went directly to the shelter and into it, then came out and darted along this side of the stream, turned back, then searched along the stream again.

"Beamer, heel!" she cried, and ran toward him. The dog came immediately. She peeked into the empty shelter. No signs anyone had been there. *Read the signs,* Nick had said, but what signs? Darkness was closing in. Beamer must have lost Laird's scent. Maybe he'd crossed the stream here. She'd heard of escaped prisoners who walked in water when the hounds were tracking them, then came out somewhere else up ahead. Before night fell, she had to get them across that water and pray Beamer could pick up the scent on the other side.

But could Laird be watching, even in the thickening dusk? She'd seen a half-moon last night, but would that be enough, even with her flashlight beam? *Don't make yourself a target by shining it after dark,* Nick had warned. If she plunged into the woods ahead, it could be very dark. Laird could be behind any tree. Maybe she should spend the night in the shelter. But that could be a setup; he could close her in, trap her there, tie her up or worse.

"Beamer, heel," she repeated, putting him back on the lead wrapped around her wrist. No, she wasn't stopping in a place that seemed to offer shelter. She had to get across the stream, trusting Beamer not to fall in and drag her with him. The water didn't look deep, but a slip could mean being battered against the rocks and being soaked out here for a long, cold night.

Tara stepped out onto the first boulder of what appeared to be the best stepping-stone path over the rushing stream. She leaped to another rock, one not underwater but slippery with wet moss. Praying Beamer would not fall in, she took another rock, then another, with Nick's wonderful dog leaping behind her.

She sprang onto the other bank, crunching small stones. Beamer jumped beside her, and she knelt to hug him. He was wet from his belly down. At least one paw was bleeding where he must have opened a cut again. She wet a strip torn from her blouse and took him up under a tree near the stream, then cleaned and wrapped his paws.

Hidden in the trees, Tara fed him half of the lunch meat and let him drink from the stream while she downed the small can of juice and several pieces of sourdough bread. She praised Beamer and rubbed his ears as Nick had taught her.

Darkness descended like a door being slammed shut. Beamer leaned into her, and she was grateful for his warmth. On this side of Crooked Creek, if that was its name, the surroundings looked different, somehow otherworldly. Lichen hung from the trees, resembling white hair blowing in the black breeze. Hemlocks predominated here, with drooping fingers reaching down from spiky limbs. Some sort of fog or mist was setting in, which made the moon and clouds look shapeless. The burble of the stream sounded like chains being dragged across the ground.

Stop it, she told herself. Stop the fear now, before it devours you. She'd tell Claire about this place when she got back, tell her it was like the haunted woods in some of her favorite fairy tales, and those always ended happily ever after.

She prayed for safety and guidance, prayed for Jordie and for Nick. Raking up dried leaves around her for some warmth, she huddled against Beamer with her back to a big, solid tree. She was suddenly exhausted. Just a little rest . . . Surely, with Jordie, Laird would need that, too, let her boy sleep. The child was no baby; carrying him so fast and so far must have made Laird's muscles ache.

She hugged Beamer again. Her arms ached to hold her son. To hold Nick. Yes, they would rest here, at least for a few hours, so Beamer's foot could scab over. She didn't want to come up on Laird if he was waiting for them in the dark. If he'd seen that she had the dog, she didn't want to be misled by a false trail or a trap he had set.

Nick. How was Nick? Maybe, with the opening in the hills for this creek bed, she could call him. Tara took out her phone and punched in the number of Nick's cell. The little window of light seemed incredibly bright. *Roaming,* it said. *Roaming.* Then, *No service in this area.*

Tara choked back a sob. She had never felt more scared or helpless, or alone, even

444

with Beamer. But she wasn't turning back. Come Laird or high water, she was going after her son.

26

Something woke Tara. She jolted alert, every muscle taut. Beside her, Beamer lifted his head, ghostly white in the predawn. Morning! She'd slept till morning! What if Laird had put miles between them? What if he'd called his father to send a chopper, and Jordie was gone from her forever?

She saw what had awakened her. Two beavers gnawed noisily at trees on the other side of the stream. She had to get going. Surely Beamer could pick up Laird's trail on this side of the water.

Keeping a good eye on the beavers, Beamer ate more of the deli meat while Tara relieved herself behind a tree, then Beamer followed suit on the same tree, his leg lifted high. So, she thought, it had come to that, down to basics. Beamer was not Nick's partner now but hers. How she'd come to love this dog. And Nick had loved her enough to give — maybe to sacrifice — his beloved old pal for this grueling search.

It seemed every muscle in her body ached; her head pounded with pain. Though she didn't feel like doing anything but throwing herself flat on the damp ground to scream and cry, she took a piece of bread to eat as they went along and scented Beamer with Laird's sock again. "Find, Beamer. Find."

It took almost five minutes but he found the scent farther upstream, on higher ground, where she didn't think Laird would go. Maybe, as Nick had said, Laird had a place to use his cell among these hills and mountains, a cleared location where his call could be picked up, so he and Jordie could be rescued.

She pushed herself harder to stay with the eager dog. He seemed to sense how crucial this was, as if he knew a child's future — please, dear Lord, not his life, too — could depend on this trail. Maybe Laird was tiring, too, she thought. Jen didn't think he'd taken food, though who knew what he'd had in the Humvee. But the vehicle had been so neat inside; he'd never been one to clutter up his vehicles with anything.

When she could actually discern a man's tracks, she felt better. Assuming the tracks were Laird's, she tried to read the pressure points as Nick had taught her. Laird was moving fast, his strides wide. Yet he was dragging his feet, too, no more clean prints. These imprints didn't look dried at all, so they must be recent. But they started to waver before her eyes as if phantom feet were pressing into the soil and moving the mud even now. Was this what Nick had called ground surge, or was she just hungry and exhausted, almost dizzy?

She forced herself to lift her eyes from the trail for any sign of him ahead. Beamer went even faster, and so she did. Dead tracking. The very term scared her now.

They came to another stream, cold and clear, rushing down from the Cascades or their foothills. She had no bearings now, no real idea where she could be. As Nick had surmised, numerous streams slashed through the area. But where was the waterfall Jordan had mentioned to Veronica, near his and Laird's hunting place, the place they'd had their dead prey taken out by air?

She glanced again into the rushing water. This stream was full of cutthroat trout, silvery brown, racing below the surface as if they had somewhere important to go. The cold current was so fierce that they had to work hard to stay in place. She wasn't sure if that kind of trout made a yearly run back to their birthing place. Birthing place. She'd borne her son at the clinic in the cold of winter. She almost remembered some of it, the pain and panic, if not the joy. And that crying, crying she'd heard: her son in the other room, taking his first breaths, then being taken away from her.

Beamer halted and cocked his head. She wondered if he heard something she did not. He sniffed in a circle where there seemed to be a path through deep woods, heavy with drooping hemlocks and thick with frosted ferns, now gone deathly brown. Yes, Claire would think this, too, was a haunted forest in one of her fairy tales, where some witch was waiting. Tara prayed that Laird had not gone in that direction. But that was the way Beamer turned, so she strode after him.

Nick's pain was so bad that they gave him what they called an amnesiac sedative before they set his leg. He was in the Cascade Valley Hospital in Arlington, Washington; he'd caught that much. He'd managed to talk to the park rangers before they'd carted him out on a stretcher, jolting him into the pain of oblivion. They'd told him in the ambulance that he had a fever and was talking as if he'd been in the desert and two guys had been killed. They'd asked if he was a soldier and had post-traumatic stress disorder, but he couldn't recall what answer he'd given them. He evidently had given them Veronica's name and where to find her.

The moment Veronica arrived at the hospital, she'd told them everything, then said to him, "Tara's fighting back, Nick. I told them that the only hint I could give them was some waterfall."

They said they'd keep him overnight, then evidently had strapped him down, because he kept insisting he had to get up to save Tara. He slogged through forests and streams in nightmares where she stayed just out of sight, out of reach. When he opened his eyes, Veronica sat there, staring at him. She popped out of her chair by his bed and put a hand on his shoulder.

"I hope I can call you Nick," she said at first. "I believe, once we get Tara back, we will be friends, a family of sorts."

This feisty family matriarch was Jordan Lohan's wife? She had helped him and Tara, so he could trust her.

"Thanks for being here," he managed. His tongue felt too full for his mouth. What in hell had they given him? His thoughts all ran together.

"It's quite a bad break," she told him. "I

decided to fight Laird and Jordan for all of us. The good Lord knows I haven't done enough of that. Do you recall that I told the hospital to inform the park rangers all about Laird taking the baby and Tara going after him? And, you know," she added with a sparkle in her eyes, "I believe I forgot to tell them Laird was the boy's father. I just didn't want to complicate things until he was caught."

He tried to lift a hand to take hers in thanks, but he was still tied down.

"Oh, dear," she said. "I absolutely hate that. They did it to Tara and me at the clinic, you know. Are you sure you are not going to insist you have to save soldiers and their dogs in the desert the way you've been talking?"

"Yes, ma'am. I think I've come to terms with that now. I'm looking forward, not back, with Tara, if we can just find her."

"So you will stay put in this bed?" When he nodded, she added, "Then I'll undo these Velcro ties."

"Veronica," he said as she freed his arms, "what's Laird capable of, if she corners him and he has Jordie there?"

She frowned and shook her head. "All the Lohan men are so crazed for heirs, but even more protective of family reputation and wealth. I don't know, Nick. I have always admired Tara for standing up to them, but if she does it now — I just don't know."

Nick lay helpless in the bed, holding Veronica's hand, thinking he'd give anything if Tara could just come back to him with her son in her arms.

When they came out into an alpine meadow, Tara saw they were high enough to have moved from patches of mist to random pieces of clouds resting on the rocky out-crops here. The air seemed thinner. Was it raining somewhere in the distance? She thought she heard an approaching storm.

Overhead, vultures soared on the ther-mals. Was something dead nearby? Were they stalking her or the dog? Beamer had been tiring, panting harder, but he pushed himself and her on and on. For his sake and Nick's, too, she should stop, let Beamer rest. Other than a long drink at the last stream, he'd had no sustenance, but she wasn't sure if he'd eat bread. She should try to bandage his feet again, because he was leaving his own reddish trail on rocks they crossed.

"Beamer, sit," she said. The moment she stopped walking, she realized how cold it was. If they stayed out in the open, sweating like this, they'd both get sick. They had to go on, at least to shelter.

She'd tried her phone two more times since the meadow, and wanted to again. Nothing had worked so far. *Roaming,* the message had read. Roaming, just like her and Beamer. Why would Laird have come so far with her baby? Had he come all this way to give his father time to fly to the area and rescue him, get him a false identity or call in a chopper, like the one that had rescued Marcie before her death?

And then she thought she heard the falls. A muted roar, not distant thunder. Yes, that must be where Laird had been going all along. Veronica had said something about hiding under the falls. Would he do that with little Jordie? Wait for the exact time to reconnoiter with his father or a chopper?

Despite her exhaustion, she started to run, almost side by side with Beamer. If Laird gave her the chance to go with them, she wouldn't dare, or they might throw her from the chopper as they had Marcie. But she could not bear to see Laird fly away with her boy. With their money, all three generations of Lohan males would disappear, the way they must have spirited away her clinic doctor.

Between a cleft in the hill they were climbing, the view opened up to an alpine tarn with a tall waterfall thundering into it. The roar was instantly louder; the slant of land and rocks must have muted it before. "Beamer, sit," she said, and hunkered down beside the dog. Below her, at least a football field away, she could see a man and a child at the water's edge. It looked as if they were both throwing stones into the ice-blue lake.

Dear God, she prayed, don't let them be rescued and taken out of here before I can get down there. But should she leave Beamer here or take him with her? He was exhausted, bleeding, her hero. No, she needed Beamer. Maybe he could distract Laird or amuse Jordie. Nick would want her to keep Beamer with her.

"Beamer, heel," she said, and started down the slant of grassy hill, hoping that Laird was looking only at the lake or sky. But if and when she got close to him, what then? What would she say and do? She wished she had a gun — yes, she who hated guns. With the blood roaring in her ears loud enough to rival the waterfall, she descended into what Laird must think was his own personal valley.

She was only about twenty yards from them when he looked around and shaded his eyes. Feeling like a fool, she waved, rather gaily, she thought, as if they were the fondest of lovers and she'd merely been off hunting flowers for a few minutes. Laird picked Jordie up and headed for the falls.

She was terrified at first he would do something dreadful, but she saw them disappear between two rocks. Veronica's memory must be correct; you could walk behind the falls. She ran toward the spot she'd seen them go. Water crashed down from at least four stories high to the rock-strewn pool below.

But when she approached the place they'd disappeared, she hesitated, looking up. Beamer tried to pull her on as if he were still tracking. "Heel," she said, and craned her neck to be sure there were no rocks overhead that could come crashing down on them. She did not believe Laird was directly to blame for her nearly being flattened at Red Rocks, but she wasn't taking chances.

She almost laughed aloud at that thought. Wasn't taking chances? What about all she'd done since her new doctor asked her two weeks ago when she'd had a baby? And she had not come all this way to let Jordie — her Danny — slip away now.

Still holding Beamer's lead, she started around the back of the falls. The sound of the water reverberated off the rocks; the noise was deafening. The pathway deep into the rock was as slippery as glass. That damned Laird could fall, with Jordie in his arms!

Pressing her back to the slick rock behind her, doused at first by a blinding curtain of mist, she sidestepped under the falls. She'd thought she'd need her flashlight under here, but an eerie, bluish, rippling light lit a cavern the falls must have carved out centuries ago. Puddles, some shallow, some ankle-deep, studded the uneven path above other rock ledges and a lower pool. Some puddles were lined with slimy-looking algae. Beamer came behind, the bravest dog she'd ever seen, but then, Nick had trained him. *Nick.* If only she could have a life with him, with Claire, with Jordie and Beamer, too!

As she looked ahead through the shimmering mist, she did not see Laird. Where had he disappeared to? Enough diffused light came in to see he was not under here. Then, through the drift of wayward spray, she saw him, as if in a spotlight on the other side, exiting the falls. She hurried faster and fell hard to her knees, sprawled on her stomach in a puddle.

"Oomph!' she cried as the breath slammed out of her. She hit her chin, biting her lip. Her cell phone skittered away, over the ledge, just as Clay had kicked it away the day he'd killed Alex. Damn, why did she have to think of that now?

Beamer nudged her, licked her cheek. She got to her knees; her hand on the sturdy dog's back for support, she stood. Five feet below, her phone lay in a pool of water. At her feet, her plastic sack had broken open and spewed everything into this puddle. She gathered the things up hastily, jamming them into her pockets. All that mattered was that Laird must have just gone out to the other side of the lake.

Ignoring her pains and cuts, she pressed on. It got lighter again. But was a trap awaiting her, another boulder when she stepped out from under the falls? Still pressed to the slick rock face, she shouted, "Heel!" to Beamer and darted outside. She scrambled, apparently safe, up the rocky, twisting path ahead.

No Laird. No Jordie. She stared across the falls-fed tarn. He had not fled to this side of the lake. They must have gone up this jagged path toward the top of the falls. Could Beamer pick up a scent on water-washed rock?

She pulled Laird's sock from her pocket. "Find, Beamer. Find!" she commanded, thrusting it at the dog. He sniffed. He went

457

in circles. He started up the rocky path, then came back. Then he sat, looking up at her, with his head cocked as if to ask her for more help.

No more help from Beamer, at least not here, she thought, starting onward with the dog coming behind her. Was Laird even up this way? Did he have some other hiding place once he emerged from under the falls? If he'd fled again, maybe Beamer could pick up his now-familiar scent once they got off these wet rocks. But, of course, above must be a wild river. Would everything be water-washed up there, too?

Out of breath and drenched with mist and sweat, Tara emerged above the falls. About twenty feet away, evidently waiting for her, Laird stood on a rocky ledge above the roiling river rushing to plunge over the edge. And in his arms, he held their sobbing, kicking son.

27

Tara's first thought was to get close enough to Laird to snatch Jordie from him, but any sort of a struggle could tip them all into the water surging over the falls. Her second instinct was to comfort the upset child. At least Laird had him warmly dressed with a hood pulled up over his head, as if he still could hide the child's reddish roots from her.

"Hello, again!" Laird shouted as if he hadn't a care in the world while he stood on the jutting ledge. "Welcome to one of the most beautiful spots my father and I have ever found. Shall we chat about the good old days or the bad new ones? See, Jordie, the lady has a dog. Doggie, see?" he added, bouncing the boy. "Don't cry. Quiet now so I can talk to the lady."

With Jordie being almost dangled over the falls, Tara knew she had never hated or feared anyone so much in her life as she did

Laird right now. But she'd never been more certain that she would do absolutely anything it took to get Jordie away from him — though that did not include walking toward him, where he could push her over the brink. Did he think she would actually fall for this charmer routine?

She dug in her jacket pocket where she'd stuffed the small sack of candy. Most of it, she knew, was smashed. She had the peanut butter jar in the other pocket, but no more bread.

"Hi, Jordie," she called, forcing a trembling smile and blinking back tears. Laird and Jordie looked as if they stood in a halo of mist. The roar was not as loud as it was below, but enough that they had to almost shout at each other. "I brought some candy for you. Are you hungry, honey? Would you like to play with the dog — doggie, like Daddy said?" she asked in a frenzied outpouring of words, as Beamer pressed tight to her legs.

At first she thought the dog was wheezing, but she realized — more through touch than sound — that Beamer was growling. Did he instinctively know that Laird was the enemy they'd been tracking, or did he think that he was going to harm the child? Beamer and Nick had tracked both escaped felons and lost children, so maybe the dog had a sixth sense about this.

Jordie stopped crying, swiped at his eyes with one fist and nodded. When Tara extended the candy to him from where she stood on solid ground, Laird shouted, "You're crazy, Tara! Always have been, messing with down-and-outers who don't pay you half the time. Just stay back. You found us with the dog, didn't you? I didn't know you had one with you, but I do know trackers are not trained to be attack dogs."

"Really? This one's trained by a man who's been living for years with the Delta Force in combat with the Taliban. Are you certain he only trains dogs to do tracking?"

Laird's eyes narrowed. He looked suddenly unsure of himself. If that bluff seemed to work, maybe she could use others. Yes, conning Laird like she'd never done anyone else.

"Why don't you just marry him?" he demanded. "Go east with him and his niece and have your own kids."

"Obviously, because I already have my own kid, who has been abducted for nearly three years. Laird, you took a child from his *m-o-t-h-e-r* when she didn't even know that he —"

"Never mind all that coddling social work

461

crap again. Too late."

"Too true. But that doesn't mean I'm going to let you take my child."

"I hungry, Daddy," Jordie screeched, twisting to be put down. "I want candy!" To Tara's horror, the child bucked in Laird's arms, almost throwing them off balance. She detested Laird for standing at the edge of the rock as if to say, *One wrong move and I might drop this child.*

"I have peanut butter, too, with jelly in it," she said, producing the jar of it. "Grandma sent it for you, Jordie. Laird, you brought that child out here without food? But then, you didn't plan to be here long, did you? Is Daddy Dearest coming or his lackeys, maybe in a similar helicopter that pulled Marcie Goulder away from me and then just dumped her?"

"Daddy Dearest," Jordie repeated. "I want candy!"

"Let me at least roll this jar of peanut butter to you, Laird. Let him get some protein in him."

"Ah, the mother-knows-best approach. How do I know there isn't something in it to harm him?"

"Harm him? You're the one who's been harming him! How dare you let an alcoholic take care of my child! She's probably only been hitting the bottle because you were so awful to her when she found out she couldn't be your next broodmare!"

"Now there's the real Tara. Too clever by far."

"Of course, you're planning to get rid of her now one way or the other," she plunged on, ignoring his accusations. "How about this scenario? You help her fall down some stairs when she's on the sauce. She supposedly hits her head and goes into a coma that you can drag out at the clinic until you —"

"I should have just let Dad get rid of you!" he exploded, almost screaming, despite the fact Jordie started to cry again. "I told him no, the mother of my son had to be protected, even if she had no intention of giving me that son. I was furious when that loose cannon Rick Whetstone actually tried to roll a rock on you. I said he needed to go, but I didn't realize that would mean — mean what happened. Then his girlfriend took over and got really pushy, but I didn't have anything to do with that. I really didn't want you hurt, Tara."

"Didn't want me hurt? What do you think you were doing by keeping me comatose, by letting me think I had a daughter who died, by taking my son away from me?"

"Just shut up. I don't want any of that to

upset him, even though, at this age, he won't remember it later."

"Not upset him? That's laughable — pitiful and criminal. You haul him out here without food. You plan to take him from the only stability he's known, and you think I'll upset him? You're planning to ditch the one he thinks is his *m-o-t-h-e-r,* his second *m-o-t-h-e-r* you've taken from him, and you're trying to make me feel guilty for wanting him? I can't say wanting him back, can I, because I never had him? And now, you're standing on a precipice, over an abyss that could be the end of him!"

"Then just back off! Take that dog and get out of here!" he shouted with another nervous glance at Beamer. "If you do, I'll tell my lawyers to work on joint visitation rights, I swear it. You cooperate and, once I arrange things with Jennifer, I'll see that we share Jordie, you know, alternate weekends or vacations . . ."

What a story he continued to spin for her. She'd been expecting some sort of salesman's pitch, but she could play that game. She'd do anything to get Jordie back from the falls and a chopper that could take him away forever. She'd already lost almost three years of his life, and she could not bear to lose more.

"All right, I'll take that bargain," she told him. She was lying now for all it was worth. "A child should definitely have both parents, and you and the Lohans can offer him so much over the years."

She was almost sick when she said that, but it was something he believed, something he would go for. "But on one condition," she added. "That you let me hold him and feed him now before I go. Laird, please. I've never touched my son since he left my body."

He frowned but nodded. Maybe the boy's crying and struggling was wearing him down. As she had suspected, Laird seemed to be the sort of father who wanted his son to learn to play golf far too young, to make him proud, compete with his cousins and impress his grandfather, but not one he really wanted to take care of on a daily, boring basis.

Not budging from where she stood, with the candy sack in one hand and the peanut butter jar in the other, she held out her arms. Laird took five steps, stopping about three feet away. With a nervous glance at Beamer, he handed Jordie to her. As he'd approached, she felt Beamer, glued against her left leg, stiffen and growl again. Would the dog protect her if Laird attacked?

Frowning down at Beamer, Laird still stayed close.

Jordie weighed more than she'd imagined. He filled her arms and her heart. She told herself she had to be wary of some trap or trick from Laird, but, for one wild moment, she almost didn't care. Her own son was in her arms, cuddled against her, sheltered from the brisk wind and drifting mist, and not fighting her as he had Laird. It was the promise of candy and peanut butter, of course, but it still warmed her to the depths of her soul.

"Since we're going to be civil to each other," she said to Laird, taking a couple of steps away from him when he still hovered, "I would like you to stop dying his hair."

"Sure. Of course. There'd be no reason to then anyway."

Too agreeable, the little voice in her head warned, but she felt besotted with Jordie's expectant expression as she popped a mashed piece of chocolate in his mouth, then dug her index finger into the peanut butter jar to feed him that, too, with Laird watching every move she made. Like a little bird, Jordie opened his mouth, so she scooped up more and put it in. He sucked on her finger, his eyes wide on her.

She would have nursed him, would have

had wonderful moments with him like this. Could he feel her love for him, her frantic need to protect him? She hugged him as best she could with the jar in one hand and her other hand poised to feed him more. With his small arm around her neck, he did not protest when she kissed him lightly on one dirty cheek.

"Good p.b.," he told her.

He called peanut butter p.b., Tara thought. She had so much to learn about him. But the time to act was now or never. She could see a speck behind Laird's head that she had thought at first was another vulture, but it was growing bigger, bigger. It must be the chopper. With the roar of the falls, Laird couldn't hear it yet. He'd soon have reinforcements, and then it would be too late to keep Jordie or save herself. She knew too much. Laird's lies aside, Jordan would insist on getting rid of her. And she could only think of one thing to do, desperate or not. Nick had said once that Beamer had jumped a guy who tried to rob him. But had Beamer done that on his own? What command would he need?

"Beamer, get him!" she shouted. Then she added, "Elk, elk!" since the dog had always been disturbed by them.

With a single bark, the dog leaped at Laird

and pushed him back. Clutching Jordie to her, Tara tore the way she'd come, down the path that led beneath the falls.

She could hear Beamer barking, but also Laird cursing and running after her, half skidding down the path. Burdened with the boy, she was too slow. Laird spun her around, slammed her into a rock.

"You deceitful bitch!" he shouted.

She actually saw stars, but she held Jordie to her as Laird tried to rip him away. Beamer was at him again, biting his pants, maybe his leg. He swore and tried to kick the dog off, slamming Beamer into the wall.

The sound of the hovering chopper above them vied with the roar of the falls. "Went after Alex when I told you not to get involved with that stupid business of yours. The coma was all your fault! You had a duty to me, to the Lohans!"

Jordie was screaming in her ear. She was dizzy. Laird pried the child from her arms and set him down on the path, sobbing and kicking. "Stay here, Jordie!" Laird shouted, holding her against the rock wall with one arm straight out so she couldn't scratch or hit him. "Stay right here until Daddy gets you! Grandpa's here to take us for a plane ride, so you stay here!"

Tara wasn't sure where Beamer was.

Jordie's screams, the waterfall, the chopper's rotors roaring . . . her head. She glimpsed a long, black corridor stretched out before her, but she fought to find the light. Laird was dragging her, partly by her jacket, partly by her hair. Her head hurt so much. Up, up out over jagged rocks where he had first stood, to the edge of a foaming maelstrom below.

He was going to shove her over the falls! Right in front of his father and at least one other witness. They would probably applaud. Finally, the rebel, the family traitor, would be gone.

Tara stared straight down into the swift suction of green-white water as it plunged over the edge to the rocks below. Seething death. Was she already spinning down into it? Which way was up? But she had held her son. She had loved him, if only for the few hours she'd known he was hers, or maybe from the moment she saw a picture of him. And Nick — she'd loved him and he loved her, and Claire . . .

Her senses came back, her equilibrium righted as he started to roll her off. Then suddenly he screamed and dove over her toward the water. Beamer slammed into her, on top of her. Her breath whooshed out. Where was Laird? Had the dog shoved him over?

Pain chattered at her, but she twisted to look down. He had not fallen to the water. About four feet below her, he was sprawled on a narrow ledge, like her, half on, half off. Despite the fact they both might die, she was furious that he had left Jordie alone where he could wander up or down that path and get hurt.

"Tara, Tara, help me!" Laird demanded, and dared reach a hand up toward her. She shoved the barking dog back from danger and leaned on her belly over the edge, looking down at Laird, silhouetted by raging water. If she stretched out her arm, she could probably grasp his hand, but he could still try to pull her over the ledge. But then, again, for good or ill, this was her son's father. She should try to save him, but the chopper would land and she'd be trapped. She had to get back to Jordie, get away. Let Laird's father save him.

"Get my father," Laird was screaming as if he'd read her mind. "Get him to help me-eee-e!"

The helicopter hovered lower, blocking out the sun. Laird gasped as he looked up, so she did, too. Clearly painted on the belly of the chopper were big, bold letters that spelled out, *U.S. Govt. Nat. Forest Dept. of the Interior.*

Unless Jordan had commandeered a government chopper — which she did not put past him — this meant a rescue for her, not Laird. Perhaps he knew it, perhaps he realized that his lies and money and might would not get him out of this. And that he'd cause the Lohans devastating scandal.

Because, although he could have tried to hoist himself up farther onto the ledge, with a dreadful frown and furious cry, he deliberately let go of his single handhold. He rolled off the edge, tumbled once, then the swift current swallowed him.

In shock, Tara lay there only a moment as a metallic voice came from overhead, a megaphone perhaps: "Tara Kinsale, do not move! U.S. Park Rangers. We will rappel a man to help you!"

But she was having none of that. Laird had left her son alone, now in more ways than one. She scooted backward, where Beamer was waiting for her. More than the cut on his paws looked bloodied; the dog had pinkish smears on his face and chest. He whined as she gave him a swift hug, then he followed her down the path.

Oh, no! Where was her son? She prayed he hadn't seen his father fall, or if he'd gone down the path under the falls, that he hadn't seen Laird's body go over. Surely he hadn't fallen in himself.

She tore under the curtain of the falls. There sat Jordie, his hand in the peanut butter jar, which she must have dropped when Laird slammed her into the rock wall.

"Hi!" Jordie said. Tears streaked through the dirt on his face and mingled with peanut butter around his mouth. "Where's Daddy? He's mad at me."

"No, Jordie," she said, kneeling beside him as Beamer came up, "he's not mad at you, but he's gone away."

"In the plane?"

"No, but I'm going to take you in the plane. Would that be all right? And Beamer?"

He nodded uncertainly but reached out to touch the dog. He grabbed his wagging tail. Beamer, as beat-up as he was, sat close to the boy and let him hold it.

"What's your name?" he asked her, holding out the nearly empty jar to her.

"For now, you call me Tara. I used to be a friend of your mommy, and I knew your daddy, too."

"He doesn't like you. But I do."

It took every remnant of strength she had to not burst into hysterical sobs. She had to find out how Nick was. He or Veronica must have sent the helicopter. As she stood with Jordie in her arms and limped toward the path that would take them up on top again, she looked around this magic, lit cave where she had finally found her lost child.

Hugging him to her, with Beamer at her heels, she walked out from the cavern under the falls and climbed the path toward the sun. Above her, two men in uniforms hurried toward her, but her real rescuers were at her heels and in her arms.

28

One year later . . .

Resonating through the clinic chapel, the last notes of Veronica's organ recital of patriotic songs ended with "This Is My Country." In the front row, Nick and Tara sat with Claire between them and Danny on Claire's lap. She was loving being an older sister, and Tara understood her joy. Her marriage to Nick and their mutual decision to stay in Conifer had made her realize the heights and depths of happiness that were possible in this life. Tara joined in the applause from clinic staff and patients, Nick's Canine Training Academy staff and members of the press who had been invited. On the other side of the center aisle, Thane, Susanne and their three children were clapping, too.

Tara wondered what Jordan was thinking today, incarcerated across the state in the same prison where Clay Whetstone was being held. Jordan was sentenced for accessory to two murders. His lawyers had managed to get him only twenty years, but Tara figured, if he lived that long, he'd be out sooner than that for "good behavior." The trial had shamed and broken him, as had his loss of Laird. He'd threatened to bring murder charges against Tara, but Laird's death had been witnessed by government park rangers, who had testified that he had tried to kill Tara but she had not harmed him.

She felt Nick's gaze, warm on her again. When she turned to smile at him, her foot bumped Beamer's belly, but the dog didn't budge and only put his head down on his paws again.

Veronica walked from the organ to the podium and gestured with both hands for quiet. She had told Jordan she would not divorce him or make public the way he had treated her if he treated her better now — namely, give her full oversight of the clinic and control of their family finances. When he'd agreed and she had signed the papers, she had promptly offered Nick and Tara one-fourth of the clinic land for his canine training school. She had also deeded them the cottage closest to that newly built facility, the isolated one where Tara had been cared for in her coma.

"All right, now, we have some other business to attend to," Veronica said into the microphone. "As I mentioned, that medley was in honor of our servicemen and the trainers here who are preparing tracker dogs for the armed services. Today, we formally dedicate the MacMahon Canine Academy — usually spelled K9," she added, drawing in the air that letter and number with her index finger. "I know you will want to tour those facilities. The dogs will be trained not only for our far-flung Special Forces but as local search-and-rescue dogs. And, I am happy to announce, that the very presence of these wonderful, bright animals will also benefit those who come to use the clinic's facilities. I give you Nick MacMahon to explain a bit more about that."

"Beamer, heel," Nick said, and went up the steps to the podium with Beamer right behind. Sometimes Tara wondered if the dog knew he'd been hailed as a hero in both the Seattle and Denver newspapers. Even Thane and Susanne had been supportive lately and, through Nick, had bought a Labrador for their kids to play with.

As Nick took Veronica's place on the low stage, she came to sit in his chair. Danny crawled onto her lap. Veronica had become

476

a great grandmother, not only for Jordie in his transition to becoming Danny MacMahon in Tara and Nick's home, but she'd been wonderful to Claire. This summer Veronica had taken her and her friend Charlee to New York to see two Broadway musicals that smacked of fairy tales; last spring, she'd taken Nick, Tara, Claire and Danny to Disney World in Orlando. As Claire had said more than once since they'd been back, "Like Jiminy Cricket says, 'A dream is a wish your heart makes.'" Blessedly, there had been no more nightmares for Claire.

"I'm honored to be a part of this beautiful Lohan Clinic facility and grounds," Nick began. Tears blurred Tara's vision of her big, rugged man. He still kept his hair short. After months of physical therapy, he'd finally quit limping from his severe leg fracture. She had never been so proud of him, of the way he'd become a father not only to Claire but to Danny, who adored him.

"Our work here on the clinic grounds is really a two-way street," Nick went on. "The generosity of Veronica Lohan and her family trust will be repayed, at least in a small way, by our tracker dogs visiting the patients here. I'm sure you know that the mere presence of an animal can calm stress and fears.

Also, if patients opt to do so, they can apply to help care for and/or adopt our dogs when they are retired. Another debt my wife and I owe to Veronica and her fine staff is that clients released from the clinic can choose to rear our young puppies until they are ready to be trained on these grounds.

"Many of you have seen pictures of or read about Beamer," Nick went on, stooping to pet the dog's head. Beamer sat erect and still, as if he were about to receive a medal. "He's pretty much in retirement now, but he recently contributed to the future of the academy by becoming the sire for four new pups."

People smiled, some clapped. Beamer had seen his job at the academy as guarding the "new recruits," including one female dog he'd obviously gotten to know quite well. Like master, like Beamer, Tara had kidded Nick.

She bit back a big grin, not thinking of Beamer's or Nick's conquest but of hers. Nick's willingness and passion to make what he called "mutual love" to and with her was all she had ever desired in a marriage. Her mind darted to last night, in the cabin where she had once slept a year of her life away. They'd made a little getaway from their home in Conifer there, a hiding place, where Nick could relax from his duties, and she could even take her laptop when she worked on her current cases for Finders Keepers. It had bunk beds in the living space for Claire and Danny and a huge bed in the master bedroom. And there, last night, after the children were finally asleep . . .

"So," Nick had said, pulling her to him in the middle of their king-size bed, "this is the room where you were Sleeping Beauty and bore your son."

"I'm glad Veronica gave it to us so we can change it all around. And take the curse off it," she said, cuddling against his strength and warmth. "I feel it's a good place now."

"Maybe a good place for conceiving another child," he had murmured, nuzzling her ear and gently pressing a knee between her bare thighs. She wrapped her arms around him. They traded hot kisses, wilder caresses. As ever with this man, she lost track of where she ended and he began, especially when he moved over her to press . . .

". . . express my thanks to my wonderful wife for her support of this project," Nick was saying.

Everyone turned her way, applauding again. Her face pink from where her thoughts had been, rather than from being thrust into the limelight — heaven knows, she'd had enough of that for one lifetime — she popped out of her seat briefly and waved. Nick then introduced Claire and Danny, and gave Veronica back the podium.

Veronica shifted Danny into Tara's arms, and she hugged him to her, still amazed at the reality of her redheaded little boy. Tara had offered to let Jen fly in from Seattle to see him and had suggested she enter the Lohan clinic to be sure she'd stay sober, but she'd turned her down. They hadn't prosecuted Jen, but the scandal of what she'd done had deep-sixed her high-level medical career. The last Tara had heard, she was working at a free clinic in downtown Seattle.

After the program, Nick and his staff of four quickly headed out toward the academy to give tours while Tara and Claire held Danny's hands and brought up the rear down the path. Nick had left Beamer with them; the dog trailed Danny faithfully as the boy kicked at leaves in his path.

"Excuse me, Mrs. MacMahon," came a female voice behind them, "but can I have a word with you?"

Tara turned to see a slender woman — gaunt, actually, though beautifully dressed in a black business suit and heels with a plaid wrap around her shoulders. Her makeup was impeccable. She looked vaguely familiar, but Tara couldn't place her.

"I'm sorry to bother you right now, but I have a question," she said.

With that, Tara realized she was a reporter, Kara Jeffords, from one of the Denver TV affiliates. At least, she had no cameraman with her.

"I hope it's about the clinic or the K9 academy," Tara told her, gesturing for Claire to take Danny on ahead. "I'm pretty questioned out about my past."

"No, this is personal. Not you — m-my past, my f-future," she said, suddenly stumbling over her words. When she blinked her mascaraed lashes, tears flew. "My ex-husband didn't bring my son and daughter back from his weekend visitation with them yesterday, and he's — he's gone somewhere — with them." She burst into tears, covering her mouth with one hand studded with a huge diamond ring. "I just thought — I wondered . . ." she choked out. "I mean, he's hiding somewhere with them — but . . . but I need them back, need to find them . . ."

Tara's heart went out to the shattered woman. She put her arm around her and guided her off the path, saying her familiar mantra that now meant so much more than ever before. "I'll do my very best to help you. And above all, please know that I understand."

AUTHOR NOTE

I am often asked where I get my ideas for my novels. The answer is, from a variety of sources, and it's amazing how they fit together in numerous ways to make a story. Sometimes I get ideas "off the page," that is, by intentionally researching for them. But often I get them "off the wall," or simply stumble on them.

My first germ of an idea for this book came from a series of articles in my home newspaper, *The Columbus Dispatch,* entitled *'Snatchback' system gives hope to a desperate mom* (Aug. 6, 2006). Those articles were about a child who had been taken out of the country to the Middle East, but for me it opened the realm of those who trace and recover snatched children.

Another piece of the plot puzzle fit in place with the help of Dr. Roy Manning, longtime ob-gyn in Chillicothe, Ohio. I appreciate his research and that of his colleagues on pregnancy indicators of women who have given birth and on comatose birth. The online cases of comatose women delivering babies are true.

My third major idea for the novel, tracker and trailer rescue dogs, seemed to fit right in. I first got to know the wonderful work that Labrador retrievers do through my short story, "Find The Way," for the anthology *More Than Words* (2006 edition), about a blind woman who learns to live a free life again with her companion dog, despite being endangered by a stalker. I was able to meet and observe several of the dogs trained by the excellent Puppies Behind Bars program (so-called because honor prisoners raise the puppies until they are ready to be trained). For information on that program, see www.puppiesbehindbars.com.

I also took two online courses from instructors who trace people for a living. Linnea Sinclair is a private investigator who answered many questions; Frank M. Ahearn is a skip tracer and a master at getting information through pretexting. Also, T. L. Gray's information in her course on Delta Force was helpful. Any mistakes on these subjects are mine and not theirs.

As for a setting, the days that my husband and I spent in the area of Denver and

Conifer, Colorado, with a drive through Black Hawk, were invaluable for creating the settings for the story. We had a lovely visit to the Red Rocks area; the idea that a person can push a boulder off a rock formation there is, I hope, a figment of my imagination. Thanks again to our niece and nephew, Heather and Jason Kurtz, for introducing me to Black Mountain and Shadow Mountain near their home in a beautiful spot at nine thousand feet, where elk and foxes stroll through the yard.

The settings in Washington State were inspired by my earlier trips to the Seattle area, which I also used for my romantic suspense novel, *The Falls.*

For background information from a woman's point of view on majoring in social work and dealing with abusive family situations, I appreciate advice from Karen McGirty, a social worker. Her summary comment — "It was the best job and worst job I ever had" — gave me an important glimpse into my heroine's psyche. For medical information on coma and drugs, thanks to Nancy Armstrong, R.N. I am also grateful to my author friend Susan Wiggs for her advice on Seattle neighborhoods.

As ever, thanks to my support staff at Mira Books, especially my editor Miranda Stecyk, for her wise guidance. To the Jane Rotrosen Literary Agency staff, especially Annelise Robey and Meg Ruley.

And always, my heartfelt appreciation to Don, travel companion extraordinaire, who even tolerated altitude sickness to research the mountain settings. Please visit my Web site at www.karenharperauthor.com.